P9-BZG-343

Quinn Fawcett

Against the Brotherhood

A MYCROFT HOLMES NOVEL

TOR®

A TOM DOHERTY ASSOCIATES BOOK
NEW YORK

This is a work of fiction. All of the characters and events portrayed in this novel are either fictitious or are used fictitiously.

AGAINST THE BROTHERHOOD

Copyright © 1997 by Quinn Fawcett

All rights reserved, including the right to reproduce this book, or portions thereof, in any form.

A Tor Book
Published by Tom Doherty Associates, Inc.
175 Fifth Avenue
New York, NY 10010

Tor Books on the World Wide Web:
http://www.tor.com

Tor® is a registered trademark of Tom Doherty Associates, Inc.

ISBN: 0-812-54523-0
Library of Congress Card Catalog Number: 97-13322

First edition: October 1997
First mass market edition: October 1998

Printed in the United States of America

0 9 8 7 6 5 4 3 2 1

Chapter One

IT WAS IN June of 1887 that I came to the employ of the most remarkable man it has ever been my privilege to know: Mycroft Holmes. This unique gentleman was beyond my usual experience, being a man of enormous intellect, combined with rare acumen and sensitivity of nature which required he live in a manner most would find difficult to endure, although he thrived on it. He was then about to celebrate four-and-forty years, a tall, portly, long-headed gentleman with heavy brows, aquiline nose, and profound gray eyes. He had schooled himself to reveal little of his thoughts with his features, but a white line around his lips occasionally revealed anger in spite of his intentions, and he had a nervous habit of twiddling with his watchfob when distracted by thought. Although he was at that time most often a man of sedentary and private habits and a strict routine which he rarely varied, his journals tell of a more active and dangerous youth. He himself admits he had a few tight scrapes in those years which I surmised at the time had left their mark upon him and upon his character. I noticed at the top of his collar on the back of his neck there is what I take to be the beginning of a long scar, but, I have never learned what caused it, or how severe the injury was.

Mycroft Holmes kept rooms in Pall Mall, a short walk across the street to his club; a second-floor flat with a sitting room, a study, a bedroom, a kitchen, a bath, a parlor, and a room for his manservant. The furnishings were largely antiques of the Stuarts' time, though he had a few diverse items, such as his secretary, which was set up in his parlor; this piece was French, from the time of Napoleon, and Mycroft Holmes claimed he had it from his French grandmother. The carpets throughout the flat were Turkish, of first quality, one of them considered to be worth more than all the others combined. There were a number of antique brass vessels from the East, most of which were pressed into service as planters for the exotic herbs and flowers Mr. Holmes grew; his interests in horticulture had more to do with the properties of the herbs than their beauty. He had an especial fascination in poisons and opiates, and maintained a small nursery of deadly blossoms which none but himself was allowed to touch. Although never unclean, the rooms were often cluttered, for Mycroft Holmes was a man who wanted everything of interest readily to hand. No artwork adorned the walls, but there were a dozen framed maps of India, Russia, and China in the parlor and sitting room, clearly the legacy of his early service, for two of them were torn and one had a suspicious dark stain blotting its left-central quadrant that Mister Holmes had assured me was nothing more than whiskey. Four good-sized brass urns stood in the entryway of the hall, with curving Arabic script around the mouths which Mister Holmes informed me was a standard text from their sacred writings and in no way sinister, as I first supposed.

At the time I became his personal secretary I had but recently arrived in London from Stirling, where I had been the confidential clerk to Mister C. T. J. Andrews-

Nimmo, who had engaged me as soon as I left school because of my facility with languages. It was the recommendation of Mister Andrews-Nimmo that brought me to the attention of Mister Holmes, and I am forever grateful to him for his introduction to my present employer. Incidentally, my name is Paterson Erskine Guthrie. I am the son of a minor staff officer who had died of disease in the Crimea. I was then in my twenty-ninth year; my betrothal to Elizabeth Roedale had been understood by our families practically from the cradle, and so my acceptance of the post Mister Holmes offered me was cause for rejoicing for both our mothers. There is nothing outwardly remarkable about me but that my right eye is green and my left blue, and I am left-handed.

It was my custom in those early days to be up at six o'clock to break my fast before putting myself at Mister Holmes's service promptly at seven, at which time it was my duty to copy and file all his memoranda of the previous night: Mister Holmes himself rarely rose much in advance of nine, at which time he wanted nothing cluttering his thoughts or his desk, the better to start his daily assessment of information supplied to him by many sources for his work on behalf of Her Majesty's government.

This particular morning, however, a warm Tuesday in the middle of October, I arrived to find him awake and fully dressed in swallowtail coat, black waistcoat, and dark striped trousers, seated at his dining table over a breakfast of baked eggs, beef sirloin, and muffins. He looked up at me as I came into the parlor, and gave me a terse greeting. "Guthrie. Come in."

Perplexed as I was to discover him already awake, I inclined my head as I would have done at any hour. "Good morning, sir. I trust I see you well."

"You see me in good health, but you do not see me well. You have your notebook ready?" he asked without ado.

"Certainly, sir," I said, indicating the leather portfolio I always carried. "Pencils sharpened, as well."

"I need not have asked," said Mycroft Holmes, and indicated his table. "Have a cup of tea if you like. Tyers!" This to his patient manservant, a former denizen of the branch of government where Holmes had his start. Now beyond service age, Tyers was in Holmes's employ and had been for more than eight years. As Tyers appeared in the doorway, Holmes said, "Tea for Guthrie. Make it strong. And a scone or two as well, with butter and clotted cream, I think."

"Actually, sir, I would prefer a cup of strong tea; I've eaten already," I said, hoping I had not offended Mister Holmes or Tyers.

"As Guthrie likes," Holmes said, making light of my request. He considered Tyers a moment. "It is a difficult time, but I rely upon you to continue your journal, Tyers. Your impressions can be most valuable during uncertain dealings. There is no substitute for a first keen observation."

"As we saw in Cairo. Yes, sir; I am continuing my journal." Tyers bowed his badger-gray head and went away.

I had gone to Mister Holmes's writing table and was looking over his notes of the night before. There were not as many as usual, which surprised me, given the level of his unwonted morning activity. "Has there been news, sir? Has any news of the treaty leaked out? Are there developments in the Bavarian negotiations?" I asked him as I puzzled over the cryptic note I had just taken into my hand: *Mister Holmes,* it read. *If you will forgive this importunity, I must beg you to look over the documents I enclose. How I came by them I cannot tell you, for that would bring intolerable danger to you, and I depend upon you to right the great wrong that is contemplated here. It would be catastrophic if the activities of these dire men go unchecked, and I can think of few who have the acumen to prevail against them. As prevail you must. Suffice it to say that it would mean my life if ever the authors of them learned of what I have done. In giving you this I place my life in your hands. I trust you to keep*

my confidence, and if I have the opportunity, I will con-
tact you again when I have learned more.

It was signed, *One who is your friend.*

"You notice that there has been an attempt to disguise the handwriting, not a very successful one since the letter was plainly written in haste," remarked my employer distantly, his attention on his breakfast. "And certainly you are aware that the writer is a woman."

"A woman?" I exclaimed. "Why do you say that? I can see why you would say the writing is disguised, but what leads you to discern the sex?"

Mycroft Holmes sighed as he cut himself another sliver of beef and topped it with part of his baked eggs, a yellow stain of yolk spreading across the pink meat. "It is not the writing itself, which suggests a European education in its character, probably Swiss rather than French; the paper comes from Holland, if you observe the watermark. It is a matter of *style,* Guthrie. The way in which the writer addresses me is womanly. The manner is female."

"Or that of a desperately frightened and helpless young man," I proposed, and looked at the documents under the note. Immediately I saw them, I frowned. "Lord Harry. These are in code."

"No doubt why she sent them to me. And based on German, too, from what I can tell, which is at least consistent with the rest. Ah, well. I will need a part of the morning to decipher them, I suspect." This with no trace of boasting, though we both knew that it would ordinarily take a team of men several days to break the codes. His skill in this regard was formidable to everyone but himself; he chafed at his own desire to be faster. He saw Tyers return, bearing a tray with a pot of tea and a single cup. "Very good, Tyers. You will not be needed for another two hours. Take them for your visit to your mother. If you are a little late returning, it will not be any great inconvenience to me."

"Thank you, sir; you are most kind," said Tyers as he

placed the pot and then the cup on the table across from Mycroft Holmes. He offered Mister Holmes a short bow. "I will return as quickly as possible." He withdrew promptly, without speaking again.

"The poor man," said Holmes, cocking his long head in the direction of the door where Tyers had departed.

"Why do you say that?" I asked, for in the eight months I had worked for Mister Holmes, I had never heard him remark on Tyers in any way, much less to call him a poor man.

Mycroft Holmes lifted one long, large-knuckled hand. "His mother is dying and he has not been able to spend much time with her."

I understood at once. "Thus you have given him an hour to visit her," I said, coming back to the table, but reluctant to sit, for I was unaccustomed to such familiarity with my employer.

"You aren't going to drink your tea standing up are you, dear boy? Oblige me. Sit. Sit." He indicated the chair across from his and went on as I obeyed him. "Yes. It is a very sad situation. I only wish it were possible to permit him more time with her, but given the gravity of what the message you have just read implies, I fear I will need him by me."

"Why do you say the situation is grave?" I asked, pouring tea through the strainer that Tyers had left next to the spoon. When my cup was near full, I set the pot down again, removed the lid and placed the strainer there. "The tone of the note is alarming, certainly, but it may be that there is—"

Holmes shook his long head. "Wishful thinking, Guthrie. From what I have discerned, there are excellent reasons to regard these papers with the utmost misgiving. I have put some time in on the codes already, and I fear we can eliminate all the usual ones. Which means we are dealing with men of great cunning, and dangerous knowledge." He had another bite of sirloin-and-egg, chewing steadily.

"How do you mean, dangerous knowledge?" I was intrigued at his choice of words; Mycroft Holmes rarely misspoke himself.

"I mean knowledge of matters outside the realms of standard learning. Studies of the realms beyond the limits of science. You may think such teaching a sop for fools, and in the main you would be right: credulous persons are often duped by incense and candles. But there are those who have acquired specific knowledge, knowledge which grants tremendous power. The men who wrote those missives have great craft at their disposal, for their German codes are based on that ancient Hebrew work, The Kabbalah"—he stared at me to determine if I knew the work; I had, but only just—"which tells us that they are adept in hazardous disciplines. Either factor alone would be troublesome, but together, their sum is far greater than their parts."

I laughed once, and wished I did not sound uneasy; in spite of what he said, I did not want to believe him. In this day and age, a man of Mycroft Holmes's intellect would not be so gullible as to put credence in the occult. "Surely you don't suppose that old superstition has any real—"

"That old superstition, as you describe it, teaches skills that very few men have been able to master. Those who have have often paid a high price for their learning." He poured milk into his tea and stirred it contemplatively. "The secret societies and occult lodges of Europe are not often drawn into the realms of politics. But there is one such Brotherhood, and it is notorious for its relentless opposition to the rightful rulers everywhere on the continent."

"You make them sound quite sinister," I observed when he broke off his explanation and became engrossed in the movement of liquid in his teacup.

"If I have done that, well and good," he declared, looking up sharply. "I would not like you to suppose that we are dealing with credulous dreamers and mad fools. These are determined and capable enemies, of ruthless intent. We underestimate them at our peril." He finished his breakfast quickly, and I drank my tea as he did; all the while I wondered who the men he mentioned were and what he thought they might do.

When his plate was empty, Mycroft Holmes laid his napkin aside and pushed back from the table. Rising, he went quickly to the longest of the bookshelves that lined the walls of his apartments, and drew out a leather-covered volume of some age; there was foxing on the pages and the gold leaf had all but been rubbed off with wear. This he held out to me, saying, "Here. Read this. Before noon. When you have completed it, we will speak again."

I took the offered book, noticing it was written in German: *A Study of the Powers of the Unseen World* I translated, and looked at the notes waiting to be copied. I read and wrote the language competently but not with ease, and on subjects of so esoteric a nature and terms with which I was not familiar, I knew I would not progress quickly through the text. It would not be possible for me to read this volume and transcribe the notes in the time he had allowed me. I weighed the book in my hands, hoping to think of some way to inform Mister Holmes of my predicament.

Mycroft Holmes followed my implication, and gave an impatient wave of his hand. "You may do your transcriptions later, Guthrie. This is much more important, and must be dealt with immediately." He picked up his saucer and cup, and carrying them with him, began to pace. "Foremost in my mind is the letter: I am concerned for the unfortunate who wrote that warning."

"You mean the *one who is your friend*?" I asked.

"Yes. For if she is acting against the Brotherhood as I fear she is, her life may well be forfeit before the sun sets. She must be aware that she is in increasing danger with every passing hour. If she still lives as I suspect she does, she will have no protection against any action taken against her." His grave mien revealed his concern far more than the tone of his voice. "If they discover she has betrayed their cause, they will demand the highest price for her daring."

"Surely it is not so hazardous as that, sir," I exclaimed, all the while reflecting that in the seven months I had been in his employ, I had never known Mycroft Holmes to magnify a risk beyond its true scale.

"It may, in fact, be much worse. There is said to be some difficulty developing in the negotiations in Bavaria." He coughed once, a signal that he was dissatisfied with such arrangements.

"Surely there can be no connection," I protested, and went on in defense of my own theory, "If those codes are truly based in German, would it not be more likely a diversion prepared by the Russians or the French or the Turks, for that matter, than the work of the Germans themselves?"

"It is possible, but I doubt it: I will know more when I have finished with these codes," he said quietly, and rose from the table, dropping his napkin negligently on his plate where the last of the sirloin juices stained the edge of the linen red. "I will be in my study, if you should require me."

"I think I can manage," I said with deference, and rose from the table quickly, reaching for my unfinished cup of tea.

"You will need more of that before you are finished for the morning," Mycroft Holmes observed. "I will have brandy waiting for you when you are done."

"Brandy?" I repeated, somewhat taken aback. Never before had my employer suggested I take spirits while I was at my work.

"When you are done with that, you may need it," he answered cryptically.

FROM THE PRIVATE JOURNAL OF PHILIP TYERS:
Mother much worse today. She is failing steadily. Dr. J. informs me that she will not be lucid many days more and

has urged me to spend what time I can with her now.

This afternoon M.H. took time to inquire into the circumstances of Mother's ill health. I informed him that Dr. J. believes it to be a general failing of health brought about by age and the vicissitudes of her life. M.H. did not seem satisfied with this answer, and asked if, before she had been taken ill, she had suffered from agitation and had an odor of carbolic on her clothes or her bedding. I had no knowledge of the state of her bedding or clothes, but I did remark that she was much distressed and restless before her collapse brought her to hospital. My response caused M.H. grave concern, for he instructed me to investigate her clothing as soon as possible to determine if such an odor clings to them. He is unwilling to explain his reason to me until he learns more about her clothing.

M.H. is planning to send G. on a mission to the Continent for him shortly. I hope G. is ready for the work.

Chapter Two

FOR THE NEXT four hours I read *A Study of the Powers of the Unseen World*, my senses reeling between outright derision and utter revulsion. The author proclaimed that there were disciplines known of old that could increase the might of those who sought it through rituals so blasphemous and obscene that I feared my eyes would be made filthy from running over such despicable words. The goals of these heinous rites were no less despicable, for they sought to overturn the rulers of great nations the world over, reducing the countries to anarchy and worse. I have never felt such abomination in anything as I did when I first read that damnable book. That otherwise sensible, modern men could be seduced into placing their belief in these rites described was appalling; that they would be willing to practice them was profoundly repulsive.

By the time I rose from my chair at the tall secretary, I was shaken to the roots. Not in all the hoary legends of Scotland, so lovingly recounted to me by my grandmother, had I encountered such malignity, such depravity and perversion. But those legends my grandmother taught were tales intended to frighten children. These were purported to be the chronicling of actual events. I went to the door of my employer's study and knocked.

Mycroft Holmes was waiting for me, a large brandy in one hand. He held this out to me and waited while I took a generous sip. "Not very enjoyable reading, is it, Guthrie?"

"No, sir, it is not. It is appalling." I held the book out to him. "If there are men in the world who have taken this as their guide in life, I realize why you are so concerned for any who cross their paths." I was glad when he took the volume; I felt I had lost a greater burden than the weight of the tome alone. As I took the brandy and drank a little, the warmth it fired in me felt greater than the simple restoration of spirits, but rather a cleansing, as one uses spirits to clean a wound.

"That is a beginning," he said slowly. "You will have to study more before you are prepared to deal with these men and those who have become their dupes."

I laughed, my senses still in some disorder from what I had read. "*Dupes* is a charitable word. Judging from what I read there, these men are capable of the utmost cruelty in bringing others to their service. The corruption is . . ." I could think of no word sufficiently condemning.

"Just so," said Mycroft Holmes. "But you must see that they would also be adept at suborning those who are susceptible to their promises of power."

Little as I wanted to, I could agree with my employer. "They would have to be very gullible, to think that these ceremonies might have such an effect."

"Or idealistic, or obsessed, or mad, or perhaps merely seeking to be part of something greater than themselves," added Mycroft Holmes. He tugged at the lapel of his coat and said, "I will want you to run an errand for me later in the day. You will need to disguise yourself, I suspect."

"Of course, sir," I said, for in the months I had been his

employee, Mycroft Holmes had sent me out on a dozen such missions for him. The first time I had been astonished; now I accepted the assignment as I would any other. In fact, I had come to enjoy them as welcome diversions from our routine. "What sort of disguise?"

"You will want to look as if you have been in the Army, in foreign places, of course. Also, you will want to seem a little crazed, driven to the limits of endurance and beyond." He ticked these requirements off on his long fingers. "Wear the eyepatch. We don't want anyone noticing their dissimilar colors."

"If you insist," I said, for I greatly disliked wearing an eyepatch since it reduced my capacity to observe the world around me.

"Sadly, my boy, I do insist. These are very dangerous people you go to watch. You will find the clothes you need in the closet off the pantry. Choose a coat and trousers that are a trifle too large, so it will be thought that you have recently lost flesh. Then you can complain about ingratitude and other such and not appear suspect." He had that slightly distant expression in his eyes which indicated that his mind was working at a furious pace. "And muddy your hands, then clean them poorly."

"And why do I wish to do this?" I asked him.

"Because you will want to seem to be willing to undertake questionable acts as the means to restore the influence you fear you have lost in the world. Let it appear that you had the confidence of some wealthy man of industry, who unfairly dismissed you after jealous colleagues threw suspicions on you, or some such tale of injustice. Let them suppose that you were posted to a distant city, in Asia or Egypt, and that you have had to make your way back to England from there without compensation." He smiled grimly. "It wouldn't hurt if you let it drop that you follow the stars in regard to your decisions."

"But I know little of such things," I protested, for it was not only true, but it went against all the training and education I had received.

"I will have some notes prepared for you by the time you finish your luncheon. Learn what is there and you will be able to make a reasonable case for your claims." He rocked back on his heels. "Now leave me to these codes. I have deciphered one, but the second is more complex."

I withdrew at once, and set about copying my employer's notes of the night before, a task I would ordinarily have behind me at this time, and which I undertook now with flagging attention as I tried to fathom what new venture I was being thrust into.

When Tyers returned, he set about preparing our light nuncheon of cold roast beef and a bowl of Cornish soup, his face grave and his manner somber. To my astonishment, I saw his hands shake as he put the silver out for the meal. When he brought me a fresh pot of tea, I asked after his mother, and saw him flinch.

"She is failing, Mister Guthrie." His voice caught in his throat, but he strove to maintain himself. "She is not expected to last much longer, no matter what they do for her, they say. Thank you for your concern."

"Does she require much of your time?" I inquired as I poured a cup.

He spoke softly, as if the quietness would slow his mother's end. "I spend as much time as I can with her, yes. With the end so near . . . Mister Holmes is generosity itself in that regard. He knows it will not be much longer."

"Ah?" I was trying to think of a tactful way to ask when Tyers gave me the information I sought.

"I spoke with her physician not an hour ago, and he said eight to ten days at most."

"I am very sorry for it, Tyers. I only hope she will be spared suffering." I had never found any words that provided true consolation at such times, but I recited the phrases that convention had taught me.

"Amen to that, Mister Guthrie," agreed Tyers, and left me to my tea.

I had finished putting most of Mycroft Holmes' notes in order when my employer once again came into his sitting room, calling to Tyers to bring our nuncheon as he took his place at the table. He glanced at Tyers as he came in, saying, "I am sorry that your mother is now on laudanum."

"Thank you, sir. She is slipping away," said Tyers without surprise at this remark.

But I was not yet accustomed to the ways of my employer, and I challenged him as soon as Tyers was out of the room. "How did you know about the laudanum?"

He looked at me with slight impatience. "You must have noticed the spoon in the oil-wrapped cloth in his pocket? No?"

"No," I admitted. "And why should I notice it? And what makes you assume it is laudanum?"

"Tyers is a careful and methodical man who errs on the side of caution. He would not leave a spoon containing a dangerous compound lying about, and he would be careful handling it himself. Since his mother is known to be dying, what else would an observant man think?" He waved his hand to dismiss the matter, adding darkly, "Those opiates are damnable things, I can tell you. When I was young, my own mother took to salving her unhappiness with the cursed stuff, and it has continued its dire work in my brother." He shook his head and deliberately changed the subject. "I think I have broken that second code at last." He dropped a small portfolio on the table by his elbow, and began to twirl his watchfob. "It was devilishly clever, and I choose my words with great care. The author is a man of great and evil erudition. Mark my words, when we discover him, we will be looking into the Pit."

Since it was not like Mycroft Holmes to use such language I regarded him with some amazement, finding it difficult to address him in such frame of mind. At last, I decided on a simple question. "Why do you say so?"

"Because it is certain that whoever wrote these messages is engaged in the most damnable studies for the most reprehensible goals." He said it flatly enough, but there was a light in his gray eyes that shone like steel. "We will have to be very careful in our moves against this man and his associates. One false step and we both could be made to pay the price with more than our lives." With that, his left hand stole to the back of his collar and I thought I saw him touch the scar there. Then he shook his head twice, very deliberately. "You will go armed, Guthrie. A pistol and a knife should be sufficient."

"I dislike pistols, Mister Holmes; I have mentioned this before." I knew it was useless to argue with him, but the truth of the matter was that I did not like to have firearms about my person. I had often noted that the very presence of a pistol made violence likely.

"In general, I share your convictions, Guthrie, but in this instance, you will permit me to require you to take a loaded pistol with you, and a knife in your boot, if you please. It is not ordinary criminals we seek, but men of tremendous and vile intent who have no conscience beyond their own ambitions. You will have to be prepared to deal with their rapacity, though I devoutly hope it will not be necessary. The men you are to meet will expect such a rogue as you to have some means of defense, as well."

"But surely they will not want to bring notice upon themselves," I said, seeking to find a haven in his reassurance.

He favored me with an exasperated stare. "They will subject you to scrutiny. You will not want these villains to decide you are not one with them once they can be persuaded to accept you. To guard against such misfortune, Guthrie"—he reached out and took my right hand—"I am going to give you as much protection as I can."

Before I could object, he had tugged on my sleeve, baring my wrist just at the base of my palm. I stared in astonishment as he took out a syringe filled with a deep-green fluid. "What on earth—?" I began, only to stifle an oath as Mycroft Holmes pierced my wrist and injected a small amount of the dye under my skin.

"It is similar to a tattoo, only this one may be removed with certain chemicals when this case is finished," said Holmes, consulting a scar on the inside of his right wrist as he continued to mark my skin.

"But what does this mean?" I asked, wincing at the repeated sting of the needle.

"It is the mark of the Servants of the Valley of the Kings," said Holmes, as if every schoolboy should recognize it. "And that is all you need know."

"The Servants of the Valley of the Kings," I repeated. "All right."

"Should anyone inquire as to its meaning," Holmes said as he put the finishing touches on a scarab no larger than my collar-button, "you must deny having any more knowledge than that."

"Which is true," I reminded him.

"Just so. They cannot force it from you." Holmes put the syringe aside. "I am sorry for the discomfort, but I assure you that the protection this affords makes the process a small price to pay." There was a grim light in Holmes' gray eyes. "For they will be revenged on you for your temerity if they decide you are not what you claim to be. They will make your death a warning to others who might attempt anything of a similar nature." He leaned back in his chair so that it teetered on two rear legs. "You will be on the precipice, Guthrie; I cannot emphasize that too strongly. I do not want you to fall."

"No, indeed, sir," I said, taking his remarks to heart, for there was no gainsaying the conviction with which he spoke.

My employer lowered his chair so that all four legs were once again solidly on the floor. "You relieve me, Guthrie. Now, have your meal while I go over what I want you to do. There is an inn off the Brownlow Street, near Gray's Inn. It is called the Cap and Balls, one of the few buildings in that area to survive the fire of 1666. I want you to go there, and take as inexpensive a room as you can, and make inquiries about a solicitor who is not particular about his client or his fees. Make sure they see the scarab, but do not flaunt it. And mention malign stars if you can, so that the spies of the men we seek will know that a likely prospect has emerged. You will need to be venal and willing."

I took my notebook and set it beside my fork, certain that I would have to take notes while we ate; I hoped that what he would tell me would not entirely rob me of my appetite.

By two in the afternoon I was as prepared as I could be without intense study. I had chosen a suit of clothes from those Mycroft Holmes kept for disguises, provided by the actor Edmund Sutton: a slightly threadbare coat not quite in the current mode, the sort a senior clerk might wear; the waistcoat was missing two buttons and was overlarge on me; a shirt with a twice-turned collar and cuffs to enhance the shabby appearance of the coat; and a pair of nondescript trousers about three inches too large at the waist. Add to this two badly scuffed boots and I presented the appearance of a man of modest means who had fallen on hard times.

"Very good, but you will need a hat, dear boy. Something that once was rakish, but alas, now only hints at the glories of the past." He chuckled without humor and selected a curly-brimmed beaver that was no longer in fashion which he held as he gave me a watch-chain-and-fob, but with no watch. "You will be able to complain that you were forced to sell your watch in order to continue to pay for your lodging. You might also say that you have had to part with other treasures."

"Very well," I said, fixing the fob in the waistcoat.

"Now, the eyepatch. Choose which eye you are willing to lose. And remember which one it is to be. It won't do to have you changing sides." He gave a slight huff of sardonic laughter. "Put your patch in place." He watched while I covered my green right eye, for it has a more definite color and might be identified more easily than the blue, then gave me the hat. "What a very depressing demeanor you present. A man nearly at his limit. You will want to put your hands in the dustbin, to get grit under your nails before you venture out. And rub the excess on your sleeve. Just what is needed." He gave me a bottle of pressed glass. "And this will be the crowning touch."

Curious, I lifted the stopper and made a face at the overwhelming scent of alcohol and lavender that rose from it.

"My dear Guthrie, we haven't time, or inclination, to give you the stench of a man who has gone long without access to soap and water. But we can disguise your lack of it, and this will accomplish our purpose very well."

"Do you think so?" I asked, beginning to feel anxious. I winced as I applied some of the terrible stuff to my face.

"I do. Now pay attention. Your name is August Jeffries. That is close enough to Guthrie so that it should not trip you up. You have only two pounds left to your name; be sure you bemoan that fact. Say that you have had to leave your wife and children behind in whatever city and country you have chosen to come from, and that you are desperate to make enough to bring them to London. Be careful to remember the names of your fictitious wife and children, set them firmly in your mind, for be sure that these men will, and they will use such information to test you. If you fail, they will treat you with utmost ferocity."

"I will be careful; I will use the names of my sister's children," I said.

"That would not be wise," Mycroft Holmes said with a sharpness that caused me some anxiety. "If any mishap should befall you, you do not wish these men to have any means to cause trouble to those close to you, as they would if they could discover your sister's children."

I was taken aback. "Surely you do not mean they would go to such lengths?" It seemed the height of savagery.

"It is precisely what I mean, and I hope you will hold such thoughts in the forefront of your mind. We are not dealing with anything less than those bent on destruction. This band of men has been known to butcher whole families for no greater reason than that one of its members offered an insult to a man in the Brotherhood." He regarded me steadily with his somber gray eyes and let the import of his observation sink in.

"I will not forget," I told him, and looked toward the backstairs of the flat. "I suppose I should use the tradesmen's entrance."

"Of course," said Mycroft Holmes. "And when you return tomorrow evening, come by way of the livery stable at the end of the block. Use the connecting alleys to get here, for you may be followed and watched. Do not suppose that your story will be accepted at face value, or that you will be trusted because you appear in dire straits. These people are such consummate liars that they suspect the same mendacity from all those they meet. They will be at pains to test you. You will have to gain their support, enough that they are convinced they may entrust you with one of their—ah—enterprises, and we have heard that they are planning some mischief abroad. I need to know what they are doing in Europe as well as in England. They will need to be certain of your aims before you learn these things."

"As you wish," I told him, and started toward the rear door.

"Remind me of the circumstances of your father's will, Mister Jeffries," Mycroft Holmes demanded suddenly.

"He died in Europe four years ago while with a hunting party, leaving the greater part of his fortune to the children of his second wife, my half-brothers, and what I had been bequeathed was placed in trust for the use of my wife and children so long as we lived in England, as my father considered me profligate," I answered at once, trying to infuse my recitation with a sound of ill usage.

"And what do you want the solicitor to do?" he went on.

"I want the solicitor to get some of that money to enable me to bring my family here. I want him to break the trust, if he can. I want to claim my inheritance without hindrance of any kind. It would mean falsifying certain claims, but it would provide me some very necessary funds in order to get them passage." I tried to sound avaricious as I spoke. "My father's will would allow release of the money only when my family is in England. I would have to get the solicitor to affirm that they were residents here before their actual arrival. Considering they would be with me now if my father had not hit upon so absurd a kick . . ." I looked uneasily at my employer. "What will happen if such a will cannot be found?"

"Rest assured, after some trouble in locating it, the clerks will be able to produce a will, and a certificate of death," Mycroft Holmes informed me.

"And the delay will increase my embarrassment," I said, anticipating his strategy. "So I will be eager for anything they offer me that leads to resolving my plight."

"Exactly," he said, and took his watch from its pocket.

"Time to be under way," I agreed.

"Tell me, what stars are influencing you now?" Mycroft Holmes rapped out as I reached to open the door.

"Saturn and Jupiter, both badly," I answered, recalling my instructions over nuncheon. "And at present the Moon is negatively influencing my First House. The aspect will change tomorrow, when I hope to hear from my half-brother."

"Who is?" prompted Mycroft Holmes.

"Edward Montjoy, a merchant in Norfolk in the wool trade. Recently a man of that name was forced to sell his partnership to Mister Howell, who now owns the company outright. Mister Montjoy has left Norfolk, and the understanding is that he has gone to America to make his fortune there, since he has not been able to do it in

England. His wife was named Anna and she died last year
of a lingering fever. Montjoy has taken his one surviving
child with him, and nothing is known of the lad."

"Very good; the Brotherhood can check on these facts
and they will be borne out. Richard Howell has, in fact,
recently bought out his partner, Edward Montjoy, that
much is in the records of the court. Let them discover this
for themselves. It will make your plight the more real
when you learn that your half-brother cannot help you,
indeed, he cannot be found." He smiled coldly.
"Remember that this news will be very unwelcome, in
spite of the fact that you and Montjoy have not seen each
other for more than ten years."

"Do you think anyone will believe that?" I asked, trepidation stealing over me now that I was about to start on
my assignment. "Why should I contact a half-brother
from whom I am estranged? Why should these men
believe I would do such a thing, if we are not on good
terms, Montjoy and I?"

"You will have to demonstrate to them your sincerity.
Because you have to convince the Brotherhood of the
extremity of your predicament. That is also the reason
you want a not-too-scrupulous solicitor, in order to press
your claim on your late father's estate. You may tell them
that you don't expect much from Montjoy, as there is no
close tie there. But let them know you are desperate for
his help, for any help, and are depending on family pride
to prevail over the coolness of long absence." Mycroft
Holmes held up a warning finger. "Do not let them come
to suspect you are seeking their help, or they will have
nothing to do with you. They abhor all notions of charity."

"I will contrive to do as you require," I said.

"Very good," Mycroft Holmes approved. "Remember
to comment on the Grand Cross in your chart, and lament
the malefic impact it brings to bear on the Twelfth
House." He cleared his throat. "Be alert, Guthrie, and

take no foolish chances. They will not allow you a single slip. You are my eyes and ears in that place."

"I will not fail you," I assured him with more confidence than I felt, then I picked up a half-empty carpetbag and let myself out of his flat. "You have been satisfied with my efforts in the past."

"So I have," said my employer as he prepared to close the door. "But these men are more truly our enemies than any other you have encountered. They are a danger to you and me and the whole of the Empire. They will not hesitate to make an example of you, if it suits their purposes. I, for one, would not wish their vengeance on the lowest executioner in Kabul."

That was not the most consoling notion to have as a parting benediction, I thought as I descended the stairs and let myself out through the back alley, stopped at the dustbin to dirty my hands, and went from there into the general chaos of the afternoon crush of carriages, wagons, and pedestrians.

FROM THE PERSONAL JOURNAL OF PHILIP TYERS: *M.H. informs me that the Admiralty pouch arrived ten minutes late today, the first time in four years. The delay was caused by a traffic tangle near the docks. Had I not been visiting Mother, I would have notified the Admiralty of the tardiness. M.H. has recommended the messenger be provided a bicycle to ensure prompt deliveries in future. It is essential that the schedule be kept.*

I have ventured out again this evening, to the theater where Edmund Sutton is appearing. He presented me with an outlandish costume which he claims M.H. wants for a disguise. What can be the use of such a flamboyant disguise I cannot fathom, but it is what M.H. stipulated, and so I have packed it in his trunk in anticipation of his departure to the Continent once G. has left.

M.H. has confined himself to his study for the evening, with Admiralty records all around him, for the purpose of review. One would think he were merely browsing, given the speed at which he peruses these records. Since I have come to M.H.'s employ, it has astonished me to discover how quickly he takes in such material. He claims that speed actually aids him, that to make a slower study would cause him to overlook crucial facts. He anticipates completing his review in two days, barring interruptions.

Chapter Three

IN THE STREET a number of delivery wagons were drawn up, and the sidewalks were crowded with various merchants and vendors bringing their wares to the houses that pressed together. I was ignored or scorned as being out of place in this affluent neighborhood, and it struck me that my fiancée would be distressed to see me in this seedy attire. I could not explain it to her as a necessary part of the work I do for Mycroft Holmes. She put great stock in appearance and proper behavior, and any lapse in either would cause her much dismay. I decided when I recounted this adventure to her, I would have to mitigate some of its more dissolute aspects. With this to occupy my thoughts, I passed quickly and without undue notice toward High Holborn, where the bustle was more general and a man looking as I did could go unremarked by those around him.

I reached the Cap and Balls betimes. It was a squat and ancient pub, one that might have had some distinction by its age had it not been such a squalid ruin of a place. The floors sagged and the low pitch of the ceiling was oppressive. I made myself known to the innkeeper, who was not much pleased to have me as his guest. He eyed my lamentable baggage and demanded five shillings for the room and an additional ten pence if I wanted my breakfast in the morning.

"For I'll have no racketing off leaving me without a farthing for my trouble." His shrewd face made me think he had rarely lost the price of a room to anyone. As I handed over the coins with a great show of reluctance, he chuckled. "A peevy cove you are, right enough. I know. You'll be playing off your tricks on less knowing coves than me."

"No doubt," I told him, trying to appear as if my dignity had suffered from his distrust. "Which room did you say, again?"

"Top of the stairs, go left to the end of the hall." He rubbed his hands on the filthy apron tied around his paunch. "You can have some baked cheese and a leg of chicken for your tea, if you want to give me another ten pence."

The price was high for what he was offering, and we both knew it. "Thank you, no. I would rather take a glass of daffy in the taproom later."

The innkeeper nodded. "Suit yourself."

The room he had allotted to me was small and so damp that I wondered there were no mushrooms growing under the sagging bed. One high, grimy window opened onto the small, oblong yard at the rear of the inn. Several other buildings backed onto it, making it more like a prison than a place to unload wagons; there was a single, narrow alley leading in and out of the courtyard. "What an unprepossessing place," I said to myself as I looked out into the confines of the yard.

Once I had bestowed my few items from the carpetbag—enough to give the appearance of my reduced position in the world—I hastened down to the street and set off toward the Inns of Chancery, the better to support my role of a man in search of a lawyer not overburdened with ethics. The pressure of the pistol at the small of my back was a constant reminder of my purpose. After more than an hour of showing myself in the places where I might be expected to conduct my search, I returned to the Cap and Balls, carrying myself in a disheartened way.

As I reached the taproom of the Cap and Balls, I searched for a dark corner where I might watch the room while giving the appearance of despondency.

The innkeeper charged me thr'pence for a very bad glass of gin, which I carried over to the inglenook by the hearth and hunched over, thinking as I did that there are few things I would like less to drink than the stuff currently in my glass. At least I would have no trouble delaying its consumption.

As the afternoon faded, a number of men came into the taproom, not one of them more sinister than a lanky dealer in secondhand clothing. He took a quick look around, passing over me as unpromising, then ordered a mug of punch. He exchanged half a dozen words with the landlord, then settled into steady drinking.

By the time the lamps were lit, the taproom was boisterous and the innkeeper had rolled out a barrel of ale. By the smell of it, the quality was about as poor as the gin. For the next two hours I watched the men in the room make merry; no one struck me as sinister, or intent on overthrowing the governments of Europe.

And then a figure crossed the threshold. What there was about him I cannot say precisely that gave him his arresting and malignant presence, but it was as if he walked in a shadow of his own making, an engulfing darkness, potent and dangerous. He chose one of the tables not far from the hearth and raised his hand. "Landlord! My port."

The innkeeper achieved a sour smile, but hastened to obey the summons, taking down a bottle from the back shelf and pouring a fair serving into a large, clean glass. He carried it to the man's table—an unusual courtesy in this establishment. As he put it on the table before the new arrival, I saw his hand shake.

"Good man, Holt," said the sinister guest as he gave him a crown for his trouble. "Do not disturb me unless I summon you."

"Most grateful, Mister Vickers," said Holt, bowing and withdrawing at once. Ordinarily this sum would have been enthusiastically welcomed, but now, the innkeeper took it as if it scorched his fingers. He took refuge behind the bar hurriedly, and around the taproom the raucous conversations quietened.

Vickers gave no sign of noticing the impression his presence caused. He was content to sit and drink his port slowly, his deep-set eyes brooding on the middle distance. I saw that he was watching the door in a covert way, as if in anticipation of new arrivals. I did not want to make my surveillance apparent, so I feigned drunkenness and did my best to make it appear that I could not hold focus with my single eye.

It was not long before the crowd in the taproom dispersed, leaving two inebriated carters leaning on the bar arguing over some matter of customs, Vickers at the hearth table, and me in the inglenook, bent over my glass of dreadful gin. The waiting was difficult, for the palpable sense of ghastliness that came from Vickers and my own sense of being observed by him. I felt as if I had been covered with a thin, viscous film of debasement.

Finally the innkeeper approached his dire guest, saying subserviently, "There's a butt of pork and stewed onions tonight, Mister Vickers. And trotters. If you should want any."

The look of condemnation this menu brought made Holt step back. "I think not," said Vickers in what would have been cordiality in another. "Perhaps something later, when I am through with my friends. Though not trotters."

This afterthought made the landlord shudder and shake his head.

Holt once again escaped to the protection of his bar. He made a point of polishing this expanse with a damp cloth, all the while taking care not to look in the direction of Vickers.

When I thought I could bear this no longer, I poured the contents of my glass on the floor and called for another, making a point of sounding ill used. "And a slice or two of bread while you're at it."

"That'll be ha'penny extra for the bread," said Holt, not bothering to bring the gin to me.

I staggered to the bar, threw down the required coins, took the drink and the two thin slices of hard bread, then made my way back to the inglenook, muttering as I went. I slouched down, and took a bite of the bread; it was surprisingly good. I ate it with an enthusiasm that would pass muster for hunger.

"Is that all the supper you are having, my good man?" said Vickers, not moving from his place at his table.

I did not respond, but continued to chew my bread, my shoulders hunched.

"I am talking to you, fellow," said Vickers, more pointedly, and stared at my head as if he would burn a hole through to my brains.

"Me, sir?" I said, turning to face him. It was not a pleasant thing to look into his eyes.

"Yes. You." He gave an imperious wave of his hand. "Pray join me a moment."

"Very well," I said, taking on a servile manner to show gratitude, though I loathed myself for even pretending to accommodate him.

This seemed to satisfy Mister Vickers, who showed me a cold smile and indicated the bench across from his chair. "Sit down. I don't recall seeing you here before, sir."

"Because I have just arrived today, didn't I?" I answered, as one seeking to ingratiate himself.

"My good man, you know your movements better than I do," said Vickers with thinly veiled contempt.

"Well, I just reached London today," I said, my cringing only partly feigned. "And a sorry place I've fetched up."

Vickers looked around. "I am forced to agree."

It was tempting to ask why he came here when it was apparent he could have chosen less lamentable accommodations, but I stopped myself in time. Remembering my role, I muttered, "I'd have better if there was justice in the world. I'd stop at the Grand or the Empire."

"Who would not?" His question required no answer, and I did not venture one. "Do me the honor of telling me why you are in London," said Vickers languidly.

I knew better than to be too easily drawn in, and so I shrugged my shoulders. "Naught that would interest the likes of you." It was a surly response and should have got me a sharp dismissal, but it did not. I noticed that Vickers had caught sight of the tatoo on my wrist and I turned my hand as if to conceal it.

"Now there you are wrong," said Vickers. "I suspect you are in need of work. Am I right? Some way to line your pockets with the coin of the realm. If your complaints are not an excuse for idleness." He did not wait for my answer. "And under the circumstances, I should think you would seek to engage the support of anyone who could be of assistance to you."

"But what would you want with me?" I asked it with a sense of coldness spreading through me; he surmised something because of the tattoo, and expected that I would grasp his meaning and share his purpose.

When Vickers looked at me this time, I felt a vileness about him that shook me to the roots. "Any number of things. I have my uses for such as you, as well you know. If you are suitable to my purposes. Which I will determine when you answer the questions I put to you."

All of Mycroft Holmes' warnings, which I had thought overblown, now came back to me, and I realized that if anything the gravity of the situation had been underestimated. I lowered my head in order to avoid that baleful gaze. "I've had some hard times," I admitted, striving to maintain the demeanor required.

"So I assumed," said Vickers with a trace of amusement. "If you will be good enough to inform me of the nature of your difficulties, perhaps we can come to some agreement on a means to alleviate the most pressing of them."

"And what would a man like yourself want to do it for?" I demanded, making sure there was enough of a whine in my voice.

"I have my reasons," said Vickers, and again, I felt a cold grip me in leaden fingers.

"It's been hard, sir," I told him, keeping my eyes averted. "I can't find employment, not as I'm qualified to do."

"And what might that be?" The question was made lazily, as if it had little or no significance to Vickers.

"I've been factoring for mercers and cotton growers, sir," I answered at last. "Dealing mostly with the Egyptians and the mercers around the Midlands; Birmingham and Coventry and the like." That was plausible enough, and I knew sufficient amounts about the brokering of cotton that I could answer most inquiries about it and sound credible, thanks to a cousin who had made a respectable fortune in the business.

"Are the mills doing badly?" asked Vickers as if disinterested. "I was unaware of it."

"They're doing all right," I said sullenly, and continued on as if I could not stop myself from reciting the whole of my misfortunes. "But a whole lot I brokered, the Egyptians wouldn't make good on the delivery, and I lost my commission and the mercers won't trust me. None of them will let me in the door."

"How unfortunate," said Vickers blandly.

"If my half-brother can give me a place, I'll be off to Norfolk in a couple of days. I can be of use to him, for all he deals in is wool instead of cotton." My confidence did not sound convincing, luckily. "Edward Montjoy, in Norfolk. You may know of him?"

"I haven't the pleasure," said Vickers, on the edge of boredom. His eyes flicked over me. "But if you have hope of a station in Norfolk, why do you come to London?"

I glanced around furtively, as if I feared we would be overheard. "It's my father's damned will. He left everything in a muddle, and I hoped I could straighten it out, so I wouldn't have to depend on my stepbrother at all, but could set up for myself. I wouldn't have to depend on Montjoy if the will didn't force me to." This last sounded unreliable even to me.

Vickers regarded me steadily for a short while. "So you are looking for a solicitor? Why not speak to the man who handled the will for your father."

"Because I don't trust him, is why," I said, and let Vickers draw the rest out of me over the greater part of an hour, by which time, three more men had come into the taproom and sat down at tables flanking Mister Vickers.

"A lamentable situation, Mister. . . ."

"Jeffries," I introduced myself. "August Jeffries. No relation to the famous judge, not that I know of, any road."

"The Hanging Judge." Vickers showed his teeth. "Not a connection to boast of in polite company."

The other three men exchanged looks that were impossible for me to read in the low light.

"So you want to find a solicitor who can . . . persuade the courts to make some of the funds left to your wife and family in trust available to you for the purpose of bringing said wife and family to England?" Vickers ran his tongue over his thin lips. "An enterprising notion."

I listened, feeling ashamed of August Jeffries and his plans to take advantage of his nonexistent relatives. "I wouldn't do it if the stars hadn't turned on me as they did."

Vickers fell silent, and now directed his gaze on my eye. "How did the stars turn on you?"

I managed to make my apprehension look like awkwardness. "It is Jupiter and Saturn together. If I had not a Grand Cross, it would not be so hard, but—"

"Stop!" declared Vickers. He looked at the other three men. "He is right; the aspects are generally negative now."

The oldest of the three, a white-haired mole of a fellow in an expensive tweed suit and the air of a man of some consequence, nodded sagely, and spoke with a broad, Devonshire accent. "That is true. With Jupiter and Saturn both badly aspected, it could account for some of his misfortune." He put a heavy emphasis on the *some.*

"But the Moon," I interjected. "Tomorrow it moves into Aries, and—"

"It is more favorable to your endeavors," Vickers finished for me. "Perhaps the Moon is working a little ahead of itself, Mister Jeffries. For I think we can be of some help to you."

I stared at him, doing my best to look grateful. "If you could put me in the way of finding a solicitor, I would thank you most heartily, sir, and no doubt about it."

Vickers nodded, and looked steadily at me. "And in return," he said with gelid assurance, "you will help us."

"At your service," I said, deliberately sounding a bit wild, so that it would appear I did not entirely trust to my good fortune, or had taken a spot more gin than was good for me, which was truly the case with the Blue Ruin they poured here. I made sure I reeled a bit as I got to my feet and saluted in very bad form indeed. "Yours to command."

"Without a doubt," said Vickers, smiling with all his teeth. He made a signal to the other men and got to his feet. "If you will give my companions all the details of your plight, I will engage to help you out of this coil, if your responses are satisfactory."

"Satisfactory in what sense?" I asked, my ill usage only partly feigned.

Vickers shrugged elaborately. "In . . . oh, in regard to that tattoo on your wrist, for example."

I felt most apprehensive. "This—I can tell you nothing about it."

Vickers gestured to one of the men, who took a poker and stuck it deep into the fire. No one else in the taproom paid the least attention to any of this. "We shall see," he mused. "When it is glowing, bring it here and lay it across—"

"What?" I demanded, ready to jump up.

"It will not be necessary if you will tell me what the significance of it is," Vickers told me as if he were describing a day in the country. "It will spare you suffering, and what is the trouble with that?"

"No trouble, except that I can't oblige you," I said, doing my best to sound more resolute than ignorant; I was convinced that any sign of weakness now would set Vickers against me and I would fail in my mission for Mycroft Holmes.

The man he had ordered tested the poker. It was red but not yet glowing; he put it back in the fire.

"Think of all I can do for you. And in return I want only to know the importance of that . . . unusual tattoo." Vickers looked toward the window. "Such a minor thing, really."

"It may be," I said, swallowing hard. "But I can tell you nothing. Do what you will, I cannot tell you."

Vickers sighed. "Bring the poker."

This could not be happening, I thought as the man approached me. I knew these men were dangerous, but I had not supposed they were mad. I could not move from my place without falling into their hands, so I did my best to maintain an outward composure. "I can tell you nothing," I repeated as the poker—now seeming the size of a loaf of bread—was brought near enough for me to feel the heat of it.

"Suppose we should burn it off?" Vickers suggested.

I recalled the scar I had seen on Mycroft Holmes'

wrist, so small I had not thought it worth notice, and I realized it was a burn scar. Good God, had they done this to him? "I still can tell you nothing," I said. To my astonishment my voice did not shake.

The glowing metal was near enough now to singe the frayed cuff of my jacket. Vickers studied me. "Well?"

"I have nothing to say," I told him.

"Not even about the Valley of the Kings?" he asked, and signaled his man to move away. "For now, I am willing to assist you."

I was startled at the suddenness of his offer, at his abrupt change of demeanor, which did not diminish my conviction of his sinister intent. In the persona of August Jeffries, I demanded, "What are you talking about? You were prepared to maim me, and now you extend yourself as if there were no . . . question, or bargains? You are not a charitable man, of that I am certain. So what benefit do you expect?" I managed to sound scornful and pleading at once, and decided that the hours I had spent with Edmund Sutton were not wholly wasted.

"Oh, there are questions, and you have answered the most pressing," said Vickers, and his voice was as cold and piercing as a hangman's pity. "Rest assured, you have given the answer." He turned on his heel and strode out the door without looking back.

The Devon man glowered at me. "Let's go over the terms of your father's will, shall we?"

I made a half-hearted and truculent protest, then sat down again and let them draw my story out of me; all the while I wondered what I had said that had so changed Vickers' mind I reckoned I must have given him the response he expected in the denial of all knowledge of the meaning of the tattoo. But what did that denial mean to him?

FROM THE PERSONAL JOURNAL OF PHILIP TYERS:
G. has been started on his mission. M.H. told me that he is apprehensive about the assignment for there is much

*we do not know, and G. is still untried. Once enmeshed in
the intrigue it may‑be difficult to extricate G. from it. If,
indeed, we have such an opportunity. So much depends
on G. himself.*

*There was a note from G.'s fiancée delivered here, sum‑
moning him to a fête tomorrow night. M.H. has sent her
a note, informing her that G. will not be available for the
occasion, being as he is on business for the government.*

M.H. was displeased to read in The Times *that there
are yet again rumors of another naval scandal. The
author of the article claims that an effort is being made
to conceal any evidence of wrongdoing, for it is feared
that another blow to the government could lead to a vote
of no confidence. In these uncertain times, even the
appearance of mismanagement might be sufficient to do
the government severe damage.*

*The messenger from hospital informs me that Mother's
condition remains unchanged. It is a great relief to me
that M.H. has undertaken to pay the whole cost of her
care, for now I know she will not be deprived of any help
or comfort the medical profession can offer her. Had I
been the one to shoulder all the cost, she must have had
far less skillful care than she now receives,*

Chapter Four

THE NEXT MORNING, true to my assignment, I left the Cap and Balls with my head ringing from gin and lack of sleep. I could feel welts on my body where it had been nibbled by the permanent denizens of the inn; I contrived to keep the itching from annoying me by recalling all the details I had offered to the three associates of Mister Vickers. They had been very interested in my supposed wife and children, as well as the nature of my fictitious father's death. As I made my way toward the law courts, I realized a puny man with a beak of a nose was keeping pace with me, roughly twenty feet back. So Mister Holmes had been right in warning me against being followed. I did my best to ignore that unwelcome companion and to keep on my way.

As I neared the law courts, I made a point of stopping men in legal robes, making it appear I was searching for a man to take my case. I was not given a very encouraging reception by those I accosted, which was my intention; I continued my efforts in as surly a manner as I could summon up. Finally I saw Pierson James, Mister Holmes' current personal courier, coming toward me, clutching a large leather portfolio, his solicitor's robe so frayed and threadbare at the collar that I could not help but wonder if he had got the garment from Edmund Sutton. He very nearly stumbled against me, and began to apologize.

"I never intended . . . your pardon, sir." He held me by the arm to get my attention. Though not much older than I, James had the air of a man in his middle years, and he carried himself with a formality that went well with his lawyer's garb. Spectacles dangled from a dark ribbon around his neck.

I recognized the sharpness of his eyes in no need of lenses. "It is no matter," I said, and launched into a request for representation, for I could see that the beak-nosed man had edged nearer.

"A will is in question, then?" said Pierson James eagerly. "Why, yes, I might be able to advise you. If you will do yourself the trouble to come with me."

"Certainly," I said, making a show of cordiality that rang false to me, and I trusted appeared the same to the man with the beaky nose. "I am grateful to you, sir, for being willing to consider my case."

"A man in your position must find it hard to come by representation," said James as he led the way down a narrow street toward a number of buildings housing chambers. "I will hear you out, without charge to you, and then decide if your case merits my attention." He turned into one of these and led the way to the end of a dark, narrow hall. "I suspect that whoever is watching you will now find a place to observe the front of this place," James remarked to me over his shoulder as he opened the door to reveal a fine suite of rooms; in the second of these Mycroft Holmes was sitting, appearing to take his ease in a high-backed, overstuffed leather chair.

"How do you do, Guthrie," said my employer, regarding me carefully. "What luck have you had thus far?"

"I think I may have been more fortunate than we anticipated." I looked toward Pierson James. "Is it all right—?"

Mycroft Holmes motioned his courier away, calling after him, "Do not leave the building. I will need you to escort Guthrie back to the street when we have done here."

"As you wish, sir," said James, and left us alone.

"Now then, tell me of what you suspect may be good fortune?" He leaned forward and braced his elbow on the arm of the chair. "Someone approached you at the Cap and Balls?"

"Yes, sir," I said, and quickly summarized my meeting with Mister Vickers, and described his three lieutenants, in particular the older man with the Devonshire accent, who I was certain could be identified. I finished with my impression of Vickers himself. "He has awakened the gravest misgivings in me. I cannot tell you precisely why, but I suspect he has within him the capacity for great evil."

"There you have the right of it, for I have known Vickers of old, and have every reason to suppose he has not redeemed his character." Holmes stared up at the ceiling. "If Vickers has been bold enough to approach you now, it must be because he is seeking some dupe, as I suspected he was." He regarded me closely. "Do you anticipate his return this evening?"

"I don't know," I said as candidly as I could. "I do have the impression he wants something from me, which accounts for the notice he has paid to me." I put my hands into my waistcoat pocket. "I have done as you suggested, and made it clear that I seek legal advice in order to deal with gaining the money I, as Jeffries, believe I am entitled to have."

"Very good. I think it will be as well that you continue this ruse, my lad. Let them know you have happened upon a solicitor who is willing to undertake acting on your behalf, but in order to accomplish this, you will have to give him thirty pounds."

"Is that a large sum for such services?" I asked, uncertain of the amount. "If the charge is too high, Vickers may wonder."

"It is not as great as many would charge, but it is well beyond August Jeffries' means, and that is all that need concern us at this juncture."

I hesitated. "You intend that I will have to avail myself of Mister Vickers' offer for help?"

"Certainly, my dear Guthrie. You will have to be caught up in his plots if we are to learn anything of his intentions, as distasteful as that may be to you." Holmes rubbed the bridge of his long nose. "I can understand why you do not welcome such a predicament. It is never pleasant to place oneself in the way of harm, or to be required to deal with individuals of such reprehensible conduct. And I sympathize, Guthrie, I truly do sympathize. But it is necessary that we penetrate to the heart of the maze."

I stared at him. "But these are dangerous men. They were prepared to put a . . . a red-hot poker on my wrist, where you made that infernal tattoo."

"You have my gratitude," said Mycroft Holmes with such sincerity that I was momentarily taken aback. "They will say nothing about the tattoo again unless you yourself bring it up."

"How odd," I said, unable to keep the sarcasm from my voice.

"You have been established as one of a most secret society. They would be risking more than hot pokers if they questioned you again." Holmes achieved a grim smile. "You are right. The man is dangerous. I have been aware of his nefarious activities these twenty years and more, and there are few men I would consider more formidably evil than Mister Justin Oliver Beauchamp Vickers." He got to his feet and took a turn about the room. "Odd as it may seem, I am pleased that you are aware of what risk you are running with Vickers. Do not forget the peril he represents, I beg you."

There was a history here, and one I sensed was particularly bitter for Mycroft Holmes; I sought to learn the whole. "He has done damage before?"

"A great deal of it, I regret to admit," said Mycroft Holmes grimly. "I cannot be more specific than that now. In time I will tell you the entire sorry tale." He reached for a bell to summon James. "Go back to the Cap and Balls, and let it be known that you need money to pay your solicitor. Do not be apologetic about it. And be firm in your choice, so that Vickers cannot foist another man upon you in James' place, though I doubt they would try, now that they are convinced of your associates." He made a gesture to encompass the suite where we sat. "I will be here tomorrow in the morning, and if you have word for me, come here yourself. Vickers will know this is where your solicitor keeps his chambers; any inquiry will reveal that P. N. James practices law here."

"I will, and I must," I said, wanting no part of any more dealings with Mister Vickers.

"As soon as you have some sense of what this fellow is up to, let me know of it." He looked at me directly once more. "I am sorry that I must require so much of you, Guthrie, but I have no other I can trust in this instance, and no one who is able to gain such direct access to Vickers without attracting unwonted suspicion." He came and put his hand on my shoulder. "I wish I could remove you from this role you have assumed at once, but, alas, that cannot be, not if I am to fulfill my sworn duty to England and the Crown."

"Is the matter of that magnitude?" I asked, feeling a shock that was also a thrill. "Am I in immediate danger?"

"Not immediate, but the situation is precarious. There are certain delicate negotiations that might be irreparably damaged if Vickers and his lot could have their way in the matter. We must have some knowledge of their intentions if England is not to be badly compromised in this matter." My employer looked across the room. "I did not think the case was so desperate yesterday, but word has come to my hand that makes it imperative we know what Vickers and his Brotherhood are doing, or risk having crucial diplomacy come to nothing."

"Of course," I said, ashamed that I should have allowed my fright to overcome my obligations.

"I am grateful to you," said Mycroft Holmes, moving away from me once again. "It is a thankless task I have set for you, and doubtless, inexcusable in me to require so much of you. But I fear I must."

I nodded, hoping to find words to express my respect for his judgment. All I was able to say was, "I will do as you ask."

Mycroft Holmes rounded on me with purpose. "Then give me your close attention, Guthrie, and prepare yourself to enter the very gates of hell." For the next ten minutes he reiterated my instructions, and provided additional information which served to convince me that I would have to persevere in this venture. "It is fitting that you ask questions of Vickers. The character of August Jeffries, being no honest man himself, will question the acts and requests of others, and assume the worst of them. Use this to your advantage, and impart to him the full catalogue of your misfortunes, with as much self-serving remarks as you can summon up. If, for example, you are asked to travel, complain of the scale of accommodations you expect to be given or the time of the travel as inconvenient, to say nothing of the cost you will not wish to bear, and demand time to pursue your own interests while abroad."

"Abroad?" I echoed, much struck by this new development. "Sir, I surmise you expect that such an offer will be made."

"Why, yes," said Mycroft Holmes blandly. "I expect you will be asked to venture as far as Bavaria, or possibly even to Vienna."

"Can you tell me why?" I did not want to require him to reveal more than was prudent.

"Let us see if the offer is made first," he suggested. "I

would not like you to have a greater burden to carry than is yours already."

I inclined my head to acknowledge the difficulty of the situation. "And you do not want it to seem to Vickers that I know more than I ought."

"Precisely." He was relieved. "That would increase your hazard, not lessen it."

This time I recognized the wisdom of his reservations. "One thing, then, if you will, sir?"

"What is it?" He had heard the supplication in my words.

"Will you have a note delivered to my fiancée for me? I have not been able to show her the attention I had thought I would. I know it would disappoint both our families if I were to fail her now." I had not thought I would be so long absent, and knew Elizabeth would expect an explanation. "Miss Roedale is unaware that I am not available to her at present. She is disinclined to tolerate slights."

"Dear me," said Holmes. "Is she such a stickler?"

"I begin to think she is," I admitted, feeling disloyal for saying it. "If I continue to disappoint her, I will be worse than a cad to her. You may have noticed that she has a strong sense of what is due her. She has informed me that she expects us to choose our wedding day within two months."

"That may not be possible," said Holmes, carefully continuing, "How profound is your attachment?"

I felt my face redden. "I cannot answer that, Mister Holmes, not as a gentleman. I will confess I have never given the matter much thought. We have been promised to each other for all our lives. Our families have long anticipated our union."

Holmes waved this remark away. "Yes. I understand." He frowned, then told me, "You may write to her if the note is brief and reveals nothing of the nature of your mission. I will most certainly arrange for it to be delivered.

You may be satisfied that she will hold the missive in her hands by tomorrow morning." He pointed to a box of stationery on the writing table. "Write now, if it suits you."

Doing my best to order my thoughts, I sat down and reached for the inkwell and pen.

My dearest Elizabeth,

I write to inform you that my employer has instructed me that in the execution of my duties I must be absent from London for a period of time, which length cannot at this instant be accurately determined. Therefore I ask that you make allowances for this and hold me in your thoughts and your prayers while I discharge the obligations my employer has laid upon me. I will certainly keep you in my thoughts and prayers while I am gone.

I realize my travels may inconvenience you, and I ask your pardon for the same. I have no reason to suppose this will prove to be an isolated event, and I apologize for the awkwardness imposed upon us.

I will send you word as soon as I know the hour of my return, so that I may once again have the honor of visiting you and your parents at Twyford. Rest assured that I will inform you at once as soon as I have returned. You have my word that I will do nothing that will betray your trust in me.

> *With my most profound affection and esteem,*
> *Paterson Erskine Guthrie*

It was not as elegant a letter as I wanted to write, but under the circumstances, I felt it conveyed my most pressing concerns in a way that would not displease Mycroft Holmes or Elizabeth Roedale. I gave it to Mister Holmes to peruse.

"Very good, Guthrie," he approved as he handed it back to me. "Tyers will carry it to Twyford when he has completed his daily visit to his mother."

"How is she?" I asked, recalling how dire her case was. I folded the letter, put it in an envelope, and sealed it, writing Elizabeth's full name and direction on it.

"Failing," said Holmes. "Tyers expects to be summoned for the end at any moment. It is very sad."

"Will you extend my sympathies to Tyers," I requested as I handed the letter to Mister Holmes once more.

"I will," said Mycroft Holmes. "And now, I think it would be best for you to leave with James. You have been in here long enough to convince those watching that you have caught the interest of a solicitor. Make sure you do your parting from him abruptly, so that your watcher will know that all did not go to your satisfaction." He gestured to the door before handing me ten shillings. "Carry on. I will expect to see you tomorrow."

"God willing," I replied, and went to the door. "How do I account for this money?"

"Any way you like. Theft would be one explanation, and not an unexpected one," Mycroft Holmes suggested with a wicked twist of his lips.

"Theft," I repeated as I left him alone.

James was sitting behind the desk in the outer room, bent over a stack of papers. He looked up as I came up to him. "You are done?"

"For today. I will come again tomorrow, if there is anything to report." I noticed that James was preparing a brief, and this startled me.

"I must convince the world at large that I am a solicitor," he pointed out to me. "Or this deception becomes more dangerous to all of us."

"And are you a solicitor?" I asked, thinking that it was possible.

"I am a barrister, in fact," said James with pride. "I am on the Prime Minister's staff." He raised his head as he reached for his well-worn robes. "He assigned me to work with Mycroft Holmes when the matter of the Freising Treaty began."

"That was last year, was it not?" I asked, mentally reviewing the many notes I had transcribed in the last few months. "Some dealings with Germany."

"It was; Bavaria, actually. The matter was assumed settled, but it now appears there may be some difficulty. A few of the less public provisions . . . you understand." James clearly disliked difficulty. He gathered up his papers and consigned them to his portfolio once again. "This way, if you please."

I followed him down the hall, doing my best to resume the manner of August Jeffries as I went, so that by the time we stepped onto the narrow street, my expression was truculent. "I'll get your damned money, then," I said, loudly enough to attract the attention of several persons passing by.

"I will wait for your call, Mister . . . Jeffries, is it?" James was able to make himself subservient and arrogant at once, and I admired this talent even as I prepared—in Jeffries' character—to despise it.

"And right well you know it is Jeffries. August Jeffries; you will hear my name again, I give you my word, sir," I snarled, and turned away toward the Cap and Balls, letting my shoulders hunch as with anger and despair. I noticed that the beaked man was twenty yards or so behind me, ambling along as if distracted by the activity in the street around him.

Mister Holt was in the taproom by the time I got back, and he poured out a serving of gin as I came through the door. "You look like you could use it."

I took the drink and threw twice the cost of it on the bar. "Make sure I have a second," I snapped, and made my way to the inglenook. The odor of junipers was so strong that I nearly gagged as I brought the glass to my lips. Belatedly I thought I should have asked for a slice of beef and some cheese while I was with Mister Holmes. I decided I would not be so foolish in future. Realizing I should make some display of the few coins in my possession, I drew two of them out of my pocket and held them up. "Tonight I'd like a bit of supper, Mister Holt."

"Oho, so you made a few pence today," the landlord declared. "Well, what would you like?"

"You might say that I made them," I answered, being deliberately evasive. "And it's shillings, not pence."

Holt shrugged. "It's all one to me how you came by it, so long as you meet the price here."

"Well, this should get me enough to fill my belly." I put my hand squarely on the small tabletop. "And none of those portions that are all fat and gristle, if you please. Let me have the best meat here."

"It's a mutton stew today," Holt informed me. "A bowl is ten pence, bread and cheese with it, fourteen pence ha'penny."

"I'll have the lot," I said, tossing him one of the shillings. "And a pot of mustard for sauce."

He caught it easily and tucked it away in his apron pocket. "I'll be back with it fast as you can say knife."

I hunched over the gin as I waited; I saw the beak-nosed man come into the taproom and settle himself near the door where a pair of draymen were muttering over their beer. He made no sign of seeing me, and showed no interest in anyone in the taproom, but I knew that if I rose to visit the necessary house, he would not be far behind me. As Holt brought the bowl of stew I had ordered with a plate of bread and cheese, I noticed my observer look surprised.

"There you are, Mister Jeffries, and may you enjoy your supper," said the landlord as he put it before me. "Food and drink enough for any man."

"True enough," I said, and sniffed at the stew, which seemed flavored only with pepper. I would need the mustard to make it edible.

"You'll have another glass when that one is empty," Holt reminded me before he went back to his station behind the bar.

I was hungry enough to enjoy this unpromising fare; it would absorb the worst of the gin, or so I hoped, for tonight I reckoned I would need my wits about me if Vickers returned.

FROM THE PERSONAL JOURNAL OF PHILIP TYERS: *Today Mother was much worse, sunk into a dreamy state that does not bode well for her life.*

M.H. has been about errands for the Bavarian treaty; he returned here in a country squire's riding gear and the look of a man who had taken a nasty fall riding to hounds. Upon my examination of him, I discovered he was bleeding in the shoulder, whereupon he produced the weapon which had inflicted the injury—a small skinning knife with a thin, wicked blade. "Much more of this," he told me, "and I'll have to send for Sutton ahead of schedule." During his absence from this flat, he has learned that there is likely to be an attempt to steal the treaty before it can be signed. No amount of coaxing on my part would persuade him to tell me more than this concerning his escapades. He hopes that G. will provide the information necessary to prevent such a theft, for it would be a disaster.

Chapter Five

IT WAS AFTER nine when Vickers at last put in an appearance in the taproom of the Cap and Balls. By this time I had almost assumed he would not arrive that night, and was on the point of going to my damp and unpleasant little room, and so was not as fully prepared to deal with the man as I had been rather earlier.

"Did you achieve your goal today, Mister Jeffries?" asked Vickers without any salutation whatever. He had obtained a glass of his port from Holt, and had taken up the same place he had occupied the night before.

"I found a solicitor who is willing to undertake my case, if that's what you mean. For thirty pounds." I spat this last out, making a show of my anger.

"A goodly sum, but surely worth it if he can expedite securing the funds your father left you?" He lifted his glass in my direction, and I had to hide the qualms he gave me by this civility.

"It's robbery, and no mistake about it. Just because he may have to dodge around the terms of the will a little." I scoffed as I laughed. "That's what lawyers are supposed to do, isn't it?"

"There are those who think so," said Vickers. He watched me for a short while in a silence as stretched and miserable as a miser's purse strings. "You have had supper, or so I gather."

"I was hungry," I grumbled.

"But with so little . . . pardon me for mentioning your straitened circumstances, but it is not what I would expect, this dining." He showed me his teeth. "You must have had unexpected good fortune today."

"I . . . came across a little money, and I decided to eat," I told him, doing my best to appear boastful about it, and sly at the same time.

"And how did you . . . er . . . come across it, pray?" Vickers persisted.

It was an effort to answer as he stared at me. "I saw a gent leave a pouch. In the solicitor's chamber. He didn't look back for it, so I picked it up when he was gone. There weren't much in it." I was able to sound ill used by this unfortunate trick of fate.

"Still, to have a few shillings just now must be welcome." Vickers met my look with his own, far more predatory stare.

"Amen to that, Mister Vickers," I said, lifting my half-empty glass of gin to him.

He sprang his trap. "And I imagine you are not above undertaking something not quite within the law in order to—"

"Hey, now, Mister Vickers. I won't risk no Brixton holiday for a handful of shillings." I shook my head emphatically.

"No, of course, not for a few shillings," Vickers agreed. "But if you could gain, say, thirty pounds, what then?"

"Thirty pounds," I said as if the amount were new to me; I used Vickers' own words back at him. "A good piece of money, is thirty pounds."

"Good enough to pay a solicitor named James to break

your father's will, which is what must be done for you to touch a penny of what he left you. You would need to have your family here to come by the inheritance legitimately," said Vickers smoothly. "Last night I offered to help you out of your current . . . shall we say embarrassments? I have given the matter a great deal of thought, and it strikes me that you are the sort of man who would not tend to be overly nice in his requirements of employment. Surely I am not in error?"

My shock was only partly false. "How'd you know about the will?" I demanded, hoping my indignation rang true for August Jeffries. "I won't say as you're wrong about me, but I don't like anyone messing about in my affairs."

"I am interested in you, Mister Jeffries," Vickers assured me. "When someone interests me, I am at pains to learn all I may about them."

"But I said nothing of the terms, at least not—" My bluster had the right undertone of desperation to it, which pleased me.

"Some of my men have taken it upon themselves to discover how truthful your accounts have been." He smiled at me again, and I knew how a deer felt when the wolf crossed its path.

"How did you get into the records of the law courts?" I demanded, aware that he must have bribed someone in an important post to secure the information in so little time. "It is no easy thing to get the terms of inheritance revealed if you are not party to it."

"And so quickly, too," added Vickers. "I went to those who are able to help me and inclined to do this for me." He saw my glass was empty and ordered another glass of that appalling gin for me.

"It weren't right of you to do that," I complained, but softly, to show that I was momentarily cowed by this sinister fellow.

"But I needed to assure myself that you had not lied overmuch to me. I thought a few of your statements in regard to the terms of your father's will sounded a bit questionable, and now I have my suppositions confirmed." He leaned forward, his expression growing more lupine than it had been earlier. "I would think you would be willing to undertake the commission I propose in order to lay your hands on thirty pounds." He rubbed the tips of his fingers together, an expression of malicious anticipation on his sharp features. "Shall I sweeten the pot by, say, another fifteen pounds, plus the expenses of your travel?"

"That'd be near fifty pounds," I said, as if I had been offered the Crown Jewels.

"So it would," Vickers agreed. "To journey to a place near Munich, in Bavaria."

"Bavaria," I repeated, thinking of what I had learned earlier that day. "What is in Bavaria?"

"There is a man there who is bringing a document from there to England. The man is married to a German noblewoman, but is, himself, a Scotsman. It would be his second marriage. What I propose is a ruse of sorts. I must know what is in that document, what it says and how it is to be enforced." He was growing restless with purpose. "I will pay you forty-five pounds as well as all your costs of travel to obtain that information for me before the document reaches England."

I shook my head. "How do you expect the likes of me to do that?" I asked. "I can't think of any reason such a man would permit me to get near him."

"He might take you to help him if his own valet should meet with an . . . accident." The real meaning of that last word was dreadfully plain; the accident was expected to be fatal.

"You mean you expect me to kill a man for thirty pounds?" I exclaimed, my dinner settling like clods behind my belt.

"Forty-five, Mister Jeffries. Forty-five pounds, at the least. Given the expense of your travel, I would think that it may well be closer to sixty pounds before the venture is done." He chuckled. "Don't tell me a man of your cut would balk at a murder?"

"I never killed no one before," I said, making it sound as if the notion was truly offensive. "And not for such a sum."

Vickers looked thoroughly amused. "Then this will be a new experience for you, no doubt," he said, and settled back in his chair. "I want your answer tonight, Jeffries. I do not want you to spend the night fretting over your decision, for that will always lead to the circumspection that is not welcome to me." He steepled his fingers once again, and looked at me over that peak. "It would be folly for you to hesitate, for even with thirty pounds, your solicitor may find his work scrutinized by the courts and your machinations could be discovered, which would have severe consequences for you."

I glowered. "I can't have that."

"No, you certainly cannot. So it would be worthwhile for you to give me an answer in the affirmative." He watched me closely, though he made it appear he had no interest in me at the moment.

"This man, then, the Scotsman. What would I have to do?" I begrudged the question as if I disliked having my hand exposed.

"Read the document he carries and return here in advance of him with all the details I have stipulated. I will need to know before the Prime Minister has read it what is contained in it." His answer was swift.

"And the Scotsman would not have to have an . . . accident?" I was pleased at how avaricious I sounded, and how unprincipled.

"No; in fact he must not be allowed to suspect anything. If he has the least suspicion that his mission has been compromised, he will make this known to those around him and that would be worse for my purpose than having the document arrive here without benefit of discovering its contents."

"What sort of document is it?" I asked, anticipating a lie for my answer. I was not disappointed.

"I have no idea," said Vickers, making no effort to hide his mendacity. "And that is the source of my trouble."

"I see. You may need to act if there are certain proposals within the document which would not favor you. That is why you want it examined and your questions about it answered," I said, as if grasping the whole of the problem.

"Yes. You see, if it turns out that certain enterprises of mine are at risk because of the terms of the document, I must have advance warning of it in order to minimize the losses I would suffer because of it. Surely in your factoring for cotton buyers, there have been times when a little advance knowledge has saved you from serious difficulties." This last was another open appeal to Jeffries' capacity for larceny.

"It would be a challenge to try to discover the details of the document," I said, as if warming to the prospect. "It might even be that some of the information could be turned to my advantage."

"It is possible," seconded Vickers, again offering his temptation.

I took more of the gin in the glass Holt brought than was prudent, and hoped as I did that it would not go to my head. "Fifty pounds, perhaps sixty, to go to Bavaria and deal with this Scotsman and the document he carries."

"That is the enterprise, yes," said Vickers. "And if you can turn your labor to your advantage, so much the better."

It struck me then that Vickers was planning to have me—as Jeffries—killed at the conclusion of the venture; he had no other reason to be so expansive and helpful as he made himself appear if his intentions were less fatal; I tried to look more fuddled than I was, and slurred my words when I said, "Then you had better tell me when you expect me to leave, so I can be ready betimes."

"I think there is a packet leaving tomorrow evening for

Amsterdam. If you take the train down tomorrow, you will arrive in plenty of time to be aboard her." He clapped his hands together. "The sooner you begin, the sooner the money is yours."

"Amsterdam is a strange port for Bavaria," I remarked.

"You do not want to go the obvious way," said Vickers. "In case your actions are traced later, you would not like the destination and purpose of your travels to be too readily apparent."

"Yes, I take your meaning. Very well, Amsterdam it is," I agreed, doing my best to seem eager for the work. "But I will have to call upon solicitor James in the morning, to inform him I will shortly have the money he has demanded of me."

"Of course," Vickers agreed, so quickly that I was certain that my impression of his intentions where I was concerned were correct. "Do that. And prepare a note for any relative you might want to be alerted to your whereabouts. Your half-brother, for instance, may want to know where you have gone, To say nothing of your wife; you would not want her to worry." He put his hands on the arms of the chair. "I will see that they are delivered at once."

"Good of you," I said, lifting the glass to him and steeling myself for the hideous stuff.

"I will meet you here at eleven in the morning. I will accompany you to your train and I will give you your instructions then, and all the money you will need for your traveling." He rose from his chair in a single energetic movement. "Until then, let me congratulate you on your decision. You have made a wise bargain." He held out his hand, and I did my best to hide my reluctance as I took it.

"It's a privilege to be doing work for a fine gentleman like yourself, Mister Vickers. You won't have any cause to regret it; my word on it." I tried to make it sound as if I was completely won over, but I feared that my inward consternation was not adequately disguised.

"Sleep well, Mister Jeffries," said Vickers. "You will need to be alert tomorrow."

"I'll take myself off at once, if it please you, sir." I bowed my head slightly to him and made myself smile ingratiatingly.

When Vickers strolled out of the taproom, I felt a pall had been lifted from the place. The fire seemed to burn more brightly, the lamps were cheerier than they had been while Vickers occupied the place.

I glanced toward Holt and saw him shake his head once as if in sympathy or unhappiness. I discovered in myself an urge to tell the man I was not deceived by the blandishments and tantalization offered by Vickers, but I was able to stop myself in time. I tossed him a thr'penny bit and left the taproom whistling.

Once in my room, I began to make a number of notes to myself, which I quickly destroyed as it occurred to me that I might well still be observed and subject to unwelcome scrutiny by Vickers' agents; if I were foolish enough to make a record of my impressions and thoughts, I might not be alive come morning. As I burned the last of these notes in the candle, I heard a sharp rap at my door. "A moment," I called out, and put the ashes into the pocket of my coat so as not to draw attention to what I had been doing. I made a point of taking my pistol as I went to the door.

The elderly man with the Devonshire accent stood in the doorway, a cordial smile on his pinched features. He wore a hacking jacket of west-country weave, as if he had just come to town for the day. His breeches were chestnut-colored and his shirt was so white he could not have ridden here directly. The waistcoat was of a tapestry brocade. The country squire-scholar to the life. "Good evening, Mister Jeffries. I am informed that you have agreed to undertake a short journey on Mister Vickers' behalf."

"That I have," I said, making no move to invite him into the room, or to apologize for my pistol. "Though I don't know what business it is of yours."

"Ah, Mister Jeffries," said the Devon man, "I don't mean to intrude in your affairs, but I would appreciate a minute of your time. You follow the stars, and when a man commits himself to a venture of so uncertain a nature, I would hope he would allow his stars to guide him." He moved nearer so that I would be forced to admit him or close the door in his face.

I was curious about the man and his purpose for coming, so I gracelessly held the door open for him, and indicated the single chair in the room; I went and sat on the corner of the bed. "What's this about, then? And tell me quickly. I don't have hours to spare."

"I have reviewed the information you provided me in regard to your birth, and I wished to remind you that there is a very powerful transit coming up in regard to your natal sun." He continued to smile at me as if he were a painted puppet.

"Yes," I said, wondering what this man was actually looking for, as it certainly was not to inform me of what I presumably already knew. "And they will be most powerful on the eleventh of next month."

"And the twelfth," said the Devon man. "I hope you will let me offer you a little advice in this regard." He folded his hands, looking for all the world like a small, earnest, nearsighted animal with glasses perched on his nose.

"What do you want to tell me?" I asked, beginning to think the man's naïveté was genuine.

"That it would be folly for you to suppose you may use the favorable conditions of the stars to push for advantage with Mister Vickers. He has much more at his command than the influences of Jupiter and Mars. He will not excuse any lapse on your part, once he has entrusted you with a task." He scowled and looked down at the toe of his polished boot. "Play him false and you will suffer for it as you have never imagined possible."

"Very well," I said. So this was what the man was doing—delivering a threat for Vickers.

"He has many servants in this world; some of them are

in Germany as well as France. Do not think you will be unobserved while you are on this mission for him. And if you think to escape him, you will discover that there is no place on earth he cannot reach you and exact vengeance for your betrayal."

"I will strive to remember that," I said, as a grue slid down my spine. I had no doubt that this last was true.

"He is a very powerful force in the world," the Devon man said, for emphasis. "Keep that in mind." He rose from the creaking chair. "You might want to read the accounts in the papers two years ago of Henry Gordon-Hughes. There is coverage of the case in *The Times*. It would be instructive to you to familiarize yourself with the case." He went to the door and opened it.

"Henry Gordon-Hughes," I repeated as if the name were strange to me, though I recalled the dreadful matter well enough: Henry Gordon-Hughes was found on a stretch of sand by the North Sea in Holland. He had been flayed alive.

"Yes. He failed to complete a mission for Mister Vickers." And with that, the man with the Devonshire accent was gone, leaving me with a number of distressing thoughts to bedevil my sleep.

FROM THE PERSONAL JOURNAL OF PHILIP TYERS:
M.H. sustained a visit from Miss Roedale of Twyford shortly before noon; she was much distressed that her fiancé has been called away from her at this time. It appears that there is to be an important gathering of her family which G. was supposed to attend and now will not be able to. Miss Roedale informed M.H. that she had not anticipated such disruptions in her life when she learned that G. worked for a member of the government. M.H. did what he could to assure the young woman that this mission could not be helped or set aside, which somewhat mollified the young lady.

Chapter Six

"I AM SORRY, my dear Guthrie," said Mycroft Holmes the next morning as he arrived at the chamber of Solicitor James about twenty minutes after I had sent word through James that it was urgent I see him. "I would have been here earlier, but I did not want to attract any undue attention to our meeting here. And I was inconvenienced when I found my flat had been thoroughly and messily searched when I returned from my club last night. Tyers was visiting his mother at the time, and that left the culprits free to cast about like wild men."

"Good God," I said in dismay. "Was anything of value taken?"

"Not that I have been able to determine after a cursory examination. Tyers is setting the place to rights now, and I will learn more later." He took my note from his pocket. "So Vickers wants to send you to Germany today. He is not taking any chances that you might change your mind, or have the opportunity to learn too much to his disadvantage."

"So it seemed to me," I agreed, trying to put as good a face upon matters as I could. "He has already done all that he can to ensure that I will be beholden to him."

"And he will try to do more," said Mycroft Holmes. "It has long been his pattern to bind his servants to him with fear and indebtedness of all kinds. You will have to make it seem you are willing to be one of his creatures." He paced down the room, hands clasped behind his back. "I can only think it is indeed the Freising Treaty he is seeking to obtain, and that is not welcome intelligence."

"What is it about this treaty that troubles you so much in this regard?" I asked.

Mycroft Holmes halted and gave me a long, direct stare. "This treaty may not be particularly significant in and of itself, but there are ramifications to it that cause me the gravest concern. This treaty may be the last chance to prevent a destructive war that could tear apart half of Europe. I dare say it may drag us into another calamity like the Crimea. And it is all the result of folly." He took a cigar from his case and returned the case to the inside pocket of his coat. "Nations, very much like people, need to grow."

I watched Holmes, wondering if he intended this last reflection to apply to my youth and inexperience. But he was snipping off the end of the cigar, apparently unaware of my presence. As he lit the cigar, he gave a quick glance in my direction, then stared up at the ceiling.

"There are so many young nations today," he explained, luxuriating in the first puff of rum-flavored smoke. "Some are not much more than children in the scheme of things. In the past such new nations looked to older, wiser states for direction, and to curb their impetuousness. But not now, not with the powerful German states uniting under the Prussian banner and the hand of Otto von Bismarck. This rapid emergence has been at the expense of the Hapsburgs. Austria as we knew it is fading rapidly, and it is being supplanted by a nation with no tradition of responsible government, much less any diplomatic sagacity." He studied the graceful arabesques from the glowing tip of his cigar as if a code were hidden there that he might break.

Although I had not yet fully grasped the extent to which my employer was involved in foreign affairs, I sensed that he had more than an academic interest in European developments. When he ventured nothing more, I asked, "Is there to be a treaty between Germany and Austria?"

"Actually, no. Their problems cannot yet be addressed. There are other, more pressing matters to be settled before those questions may be answered." He flicked the ash off his cigar. "This treaty was negotiated by England as a neutral party in order to prevent a particularly disruptive war from erupting in the Balkans. A most unsatisfactory region, the Balkans: everyone is eager to rule himself for the specific purpose of being free to slaughter his neighbor."

"If the region is as volatile as you say, why should we bother with such pugnacious peoples?" I asked. It hardly seemed worth the effort to me.

Mister Holmes sighed and commenced to twirl his watchfob. "Yes. Ordinarily it would be a useless venture. But their interminable struggles do not involve only themselves. Every nation in the area, including Italy, feels the need to demonstrate its influence in the disputes. More than that, they all fear loss of importance should they fail to take action. The great powers are trapped by their sense of national honor as well as their fear of appearing weak or indecisive. Thus they mobilize their armies over questions of endless dilemmas of regional borders and the duty charged on fox pelts."

"But surely," I began, hoping to glean some reason from what he had said, "this need not result in war?"

"Need not, but very nearly did." Mycroft Holmes stopped twirling his watchfob and spoke more thoughtfully. "Two nations, neither as populous nor as advanced as England, were just on the brink of coming to battle. Unfortunately every major nation except England has agreements that would require them to intervene in this conflict. None of them felt secure enough to turn away from the impending crisis."

I took up his tone with more indignation. "And because a handful of hill-people cannot agree on their—"

"This was not simply a matter of a few peasants potting away at one another. We could have had all Europe and Russia joining in the argument. We came very close to Armageddon last month."

"Then what does Vickers want with the treaty? Your book said the Brotherhood seeks the downfall of European states; why not let well enough alone, and let the war come?" I could see where those in high governmental positions might oppose this treaty, but I could not guess what a man of Vickers' interests would gain from compromising it.

"Ah, that may be the heart of the issue," said Mycroft Holmes. "He is indeed part of the occult Brotherhood— as you say, you read something of their history the other day—which seeks to bring about the downfall of all royal houses in Europe and Asia. Its goal is the complete destruction of all nations and empires so that they may assume total power in place of the legitimate rulers." He shook his head. "They must not prevail."

"No, certainly not," I said at once finding the whole notion dreadful.

"And you will have the task of preventing their interference with this treaty. For if it fails, there will be more and greater difficulties because of it." He drew on his cigar and blew out the smoke. "For now the Balkan crisis has been diffused. The treaty we are concerned with gives guarantees by England to one of those countries involved—enough so that they have prevailed upon their smaller ally in the Balkans to give ground. The treaty has been most aptly named the Treaty of Reassurance."

I shared his ironic smile. "An interesting touch."

"Isn't it," he said, and went on, "Our problem now is that there are nations, some who are numbered among England's friends, who would not entirely approve certain secret clauses in the treaty." He set the cigar aside. His voice was now more solemn than I had ever heard it before. "The matter is too grave for rumor and suspicion to prevail. The exposure of those secret clauses as we have signed and sealed them would bring about the very war it is supposed to prevent. I have striven too long to permit peace to elude us now. Only two copies of the entire treaty exist. One is safely under the domes of the other signator's capital. The other, due to the peculiarities of the messenger entrusted with its safe escort to London, is at risk."

"You mean it would be possible for the Brotherhood to obtain it?" I asked, much shocked.

Holmes waved his hand, and the cigar left traces of it in the air. "Diplomacy often goes down some very strange roads, Guthrie. In this case, the messenger was agreeable to both sides, peculiarities and all."

"But if the Brotherhood steals the treaty—" I exclaimed.

"Exactly. Such a disaster is what the Brotherhood desires most, and what we, Guthrie, you and I, must prevent at all costs." He repeated the last grimly. "All costs."

I had not reckoned on such high stakes in this venture, and was attempting to find a way to express my misgivings when it struck me that much of this conflict that so troubled Holmes must be ongoing. "When did all this begin?" I asked him, hoping to learn the source of the trouble.

"It started long ago," said Mycroft Holmes, "in Europe with a group of renegade Masons and a lodge of occultists, who decided they would have to band together if they were ever to achieve the downfall of the great houses of Europe. They combined the most radical of Masonic notions with the manipulative strength of the occultists into one, hidden, subversive movement that had support from many ambitious nobles, those who had sought advancement and had not achieved it. The alliance has continued to this day. It is often at the very heart of the most nefarious plots that strike at the seat of power. I am personally aware of six lodges of this Brotherhood currently active in England and Europe. And I know that Vickers is the leader of the lodge active in London." He lowered his voice. "In addition, I am aware of more than a dozen murders committed by this one lodge in the last five years alone."

"Henry Gordon-Hughes," I said.

Mycroft Holmes regarded me steadily, saying in a low voice, "Why, yes, he was one. There have been others, I am saddened to tell you." His frown deepened as he stubbed out the end of his cigar. "I am loath to send you on this mission, but there is no one else whom Vickers will accept at this point, and so, with notice much shorter than I anticipated a week ago, I am afraid it will have to be you, or we must face the possibility of failure with the treaty. Which I dare not contemplate." He rocked back on his heels, which I had learned meant that he found the matter under discussion unacceptable.

"I will go, of course," I said, hoping I did not sound as frightened as I was. What had my employer put me into? "But I am a secretary, not a man of action, and I may not be able to—"

"My dear Guthrie, you are young, you are intelligent, and you are resourceful. I have great confidence in your abilities." Mycroft Holmes put his hand on my shoulder. "I can think of no one else in whom I could repose the confidence I have in you."

This encomium was much more than any I had expected. And if his motives for giving it were less than pristine, I could not make myself question them. Though were the mission not for the protection of my country, I might have felt I had been taken advantage of by both Vickers and Mycroft Holmes. The importance of the task overshadowed all other considerations. "I will do my utmost to discharge my duty to your satisfaction."

"Excellent. I was convinced I could not be mistaken in you." He went to the desk and sat down, pulling a map from one of the pigeon-holes and spreading it out. "As you see, your destination is very near Munich, in what was once the Bishopric of Freising in the Electorate of Bavaria, according to the terms of the Peace of Westphalia—"

"That was 1648, as I recall," I interjected, to show I was not wholly ignorant of the history of the region.

Mycroft Holmes nodded once, his manner decisive. "You are correct. Being near Munich and controlled by the Church made this odd little sliver of land much more important than its acreage might appear to suggest. Even today there are crucial alliances in that region which are vital to English interests in Europe, as you have gathered from what I've told you."

I listened in growing apprehension, for it seemed to me that as determined as I was to succeed at my task, there were those opponents who were as determined as I to see it fail.

"If you are not feeling the ill effects of that horrible inn, I hope you will permit me to provide you with a light meal before you leave." He smiled at me pleasantly, and went on in response to my look of surprise. "Well, you are heavy-eyed, and your stomach has growled twice since you arrived."

"I hoped you had not noticed," I said, feeling embarrassed.

"With what you must have had for fare, I am astonished you are not quite green about the gills," said my employer. "A mutton pie and some cheese will put you to rights again."

"Thank you, sir. It would be very welcome." My mouth was watering.

"There are just a few more matters to tend to, and then you may have your pie. Tell me, Guthrie, what do you think is the most important thing you can do at this time?" Mycroft Holmes regarded me with expectant cordiality, as if he were confident of my answer before I had even decided what it was.

"Follow the instructions Vickers gives me?" I suggested.

"I knew I was correct to employ you," he approved. "Yes. Do nothing to alert him to your real purpose. Let him think he has suborned you—meaning August Jeffries—with the promise of money and an end to the restrictions of your father's will. Make him think you are venal and greedy, so that he will not be inclined to know more of you. If he is persuaded you are his tool, you will be able to penetrate the maze of his lodge, and, perhaps, the Brotherhood as well. Which service would be of greatest importance to England and the Crown."

It was, I admit, thrilling to think my activities could have such overwhelming importance, and I was not immune to pride as I listened. I was also keenly aware that I could not accomplish this assignment without help, and I summoned my courage to say so. "I will need a way to contact you, for I will have to relay information and receive your instructions as I travel."

"You most certainly will," said Mycroft Holmes, his manner at once approving and measuring. "To begin with, you will send a telegram to these chambers, to your solicitor, asking if he has had time to review the will yet. That will inform me that you have arrived in Europe. If your port of entry has been changed—and it would be like Vickers to do such a thing—add that you expect James to contact your stepbrother as soon as possible. You will telegraph your solicitor daily, asking for reports on his progress. If you have significant information to pass on to us, add your concern that the matter ought to be settled before the end of the year. If you perceive a greater risk than we have discussed, inform James that you are not satisfied with his efforts. If you are convinced you are in danger of being discovered, appeal to James on behalf of your wife and children. There will be telegrams sent to you as well, from James. If he says that press of work delays him, it will mean that we have more information for you. If he tells you that he is not pleased with the terms of the trust, you will have a packet waiting at the next stop along whatever line you travel. If he apologizes for failing to have your brief prepared, it will be a signal that you are in danger of exposure." He studied the map. "As soon as you make contact with the Scotsman, send a telegram assuring James of payment."

"I hope I will be able to remember all of this," I said.

"You will be astonished the number of things you can remember during missions of this sort." He took out his watch and studied it. "You will have to be away shortly. James will provide you with the key for the code we will use. It is a fairly simple one, but that can't be helped with so little time." He held out his hand. "Vickers is not the only one who has helpers in Europe. I will do what I can to provide you with trustworthy assistants. The recognition signal will be my brother's address, but C instead of B. The countersign will be the Cap and Balls. Anyone offering you that address is someone you may rely upon, no matter how unlikely a person it may be."

"All right," I said, starting to feel a trifle giddy at the prospect of the undertaking before me.

"You will find the Scotsman a challenge to your ingenuity, I think," added Mycroft Holmes with a wry smile.

"Why? Is he an ogre? Or is he part of the Brotherhood?" This last gave me a pang of anxiety.

Mycroft Holmes was quick to banish my apprehensions on that head. "Nothing like that, no. But he is a good friend to those in high office; he is important in his own right. Cameron MacMillian, while not The MacMillian, is a most influential man. His position in his clan is unassailable and his wealth is immense. His father, who is still alive, controls most of the manufacture of engines for our country's warships. He is the pride of the Scottish engineers, and his influence extends beyond the Admiralty to Number Ten."

I sighed once, thinking how position and worth did not often walk hand in hand.

"As your expression reveals," said Mycroft Holmes drily, "you understand how it comes about that this man was chosen as the messenger for the treaty. But you do not know what a reckless decision it was."

"Surely such a man is loyal beyond question," I blurted out.

There was a slight line between Holmes' strong brows; it deepened to a furrow as he continued. "He is certainly loyal to his clan and King. His record as a Hussar officer is beyond question. It is not his loyalty but his judgment that concerns me."

"His judgment?" I echoed.

"Yes. Some years ago Cameron MacMillian married a lovely young woman—an American, as I recall—who died tragically while pregnant with their first child. MacMillian did not behave well. He began to assuage his grief, which, in fairness, I know to have been considerable, with strong drink and the company of women of a certain station. He was careful at first, but grew careless with time, sometimes arriving in the company of obvious ladybirds and not in full control of his faculties. None of this embarrassed him in the slightest, for he was protected by his family name and his tremendous wealth. When intoxicated, he is not above baiting those he is certain will not strike back at a man of his position. Of course, in time he became unwelcome in polite society. He was not invited to court after one truly appalling breach of conduct. Bereft of the company of those of his own station, he plunged into debauch. Finally, when his father would permit no more, he was dispatched to the Continent to . . . em . . . manage certain family holdings there. It was hoped he might marry again for the family. That was three years ago. I gather there was some bitterness upon his departure, and he has, by all accounts, neither reformed nor voiced a desire to return."

I was more at sea than before. "If that is so, why should he be the one chosen for so delicate a task?"

Holmes held up one long finger signaling me to hold my question. "The gentleman who headed the team that negotiated the Treaty of Reassurance was Sir John Drummond. You may recall the name?"

"Yes," I said, having seen it on a number of courier packets and telegrams.

"Those communications came, as you may be aware, from St. Petersburg," said Mycroft Holmes. "Fellow Scots Drummond and MacMillian were at Balliol together, and you know what the Oxonian ties are. I was unable to dissuade Sir John of the lack of wisdom MacMillian represented. Perhaps he thought he was doing MacMillian a favor, providing him with a way to redeem himself. Sir John himself is still in the East, continuing his mission."

"Sir John chose MacMillian as his personal messenger." I said it as if hearing it aloud I might convince myself of it.

"Yes. And though it may be that Cameron MacMillian's motives are of the highest order, it is difficult to conceive of a less appropriate courier for secret and sensitive papers." He made a gesture to show the matter was beyond him.

"I see what you mean; very high in the instep, and without cause," I told him, and decided that I would need to keep a very civil tongue in my head if I were to be admitted to his staff.

"At the least," agreed Mycroft Holmes. "Now, I must be about my own arrangements." He moved briskly, with more energy than one would suppose he possessed from his air of general, scholarly indolence.

"What are your plans, sir? May I know, if they impinge on mine?" I did not like the notion of not knowing where my employer was now that I was being sent on such duty at his behest.

"I must spend a short while with Edmund Sutton this morning; I trust I shall find him awake, though the hour is early for him." He snapped his fingers restlessly. "He will have to prepare for his standard assignment." By which he meant the actor would impersonate him, keeping to Mycroft Holmes' strict schedule and providing the illusion that Holmes was, in fact, in London. It was a device that had served him well in the past, and doubtless would serve him in the future. "I am also expecting word from my brother in regard to that fellow with the Devonshire accent. He knows such a catalogue of rogues, criminals, and ruffians that I do not doubt he will assist in identifying this individual."

"How will you get word of it to me, if I am expected to depart so soon?" I did not relish going into the hands of these men without knowing as much as possible about them, for though I realized they were indeed desperate, I was also aware that my only hope against them was information.

"You will be delivered two new shirts at the Cap and Balls. They will come from a shop two blocks from here. Folded in the sleeves will be a report, as well as any necessary changes in our system of codes." He indicated the door. "You must be off. For if you linger, the man assigned to watch you may become suspicious. James will tell you where to find the haberdashery I mentioned. You should stop in there on your return to the inn so that it will be understood that you have reason to accept the shirts."

"Of course," I agreed, impressed at the quickness of Mycroft Holmes' mind.

"I will also alert you to any changes in our arrangements with the Scotsman, so that you will be prepared to deal with him when you meet him." He looked at his watch again. "Well, off you go, Guthrie. Godspeed." He made a gesture to dismiss me and then stopped as one more thought occurred to him. "Take no gift from Vickers or any of his men. They will probably offer you some minor token. Find a good excuse to refuse it. And avoid a high-born churl called von Metz."

"All right," I said, curious as to why, and who was von Metz.

Mycroft Holmes sensed my unspoken question. "You

have read of some of the rituals of this Brotherhood. They will seek many ways to control you."

"And superstitious fools let themselves be persuaded by chicken-claws and rattles. You will find I have a sterner mind than that, sir," I assured him. "I am a rational man, educated and well informed. Those—"

"It is not only ignorant savages in Africa and India who resort to such devices. Vickers and his cohorts have skills enough to use these techniques with deadly purpose. Your doubts will not help you if they decide to turn their efforts against you." Again he motioned me to the door. "Keep your wits about you, Guthrie, and do not relax your guard, for that way lies worse things than death."

My time in Mycroft Holmes' employ had taught me that he was not one to engage in rodomontade, or similar hyperbole, and for that reason alone, his warning struck me to the heart. I bowed slightly and left him.

FROM THE PERSONAL JOURNAL OF PHILIP TYERS:
I have at last completed the restoration of M.H.'s flat. Whoever undertook to search the place must have done it with speed his most important concern, for everything he touched was in disarray. Papers and books flung everywhere, cushions pulled out and ripped open, drawers overturned and their contents strewn about. At M.H.'s instruction, I have completed a thorough search of all the rooms that were disturbed—though the kitchen and the pantry were left without any disruption, and the sitting room was only half searched. It is my belief that the miscreant was interrupted by my return, and was forced to flee with his purpose unfulfilled, as we can determine that nothing is missing. Were it not for the reason for my absence, I would chastise myself for failing in my duty to M.H.

Mother continues to fade. I have asked that the minister give her what comforts he can, as it is not likely that she will be truly conscious again before the end. M.H.

was kind enough to permit me to visit her again this evening, for he became aware of my lack of concentration on my work here. I cannot express the depth of gratitude I feel toward him for his kindness in these dark hours.

Chapter Seven

"So you purchased new shirts," approved the other man sharing my compartment on the train for Dover. He was thin and professorial, about forty, a gray-faced academic sort in old tweeds, with a short beard and spectacles clipped to the bridge of his nose.

"Two," I said, glaring at him with a suspicion that was only partly feigned.

"Good. If your collars and cuffs are freshly laundered and starched, it should be satisfactory. You will present a less unfortunate appearance." He settled back against the squabs and regarded me speculatively. "Not that you are very prepossessing, as it is."

I was pleased I had not taken the two small notes I had found concealed in the sleeves of the second shirt out to read in this train compartment, for surely that would have caused suspicions in the mind of this fellow, suspicions I could not afford. "I do the best I can; and I will thank you not to question me too closely. I have said I will undertake this work, and you may be sure I will." My umbrage was more genuine than I liked to admit.

"What pride and delusion," said the man, as if remarking on the clouds overhead. "You will have to curb those impulses when you reach Germany or there will be hell to pay." He chuckled, his face as unchanged in expression as if it had been carved in stone.

"I'll thank you to keep your thoughts to yourself, sir," I grumbled, and hitched my shoulders higher to do what I could to cut myself off from him. I moved my aged carpetbag—another of the inestimable Edmund Sutton's contributions—nearer to me on the seat, as if I feared my traveling companion might attempt to snatch it or rifle its contents.

"To be sure," said the man, ignoring my rudeness with such determination that I realized his manner was deliberate. "But you may have need of them before we reach France."

"You're mistaken, sir," I grumbled, hoping that my dismay was concealed. "I am bound for Amsterdam."

"No, Mister Jeffries, you are not. Your travel itinerary has been changed. You will make the crossing to Calais, and there go to Paris, and then east into Germany, by way of Luxembourg. From Luxembourg you will go to Mannheim, to Würzburg, from there to Ulm—that is a bit indirect; it can't be helped. At Augsburg you will be met by a Herr Dortmunder. You need not know anything about him, for he will have a description of you to guide him. He will identify himself by asking if you have any English coins you would like to exchange for German ones. He will give you further instructions." All goodwill had vanished from my traveling companion, and I could not help but be aware of the intensity of his purpose.

I regarded him with an expression I hoped was sullen; my eyes fixed on the top of his tie and I muttered, "Why should I believe you?"

"Because I have authorization, and a note from Mister Vickers. I also have the tickets you need, and I will take those you already possess. Do not think to deny you have them: I know very well that you do. You have them in your inner coat pocket, or so I am told." He achieved a grimace of satisfaction. "Oh, yes. I am under instructions, too, to make your journey for you so that if there is anyone supposed to watch you, they will have a target for their efforts. We do not want them casting about for you." He pulled an eyepatch from his pocket, removed his spectacles, and set it in place. "Doubtless they will be searching for this." He fumbled with his spectacles, trying to keep them in place on his nose without success.

"Mister Vickers is a knowing cove," I said, and took the large envelope he held out to me. Inside was another packet of flimsies, not all of them British, and a purse of coins, everything from French to Austrian. There were also a number of train tickets and timetables. I took one out and started to read it.

"You'll notice that there are a number of departures marked. Those are the ones you are expected to try to take; there is plenty of leeway in the departure time so that it should not be impossible, even for you. If you cannot reach the latest on the list, you are to send a telegram to the station where you are to transfer, to a Father del Franco, advising him of your late arrival." He leaned forward to emphasize his next words. "Should you fail to make a connection and not send word ahead, the Brotherhood will assume that you have played them false. They will then be forced to hunt you down and exact vengeance for your betrayal."

At another time I might have found such pronouncements a trifle overblown and melodramatic, but in this place, and for the purposes involved, I could not make myself regard the threat as anything but of deadly sincerity. "I'd be a fool to hop the drum, with such a huggermugger lot as you are," I said, and noted that my traveling companion understood that bit of street and army jargon. "I'll do what's necessary for you—I said I wouldn't rat, and I won't."

"You had better not. We dispose of those who have no use to us, and those who defy us we destroy," he said with as chill a tone as any I have ever encountered before.

"Indeed," I said, and continued to examine the items in the envelope.

"You will tell me if you have any questions before we reach the coast." He sounded bored now, and he leaned back against the squabs, holding his spectacles with one hand to keep them from falling.

"It says here that I'm to stay at the Red Lion in Calais," I remarked as I went over the instructions. "I could probably get a good way to Paris if I slept on the train."

"You probably could," said the other man, his attitude one of casual contempt. "But Mister Vickers has deputies in many places, and he requires that you be in a site that is useful to him, should he have any reason to change your plans again. And he may change them if he feels it wise to; you must be prepared. So it will be the Red Lion. You will find a room has been engaged for you." He showed no inclination to say more, and I went back to my perusal of the contents of the envelope, all the while wondering how I would get word to Mycroft Holmes without endangering myself and this mission. I recalled my instructions in regard to telegrams, and suddenly I thought we could not arrive in France too soon.

My traveling companion noticed some shift in my manner, and said, "Well? What is it?"

I frowned. "I left with matters unsettled with the solicitor. I suppose you know about that?" I did not wait for his answer, but went on, "And I notice there is not much time to reach the boat once this train arrives. So I suppose I will have to wire him from France." I did my best to look disgruntled. "That will be another expense."

The man sighed. "I will attend to that for you," he said, his demeanor condescending and sour. "Write your message and I will see it sent from Amsterdam, upon my arrival."

I shrugged, although I was becoming steadily more

apprehensive. "All right," I told him, and drew out a small notebook from my pocket, and found a pencil. I licked the point as I thought of the best way to phrase the message so that this man and Vickers himself would not be alerted.

Pierson James, Solicitor
Steyne Chambers
London, England
James:
Contact Edward Montjoy. Imperative you act immediately or estate will not be settled until year's end. Will wire again tomorrow. A. Jeffries.

The man read it, his brows drawing together. "Why should you contact him again?"

"Because he's a bloody lawyer, that's why," I said truculently, hoping that the sullen manner would not betray the fear that went through me. "If I don't keep goading him, the estate will never be settled, and my stepbrother might well be off to Australia before James can reach him." I scowled at him. "You send it."

"I said I would." He pursed his lips as he continued to think. "I suppose once you are in Europe there would be no harm in sending telegrams. If the solicitor is expecting to hear from you . . ."

"Well, he is, see," I insisted. "And if he doesn't hear from me, he'll probably have questions about it. Then you'll have trouble throwing him off the track, if you can, lawyers being the natterers they are. Best send the telegram and save us both trouble." The last was more improvisation than certainty, but I trusted it would convince the man.

He folded the paper and slipped it into his pocket. "Very well. Unless Mister Vickers gives me orders to the contrary, I will go along with your plan." He shook his head. "Solicitors are the very devil; you have the right of it there."

"That they are," I agreed with as much of good fellow-ship as the two of us would be able to share.

The train reached Dover ten minutes late, and so the rush to get aboard the boat was greater than I had antici-pated. My traveling companion took his case from the rack above his seat and said, "Your message will be sent from Amsterdam. Have a pleasant crossing, Mister Jeffries. And remember, as long as you are on a mission for Mister Vickers, you are not alone." As I studied the tickets he had given me I recalled too late the warning Mycroft Holmes had given me about accepting anything from these men.

His wish for a pleasant crossing was not to be fulfilled. The Channel was choppy and we lurched from Dover to Calais, and by the time I set foot on the shore of France I felt as if I had been racked. Much the worse for wear I went in search of the Red Lion, and stumbled into it after ten minutes of casting about, my head ringing and my gut sore.

It was one of the old coaching inns which had had its heyday in the sixteenth century, with private parlors and a plenty of rooms that once were used for servants; now the parlors had been divided in half, and the servants' rooms were let out to guests. It wore its age and fall in station with a kind of resigned gentility, like a bankrupt duchess living in dignified but reduced circumstances.

The landlord scowled at me and was about to refuse me a room—and I had to admit I was a very unappealing prospect—when I mentioned that Mister Vickers had reserved a room for me, and that I was traveling on his instructions. As I said Vickers' name, the landlord's expression brightened so desperately and dramatically that I supposed Vickers must have some terrible hold over the poor devil, for there was no other reason for such a startling change of demeanor.

"Ah, yes, Mister Jeffries. I have been expecting you." His English was excellent for a Frenchman. "The room on your left at the top of the first flight of stairs is ready for you. I will have the chambermaid go and warm the bed if you wish to retire at once."

I must truly be a sight, I thought. "No," I said, doing my best to sound as rude as possible. "I think I had better have a bath first. And if there is someone who can have my clothes brushed and sponged for me?"

"Certainly," said the landlord with a nod as he indicated his registry and the place I was to sign.

I scrawled *August Jeffries, Norfolk and London, England* and listed my occupation as *personal representative,* which seemed vague enough for a fellow like Jeffries.

"Very good, Mister Jeffries," said the landlord, and with a disapproving stare at my luggage, he snapped his fingers for one of the servants to come and carry it up for me.

"Never mind," I said, picking up the carpetbag myself and nodding in the direction he had indicated, "I'll see to stowing it. You get that bath heated up, and see that the boots gets my coat presentable again." With that I accepted the key and made my way up the steep stairs.

The room was nicer than I had expected, far better than my place at the Cap and Balls, a good-sized chamber with a formidable armoire of considerable age against one wall, a commode under the two high windows, and a bed large enough for a pair of opera singers standing out at right angles to the armoire. There was also a writing table and chair, as well as a shaving stand with a filled ewer of water against the third wall. I tossed my bag onto the bed and removed my limp collar and cuffs, deciding as I did that these should be ironed and starched while my jacket was sponged.

I had just finished setting out my brushes and shaving kit when there was a timid knock at the door, and a small voice said in French, "Your bath is ready, sir."

Ordinarily I would have given the youngster tu'pence for his trouble, but Jeffries was made of coarser stuff, so I only shouted through the door that I would be in to bathe in a moment. I realized I was being hurried, and I supposed it was the landlord's desire to please Mister Vickers' deputy. I dragged my robe from the carpetbag, thrust my pistol under the pillow at the head of the bed, tucked my knife into one of my robe's capacious pockets, and made my way along the hall to the end of the hall where the door was prominently marked BAIN.

The room was steamy and growing dark as the day sank down to dusk. If there were lamps in the room they had not yet been lit. I considered going back to my room for a book of matches, then decided against it, as I would not be so long bathing that I would have to worry about nightfall. Besides, it was pleasant to have the fading, gentle light of gloaming around me, or so I thought. There was a tin of bath salts standing next to the tub, and I added them to the hot water without hesitation. Satisfied that my soap was near to hand, I tossed my coat over the brass valet-stand, and then peeled myself out of the rest of my clothes, and glad to be rid of them, then, without further ado, I sank down into the high, old-fashioned tub, my feet resting near the taps. At any other time I would have removed my eyepatch, but I remembered my mission and left it in place, disliking the sensation of something on my face. I was aware of an odd scent in the room, which I attributed to salts or soap, and not long after, I began to doze.

FROM THE PERSONAL JOURNAL OF PHILIP TYERS:
M.H. has surmised that since there was nothing missing that we could determine, it is possible the searcher achieved his ends by taking something that should have been delivered. He has demonstrated his assumptions by pointing out that only the secretary and desk were broken into, and the correspondence boxes had been gone through quite thoroughly, while several objects of considerable value were left untouched. Coupled with that, M.H. has shown that in spite of the chaos left behind by the perpetrator, all that was disrupted were items that were written, from books to journals to files.

There was no packet from the Admiralty yesterday, and he has sent word to learn if anything was sent, and if so, when.

It would be a terrible thing if the thief has taken anything from the Admiralty, and M.H. has said he will have to delay his departure for the Continent until the matter of the delivery—if there was one—is cleared up. He has sent word to Edmund Sutton to postpone his coming here for a day at least, but to be prepared to present himself on short notice once this has been settled. "For mark my words, Tyers," says he, "Guthrie is going into more danger than I thought when he left. And the longer I am forced to remain here, the greater his danger becomes."

Mother has slipped further away. She cannot be fed and what little water can be coaxed past her lips will not sustain her for much longer.

Chapter Eight

I HAD THE oddest sensation of floating, not just on the hot, soapy water, but in the air. There was a strange, bitter odor in the room that I had first assumed was bath salts, but now I began to suspect it was something else, more pernicious. My head felt enormous and light, like a bubble, and my vision was obscured by more than the steam in the room. Everything had the appearance of being haloed in rainbows, and at another time I might have found this enjoyable, but not now. Deep inside my mind, I could sense a terrible, muted panic rising, as if I were trying to scream through a pillow. But my limbs were filled with such lethargy and my will appeared to be altogether absent; nothing I thought of seemed to reach my body. My head lolled back and I tried to prevent myself from sliding dangerously low in the tub.

I did not have to worry on that account, for there were footfalls in the room and then I felt strong hands fix themselves on my shoulders and pull me higher up in the bath so that my head and neck were above the water. "Now then, you must wake up," said a male voice with a distinct German accent. "It is time we had a little talk, fellow."

It was useless to try to focus my eye; I could distinguish little more than smears of faded colors in the steam. Nightmarish as this was, I could not summon up the strength to oppose it.

The man with the German accent said, "You are the messenger for Mister Vickers, are you not?"

My tongue felt like a length of cotton wool in my mouth but I did my best to answer. "I am."

"And you are going to Germany for him, aren't you?" He spoke slowly and distinctly, which was necessary for me to understand him as there was a great roaring in my ears as if I were still at sea.

"I am," I answered after what seemed forever. I did not want to give the man any answer but defiance, but I was under the compulsion of whatever damned drug was in the air, and I could not resist it. Vaguely I wondered why my questioner was not affected by the drug that held me.

"Is there anything else you are doing?" the man asked with false geniality.

There was something in the question that caused me alarm, but my thoughts were so muddled it eluded me. "Yes."

All pretense of good fellowship left the man then. "What is it?" he demanded as if I were a recalcitrant horse.

"Scottish fellow," I muttered, fighting an echo of dread. I was determined to hold something back from the man. "Have to find him."

"Yes," said the German impatiently. "That is what Vickers told you to do in Germany, isn't it?"

"Yes," I agreed, pleased to be able to comply, for I suddenly thought I might be in great danger if I displeased the man.

"Is there anything else you are doing in Germany?" the man demanded.

To my distant-but-anguished dismay I heard myself say "Yes," in the same dreamy tone I had used before.

"And what is that?" The man was growing furious, and my fear, though banked behind languorous clouds, grew stronger.

Say nothing, say nothing, say nothing, I ordered myself, and heard myself answer, "Make my fortune." I felt giddy with relief that I had revealed nothing of my true mission, and I strove to let none of this show in my manner.

The man shoved me under the water and held me there until my lungs seemed about to burst. My eyepatch came close to sliding off my face, and I could do nothing about it. That may seem a small thing, but at the time it was of enormous importance to me. I have never been so thoroughly disoriented in so small a space. It was well nigh impossible for me to determine which way was toward air, and which way was not. To make it worse, I had so little strength that I could only thrash feebly, and did little more than make the man wet. The event had one beneficial effect, however, and that was to clear some of the cobwebs from my mind, and bring more of my own control back into me. I felt a hand in my hair and then I was dragged upward into the air again.

"How will you make your fortune?" the German asked with a single, swift glance at the tattoo on my wrist. He averted his eyes almost at once. "I am sorry so much water has been splashed about."

"There is a will. Father's will," I said, sticking to the rehearsed story. "The money will get it set aside. It's mine by rights in any case." I made an effort to show the same somnambulistic lack of concern that I had until he had attempted to drown me. It was a greater effort than I had anticipated. I wanted to launch myself out of the tub and strangle the man. "Need money for the lawyer and the courts, damn them all."

"Oh. Yes. That." He released his hold on me and strode away toward the door, slamming it shut as he went out.

As soon as he was gone I began, to my distress, to tremble, as cold panic took me in its unrelenting claws. Until that moment I had thought I had handled myself rather well, given the circumstances, but now it was borne in upon me how easily I might have perished, and how ignominious such a death would be. Had Vickers sent this German to be rid of me? Was Mycroft Holmes mistaken in his conviction that Vickers recognized the tattoo? Had Vickers somehow learned that I was not the man I seemed to be? I huddled down in the hot bath and did my best to keep my teeth from chattering. The soporific phase of my drugged state—for surely I had been drugged—was over. My head was beginning to hurt now with a ferocity the Channel crossing had not approached. My chest felt closed as well, and I did all that I could to get into position to haul myself out of the tub while I could trust myself to move. I thought of my codebook which I had been at pains to keep with me, surely soaked and illegible, and cursed myself for such carelessness. My head raged afresh.

When I came to myself again, the water was cold and the room was dark. My head rang like a distant gong and my joints were as stiff and creaking as a frozen gate. I struggled to pull myself to my feet, and, shivering with cold I wrapped myself in a towel and tried to warm myself with brisk action while drying off. My results were mixed. I was still as cold as if I had come out of the North Sea at midwinter, but my mind was less clouded and when I moved I no longer felt about to collapse with fatigue. As I drew on my robe and reached for my clothes, I realized, without much surprise, that they had been thoroughly searched and my knife was missing.

As vexing as it was, I knew I had to complain, or questions might be forthcoming I would find less pleasant to answer than those my interlocutor had posed at the edge of the tub. So I pulled my robe around me and made my way down the stairs, calling loudly for the landlord; nothing conciliating in my manner or the sound of my voice.

Hearing my outcry, the landlord bustled out of what I supposed must be his private dining parlor. I stood in the hall, hands braced on my hips, ready to confront him in the person of the ill-tempered Mister Jeffries. "What sort of a house are you running, when a man traveling on behalf of his employer is subjected to abuse and possible theft?"

"Mister Jeffries," said the landlord, his lugubrious expression reminding me forcibly of one of the less endearing hounds. "Pray, sir, keep your voice—"

Immediately I began to bellow. "Oh, don't want the others to know what may become of them in this place, is that it? You want them to be attacked as well?" I took a hasty stride forward; to tell the truth, my head was still aching as if mice were getting at the inside of my skull, and the band that held my eyepatch in place felt as if it were made out of red-hot bands of metal. "Well, perhaps I should just warn them of what you countenance in this place?"

"Mister Jeffries," the landlord protested.

"Yes," I said belligerently. "I think it might well be my duty to warn them. What do you think?" I achieved a sneer that must have been more successful than I supposed, for the landlord cowered back.

"If you would tell me first what has transpired? I perceive you are upset."

"Upset, you call it?" I said with furious incredulity. "And bloody right I should be. Anyone who wouldn't be would be barmy in the brain-box." I longed for a cool cloth over my eyes and a proper lie-down, but I could not let myself be lured away from my purpose. "Well, since you will have it, I was no sooner in the bath when a great brute of a man comes into the room and proceeds to attempt to drown me."

"Drown you? But why?" asked the landlord.

"Well you may ask," I said darkly, hoping to control the nausea that rose in my throat when I moved my head too quickly. "He was determined to get information from me and was not above using violence to do it. He threatened me repeatedly. I think he also slipped me a Shanghai nightcap, for I cannot think how else I come to have such an ache in it. My employer will be displeased with your service." I watched him for his reaction to this threat.

"*Par bleu,* who would want to do such a thing?" There was a lack of steadiness in his eyes which suggested he knew the answer, though I doubted he would reveal it. He was frightened, but not of me. So the man who attacked me had probably not been an agent of Vickers, or the landlord would not be afraid of anything I would report. Then who was the German and why had he wanted to drown me?

"Then you had better tend to your other guests, in case this blackguard should try to take advantage of one of them. As it is, Mister Vickers will not be pleased." This last threat I threw in with the hope that it would cause alarm to the landlord. I was surprised to see the man blanch and cross himself. "Oh, you wouldn't like that, would you? Well, then try to find out who did his best to drown me." With that, I set my teeth against the pain in my head, turned around, and made my way to my room with the exaggerated care of one who was intoxicated.

As I closed the door, I saw that the room had been gone through. My clothes were tossed all about the floor, the drawers of the chest had been pulled out and turned over, the bed had been torn apart and the mattress shifted off the leather slats onto the floor beside the bed. The pistol was nowhere to be found. While I was not surprised, I was disheartened, and decided that I would save the inspection of my luggage for tomorrow, when I hoped my head would be working better and ache less. I did not trust myself to do a good job of such an examination now, so I did little to repair the chaos, but cleared myself a place on the mattress, dragged the covers and a pillow into place and made preparations to retire.

I slept badly, my dreams tumultuous and haunting, and I woke at cock-crow, heavy-eyed and queasy from the aftereffects of the drug. A vague but persistent unease had got hold of me and filled me with disquiet. I could not decide why the German had attacked me. I was satisfied Vickers had not sent him, had no reason to send him. Then who would take so bold a chance, thinking that I was in Vickers's employ? Realizing that no matter how tired I was, I would not be able to sleep any longer, I sat up on the mattress and began to make a mental list of all I could remember from the night before. Were these men enemies of Vickers's Brotherhood, or were they attempting to stop a mission ordered by Mycroft Holmes? I dared not put my thoughts on paper, for I was certain now that I was being observed by at least one group of men who were suspicious of me, if not two.

The landlord did not strike me as dangerous in himself, more an unfortunate pawn in the hands of ruthless opponents. The German must have been waiting for me at the inn prior to my arrival, for he was too providentially placed to have stumbled upon me by accident. Therefore someone other than Mister Vickers knew of my travels and had pursued me. The implications of this last realization did nothing to restore confidence in my soul.

I decided I had better look through the jumble of my clothes and bag, as well as make an attempt at setting the room to rights before the chambermaid brought me coffee and pastry for breakfast. My joints objected as I rose, and I felt as if I had aged four decades in a night. My hands shook as I reached for my clothes, and my shoulders were stiff as rusted hinges. Grimly I set about putting all in a semblance of order, and then went to the basin to shave.

My razor was missing. That was the one item, aside from the gun, I had not been able to find, and now, as I contemplated the stubble on my jaw, I wondered why they should want to take my razor. Then a nasty thought occurred to me: the razor was imprinted with my initials. My own initials, not those of August Jeffries. I scowled at my image in the glass, and tried to anticipate what use could be made of this, and how I could prevent it happening. Thinking was an effort still, but I was spurred on by dread, and by the time the chambermaid knocked on the door, I was ready with my tale.

"Is the landlord up?" I demanded as the young woman came in with a tray. "I want to talk to him."

"He . . . he is at breakfast," she said hesitantly.

"Tell him I want a word with him. As soon as he is done. I will be ready to leave in an hour and I expect to speak with him before that." I glared at her. "My razor was stolen."

"Stolen? Your razor?" she said, as if she were uncertain of the meaning of the words. "But . . ." She put the tray down and made a hasty departure, her eyes huge in her young face.

The coffee was very strong and the cream provided was thick and yellow, so that when I tried to mitigate the harshness of the coffee, the result was an unappetizing jaundiced mixture that I could only endure a few sips of before giving up on it entirely. Had I felt more the thing, I might have attempted to get through the whole of it, but not that morning, with my head still aching and my residue of fear making me apprehensive at the sight of unfamiliar shadows.

The landlord was hovering near the foot of the stairs when I at last came down from my room. I favored him with the kind of condescending nod I was certain August Jeffries would give, and said in a surly way, "Not content with trying to kill me, the fellow has made off with my razor."

"Yes, there was a mention of theft," said the landlord cautiously. "I did not know of it until now."

"Well, now you do, fat lot of good it will do," I said as gracelessly as possible. "It were a nice new one, too. I had it from a shop in Gull's Lane, just off High Holborn. Nearly new, it was, and with a monogram on the handle. I paid three quid for it." I did my best to sound injured by this loss, and I saw the landlord regard me speculatively. I realized then that he knew more than he would let on.

"Monogrammed, was it?" he asked me, his eyes open and candid as oysters.

"That it was. A large, decorative *G* on it. *G* is close enough to *J* to suit me, and so I paid my money and the razor was mine." I straightened myself as I watched him. "I had an old one, but I got rid of it when I found the toffy one."

"Well, I will have the servants keep a lookout for it," said the landlord, so glibly that I was sure he had more knowledge of what had befallen me during the previous evening than he had felt necessary to tell me. He indicated his registry book. "Your room was paid for in advance. You need only sign your name and go." He had that look of greed in the glint of his eyes, but I gave him no heed, fully aware that Jeffries would not be persuaded by so obvious a ploy.

I tipped my hat to him and went in search of the train station, all the while resisting the urge to look behind me to see who was following.

FROM THE PERSONAL JOURNAL OF PHILIP TYERS: *There was a delivery from the Admiralty, as M.H. suspected, which should have arrived while he was at his club. Ordinarily I would have been in the flat to receive it, but I was not, which afforded the culprit time to begin the search, and then to take charge of the packet when it arrived.*

M.H. is convinced that is the reason the wild disarray was incomplete, for the man who made the search had no reason to continue once the packet was in his hands. "It is not what was missing that was his target, but what arrived," M.H. announced when he received word of the delivery. He has fixed the time of the theft from the records of the Admiralty delivery records. Had I returned but ten minutes earlier, I would have been able to prevent the whole, but I was with Mother. M.H. is once again reviewing a copy of the records sent to him, spreading them around him and running his glance over first one and then another, making comparisons so swiftly that I am not able to follow it. He admits that now he is pressing himself to greater effort. "For the sooner we learn the perpetrator of this theft, the sooner I may follow Guthrie to Europe."

Chapter Nine

THE TRAIN WAS just pulling into the station when I arrived there, sent my next telegram to James, and secured myself with the ticket I had been given on my way to the Channel. My head remained thick and sore, the after-effect of the drug, and my stomach was unsettled. So I was relieved to see the ticket procured me a place in a first-class compartment, where I hoped to have a chance to catch up on the rest I had not been able to enjoy the night before. I had no desire for conversation, let alone company. I put my case on the rack above my seat and did my best to find a comfortable position for the next leg of my journey. I thought again of what I had said in the telegram: *Not satisfied with efforts to date. Persevere in all efforts to hasten settlement.* I hoped I had remembered the code correctly. After my efforts to reconstruct it, I was still not sure I had recalled it accurately; the thought of failure made me surly with myself. If only I had not soaked the pages, obliterating the ink. Fine operative I was turning out to be, and after all Mycroft Holmes had done to establish Jeffries's identity. I even begrudged the loss of one shirt—the ink had stained it beyond laundering.

By the time the train rumbled out of the station, I was attempting to drowse, my thoughts drifting over all the events of the last thirty-six hours, and feeling much abused by fate, Vickers, and Mycroft Holmes. I was trying to sort out the developments and complications when a young woman dressed in deep mourning came into the compartment I occupied.

"Oh," she exclaimed in English, "I had no idea . . . I thought I would be alone."

"I am dreadfully sorry," I said without thinking, and then recalled the persona expected of me and did not rise. "My ticket's for this compartment."

"And so, I fear, is mine," she said, watching me unhappily. Her features were concealed by the veil of her wide black hat, but I thought I saw a blue eye and a wisp of fair hair. "This will be very awkward."

"I hope not," I answered, trying to preserve a modicum of the good manners I had been raised to have without compromising my role as August Jeffries. "Died recently, did he?"

She looked shocked. "My mother has been dead for two months, if you must know." Her accent was from the region of Warwickshire, and of a class that was privileged enough to have educated her well.

"It's just that it looks odd to me that a woman in mourning would be traveling alone on the Continent," I said, beginning to be more brash, for the truth was I felt suspicions rising in me. Anyone coming within my ken seemed to me to possess questionable motives. My annoyance was fueled by my headache, and though I knew my conduct was bad, I excused it on behalf of Jeffries' persona.

"I am going to join my brother, not that I have any reason to account for myself to you. He is expecting me in Basel where he works for the Ambassador. The British

Ambassador." She took a seat on the opposite side of the compartment to me, and opened her traveling bag to take out a book, which she made a determined effort to read.

"What kind of brother leaves a sister to travel alone in a strange country, that's what I want to know," I said as I watched her open the volume *Adam Bede* and try to find her place about a third of the way into the narrative. "How does your brother, who works for the British Ambassador, come to let you travel alone? Taken leave of his senses, has he? I wouldn't let my sister go racketing about France on her own, not any road."

"It is none of your concern," she said with enough hauteur to frost a desert bloom.

"Or are you doing this on your own?" I ventured, thinking it outrageous of me to make such a suggestion. "Did you simply wire him and inform him of when you were to arrive?"

"There is no reason I should account to you for my actions," she said, and fussed with her veil.

I watched her a short while, and then turned away, prepared to doze as the French countryside rolled by outside the windows.

We had been traveling for perhaps an hour when I saw, out of my half-closed eye, my traveling companion rise, set her book aside and move as stealthily as the motion of the train allowed toward my side of the compartment, all the while looking at where I had put my valise. She did her best to reach it without touching me, but a bend in the track flung her against me. She cried out and strove to brace herself to keep from any more contact with me, but she did not succeed, and a moment later, she was sprawled gracelessly across my legs, her hat and veil in disarray, her dress caught on the heel of her shoe so that I saw an expanse of well-turned ankle and calf that would be more appropriate in a music hall than a train compartment.

"What the devil?" I muttered and pretended to be roused from half-sleep. I stared at her for a moment, and then said, "Well, what have we here?"

She was distressed, though I could not tell for what reason beyond her immediate embarrassment. "I'm . . . very sorry, sir. I hope you will . . . forgive me." All the while she was struggling to get to her feet once more.

I held out my hand to help her up. "Caught you unaware, did it?"

"I . . . I suppose it must have," she said apologetically as she tried to restore her garments to proper modesty. "I didn't know the motion of trains could be so . . . so . . ."

"Dramatic?" I suggested. She was very pretty in that Dresden sort of way some English girls are, though her hair was a pale rosy shade and not flaxen; I decided she was about five-and-twenty. Not what I would expect to be working for the likes of Vickers, or Mycroft Holmes, for that matter, or any other sinister group. Even I could see that, with my eyepatch in place and the tatters of a headache playing old hob with my skull. I steadied her up and looked at her face, and could not resist asking, "Were you wanting something?"

"I . . ." She blushed deeply, and her slender hands trembled as she strove to put her veil back into place; she did not succeed entirely, and her dignity of manner eroded still more.

"Well, if you tell me what you wanted, perhaps I will give it to you." I was astonished at my forwardness, and sternly reminded myself that I was an affianced man, not at liberty to indulge in flirtations. But doubtless Jeffries, though supposedly married, was the sort of ill-mannered man who would direct his unwanted attentions at this young woman, and I had, for the nonce, assumed his vices with his—admittedly few—virtues. I made no attempt to apologize for my behavior, and pressed any supposed advantage with a one-sided smile.

"I . . . didn't want anything," she said defensively, her face set in severe disapproval, at least as much as she could achieve, given the awkwardness of the circumstances. "I only hoped that there might be a map, so I could watch our progress."

I was reasonably certain that this was a lie, but I was willing to pretend I believed her, at least for a short while. "If you'd wakened me, I could have told you I don't have one. Trains go where they go. This one will reach Paris soon enough. It can't leave the track and junket about the countryside."

Again her cheeks reddened. "I didn't want to . . . make any scene."

"Well, you're doing that now, aren't you?" I said back at her, my manner as curt as I could bring myself to make it. I did not want to make her think she had won me over, if that was her intention. "Or had you something else in mind? Did you truly want a map?"

"What . . . what do you mean?" she asked, doing her best to appear affronted and looking more like an outraged kitten, as much confused as angry. I noticed that she had a talent for this, and my suspicions about her grew. It could be that she was just who she said she was, but what if Vickers had sent her to keep an eye on me? Or the German from the night before hoped to learn what he could not with threat of drowning? "Why are you staring at me in that horrid way?" she asked, cutting into my unpleasant thoughts.

"You might have wanted to get your hands on my flimsies," I said in the insinuating way someone like Jeffries would do. "Well, I don't keep it where you can reach it, and that's a fact."

"You think I wanted your money?" she said in rising accents. "Just because I looked in your luggage?"

"Looks that way to me. Why else would you try to prig my luggage, is what I want to know?"

"Well, I was." This confession took us both by surprise. She looked away from me, her neck quite red above the high collar of her dress. "I . . . I . . . my money was stolen last night. I haven't got very much left, and I thought if I could find five pounds or so, I would have enough to pay for my meals until I reach my brother. I'm afraid I will run out of funds before I reach him."

It sounded absurd that such a young woman would have that misfortune befall her; like the rest of her tale, it seemed ludicrous, and I did not know what to say to her that would not reveal my doubts. At the same time, I knew it was just possible that this story, ridiculous though it was, was the truth and that she was more naive than she wanted to appear. I stared hard at her. "Did you have breakfast?"

She shook her head. "I'm quite hungry." She looked at her hands in her lap while she wrapped a black lace handkerchief around her gloved fingers. "I don't mean to throw myself on your kindness, but . . ."

"Well," I said to her, trying not to be too caught up in her tale, "when we reach the next stop, I'll let you a few francs so you can nip off and buy yourself a pastry and a cup of coffee." I tried for a smile in the Jeffries manner, and hoped that I achieved the mix of gallantry and lechery I was aiming for.

"Oh, would you?" she said, giving me a melting look that must have cost her father a great deal while he lived.

"If you don't try any more high jinx with me, I would. It happens I don't like to see anyone go hungry," I said, as if I had just performed an act of great magnanimity.

"I won't try anything more," she assured me with the look of one who has brought grief to a score of governesses. "I am very grateful to you."

"No doubt," I said drily. "And if I were not a gentleman, you might have to show me just how grateful you are." I finished this off with a wink.

She drew back as if from something rotten. "How can you?" she demanded. "I shall have to find another compartment if you continue this way."

"Not until you have your pastry," I appended to her protestation. "It wouldn't be a good trade as things stand now."

"Surely you wouldn't dishonor me for the price of a breakfast?" she asked, one hand to her throat.

"Women have been dishonored for less," I said, astonished at my own cynicism and temerity. I decided to try to be less of a lout without letting down my guard entirely. "But you need not put yourself in a taking, Miss." I saw she was truly shocked by what I had said. "If you're going to cut up rough, I'll say nothing more about it."

She looked huffy, and emphasized this by fixing her veil more completely across her face. "I think you owe me an apology, sir."

"Why? Because I spoke the truth? I won't apologize for that." I looked directly at her, my eye fixed on hers behind the veil. "It's all very well for girls like you to fly your colors and faint to learn what your sisters do every day of their lives. But I have seen something of the world, and I know how little honor may be bought for, even in the backstreets of London. You need not go to Africa or India or China to find it."

"You are an odious man," she informed me roundly. "I want to hear nothing more from you."

"But you do want me to buy you something to eat, don't you? So keep a civil tongue in your head until you've eaten. You don't want me to change my mind about the breakfast, do you," I advised her, and leaned back in my place once more, pretending to doze again.

She sat very straight; as I watched her through my half-closed eye, I could see that she was more frightened than offended by what I had said. My headache still had a grip on me, but I no longer felt as if the upper part of my skull were about to burst to pieces. I occupied my thoughts with what little I had learned about her. She claimed to be in mourning for her mother. That could be true; her clothes were black and severe, with no adornments beyond simple pearl earrings, which were suitable for mourning wear. She had made no mention of a father, and since she claimed to be going to visit her brother, I had assumed her father was dead. But what if he were not? Could there be some reason why she did not like to mention a father? If so, what could that reason be? And was it enough to impel her to travel alone in a foreign country? Or was the whole a fiction, or enough of it to render any conclusions I might reach invalid from the start? If the misadventures of the night before had not caused my head to ache, these ruminations certainly would. I wished I dared to make notes, or to prepare a report for Mycroft Holmes. The patch over my eye felt itchy, and it was all I could do not to scratch.

The conductor came by to punch our tickets and to check our travel documents. He remarked that I would have to change train stations as well as trains in Paris, adding that I had been wise to schedule a night in that city. "It is better to spend the night in Paris than in Amiens or Charleroi." The suggestive roll of his eyes made it apparent that he had his own ideas on how a man might entertain himself there.

"Will we be stopping soon?" I asked as he handed back my documents.

"*Oui*, in about thirty minutes. It will be a twenty-minute stop." His expression was suggestive. "Will that be enough time for you?"

"Time enough to purchase a croissant or brioche and some coffee, I should think," I observed.

"Yes; there are sellers at the station. They will be on the platform. You need only lean out the window. You do not need to trouble yourself to leave the carriage."

"I must catch a train for Dijon, and from there to Basel," she said to the conductor as that worthy examined her papers. "Will I have to change train stations?"

"There is a train that departs to the southeast from your station. It will reach Dijon in the evening, and there will be a train to Basel in the middle of the next morning." He tipped the beak of his cap to her, nodded to me with a knowing wink, and departed the compartment.

"He is a very rude person," said my traveling companion. "I think he was amusing himself at our expense."

"Perhaps," I allowed, and regarded her with more concern. "Just what is it your brother does for the British Ambassador in Basel?"

"He is an undersecretary," said my traveling companion with the sort of disdain that can only be called sad, for such a post was not worthy of such grand airs. "He has been in his position six years."

"In Switzerland," I said, as if I meant Samarkand. "How fortunate for him."

The train began to slow for Sainte-Cecille, where passengers wanting to visit the bathing hotels at Plaige Saint-Cecille would depart, and those returning from such recreations would come aboard.

"It is a very good post. My mother said so often and often," she said.

I reached into my jacket and drew out the small purse of coins. I handed this to the young woman and said, "We'll be in the station shortly. You'll want to be ready."

She took the coins so eagerly that I was hard-pressed to doubt her sincerity. I watched as she worked the window open and stood in order to reach out farther. "I'm so grateful, Mister . . ."

"Jeffries, at your service. August Jeffries, of Norwich." I bowed a little, to show the remnants of good conduct.

"I suppose sharing a first-class compartment on a train constitutes an introduction, under the circumstances. I am Penelope Gatspy, of Kenilworth." She held out her left hand for me to kiss.

I complied, thinking as I did that it would be very easy to fall into conversation with her now that we had exchanged names. That would be a very dangerous thing to do, for her, if not for me, so I merely watched as she purchased two croissants and a jug of coffee, and sat consuming them while the holiday departers replaced the holiday arrivals, and the train continued on its way to the River Somme.

FROM THE PERSONAL JOURNAL OF PHILIP TYERS:
M.H. has been occupied with the Admiralty records for many hours. I now believe he has made layers of information around him, for otherwise, I cannot conceive how

he is able to keep everything in order in his mind, for it is certainly not orderly in appearance. Yet he claims success in his endeavor. He has found a pattern of pilfering that he is following to the full extent of its possibilities. He has already sent word to the Admiralty requesting them to detain four clerks in anticipation of his determining which of them has been altering the records to his own ends. He has not informed me of how he will do this, but I am confident that he will, for he has always prevailed in the past. Eventually he may tell me how he has determined it must be one of these four clerks, and what in the records pointed his way to them.

I have had word from hospital and must leave shortly in order to consult with the physician tending my mother. M.H. has said I may have the next four hours for this purpose. He has asked that I go by the Admiralty on my way back and obtain copies of the handwriting of the four clerks in question.

Word from G. has caused M.H. increasing concern for G.'s welfare, and he is attempting to bring this Admiralty matter to a swift conclusion through the discovery of the criminal so that he may depart as quickly as possible for France. Such a resolution will be welcome to the Admiralty, for it would provide a means to keep any scandal to a minimum, which is fervently desired. I know M.H. is more keenly aware of this than I, and that he will strive to serve the interests of the government in this matter as in all others.

Chapter Ten

By the time we reached Paris, Miss Gatspy had told me a great deal about her family: her father had caused a scandal of some sort when she was a child and had left England under a cloud. Her mother had removed from London to Kenilworth and stayed there in quiet retirement from the world since Penelope was nine. Her brother, some years older than she, had remained in the care of an uncle in London while he completed his studies at Harrow and then had gone on to Trinity College, Oxford. It was apparent that Miss Gatspy and her brother were not well acquainted and had had little contact for many years. If, I kept reminding myself, any of this is true. It may all be a whimsy to mislead me.

"So you see, I must go to Bertram now that mother is dead and ask him to lend me his support, or reveal what, if any, provisions our father may have arranged for me before his disgrace. My mother's will gives me a competence only, and it was my understanding that father had made arrangements for some monies to come to me upon mother's death." Her conversation was artless and beguiling, and it was an effort not to be wholly caught up in it.

"I surmise your brother did not attend your mother's death," I said as we rolled along the north bank of the Somme.

"No; he was not able to obtain leave from his post," she said, looking downcast. "It has been years and years since I have seen Bertram. I only hope I will recognize him when he meets me at the train."

I regarded her with a mixture of sympathy and reserve. "Bertram Gatspy," I said, trying to recall if I had ever heard Mycroft Holmes mention such a name in his encyclopedic accountings of the diplomatic corps. Nothing came to mind, but I was aware my memory could be faulty.

When at last we reached Paris, I left Miss Gatspy with mixed feeling. I made my way through the horrible crush to the telegram desk, gave my address as 221C Baker Street London and asked if any messages had been received for me.

"Yes, Mister . . . ah . . . Jeffries," said the clerk in passable English. "It arrived five hours ago." He handed over the telegram. I tore open the envelope, noticing that the seal was not as secure as it should have been, and found the following message: *Terms of trust appear questionable. Am awaiting word from Luxembourg. Pierson James, Attorney-at-law.*

I considered this information, remembering my instructions, and concluded that there would be a packet of some sort waiting for me in Luxembourg. I folded the missive and thrust it into my inner jacket pocket and handed over my new message to be sent to my employer.

Efforts still not satisfactory. More options are needed. I hoped that this second sentence would convey my concerns about Miss Gatspy, by implying that I could not tell Mister Holmes enough with our codes as we had arranged them in advance.

As I hurried out of the train station, I caught a glimpse

of a woman in mourning, who might have been Miss Gatspy, climbing into a cab. I could not help but be puzzled by this, and it distracted my thoughts as I summoned a cab for myself and gave the address of the hotel included in my instructions from Vickers.

The stay was less eventful than my night at the Red Lion had been. Before I checked into the hotel I purchased a new razor and a packet of sticking plasters in case I should cut myself with the unfamiliar instrument. At the hotel I was given an odd-shaped, dark room, and an indifferent meal by a waiter who had as much interest in me as he would have had in a herd of sheep. I slept through the night and awoke at the first summons of the chambermaid. Some of my previous apprehension faded as I prepared to depart for the station.

I was surprised to find a message from Vickers waiting for me at the desk when I came down in the morning: *Performance to date satisfactory. Proceed according to instructions. Dortmunder will meet you as arranged.* It was signed, ominously as I thought, *Vickers for the Brotherhood.*

Breakfast was provided, such as it was, as part of the price of the room. I had a stale pastry and a cup of very strong, tepid coffee, all served by the same massively indifferent waiter of the night before. The landlord made sure I had my bag, asked for his money and sneered at the tip I offered. And then I was in a cab pulled by a horse with a loose off-side rear shoe and bound for the next leg of my journey.

No one disturbed my peace this time, and I stared out the window at the French countryside, the little villages and the rolling hills, the occasional spire of a church. It was enough to lull me into a sense of safety that I was aware could evaporate in an instant. Finally we came to Luxembourg just at sunset. I called at the telegraph desk and was told nothing had come for me. Recalling the telegram, I experienced a sense of apprehension, but I was assured that the staff handling the telegrams was conscientious.

Disappointed and mildly troubled, I left the train station, thinking that I ought to find a way to contact Mycroft Holmes and inform him that I had not received his information as I made my way to the hotel suggested by Vickers. It overlooked the gorge that had made the little country so strategically important when wars were fought on foot and on horseback only, without trains and powerful guns to change the balance as they had done in the last twenty years. I was so interested in the place that I went to take a walk along the precipice, to marvel at how nature had contrived so useful a barricade.

I had gone some distance along the top of the gorge, marveling at the narrow roads leading down to equally narrow houses clinging to the side of the chasm, and impressed with the ingenuity that made it possible for men to put up such structures. I was about to turn back when two figures leaped out of the shadows and rushed at me. I might have been able to run from one of them, but with two it was impossible. As they overtook me, I prepared to fight them, thinking them nothing more than common footpads, out to steal from an unwary foreigner.

They were both dressed in nondescript dark-gray coats without capes or anything that would provide purchase for an opponent. One was tall and lean, with wide shoulders and fair hair. The other was not as tall, somewhat blocky, with light-brown hair and intense blue eyes. They walked with the practiced elasticity of movement that promised athletic ability and strength.

I looked about in the hope that we were observed, but I saw no one on the street or in the houses below who might raise the alarm. I did not think of myself as an adept fighter, but I had been the middle of five sons and learned a thing or two about holding my own in my youth.

The first, taller man swung at me, and I saw that he had

a knife in his hand. I stepped back to avoid injury and nearly lost my footing. My arms swung wide to preserve my balance and I noticed how near I was to the edge. It was an unpleasant revelation, being so badly placed to fight. That caught me up short, for a plunge into that chasm would surely be fatal. I took a stance as best I could and prepared to fight the two ruffians off.

How I longed for the weapons that had been taken from me in Calais. If I had had the pistol, or even the knife, I would be able to face these men without fear for my life. But those invaluable aids had been taken from me, and I was left with my skill and wits alone for defense, and I was not certain they would be sufficient to keep me alive.

The two men were quick and expert, clearly familiar with the locale, and prepared to take advantage of it. While one would rush me with a knife, the other would duck low and come up on my side, like two shrikes harrying a dog. I was able to elude the attempts to confine my arms, but in the process I was nicked on the cheek and the wrist. Neither was deep or dangerous, yet blood welled under my eye, and I cursed the eyepatch I wore, both for limiting my sight and for sticking to my face, distracting me and keeping me from being able to deal with these two. I began to tire as the attack continued, as I wove, dodged and feinted, all in an attempt to avoid their sallies. They were wearing me down, deliberately keeping me near the edge of the gorge so that I would have little room or opportunity to maneuver here, or time to think, with my heels at the edge of the abyss. I stumbled as one of them rushed at my side and my right foot dangled over emptiness. My arms again waved wildly as I strove to regain my position.

The nearer of the two attackers, the smaller man, picked my ribs with his knife: I felt a hot numbness where the blade went in, but I did not fall. The pain had not hit me yet, so filled was I with fighting, but I knew it would, and when it did, I would be at their mercy.

Angry now, as well as confused and frightened, I struck out with my arm and had the satisfaction of having the blow connect with the smaller of the two men. He staggered back as his companion rushed at me, I thought with the purpose of pushing me off-balance so that I would reel backward and fall into the deep canyon. I was so determined to prevent this from happening that I reached for his shoulder to thrust him away from me and to use a little of his rush to propel me a few feet further away from disaster.

To my astonishment, the ploy worked. The man, with my leverage added to the power of his rush, was carried out beyond the edge and he fell, screaming, into the depths.

I was aghast at what I had done.

The second man went still, and stared out over the rim of the chasm, and muttered an oath in what sounded like a Slavic tongue, then swung back at me, his knife at the ready. Determined now to avenge the death of his companion, he advanced on me with grim purpose, features working, muttering something about "that Devil von Metz, and the Brotherhood," every line of him lethal. He began to make great scything sweeps with his arm, the knife whistling with the force of his movement.

I backed up, but away from the canyon, and my pursuer did not appear to notice or to mind that I was no longer in danger of falling as his fellow had done. My breath was ragged and the first of the pain from my wound had struck, making me nauseated and cold. If I had not dreaded what the man might do, I would have broken away and run from him, but the thought of having this dire opponent behind me was more terrifying than the notion of another knife wound or a plunge into the canyon. I did what I could to keep my teeth from chattering and readied to grapple with the man.

How could I best this determined man, I asked myself as I felt my strength ebbing much too quickly; I would not be able to defend myself much longer. My vision wobbled as I made a wild jab with my fist at my remaining attacker and was about to reel from imbalance when the other man uttered a sharp oath, clapped his free hand to his neck, took three erratic, stumbling steps, and pitched forward onto his face.

I stood uncertainly, my head swimming, my side wet and sticky with my own blood. My mind was filled with the horror of having killed another human being, a realization that left me nauseated as much as the unwarranted attack disoriented me.

The fallen man was still twitching, but it was the proof of death, not any spark of life in him that led to this bizarre action. I went to bend over him, hoping to discover that life was not fully extinguished in him, or at the least, learn what had killed him, for I had heard no shot. The light was poor, and I did not want to linger where I might be questioned how I came to be fighting on the edge of the gorge, so my examination was cursory at best, but I thought I saw a feathered dart embedded in his neck, just above the collar of his jacket.

Then there was a shout as the alarm was raised, and I hurried away as best as I could toward the hotel. I had to haul myself upward to my room, using the bannister for purchase. There was a smear of blood left in my wake and I wondered what I should say to account for it, should anyone inquire about it.

Who were these men, and why had they set upon me? Were they opponents of the Brotherhood, and if so, who might they represent? What did they seek to do by killing me? And—dear God—what was I to do about killing one of them? It would leave a blot on my soul I would never be free of, whether the man was my enemy or an assassin set upon his work.

In my room, I unpacked my carpetbag, in the hope of discovering in my few toiletries something that would help to treat and bandage my still-bleeding wound. I was less concerned about my clothes, but that was because I had not seen them yet. As I pried my eyepatch off, I opened the half-dried scab and blood ran down my cheek like tears.

I spread out my shaving materials, including the new razor I had purchased in Paris, and opened the packet of sticking plasters. There were ten of them, and I knew I would need at least six for the cut in my side. I pulled my other belongings out and reluctantly decided I would have to sacrifice one of my remaining clean socks to serve as an absorbent pad for my side. I was quite cold now, and feeling stretched beyond my limits. Gingerly I pulled myself out of my coat, wincing at the protestations the muscles in my side made at this simple action, and looked in dismay at the rent in the worn black fabric. I would not be able to repair it adequately, and even if I could, the bloodstain was large and would be impossible to remove. For an instant I felt I was back at that chasm, and my first attacker was falling to his death. I pinched myself, and was once again back in my hotel room, facing the task of getting out of my clothes. Carefully I reminded myself of my necessary tasks. Next came the waistcoat, where the damage was bad but not so apparent as the ruin of the coat. I could tell that the new shirt would be useful for little but rags.

But that realization made me cast aside my sock and rend the shirt, making the pad I would need to place over the cut in my side. I went to the washstand and did what I could to examine the damage in the light of the lantern put there.

The cut was about five inches long, generally superficial but deep enough in the central part to be troublesome. I hoped that I could do something that would reduce the risk of infection, but all I had was a small vial of iodine which I carried to treat shaving nicks. I assumed it would be easy to procure a replacement for this, and so, clenching my teeth against the pain of it, I dribbled most of the contents of the vial into my wound, my eyes watering as I did.

It took me nearly an hour to complete these necessary

ministrations, and at the end of it, I felt wholly shaken and ill with the experience. My palms were sweating and it required an effort to keep from trembling. As I climbed wearily into my nightshirt, I could not help but review the last few days' activities in my mind, and thought that it was an astonishing account: I had been taken in by an organization of enemies of the Queen, sent to Europe where in a period of four days I had been drugged, nearly been drowned, and been attacked by armed men, one of whom I had killed, and one of whom had been dispatched by unknown hands for reasons I could not surmise.

Doubtless this was more than I had bargained on when I entered Mister Holmes' employ, and as I pulled up the covers I pondered what might happen next, and how I should inform Mycroft Holmes about the events of the last four days. After the attack on the edge of the gorge, I suspected that the absence of the packet of materials I was to receive was more than an oversight. This brought more unwelcome speculations, and some distressful notions returned to plague me. If those men at the abyss were mere footpads I could dismiss their attack as the misfortune of a solitary traveler. But suppose they were more than that? I could not persuade myself they were not, not even here in the apparent safety of my room. Their attack once again became more sinister in my perceptions than it had seemed. For what reason had they tried to kill me? And who had killed the second man? Was there any significance to my missing razor? To say nothing of my pistol and knife? How alarmed should I be in that regard? In the midst of such confusion, it might be nothing, but I could not afford to overlook any possibilities. There was also the unaccountable Miss Penelope Gatspy, about whom I had come to no conclusions, for there was always the possibility there was no reason to consider her more than a serendipitous encounter.

But if there had been more to it than that, I wondered what her purpose might have been, and who it was she served. Sleep eluded me as I puzzled over these very strange events and tried to decide what I should do about my current predicament. At last, more from exhaustion and pain than from any calm or resolution, I lapsed into uneasy slumber, filled with images of unknown men plummeting into gulfs so vast that oceans could be contained in them.

FROM THE PERSONAL JOURNAL OF PHILIP TYERS:
M.H. has been busy all morning with the Admiralty, who have sent three of their men to wait upon him, and has only just broken off his conference to ask me to send another telegram to the Continent. I am, of course, not permitted to know the particulars of their deliberations, but I am conscious that M.H. is seriously displeased that they have dragged on so long. He is increasingly worried about G., and if only this emergency at the Admiralty were not so ominous at this time, he would have departed for Europe yesterday at the latest. As it is, he is afraid he may have the young man's life on his conscience for the rest of his days.

"For mark me, Tyers," said he, "the Brotherhood will have him in their clutches by now, and I'm damned if I can be sure of getting him out."

He has already declared that two of the clerks under suspicion are blameless, for their handwriting is not found in any of the records in question, and their handling of the material occurs at an earlier stage than M.H. is now convinced the mischief is done. He said that had he not been able to review all the pages and entries associated with the matter, he would not have been able to dismiss the two from the pall of doubt. But since he has had all the records, he has discerned the pattern more clearly. Without question he will know which is the culprit before much more time has passed.

I must visit Mother this evening, and make the necessary arrangements with the church, for her earthly repose.

Chapter Eleven

BY THE FIRST light of dawn I rose and began to write an account of all that had happened to me since I left Pierson James's chambers. I crossed the pages and wrote on both sides of the few sheets of paper provided by the hotel, taking care to be succinct and yet to leave nothing out, and even then, when I had filled the available sheets I had not finished my account of the incident on the edge of the chasm the night before. What I ought to do with this account, I was not entirely certain. Very carefully I folded it in half and tucked it into my carpetbag, trusting I would hit upon some plan. I was not wholly sure it was safe to keep with me, though I had taken care to reveal no names in my writing, with the exception of Miss Penelope Gatspy. More than anything I wanted to find some means of getting this back to Mister Holmes in London, but had no notion how I could accomplish this.

It was tempting to think of turning back, to fly for the Channel and the protection of home, but as I wrote of all that had happened to me, I lost all hope that such an effort would succeed, for I was fully aware I was being observed, and any deviation from the course set down to me would doubtless expose me to more than the censure of my employer: I would not reach Dover alive, of that I was quite certain.

There was also the matter of my ruined coat. I would have to find some means of replacing it before I continued on my journey, for I surely could not present myself to that stickler Scotsman with my garments in tatters with bloodstains upon them. A more liberal man than he was said to be would think twice about engaging a man with so obvious a record of violence about him. I would have to procure another shirt, as well, with the one I had been wearing reduced to scraps. How could I fulfill Mister Holmes's instructions if I appeared before this MacMillian looking like the scaff and raff of the gutter? I had money, but not enough to allow me any extravagant purchases.

My side ached and my muscles were stiff, and when I pulled on my second shirt, the soft cotton felt like sandpaper on my skin. A look in the mirror for shaving confirmed my worst suspicions regarding my face: there was a great, discolored mass under where I would wear my eyepatch again, as well as puffiness from the nick. It would be useless to deny a mishap of some sort. I was so enervated that I wondered if I would be able to carry my bag to the train, whither I was bound as soon as I broke my fast.

I came down the stairs and made my way into the breakfast room where the host had spread out a variety of cheeses and breads, and an array of preserves and comfits to accompany these. I had little appetite, but I knew it was essential I eat. As I selected two wedges of cheese—one soft with a pungent rind, the other pale and firm—and a soft roll, the host himself came into the chamber, concern on his benign face.

"Ah, Mister Jeffries," he said, his Luxembourgeois accent making the name sound exotic. "I hope you have not had a misfortune?"

"As a matter of fact, I have," I declared, deciding not to deny the events of the previous evening. "I was set upon by robbers."

The fellow crossed himself and regarded me with great concern. "You have spoken to the authorities?"

I shrugged. "I must leave today, and, as the black-guards did not get anything from me but the satisfaction of my bruises in exchange for some of their own, I decided I would not bother."

"It is shocking," said the host, his hands joined to show his solicitous attitude.

"Very true," I said. "The worst of it is, the fellows ruined my coat, my shirt, and my waistcoat." Too late I noticed the distress in the host's face, and did my best to make light of it. "They struck a couple lucky blows before I got away from them."

"But this is dreadful," said the host, coming over to me. "That such a thing should happen to you in our little country." He leaned forward, lowering his voice. "If you will let me have your old coat, I will tend to it. In the meantime," he said more brightly, "I have in my closet a number of coats left here over the years. You may make a selection of them, choose whichever suits you. I would make the same offer for a shirt, but I suspect you would prefer to purchase one new." His smile was wide and beneficent.

"That is very kind of you," I said to him, trying not to question this gesture, for I could not but suppose that he was correct in saying that many items of clothing had been left behind over the years, and if he had not sold them to a dealer in used clothing, he might well still have such a trove. "I fear I will have to avail myself of your offer."

"When you are finished here, come to the front. If the landlord were here, I would not be able to do this, but as he is away in Berlin, I will take responsibility for this." He continued his smile. "It is not as if you are seeking to take advantage of our goodwill."

Remembering that I was August Jeffries, I just nodded once, and said I'd talk to him when I was done eating.

The host was about to leave from the room when he was struck with a new thought. "Is there anything I can do additionally? I believe it is fitting that since my country is responsible for the injuries you have sustained that I should take it upon myself to dispel any ill notions you may have in regard to it." His sigh was like listening to an actor expressing profound sympathy, and I was unable to determine if this might be the actual temperament of the man, or a pose to convince me of his legitimate concern.

"I'll give it some thought," I promised him, and went on with the meal. By the time I was finished, I had decided on a risky course. Taking care to do it while still at the table, I retrieved the report I had written and tucked it into the Luxembourg newspaper left as a courtesy at each table. This was folded securely and I went in search of a postage sleeve for it; I found this at the front desk, where the host declared himself in readiness to see that the thing was sent back to my attorney in London with all due haste. "He has dealings in Europe, don't you know, and has asked me to procure newspapers for him while I travel, which I have attempted to do," I temporized as I scrawled James' address upon it. "What is this likely to cost to post to London?"

He made a gesture of dismissal. "Do not worry about the amount; it is trifling, I assure you. Think of it as a gesture from Luxembourg to compensate, inadequately, for your unfortunate experience."

I had a moment of wondering if I were wise to trust the man, but decided since it was known that Pierson James was representing my cause it might not be thought too strange that I would send him a newspaper from my travels. If the missive included were discovered, I could claim I wished him to be aware of what I had been forced to undertake as a means of financing my claim on my trust. Satisfied that I had nothing to fear from sending the material to London, I nodded to the host and said, "If your employer gives you any trouble for this, notify my solicitor and he will see you are provided some recompense for your problem."

"Given what has befallen you, sir, I would venture to say that any troubles the landlord might visit upon me are trifling." He indicated the way to the closet and took a ring of keys from the loop attached to his belt. "I'll open the way for you."

As much for small talk as any other reason, I said, "How is it that the landlord is gone?"

The host shook his head. "A sad business. He was called away two days since; his sister and her family have been stricken with fever and he was summoned to attend them." He paused. "I must say, he took it badly, complaining that this was the worst possible time for him to be gone from here. But as his sister is a widow and there are no other male relatives, his presence was necessary . . ." He shrugged as he opened the closet. "He said he will return as quickly as possible."

"I hope his sister recovers quickly and fully," I said automatically.

"Amen to that, sir," the host said as he stood aside.

I went in and waited while the host struck a match for the lamp and adjusted the flame. "Gracious," I said as I looked at the two long racks on which clothes of every description of the last forty years hung. Inconsequently I thought that Edmund Sutton would be delighted to get his hands on half of the garments here. I strolled along the section of the nearer rack which contained gentlemen's coats, and at last took two from their hangers; one was too long in the sleeve, the other too narrow in the shoulder, but the third was precisely the garment I needed. It was about six years out of fashion, a long frock coat of dark brown broadcloth cut full at the sides in the German manner with a rolled velvet collar. It was in remarkably good condition, and were it not that it was no longer the mode, I would have thought it quite new; surely it could not have been worn many times before it was left here.

The fullness of the cut not only gave me the appearance of having lost flesh recently, but provided a little extra room around the improvised dressing over my ribs, which was particularly welcome to me. I let the host help me shrug into it.

"It is a good choice, sir," said the host, looking pleased. "And perhaps, while you are here, a waistcoat as well?"

I smiled. "Why not?"

The selection was varied and interesting, and I was hard-put not to choose one of those that suited my own rather conservative taste. But that was not the persona of August Jeffries, and so I took one that was a tapestry brocade of leaf-patterns in russet, rust, and dark greens. "Thank you very much, my good man," I said as I removed the coat in order to don the waistcoat. "It will suit me very well. It's better quality than the one I lost." I looked around the room again. "With all this on hand, I doubt your employer will miss these two."

The host laughed. "I am of the same mind."

"Well, it is good of you to do this for me," I said to him, and resisted the urge to give him a few coins for his trouble. "And it is right welcome, too."

"A pleasure to serve you, Mister Jeffries," said the host, and ushered me out of the closet, taking care to lock it once again before escorting me to the front of the establishment. "Will you want a cab to the station?"

"No, I think I'll walk; it isn't very far," I said, and picked up my carpetbag. I hoped that the exercise would limber me somewhat. With a jauntiness I did not truly feel I set out toward the long boulevard that led to the station. I made a point of not looking toward the gorge again, for fear of what I would see there.

Upon reaching the station, I was informed that the train to Mannheim was late, and I would have more than an hour before it arrived. I asked again at the telegram desk if any packet had been delivered for me, and was again informed that none had been received. I sent my daily telegram with a sense of fatalistic oppression. The appre-

hension I had nearly succeeded in shaking off returned
threefold. Why would Mister Holmes fail to deliver the
material he had promised to have for me at this place?
None of the answers that occurred to me lessened my
worry. I purchased a two-day-old Munich paper and did
my best to ward off my anxiety and hide my battered face
by reading of events there, including the arrival of a pair
of young giraffes at the zoo, an event that was causing
something of a public festival.

When the train finally steamed into the station, there
was a general rush toward it, and I found myself in a
crowded compartment where each man was hidden
behind his paper. I decided to do as the rest did, and
returned to my German paper as the train rattled on
toward Mannheim.

We arrived there now three hours late; I had missed my
train to Würzburg. I was informed I could take the late
train to Nuremberg which was scheduled to leave in forty
minutes, and arrive there around midnight. It was not part
of my instructions, but if I were going to arrive in
Augsburg at roughly the appointed time, I would have to
reroute myself. My limited experience of the Brotherhood told me they would more readily forgive a change
of travel than an unnecessarily late arrival. I decided it
would be better to do this, and went to the telegraph desk
to send word back to James: *Will be at Nuremberg late
tonight, departing for Augsburg tomorrow morning. No
promised material delivered. Lacking information to continue. Need to know what you are doing toward resolving
case.* I thought this would not depart from what Mycroft
Holmes had instructed me to do beyond the bounds of
what he would tolerate. I purchased a new ticket, a
second-class one, for Nuremberg and one from Nuremberg to Augsburg for the following day. Then I went to
wait for the train.

This ride was as uneventful as it was uncomfortable.
The wooden seats in the second-class car were old and
prone to leaving splinters in hands and bum as the train

jolted and rocked its way to the southeast. By the time it halted in Nuremberg I was as miserable as if I had been taken with the grippe.

Only two hostelries were willing to take in late travelers, and those of us leaving the train had to choose between an ancient, black-beamed coaching inn and a tavern attached to an old brewery with a dozen small rooms available to travelers, or those so filled with beer they could not make their way home. While I would have preferred the coaching inn, it was twice the cost of rooms at the tavern, and I knew that Jeffries would far prefer the latter to the former. Reluctantly, I went into the taproom and arranged for a bed for the night and the promise of chocolate and pastry before seven in the morning.

"That's quite a bruise you have on your face," said the parlormaid as she led me up to the second floor.

"Hazards of travel," I said, speaking my German with a stronger English accent than I had been taught to use.

"Certainly is," said the parlormaid with a speculative look at me. "Do you want to sleep alone?"

Given where I was I should have expected this. I did my best not to appear shocked, and instead I said that another time I would be interested, but just at present, what I wanted was to lie down on something that wasn't moving.

She laughed and winked, and indicated a room with one high, small window, a bed, a dresser, a shaving stand, and precious little else. There was a faint-but-pervasive smell of malt and barley in the air. "If you change your mind, I'll be up another two hours."

I could think of no reply other than to hand her a few coins as I closed the door, taking care to set the bolt in place. This was one night I had no wish to be disturbed.

But much as I yearned for sleep, it would not come. There were too many questions haunting me from the last few days. What had Mycroft Holmes sent me into? I had had no concept of what dangers I would encounter, and, in my exhausted state, I began to think myself very hard-used by my employer. Treaty or no treaty, I grumbled inwardly, I had been sent as a lamb to the slaughter. That reminded me afresh of my narrow escape, and the killings in Luxembourg, and a shudder went through me. I did my best to persuade myself that my worries were as much a product of fatigue and sore joints as any other factor, and I was able to convince myself sufficiently to fall asleep so that the trepidations I held at bay now had free rein in my dreams.

FROM THE PERSONAL JOURNAL OF PHILIP TYERS:
For the first time since the trouble with the Admiralty has come to light, M.H. has been hopeful of resolving it. This morning he has sent for two men who manage accounts for the Admiralty who remain under suspicion, and they are to arrive this afternoon at two-thirty. After his meetings of yesterday, M.H. is certain that one of the two is the guilty party, and he is determined to resolve the matter as soon as possible. "Had I the leisure, I would discover the man on the evidence, but I haven't the time to do it. Guthrie is too much at risk for me to indulge in deductive games. I will have to confront the two men and observe them carefully."

I am to carry a message round to Edmund Sutton, advising him to present himself at M.H.'s flat after one in the morning, prepared to undertake his replacement for a period of at least a week. I am also to order that the Mercury train be standing by in Calais for M.H.'s use as soon as he can depart for the Continent.

"We have either a very dangerous man to apprehend, or a venal one," said M.H. to me as he finished writing his note to Sutton. "I will hope the man is dangerous. It would be galling to think that I have put Guthrie in danger for nothing more than a small man's greed."

Chapter Twelve

WE LEFT NUREMBERG without incident, and I arrived at Augsburg no more than two hours later than the train from Ulm pulled into the station. Satisfied that I had made good time, I went in search of Herr Dortmunder, pausing on the way to stop at the telegraph desk to inquire for any messages that might have been left for me, giving Mycroft Holmes's brother's address for identification. While the agent went through his records, I noticed two men of military bearing standing on the platform, scanning the crowd with narrowed eyes. I knew that sort of soldier from times past, and I could find it in my heart to pity whomever it was they sought.

"Herr Jeffries?" said the agent, and handed me a packet roughly the size of two books bound together. "Sign for it, please."

Ah, the German love of order, I thought to myself. When I had done that, I did the one thing I had decided was prudent to do: I sent a telegram to Vickers at the Cap and Balls, telling him of my forced change of travel plans and informing him of my belated arrival in Augsburg. At least if my actions were ever questioned, I would have this to defend myself. That is, if men of this sort gave a damn about such things. Still, it was a precaution against his promise that I would be hunted if I did not keep to the schedule provided me. Satisfied that I had done what I could in the way of self-protection, I went away from the telegraph desk and the presence of the two watchers.

I looked around once more, and went toward the waiting area to see if Herr Dortmunder would find me, as I had been told he would. While I waited, I opened the package, and, trying not to appear too eager, I examined its contents. First was a telegram from James, sent with the material from Zurich, where a British exporter had added the requested information: *In hopes you arrive as per schedule. Press of work delays action. Contents should explain. When should I expect payment?*

Going over the telegram, I realized that there was more information still to be delivered, and he wanted to know when I would reach MacMillian. I was puzzling out how to answer that when I noticed a stiff-spined man with a face like something off a bad statue of Beethoven. He was looking over all those of us in the waiting room, scanning each person in the place with an increasingly serious glower. I made note of him, then began to read the contents of the bound notebooks provided by the exporter in Zurich. What was written here were catalogs of the records of criminal and political activities of members of the Brotherhood. I scanned the pages, realizing that I would have a great deal of reading to do tonight, most of it distasteful. First among the men of this list was a sinister man who styled himself Luther von Metz, though it was thought he had taken this as his own after he had started his career with the Brotherhood. That name caught my eye and held my attention for some seconds as I tried to bring to mind where I had come across it. It did not take me long to narrow the time. Somewhere in the confusion of the last several days, I had heard von Metz, perhaps more than once. If my thoughts were not so disjointed, thanks to the developments of the last few days, I knew I would recall it at once. The memories slithered away from my attempts to grasp them as readily as snakes. It was quite frustrating, and I glared at the page where I was studying the entry under von Metz's name when the Beethoven-faced man approached me, bowing a little before he spoke. He wore a long suit-coat in the German fashion, and a heavy neck-cloth. In addition, he affected riding boots and heavy postilion's spurs, with the chain leathers.

"Your pardon, but are you waiting for a Herr Dortmunder?" He spoke English like a machine, and I realized he had learned it from a book. "Are you Mister Jeffers."

"That's Jeffries. Yes, I am," I said, aware that any questioning of the man could cause more trouble than I wanted to deal with. I also suspected that his slight mispronunciation of my assumed name was intentional, done to throw off any spy or imposter.

"I thought you would be on the train from Würzburg." He made this an accusation. "I was told you would be on it."

I answered him in German. "My train from Luxembourg was delayed, and I was not able to reach the connecting trains, so I made my way to Nuremberg, and from there to here. I did not want to delay on Mister Vickers' errand. He told me it was urgent, and so I came as quickly as I could." If I had expected praise for my initiative, I did not receive it.

"You were told to come on the Ulm train," he said, his German as bookish as his English.

"I would not have arrived until tomorrow, if I had done that. My instructions were that I was to arrive today, and I endeavored to comply," I said at my most reasonable as I did my best to appear casual, tucking the two bound volumes into my carpetbag as I talked. "I regret that I did not arrive until a short while ago."

"I would have come back." He inspected me in that abrupt way I have always associated with Germans. "Your face is damaged, and your coat is brown, not black. I was not told to expect that. I am Herr Dortmunder; a pleasure," he added with feigned cordiality.

"Nor was I," I countered, beginning to weary of the man. "Expecting these things."

Herr Dortmunder stared hard at me. "Is that a witticism?"

"Apparently not," I said, my fatigue increasing with every word we shared. "I was attacked in Luxembourg by two men."

"Attacked?" Herr Dortmunder exclaimed. "Who were they?"

"I have no idea," I answered. "They did not give their names or their mission; they tried to kill me."

"And what became of them?" Herr Dortmunder's tone demanded an answer.

"They failed in their mission," I told him, reluctant for some reason I could not define to relate the whole tale to this brusque man. I did not relish having to recount how I happened to kill one of them.

"That is fortunate," said Herr Dortmunder. "We must leave at once, before you are too closely observed." He indicated my carpetbag; as his coat swung back I saw he had a pistol tucked into a pocket of his waistcoat. "Is that all you carry? Just that one bag?"

"Yes, that is all," I assured him, rose and picked up my luggage and said, "Lead on, MacDuff," in English.

Whether he understood the remark or its contents, Herr Dortmunder did not find it funny. He sneered at me and stalked ahead of me toward the front of the station where carriages were drawn up, some for hire, others private. He indicated a covered calash drawn by two strengthy seal-brown horses of a breed I did not recognize. "Put your bag under your feet," he recommended as he paused to make a series of signs to the coachman before he climbed into the carriage and said, "The man is deaf."

"Poor fellow," I said automatically, and looked at the man beside me. "Where are we going?"

"You'll learn that soon enough," he told me gruffly as the calash started off through the traffic at the station. "We will not arrive for a while; you might as well make yourself comfortable."

It was a day of uneven temperament; when the sun peeked through the clouds, it was warm, but all shadows were cold, and there was a chill in the wind that whipped color into my face and made it stiff at the same time. I tried not to let this dismay me, but I could not wholly rid myself of the feeling that all the world was warning me of my current predicament. I sat back against the low squabs and did not speak as we rolled off into the German countryside.

In mid-afternoon we stopped at a country inn and were given a meal of savory wurst, cheese, and bread, and one of those yeasty German beers to wash it down. Herr Dortmunder ate with a steady, mechanical determination, without any sign of relish or disgust for his food. We exchanged no more than a dozen words over our repast, a thing that is harder to do in German than English. Then we were back in the calash, bowling down the road at a smart trot. About an hour later, the coachman turned his pair off the public road onto a narrow track that led toward a spinny of oaks mixed with pines. Herr Dortmunder offered no explanation for this diversion and I asked no questions, not wanting to cause any problems with the fellow. A quarter of an hour later, I could see the vague outlines of a large country house, which I think the Germans would call a *schloss*. The building was hidden among the trees, and I realized it was also of an age and design that was intended to withstand siege warfare, from the days when Germany had been a collection of minor states all at war with one another. This impression was confirmed as we neared the schloss itself, which was larger than I had first supposed, and nowhere near as welcoming; a drawbridge was lowered to admit the calash.

We passed under an emblem carved in stone: an Egyptian eye.

I saw men standing inside the portcullis who carried weapons of three hundred years ago—crossbows and pikes—along with formidable sidearms of more recent manufacture. They watched the carriage as it drew up, and I saw the coachman wince as two of these formidable guards came up to take the pair in hand from him. Although they wore no uniforms, they had the look of seasoned, professional soldiers. This schloss was an armed camp, and I was the enemy inside it. The notebooks in my carpetbag suddenly seemed about to burst into flame.

"You may step down, Mister Jeffries," said Herr Dortmunder. "I think you would do well to bring your own bag. We have few servants here."

Obediently I left the calash and took my carpetbag, filled with relief at his suggestion. The last thing I wanted to do was surrender the bag. Tempting as it was I did not look around with too much curiosity because I had the strong impression that such obvious interest would not be welcomed by the people here. I watched Herr Dortmunder for some indication of where I was to go.

At last he turned to me. "You will come with me." With that he set off through the massive oaken doors of the schloss. "Stay close behind me. If you do not, the men will shoot you." With that for encouragement, I followed after him, trying to take in as much of the place as I could without seeming to do so. After traversing a drafty room, we entered a stone corridor that led to what I supposed must be the heart of the building, to a baronial hall with a huge hearth with a blazing log set within it. On the chimney was another representation of the Egyptian eye. For decorations, the arms of what I assumed were noble German houses were displayed on the walls. Here was the gold-and-black lozengy of old German Württemberg rulers, and next to it, gules with argent per fess of Austria, followed by the quartered arms of Hungary; beyond that, the displayed black eagle of Prussia, and then the three crowned lions' heads on an azure field of Dalmatia. It was then that I realized what was troublesome about the arms: all were upside down. That was clearly no oversight or accident. This place was dedicated to their defeat.

Herr Dortmunder stopped and pointed to me to sit down. I did this, on an odiously uncomfortable wooden chair with a high, straight back. We remained there for the better part of an hour, Herr Dortmunder occasionally relieving the tedium by pacing the length of the hall, then pausing to stand before the massive hearth, hands behind his back, about as forbidding as the stones around him.

I spent the time trying to place the various reversed arms. I was reasonably certain that the golden goat with the red horns and hooves on the azure field was for the Margrave of Istria, but the attenuated argent goat rampant breathing fire on vert puzzled me, as did the red device like an English label or a bishop's mantle on an argent field. The black bull's head on the per pale azure and gules also was unfamiliar to me; the colped arm emerging from a cloud and wielding a scimitar I eventually recalled was Bosnia and Herzegovina. So it appeared—if this display meant anything—that the Brotherhood was determined to bring down every noble house from Moscow to London, just as Mycroft Holmes had implied when he put me in the way of meeting Mister Vickers.

Finally, as my nerves were beginning to fray and the hall was growing dark, the far door opened and an emaciated figure entered the room, striding purposefully forward, his hand extended to Herr Dortmunder. I rose, anticipating an introduction.

None was offered. The two men spoke quickly and in whispers, then the very thin man departed again, leaving us once more in the gathering dark.

"We will have lamps brought soon," Herr Dortmunder told me, as if this were a great concession to me. "And something to eat, as well. It is growing late." He went to face the flames.

"Well, I won't say they aren't welcome," I told him, making sure my German was not as good as it could be.

"Von Metz will come shortly. He wishes to speak with you for himself." He said this as if he were offering me a high treat. I remembered then that Mycroft Holmes had warned me about the fellow back in London, and there had been a mention of him since then. I tried to remember it. It came to me at last: one of the men at the edge of the canyon in Luxembourg had said the name, calling him a devil. I once again wondered who those men were and why they had made that desperate attempt on my life. The fear that they were not simple thieves determined to prey upon a traveler returned tenfold, and left me shaken.

"I'll look forward to that," I said, doing my best to seem interested and greedy enough to convince them I was the sort of man they were searching for.

"Do not think you will deceive him. He is very powerful. Very," said Dortmunder; I thought I detected a trace of fear in him, and the manner of one who is cowed by his superior.

I did my best to look interested but slightly skeptical, as I was aware a man of Jeffries's stamp must, but inwardly I was beginning to feel much distressed.

The man who came into the room was not a large fellow; of moderate height, fair hair running to white, and eyes of so pale a blue that they seemed made of ice; unlike ice, their gaze was hot. He had on a leather hacking jacket with suede collar. I came to my feet again but could not bring myself to approach him, for there was a palpable air of evil around him.

"This is Herr von Metz," said Herr Dortmunder, with the look of one who is presenting a ruler with a capricious temperament.

"Thank you, Herr Dortmunder," he said in excellent English, undoubtedly for my benefit. "Our truant has arrived. A fortunate thing for you, young man. I do not often tolerate any departure from my plans. Had you delayed reporting to my men another day, we would have been forced to look for you. And kill you once we found you." He strolled in my direction, and held out his hand as he looked me over, though not in greeting; I felt rather like a prize piece of stock about to be bred or slaughtered, at von Metz's fancy.

"I had to come a different way," I said, feeling like a child reporting to a teacher in class.

"We knew about the delayed trains; we were prepared to accommodate the change of times. We are not entirely isolated here," said von Metz. "Some of us travel, as well. I have been kept informed of your movements since you left Vickers, with the exception of the time you spent in Luxembourg; my man there was, most unfortunately, called away, and I could not act quickly enough to fill the gap he left. Had he been there you would not have taken off on that ill-considered detour. An oversight he will answer for to me." His glance flicked over my face; it was as if he had struck me. I began to suspect that what I had been told of this man's power was not overstated. "It appears that you have had some . . . adventure getting here."

"Adventure," I said with a sudden, hard laugh. "I have been nearly killed twice."

"That should not have happened. If anyone is to kill you, we will do it," said von Metz in such a tone as I never want to hear spoken by a human being again in my life. "Tell me what befell you, from the time you left London until now. And keep in mind there are marksmen in the gallery above. They will shoot at my signal or at any intemperate act on your part."

FROM THE PERSONAL JOURNAL OF PHILIP TYERS:
They have pulled a body from the Thames, one of a young woman who was done most horribly to death. Her name is not known, but she had put a note in her mouth before she was tortured, and since it appears she was gagged, the note was not discovered by those who killed her. It was written in the same hand as the anonymous note

*M.H. received just before G. undertook the mission
against the Brotherhood, and although somewhat damaged, it is nonetheless readable. In this note, which is
addressed to M.H., the writer states that she is aware that
she has been found, and she has secured an egg of opium,
and will take it in order to keep from satisfying her
attackers.*

*This has distressed M.H. very much, and he has
informed Scotland Yard that the woman had stumbled
upon some secret which she felt was too dangerous to
impart, and who had feared for her life, with excellent
cause. He has made a copy of her note and passed it on
to Scotland Yard with misgivings.*

*When he confronted the two men from the Admiralty,
he was in no mood for nonsense. His one piece of welcome news was confirmation that the Mercury train
would be at his disposal from midnight tonight. M.H. will
leave for the coast and the Channel as soon as this matter of the A. is resolved.*

*The first man, a confidential records clerk for the A., is
Harold Worthing, a young fellow with better family con-
nections than personal resources, which is to say he is a
spendthrift and a fool, at least according to M.H. The
young man has been much in the company of the young
widowed Hungarian Countess Erezebet Nagy, and is
clearly infatuated with her. The connection is not a wise
one. She is known to work for those who pay the best and
is currently accepting fees from the Russians.*

*The second man, also a records clerk, though of some-
what lesser station, is Arthur Upton, who has been at his
post for six years without any trace of misbehavior. Yet it
was upon this second man that M.H. bent his attention.*

*After assuring these two men that everything discussed
would be confidential, M.H. announced that he had
determined that one of the two of them, or possibly the
two working together, were responsible for the purloining
of his Admiralty packet and the wrecking of his flat. He
said to them both that the amount filched from the*

Admiralty over the last twenty months was staggering—more than seven thousand pounds. "But done in shillings and pence, so that it was not very noticeable. And on the return invoices. I suppose you thought they would be less noticeable, and for a time, you were right. The device is so uncomplicated. It was simply a matter of rounding off the figures and pocketing the difference, wasn't it?" This he addressed to Mister Upton.

The fellow blustered in protest, claiming he had no knowledge of such things.

"It was your entries that were the ones I noticed. You were not so obvious at first: a few rounded figures in a list of twenty attract no attention. But success led you to greed, and in the last several months, there are more and more rounded figures. I supposed the money must be going somewhere, and a word to your banker revealed that you had opened a second bank account, supposedly for a small trust, but, in fact, to hide your pilfering." M.H. glared at Worthing. "You, sir, accepted a bribe from this man—which is preferable to accepting one from the Russians or the Turks, but still enough to dismiss you from your post—to inform him of your schedule of invoices received."

Poor Worthing was already quite shaken, and now could not wait to confess his guilt.

"You may do that later," said M.H., his expression still grave. He once again turned to Upton. "What was it? A mistress or the horses? Or gambling?" He said the last with a pounce. "Did you make the classic mistake of all men who game—that having lost, you must risk more in the hope of restoring your losses?" He pulled a notebook from his jacket. "I have here the records, supplied to me not an hour ago, from Remi des Langres, in Curzon Street. He, it seems, holds your vowels. They add up to quite a formidable figure."

"The devil's been in the games. I know I shall come about," he said, putting a bold face on his error. "I intend to repay all the debts. Truly I do."

M.H. sighed, his voice dropping to a deep whisper. "And for this petty gaming mania of yours, I have had to let a good, loyal, and brave man go into mortal danger. Your little flirtation with corruption has placed an honorable civil servant at hazards compared to which your financial embarrassments are as nothing." He fixed Upton with a hard stare. "Guthrie is a far better man than you, deserving of all the help I can provide him. He has undertaken his mission on behalf of the safety of this country—a mission you were willing to imperil for the turn of a card or the fall of the dice. You are contemptible. If he loses his life, be it on your head, sir."

Upton was quite pale now, and Worthing was trembling. "I . . . I never thought that it would come to this," he said in a strange, fawning manner.

"More fool you," said M.H. without pity.

Worthing was on his feet. "I had no notion of his reasons for wanting to know my schedule."

"But there are others who would offer you more attractive items for your help," said M.H. heavily. "Your friendship with Countess Nagy is unwise, and could easily lead you into a far more devastating error than you have made. She is not the victim of fate you think her, and once in her toils, you could do inestimable harm. Your position is what makes you attractive to her, not your breeding or your probably genuine affection. Your resignation will be accepted today." He paused, then added, "Had you been the one taking money, you would be clapped in as a traitor. As it is, you have shown yourself to be too imprudent for the trust reposed in you." Then he rounded on Upton once more. "You, sir, will find that there are officers below waiting for you. Go along with them. Let me advise you to give them no trouble, for you have enough on your plate already."

Upton shot M.H. a look of such loathing as I hope never to see again. "You think you're above it all, don't you? You think that you can never succumb. You believe you are immune to the lures of the world, and can look *with contempt on those who are suffering. You sit here in your flat and the spiders spin their webs around you, for your uses. Well, I hope your schemes fail and you come to disgrace."* He put on his hat and started toward the door.

M.H. said to his back, *"For what satisfaction it may give you, Mister Upton, I very much fear that may already have happened."*

Chapter Thirteen

IT WOULD HAVE taken a far stauncher man than I am to refuse the order von Metz gave me. Trying not to look upward for the marksmen, I took a deep breath, and began, "When I had purchased new shirts for this journey, I caught the train for Dover where a man who looked like a professor boarded the same compartment and gave me new instructions and tickets for my travels, saying that Mister Vickers, in effect, did not trust me." I managed to appear ill used as I reported this. I continued on to the attempt to drown me as it happened in Calais.

"Who was this man, do you know?" von Metz asked me. Until then I had never truly known what it was to actually shiver in my boots. Yet if pressed, I could not have described what it was that so frightened me about von Metz, for superficially he looked like nothing more than a prosperous, somewhat arrogant man who might have been a judge or perhaps a fellow in the world of business, like Krupp or one of those.

"I had no chance to ask him anything; I was drugged.

He was trying to drown me." It was no effort to sound ill used at this moment. "I do not like to think what would have happened to me if he had not liked the answers I gave him."

"How came he to know where you were?" Von Metz made this question an accusation, one that I flinched to hear.

"How should I know?" I answered with more sharpness of tone than was prudent. "He came into the bath and shoved me under the water, didn't he?"

"You say he did." Von Metz was not convinced of my blamelessness at this moment.

"And someone searched my room and my bag while all that was going on. Vickers didn't say anything about this kind of . . . trouble." That was the least I could call it. "I would have asked for better wages if I had known there would be men like that after me."

"All right," said von Metz. "Continue."

I explained about how I had searched for any losses in my things and had only been able to complain of the loss of a razor. I made my complaint to this man as well, claiming I had purchased it, nearly new and toffy, and resented its loss. I then described my journey to Paris, remarking that I had a pretty traveling companion for that leg of the trip, but volunteered no additional information about Miss Penelope Gatspy. I thought that it might be dangerous for her if these men knew of her, and she was already at great risk, if her tale was true; if it was not, then I needed to be more circumspect than ever, for there was no telling what her mission might be, or how the Brotherhood would answer her for it. Next I accounted for my night in Paris, and then described the events after my arrival in Luxembourg, including the remark I overheard on the cliff when I was attacked, calling von Metz a devil. The memory of those two men dying jolted me.

"How pleasant to be understood by one's enemies, so much more so than the approbation of one's friends," said von Metz with a degree of inner satisfaction any cat might envy. "I am gratified those hypocrites have not forgotten me entirely."

I did not like to think what such remarks might portend. "The host there at the inn let me take a new coat, seeing as mine was ruined; there were plenty in storage, and the host said he could spare one," I went on, doing my best to maintain my composure. "It was a nice one," I went on, rubbing the lapel in approval.

"A pity that Sanglot wasn't there," said Herr Dortmunder to von Metz.

"Yes. He should have refused his sister's importunities until this matter was taken care of." Von Metz came up and looked at my face again. "How badly were you injured?"

"Took a couple nasty cuts and got knocked about," I said, offering my hand and wrist as proof; for some reason I did not want to have to tell him about the more serious wound. "Worst was the tears in my clothes."

"It must have been quite a battle, if you were able to defeat two such clever assassins," said von Metz with a bit too much speculation for my satisfaction.

"A man lives by his wits long enough, he learns a thing or two," I said with all the bravado I supposed this von Metz would expect from one such as Jeffries. I did my best to put a good face on it, hoping that my queasiness did not show. "Not that it wasn't a near thing, because it was. They knew what they were doing, those two. If I hadn't had some luck going for me, I should have been put paid to, and no one the wiser."

"It does seem that you have had to endure a great deal on our account," said von Metz with the kind of sympathy that made me squirm. "We will have to remedy that in some manner."

I have rarely encountered so soulless a smile as his. I could say nothing.

Herr Dortmunder folded his arms to let me know he did not believe me. "A shame about the coat," he allowed.

"That it is," I agreed promptly, and continued my explanation of my changing trains.

"You have been asking for telegrams everywhere you stop," said von Metz in a speculative manner. "Why is that? You've sent some, as well."

"To my solicitor, feckless lot that he is, wanting money before raising a finger to pen a writ," I told him, appearing to sulk. "He's supposed to be looking into the trust I was left. It's got conditions in it that are . . . a hardship on me and my family." I nodded, confirming Jeffries's own low opinion of the legal profession. "I have a wife and children, but I can't afford to bring them to England until my father's trust is wound up so I have my hands on the ready." I had repeated this story often enough that it was beginning to seem real to me, in an absurd way. I did my best to look stricken without intending that either man be convinced.

"No wonder you are willing to do these things," said von Metz, as if this were the first he had heard of it, though I was reasonably certain it was not. "How inconvenient this arrangement must be for you, given what you seek to accomplish." His crocodile smile was intended to show sympathy—without success.

"I have to get that money, and that lawyer won't act if I don't keep at him. He's like all that breed," I temporized. "Too ready to take your money, and too slow to get the work done right."

"Alas, it was ever thus," said von Metz with a look in his icy eyes that made me sorry for any man having to represent him in court. "Well, when this is over, you should be able to pay the whole of it."

"How do you mean?" I asked.

"Considering what you have endured thus far, it is appropriate that the sum Vickers promised you be increased. You may telegraph your solicitor that his payment is assured, and inform him that you will contact him again once you return to England." His smile made the

absolute order more horrible, for it implied the gratification the man would have in making me pay for disobedi-
ence. I looked at him and felt my viscera go cold.

"If I do that, how am I to know he's doing his job,
then?" I demanded, and heard my voice three notes
higher than usual.

"You will find a way, good fellow," said von Metz. "If
ten pounds are sent to him as an installment on his even-
tual fee, he will no doubt be pressed into action on your
behalf." He came toward me; I took an involuntary step
back. "I do not want your attention diverted from your
work for us, Herr Jeffries. Given what you have said
today, it is apparent to me that we have cause to be concerned, and I must be certain you will not allow yourself
any distractions from what Mister Vickers has demanded
you do."

I did not like that word *demanded,* but I made myself
shrug. "If that's what you want and you're willing to pay
more for it, then I'll manage. I'll notify him of the money
coming, as you said, and then mum's the word until the
work is done." I found it difficult to breathe.

"Very good." Von Metz took a turn about the room. "I
don't know if Mister Vickers made it clear to you why
your work is so important. This Scotsman you are to
become acquainted with holds the key to some negotiations that are most important to me and my organization.
For some years my Brotherhood and I have watched
while fools determined the fate of our country. Yes, fools!
And what better example of it than King Ludwig, who
seeks to build nothing but fantastic palaces; and his ministers permit it. Such men have failed to see my value and
foresight. I have plans for a brilliant future for Europe,
grander than Napoleon ever conceived. I am an incisive
leader who is not limited by ordinary conventions."

I had expected much ambition from the head of the
Brotherhood, but I had not supposed the man would be
completely self-aggrandizing as von Metz was. I lowered
my head and muttered something to the effect that the

times were uncertain in so many places. I wanted to appear impressed, for less than that might cause the man to turn on me. I had a moment when I had to suppress an urge to laugh at his vainglorious ravings. But I knew from what Mycroft Holmes had told me and what I had now observed for myself: von Metz was in deadly earnest, no matter how mad his vision.

He continued on with little regard to my emotions. "The Brotherhood knows that it will take very little before the entire ridiculous cobbling called 'peace' collapses. The buffoons attempting to hold all together are desperate. War between Serbia and Bulgaria, so recently freed from the bondage of the Turks, and so naive, can be the spark that puts all Europe to flame. Then I, who have been ready for this, will make myself an alternative to chaos. I, and my Brotherhood, will ascend the heights by the acclaim of the people."

"But the Brotherhood is . . . secret," I said, wanting to show I was paying attention to him.

"It was factored into my plans. Certain of the Mad Ludwig's ministers have been brought into our ranks, so that I am sure of their support. We might have struck within the month had it not been for the intervention of England." He spoke the name of my country as if it were despicable. "But the Brotherhood is not daunted by the activities of busy little men. There are those who can be made to dance to our tune. To that end, we seek what the Scotsman has." His smile reminded me of nothing so much as the gaping maw of a deadly serpent. "So you see, I must have your full cooperation if I am to succeed in my aims. The King is tolerant of us for the moment, but he cannot be depended upon for anything but building palaces and castles. If he should take a notion that he is more in tune with the Golden Lodge, we could be exposed. Which I would not like, as I am sure you must appreciate."

I appreciated more than that: I realized that he would not let me live with the information he had given me. I also realized that he would have me killed when I ceased to be necessary to him.

Herr Dortmunder heard this out with a faint sign of approval. He was determined to impress me with his knowledge and close ties to von Metz, for reasons that troubled me greatly.

"There is a difficulty," said von Metz. "There are those in the British government who would like to stop me. They have much riding on this foolish treaty. And there is the Golden Lodge, as well." He said this casually, but I knew he was weighing my reactions. Any slip now would be very dangerous.

I stared at him. "The Golden Lodge?" I repeated, hoping I sounded as foolish as I felt.

"Yes. They used to be part of the Brotherhood, but in the last decade they have split off from us, going on their own for reasons that are as reprehensible as they are dangerous. They have declared themselves the enemies of the Brotherhood, pledged to bring all our efforts to ruin. Those men in Luxembourg were certainly with the Golden Lodge. None of the spymasters in Europe are aware of me, let alone of the Golden Lodge." He scowled and made a gesture with his hands that suggested he wanted to strangle the life out of all of them.

"Whoa there; this is getting too deep for me," I protested. "Brotherhoods and Golden Lodges. What next?"

"Very little. The two are ample," said von Metz.

"That cove in Calais—was he one of them Golden Lodgers?" I hated the question as much as I needed the answer.

"He might have been," said von Metz. "He may also have been sent by the British government, or—"

I dared to interrupt him. "Not that one. He had a strong German accent. Like Herr Dortmunder."

"Ah," said von Metz as if he had gained understanding from my words. He paced a few steps away, then turned back, as if those few steps had given him wisdom. "Then he may well be of the Golden Lodge." He paused. "Or it may be that there are men in Bavaria who have learned more than they should have and are trying to keep this treaty protected. I would anticipate such actions from them, given their determination to keep the treaty a secret."

I heard him out without satisfaction. "And what am I going to do about it?" I asked sharply. "It's my neck that's on the line. How am I going to watch out for these Golden Lodgers and half the civil servants in Germany? And deal with a King who's dicked in the nob?"

"You will not concern yourself with these issues, Mister Jeffries," said von Metz, menace infusing his simple order.

"Easy for you to say," I muttered.

Von Metz shot an angry glance in my direction. "I did not think we had employed such a coward," he said casually.

"Not a coward," I corrected him. "A cove what's careful of his skin." And given all that had happened in the last three days, I had more than sufficient reason to be.

"If you say so," said von Metz in total disbelief. "I would have thought that you would be more willing to defend yourself than you have shown yourself to be thus far, but it may be that I have misunderstood you."

"Well, you haven't. August Jeffries don't turn his back on a real fight, but I'm damned if I'll get killed for something I have no part in, and for nothing." I let my indignation override my trepidation. "How do I know you don't want me out there as a decoy, someone for those other-Lodge coves to shoot at while you do your real work? How do I keep from making another mistake about who's after me, the next time someone tries to kill me? Tell me that, will you? Do I just ask them who they're working for before they deliver the coup de grâce? Do I offer them a sign to see if they have one to give back? And how do I know that you are going to pay me a single farthing for my services? Oh, yes, you say you will, but what happens to my wife and kids if you lope off and leave me in a pauper's grave?"

"We would not do such a thing," said Herr Dortmunder, as affronted as I was.

"How do I know that? Because you tell me so? Because you have a castle and armed men around you? Because of your bloody *Brotherhood*?" I made myself give a bark of laughter. "After the last few days, I don't find it easy to believe you."

"You are offensive, Mister Jeffries," exclaimed Herr Dortmunder.

"But you can't blame him," said von Metz in a mild voice, which silenced both Herr Dortmunder and me. He went on. "I will make a deposit in any London bank you stipulate, in the amount of one hundred pounds, for your family, if that would reassure you," he offered. "This must ease your conscience in regard to your wife and children."

His very blandness distressed me. "Make it two hundred," I blustered, now more certain than ever that he would not let me live through this venture; we were haggling over my blood-money.

"Done," said von Metz with satisfaction. He rubbed his hands together and went to a bell-pull that hung beside the hearth. "We will dine, and then you will rest. Tomorrow you will continue on to Munich with Herr Dortmunder. The Scotsman is there for another two days. Herr Dortmunder will see to the disposal of his valet. The rest will be up to you. Fail us, and you will lose more than your eye." He indicated my patch, and grinned.

I heard this out with a sinking sensation, for surely I had just heard von Metz issue my death warrant.

FROM THE PERSONAL JOURNAL OF PHILIP TYERS: *At last it is arranged. M.H. leaves in two hours for the coast, traveling in a private compartment on the night train. He will arrive in France in the morning, God and the Channel willing. The Mercury train will be ready to speed him on his way to Germany. And Edmund Sutton was able to supply the necessary clothing and complements for his other personae for this journey.*

Sutton is installed now as M.H., and has elected to use his hours here to learn the role of Angelo in Measure for Measure. *He has played M.H. enough that he no longer finds the role challenging, or so he claims.*

I will visit Mother this evening, and then contact her solicitor regarding the disposal of her house in Redding.

Chapter Fourteen

AFTER AN UNEASY night in a drafty unadorned room with a bed like a sepulchre, a small hearth with an inadequate supply of wood, and an oil lamp with a smoking wick, I found myself grateful for the first time that my codebook had been ruined. I should not have wanted to have to try to conceal it in this place. I thought my few reconstructed notes were as noticeable as smelting ore, and kept them under my shirt the whole night long; they felt massive as boulders. I was awakened at dawn by one of the schloss guards, who told me I had forty minutes to dress, shave, break my fast, and present myself in the courtyard for departure.

Herr Dortmunder was waiting at the calash; the hood was raised and two bearskin rugs were lying on the seat. "It is supposed to rain this morning," he explained. Those were the first and last words he addressed to me until we approached the outskirts of the old town of Freising, where the Bishop had once maintained his See. There was nothing much to the place now, the greater part of the region having directed its attention to Munich. "Do not show yourself," Herr Dortmunder said then. "We may be observed."

There was an old church in the town, not on the Domberg with the Cathedral, St. John's Church, and the Benedict Church—for, being the center of the Bishopric, the place had more than the usual allotment of churches—but below. We went past it quickly, although it looked to have some interesting stained glass work, having the lines of a building of the late Gothic period. I leaned forward and craned my neck as we went by, hoping to see more of the place.

"That is Saint George's Church. It is in disrepair," said Herr Dortmunder, with an underlying satisfaction that caused me distress, for though I do not subscribe to the Roman Rite, I respect the history that building represented. "Sit back. Quickly."

I did as he ordered, and just in time, for Herr Dortmunder ordered the coachman with a signal to spring the horses. I clung to the arm-strap while the carriage lurched through the muddy streets. When we had to slow down, I was pleased.

Then a shot rang out, and the fabric of the hood tore as a bullet ripped through it. The off-side horse neighed in distress and tried to rear, preparing to bolt. He flung his head up, attempting to wrench free of the reins. With vociferous and incomprehensible oaths, the coachman got the horses under control while passersby in the street ran for shelter, many of them shouting as they did. One woman all but swooned and had to be carried from the street. Other drivers strove to move their wagons and carriages aside. Children screamed and wailed.

"What the devil—?" I asked.

There was a second shot, and a third. This one struck the coachman, who roared with pain and outrage, then collapsed onto his side. There was blood on his neckcloth and the side of his face.

"Down on the floor. At once. Cover yourself." Herr

Dortmunder shoved me hard as he scrambled onto the coachman's box, his postilion's spurs jangling, flinging the man aside without ceremony as he grabbed the Hungarian reins and seized the whip, shouting to people and vehicles to clear a path for us.

"Who is shooting at us?" I demanded. "And why?" I was startled to realize the team had not bolted. "Your horses—"

"Are army-trained. Gunfire doesn't frighten them. They will hold as long as we need." He looked around quickly as if to assure himself no one was coming up behind us.

"Who?" I cried.

"Later!" Herr Dortmunder thundered as we rushed through the last bits of the town, hurrying beyond the limits, and racketed along the road on the bank of the Isar toward Munich. Only when we were three miles or so from the city did Herr Dortmunder rein in his weary team and let them walk, though he continued to glance over his shoulder, as if in anticipation of pursuit.

"What was that all about?" I got up from the floor of the calash, and looked condemningly at the rents in the hood. "And don't try to fob me off with easy tales and vague comments."

"Of course not," said Herr Dortmunder. He had lost his hat in our precipitous escape and I noticed his face was flushed to an unhealthy degree. As he spoke, he kept up an uneasy surveillance, his eyes never fixing on any object for long. He made the horses walk out, though the off-side bay was beginning to flag and I could see he was favoring his on-side front foot. "That is why I told you not to let yourself be seen. There are many who do not want you to reach Munich. You will discover they are ruthless, the men of the Golden Lodge, to say nothing of the agents of the German and British governments who operate here in Bavaria. As a Servant of the Valley of Kings knows better than I." He laughed once. "But they like to think themselves as patriotic gentlemen, and often lack the will to do the things that must be done. They suppose that they will smirch the honor of their countries, and are of little concern. The Golden Lodge has no such compunctions."

"And what of your coachman? Have you no thought for him?" I did not like what that fellow's treatment implied where I was concerned.

"He cannot speak. And if they attempt to force him to reveal his knowledge some other way, he has a vial of poison, and he will use it." The cold confidence with which Herr Dortmunder spoke was truly frightening.

More than anything I wished now I could speak directly with Mycroft Holmes. I knew that he would be able to unravel this coil. I cleared my throat. "Well, if I'm going to be set upon by men of that sort, you had better let me send a telegram to my solicitor at once. So I can arrange to file my will with him." I had wanted to sound disgusted and brave, but to my own ears, my words seemed hollow, petulant and frightened.

"We will arrive there shortly. When you go to the train station to send the telegram, you will have to go in disguise. Whoever is following us, they are no longer fooled by that new coat of yours. We will have to find some other costume for you." He spat, and whipped up the pair to a trot, though the foam on their coats from the maddened rush from Freising had not yet dried. "We will be there shortly. And I will search out the Scotsman, to take care of his valet. The rest is up to you. I advise you not to fail."

I recalled how determined von Metz had been, and the armed men who guarded him, and I began to reflect on some of the things Mycroft Holmes had shown me in the time I had been in his employ. It struck me now that the stakes here were huge, for if the treaty were compromised, much of Europe could eventually fall under the shadow of the Brotherhood: even if von Metz's grandiose plot to thrust all Europe into war failed, the Brotherhood would have insinuated itself into the governments of a dozen countries. I shuddered to consider a Europe where the leaders were daily fed the venom of the Brotherhood, for eventually each country would be isolated one from another—and England by virtue of being an island, most of all—so that no peace could be sustained.

An hour later, I could see the city of Munich emerging from the splendid Bavarian scenery. I have rarely looked upon a place with such mixed emotions as I had at the sight of Munich that day. The setting, with the mountains rising grandly behind it, and the clouds towering above them all, made it appear like a city in a fairy tale, but there was danger there, more than I had ever supposed I would have to face, and that turned the delightful place to a sinister lie, like a trap set in a nightmare.

By the time we reached the train station, it was drizzling, and I was grateful for the bearskin rugs in the back. The day was closing in swiftly, the clouds masking the waning afternoon.

Herr Dortmunder drove us to a warehouse in Ortenburg Strasse, a dark and oppressive building dating from the fourteenth century, by the look of it. He stepped down from the box and rapped sharply in what I assumed was a coded pattern. Less than two minutes later the doors swung back and three armed men, much like the ones I had seen at the schloss, came out to lead the horses and carriage into the interior. Herr Dortmunder was standing in one of a number of narrow doorways that surrounded the central hall; the place was gloomy, and oppressive. I may have imagined that the muzzles of rifles were trained upon me, but I doubt it.

"You will have to disguise yourself. With the eyepatch that will not be easy, so we must improvise." He signaled me to approach.

I retrieved my carpetbag from where I had shoved it during our flight, saying, "Is there somewhere I can put this?"

"We will show you eventually," said Herr Dortmunder, his manner testy and abrupt. "You must come with me."

In this company I was not about to dispute the matter with him. I fell into step behind him, this time making little attempt to hide my curiosity about the place. "Where are we?" I asked as we continued along the corridor to a flight of stairs leading down.

"In Munich. That is all you need to know for the moment, Mister Jeffries." He was running out of patience with me, and I could not help but notice the tension that existed between him and the men who guarded this place.

We arrived at last in a cellar, with ancient, damp stones keeping the huge chamber perpetually dank, though I realized the chill of the place had more sinister origins than wet stones. At the far end of the large room, I saw a raised dais with what appeared to be an altar set upon it. It was too dim to make out the various accoutrements there, but I was reasonably certain they were not for rituals I knew or wanted to know.

"This is where you will remain until tomorrow. Then you will be disguised and taken to the train station," said Herr Dortmunder, looking more like a bad impression of Beethoven than ever.

"But I thought—" I began, only to be cut off.

"The station is being watched. It is not safe to go there tonight."

I did my best to look put-out instead of alarmed. "Who'd be watching, then?"

"The same ones who shot at us. Probably the Golden Lodge, or agents of that braggart von Bismarck." Herr Dortmunder made a gesture I did not recognize but I clearly understood its intent. I rocked back on my heels and waited for him to say something more. "They are trying to keep us from reaching MacMillian." He nodded in an infuriatingly superior way. "It is not a bad plan. In their place I would probably do the same thing." This grudging admission was more than he wanted to give, and he did it with ill grace.

"How can I do what you need me to do?" I asked as I followed him into the heart of the cellar. "I won't be able to convince the Scotsman to take me on if I'm being shot at all the time."

"True enough," said Herr Dortmunder. "And that is why I have brought us here. So these men may go out and find the assassin and bring him here. There are some questions I want to ask him."

The menace in that simple statement was greater than any I had heard from this dire man, and I began to fret that I should be in the hands of these men with no one to find me if my situation became desperate. How the last few days had changed me, I remarked inwardly, that I should find myself in a nest of villains whose purpose was the overthrow of everything I honored, and who were ruthless against their foes, and still not think of my situation as desperate. I noticed that there were half a dozen men approaching the altar, all wearing robes and hooded.

"Who are these people?" I asked of Herr Dortmunder in a low voice.

"They are members of the Brotherhood. They are going to perform a ritual that will aid your efforts. You must witness it, to ensure your success." He showed me a high-backed chair. "That is for you. Do not stir from it once the ritual has begun."

"And you?" I asked, not liking being alone in this place with those sinister figures.

"I will join the men performing the ritual." He started away from me, but paused to reiterate his warning. "Do not move once the ritual begins, no matter what happens. It would be very . . . bad for you if you do."

Looking around at where I was, I thought it could not get much worse. I sat down, my carpetbag between my feet, and tried to find a comfortable place to sit on the chair; none seemed possible, and after five torturous minutes, I abandoned the attempt and took my place squarely on it, hoping that my bones would not ache too fiercely from what was to come. If the ritual was a long one, I might expect to be in this place for over an hour, a prospect that filled me with apprehension.

Another ten minutes passed as the hooded figures brought various items to the makeshift altar: a large basin made of brass, a small mace, a pair of braziers which smoked more than they gave off light, a dagger, a large crystal, a towel with an odd design embroidered on it, a broken staff, and a set of restraints made of chain. These last made me shudder as I caught sight of them.

Then a gong sounded from somewhere along one of the echoing corridors.

The cowled figures at once took up positions at the corners of the altar, their heads lowered as I heard chanting, distorted by constant echoes, come from three of the entrances to this huge cellar. A short while later, three processions of other habited figures made their way toward the altar, all taking pains to pass through the portals set up at the far end of the altar.

I decided the language they used must be German, but an older form of the tongue than any I knew. I recognized a few words, but not enough to be certain I understood the purpose of this ritual.

Finally a man in a long red cowl made his appearance. I recognized his voice as that of Herr Dortmunder. He went to the altar and lifted up his hands, saying something in the archaic language about the power of sacrifice. The rest of the men intoned a response about the might of their work. Then Herr Dortmunder asked for the offering.

Three of the cowled men went into the nearest corridor, and I heard a great struggle, a few oaths, and then a man with a badly bruised face was half-carried, half-dragged out to the altar. Even in this light, and in spite of the blood matted in his unruly hair, I could see it was, as my mother would have said, red as a fire in a hay-rick. His mouth was too swollen for him to be able to do more than make incoherent screams. His hands were purple and badly distended from repeated blows. I suspected that all his knuckles were broken. The look of him made me queasy, for I was helpless to come to his aid, and I despised myself for not doing so. I steeled myself for what I was afraid might come.

"This is the plunder we bring," intoned Herr Dortmunder as the man was bound to the altar.

I wanted to protest, but the words stuck in my throat as I felt the hand of one of the cowled figures descend on my shoulder, and a slim blade was pressed lightly against my neck.

"Watch," the figure commanded. "And remember. Those who cross us will all die as this man dies. Do not forget."

As if I would ever forget that place and the hideous acts I witnessed. I could not believe what I saw. I sat, transfixed with fear, as Herr Dortmunder stripped the man, and with the implacable assistance of the rest of his fellow-devotees, cut out the man's tongue, and then emasculated him, putting these grisly tokens into the basin to the approving cries of the cowled men around him.

There was blood everywhere. It splashed, steaming, onto the floor, and it reddened the cowled habits of the men performing the heinous rite. The victim of this atrocity had fainted; I hoped for his sake that he would remain unconscious until he bled to death. The hideous ceremony went on, the cowled men chanting in a rough monotone as Herr Dortmunder continued his ghastly work.

The man on the altar suddenly struggled and cried out aloud, the sound of it causing my very marrow to freeze in my bones.

"This will be your fate, if you fail us," said the man beside me, as if he were speaking of a notice in the paper. "Watch and remember."

There were other terrible things done to the man on the altar. Signs whose importance I did not understand but by implication were cut into his chest, his abdomen, and his forehead. I was finding it difficult to breathe.

I stared at the altar as Herr Dortmunder declared that

this life would bring into his power and the power of the Brotherhood the life of Cameron MacMillian, and make him the willing tool of their cause.

Then, with a great cry, Herr Dortmunder took the mace and dashed the man's brains out.

FROM THE PERSONAL JOURNAL OF PHILIP TYERS:
Word has come that M.H. has reached France safely, and assumed one of the three identities Edmund Sutton has supplied him. He will not send word again until he reaches Germany, for fear of having his messages intercepted as well as wishing to take the utmost advantage of the Mercury train.

Arthur Upton has signed a full account of his wrongdoing and will face first the Admiralty and then, if it is decided that it would be worthwhile, the Bench. Acting upon M.H.'s instructions, Harold Worthing has resigned his position and is now retiring to his hunting box in Yorkshire, to wait out the worst of his disgrace. His family have done all they can to put a good face on it, but it is clear to all that they are keenly dismayed by what has transpired.

Countess Nagy has been informed by certain men in government that she might prefer Paris for the next few years. Her voluntary departure would spare her and the Hungarians the misfortune of having certain of their activities brought to light in a way that would please no one.

Inspector Cornell of Scotland Yard has sent word that he would like more information on the unfortunate young woman whose identity has still not been established. It seems that there are some odd marks branded into her body which give the Inspector grave reservations about the case. One of them, his note informs me, is the representation of an eye, and this is what is proving the most troublesome, for with so many high-ranking Masons in the government, he must tread carefully, if this eye is the same as the one the Masons represent within a triangle. I have sent word back saying that M.H. will be informed of these matters by telegram, and he will send his response directly to Cornell at Scotland Yard.

 Mother was lucid for a short while today, and I can only thank God for the opportunity to see her then.

Chapter Fifteen

I HAD JUST witnessed a murder of utmost ferocity. I was stupefied, unable to move. There was nothing I could do or say that would change anything of what I had seen. Again my danger struck me, but with renewed force, for as a witness to this unspeakable ritual, the Brotherhood could not afford to let me live. Surely they would do away with me when my work was done, possibly in a fashion as hideous as the atrocity was.

A short while later, my guard dragged me to my feet and directed me toward a room off one of the corridors leading to the chamber. I was able to keep my wits about me only to the extent that I carried my carpetbag with me, for more than ever, the notebooks it contained heralded my guilt to the Brotherhood.

The chamber assigned for my use was little more than a cell, containing an unmade army bed, a small chest with a gate-leg writing table at one end, and a commode. About eight by nine feet, it had two high, small windows which looked out on the ruins of a kitchen garden lit by three torches: I was below ground level at the rear of the building, and so isolated I might as well have been in the grave. I sat down on the cot provided and tried to make my mind work. The unsteady light from the torches in the courtyard provided irregular illumination that was much in accord with my wavering thoughts. At last one notion came to me—that I must do something about my covered eye. Desperately I tried to recall the tricks I had seen Edmund Sutton do, and set myself the task of using what my observations had taught me.

In my toiletry kit I found a wad of cotton lint. I took a little of this, my concentration driven by dread and the need to do something so that I would not feel so utterly in the power of the Brotherhood. I took also my iodine bottle and stained a little of the cotton with it. Then I rummaged in my things for my mucilage for stamps. I spread some of this vile-smelling glue on the cotton and pressed the cotton onto my closed eyelid, holding it with my fingers until it dried in place. The appearance, once the whole was set—at least as much as I could determine in the shine of the torches—was of a badly puckered scar. Satisfied that the effect might stand a superficial inspection, I then put the patch back in place, trying to find some reason for optimism in the efforts I had made.

Tempting as it was to try to find a place to conceal the notes I had been keeping somewhere in the room, I was unable to convince myself that this was wise, for any disruption of the room might bring unwanted attention to my activities, and I suspected the tattoo would not banish all doubts from the minds of my captors. I went to the chest and looked inside it for the bedding, and found old, discolored though freshly laundered sheets, a blanket—the moths had been at it—and a pillow stuffed with spent barley with a sour smell that pervaded the whole of the cell. Not very promising, I thought, doing my best to cheer myself with these mundane reflections. I set about putting the bed to rights, and wishing I had been provided a lantern, or a candle, for the darkness was oppressive and my efforts clumsy.

The night went by interminably, and I found myself sinking to the depths of despair. If these men had disposed of that poor man so unspeakably, what would be my fate if they discovered my mission? The more I tried to dismiss such concerns from my mind, the more determinedly they stuck there, like an aching tooth. I tried to convince myself I was hungry and cold, and those things accounted for my state of mind, but I knew it was not so. When I tried to sleep, I was visited by images of the man in Luxembourg falling into the abyss. By morning, I was groggy with fatigue and melancholy, and I rose feeling stiffness in my joints when I heard others stirring in the hall beyond me. I decided I should shave, and wished I could have a proper wash.

"You are to come with me," announced one of the guards who appeared unheralded in my doorway as I was shaving. As I had my eyepatch raised, I was glad I had taken the precaution the night before of making it appear the covered eye was hideously injured. I trusted that the light was insufficient for him to realize the makeshift nature of my supposed disfigurement.

I continued with my razor—the one I had bought in Paris—and prayed my hands did not shake. "I will be with you as soon as I'm finished here."

He clearly did not like this, but he remained where he was, unwilling to move until I completed my work and had put my razor away in my case and returned them all to my carpetbag. "Herr Dortmunder is expecting you." His English was good but his accent was thick enough that under other circumstances he might have sounded comical, something Edmund Sutton would use for a music hall revue about the stiff-rumped Germans. In this setting, I could find little amusing about it.

I put my eyepatch back in place. "Not surprising," I said, trying to sound unmoved by this information, as if the ghastly dealings of the night before had made no impression on me. "Well, I'm ready."

"Nasty scar you have there," he observed as he started down the corridor ahead of me.

"Better than having my brains shot out, I suppose, or so I thought at the time," I answered as casually as I could. "Thought it would be easier to lose an eye than my life."

"No doubt," said the guard, unimpressed with my sangfroid.

I followed after him, my carpetbag feeling as heavy as if it contained anvils; those notebooks might yet reveal my ruse. I was attempting to think of some way to explain them when we arrived at last on the upper level of the building, in a good-sized dining room paneled in dark oak and made cheery by a blazing fire in the hearth and a half-a-dozen east-facing mullioned windows letting in the watery morning light.

Herr Dortmunder was seated by himself in solitary state at the head of the glossy table, which was designed to accommodate twenty-four people at least. He had a number of covered dishes in front of him and a tankard of beer in one hand. His own plate was filled with fried sliced potatoes and bits of egg and cheese. "Good morning, Mister Jeffries," he exclaimed, indicating the seat beside him. His heartiness did not convince me, not after what I had seen the night before. "I have just had a most interesting telegram from Vickers." He held up the document and smiled at me. "He informs me that you notified him of your change in travel arrangements." His expression turned granitelike. "You may think this was clever, or you may have only been hoping to please him as the one who first employed you. But you will understand that Vickers as well as I takes his orders from von Metz." He nodded to my guard, who gave a kind of salute and left us alone. "Sit down."

I did as I was told, taking a chair to Herr Dortmunder's left, leaving one space between us so that I would not appear too presumptuous. "I did not want him to think I had disobeyed his orders," I said, trying for the right mix of servility and sulking. "He might have withheld the money he promised me if I had not done it."

Herr Dortmunder sighed heavily. "You are so concerned about money, Mister Jeffries. There are more important issues at stake here."

"Of course I am concerned about money," I answered with indignation. "I haven't got any, have I? It's easy to say that money isn't that important when you have it, but when you don't, then it is as important as food." I glanced at the covered dishes, though I had no appetite.

"Oh, help yourself, Mister Jeffries. There are hot pastries with sausages in this and baked apples in that baroque dish. And baked eggs and bacon with cheese in the far platter with the Bavarian arms on the lid. The crockery dish with the fish pattern contains the fried potatoes. They're very good. Have whatever you like." He continued to smile, his version of affability making me feel nauseated. "This is going to be an important day for you."

"How is that?" I asked, pausing in the act of raising the lid on the pastries with sausages.

"Today you are to meet your future . . . eh . . . employer. Cameron MacMillian is in want of a valet, and you will offer him your services, as he has just discovered his man has decamped." His chuckle was mirthless.

"How's that? You've arranged it?" I wanted to sound surprised, but my suspicion turned it to apprehension.

"Certainly." He regarded me steadily. "Well, surely you guessed?"

"What?" I was anticipating his answer already.

"Our sacrifice last night was his man," came the bland explanation. "I saw no reason for our Brotherhood to lose such a fine opportunity to further our work. You made it possible for us to get full value from the fellow. Had you not been here, we would not have dared to risk killing him because too many questions might be asked about his disappearance. Now that you are here, you will take his place, and so any inquiry as to his whereabouts is going to be cursory at best. He was a foreigner and a servant. Such persons are unreliable when traveling abroad." He opened the disk of baked eggs and used the silver spatula to remove two and add them to the mess on his plate.

"You're sure of that, are you? Someone will notice he's gone. Won't my arrival look a trifle too convenient, coming on the heels of the . . . other cove's departure?" I made myself put pastry and sausages on my plate.

"No. If the Scotsman were another sort, the authorities might question it, but MacMillian is known to be difficult. His servants do not remain in his employ for long." He picked up his fork. "But a man down on his luck, as you appear to be, can be expected to try to gain the help of such a man as he." The certainty with which he said this chilled me.

"I don't know," I said as I took my first bite; it was like eating sawdust and blotting paper. "If he's difficult, he might want a replacement he knows. Why should he accept me as his valet?"

"He is in no position to choose, at least not at present. He will not find a manservant where he is now." He took a long draught of beer. "He has been spending the last few nights at a very exclusive brothel. He will not want it known that he visited such an establishment while on so urgent a mission as he has undertaken."

"Probably not," I agreed, thinking of the stern demeanor of the Queen in regard to such things, urgent mission or no.

"So, as soon as you are done, we will take you to the place. You will say you encountered Angus at a biergarten, playing cards and drunk, who told you about his intention to leave Munich at once. You, not being one to waste a possible advantage, decided to present yourself to the Scotsman in his valet's stead. That should do well enough." He looked very satisfied with himself.

I sat at the table and ate as much as I could bring myself to take, thinking as I did that I might be nourishing a corpse.

We were away from the old warehouse in less than an hour after I finished shaving. It was a chill morning, and mists from the river made the city almost as foggy as London, but without the penetrating smell of saltwater. The calash went through the streets at a steady trot, and around us I heard more than saw the people of the city. All the while, Herr Dortmunder did his best to prepare me for our destination.

"It is King Ludwig who has made the city mad for Orientalia. He has a Turkish room at his hunting lodge, and there is a Moorish kiosk being built at Linderhoff, his latest building effort. Who knows what he will want next—an Indian castle, perhaps." His account smacked of condemnation of these excesses.

I thought of George IV's fantastical pavilion at Brighton, the one Beau Nash, or one of the other great dandies, had described as Saint Paul's having littered and brought forth cupolas, and for which I had a tasteless but genuine affection. "It could be a right treat," I said as if approving of the venture.

Herr Dortmunder rolled his eyes upward in disapproval. "If he cared for anything but buildings and the opera, Bavaria might have played a more important role in the war. As it is, Ludwig has no thought of any glory but what his architect and Richard Wagner can supply. He has gone to Bayreuth to hear every new work at least once."

"They say Otto, the Prince, is mad," I remarked.

"How do you know about that? Where did you hear it?" demanded Herr Dortmunder. He swung around to look at me, ignoring the guard driving the carriage.

Too late, I recalled it was in a dispatch on Mycroft Holmes's table. I covered my error as best I could. "Well, they put him in the loony bin, didn't they? That's what the *Mirror* said," I responded in a quarrelsome tone. "Putting the Prince away like that, he's got to be daft. Though how anyone would notice, given how royals are, I'm—"

Herr Dortmunder interrupted me. "If you are not willing to listen and learn, you will be of no use to the Brotherhood when we reach Madame Isolde's. Pay attention to what I tell you."

I took the rebuke as well as I, as Jeffries, could—that is, petulantly—and I said, "You wanted to know how I knew."

He did not dignify this with an answer. "You will begin with Madame Isolde. She will introduce you to Mac-Millian. Madame Isolde is the name Lottelisa Spanner gave herself five years ago, to suit the fashion. She has turned her establishment into an Oriental paradise, or so she claims. Occasionally she entertains Arabs and Turks there, so she must have achieved some success."

I wondered if there was another reason for selecting the place, but I said nothing more as Herr Dortmunder went on.

"In a way we of the Brotherhood are grateful for King Ludwig's passions. He reminds the populace of the glorious past of the German people, and he is so preoccupied with his projects that he leaves the affairs of state to others. Two of his ministers are members of our Brotherhood, and they have promoted our interests without impediments." He frowned. "I suspect that there are members of the Golden Lodge buried in the government as well."

"Why is that?" I asked, hoping to learn what I might be running into. I did not want to have another encounter like the one in Luxembourg.

"Because some of our efforts have been thwarted," said Herr Dortmunder in so threatening a tone that I recoiled at it.

"Tough on you, Captain," I made myself say. Playing August Jeffries was becoming more automatic even as it became more hazardous. "They probably think the same of you."

Herr Dortmunder shook his head twice. "They will answer for it." He made a sweeping gesture at the fog. "Be grateful for this, Mister Jeffries."

"Why? So like England?" I knew it was dangerous to be sarcastic with this man, but I could not bring myself to care.

He gave a vile chuckle. "Not exactly. Because no one can see us well enough to stop us." This announcement had all the unpleasant effect he had been striving for. "We have received word that the assassin from the Golden Lodge has been sent to stop us from getting the treaty. He is supposed to have arrived in Munich yesterday."

"The assassin?" I repeated, disliking the sound of it. "Who is it?"

"We don't know that, or the assassin would be in our sights," Herr Dortmunder admitted unhappily. "Which is why you must be particularly careful. You may be known to them already, judging from the incident in Luxembourg."

"You mean that the way you will find this assassin is when he tries to kill me? And it might not matter much to you if he succeeds?" I did not like the rising tone of my own voice.

"It may come to that, yes," said Herr Dortmunder.

If only I had some way to reach Mycroft Holmes. I had to know more about the Golden Lodge and this supposed assassin, or I suspected this first mission of mine would also be my last, and Mister Holmes would be in need of another secretary. Which put me in mind of another unpleasant matter: what had become of the man I replaced? At the time I took the work, I had been informed that the fellow had received a more satisfactory offer for his services, and had departed. But I had inquired no further—why should I? Now it seemed I had overlooked something I needed to know.

"Do not go into panic, Mister Jeffries," advised Herr

Dortmunder with a slight, contemptuous smile. "Your pay for risk will more than make up for this minor danger."

"Minor, you say," I scoffed, and realized I had let myself be lost in reflection. "You're not the one's being shot at, are you?"

"Not by the assassin, I should hope," said Herr Dortmunder, with great meaning. "You cannot ignore the possibility."

"If your Brotherhood doesn't kill me, then this Golden Lodge assassin may do it," I said, speaking my thoughts aloud.

"Exactly," said Herr Dortmunder.

FROM THE PERSONAL JOURNAL OF PHILIP TYERS: *Inspector Cornell is once again asking for M.H.'s assistance. Thus far I have been able to put him off, saying that M.H. is busy with Admiralty affairs, but I will not be able to continue this ruse forever, and Edmund Sutton has said he wants no part of deceiving the police. I have produced the original letter sent to M.H. by the dead woman—M.H. said I should if pressed—and that ought to satisfy them for the time being. In time, the Inspector will return and will not be willing to accept the temporizations Sutton and I must provide.*

M.H. has wired to inform us that he will be in Germany shortly, and has located MacMillian.

Chapter Sixteen

NEVER VISIT A brothel early in the morning; it is more dis-illusioning than being backstage at the ballet, and just as odorous. Beyond the discreet entrance to Madame Isolde's establishment, there was clutter everywhere: abandoned glasses, tankards, plates, cigars, and, in one corner, a pair of patent men's shoes. A sleepy butler in a Moorish tunic provided our escort through the refuse, muttering only a few words to us to prevent us from adding to the shambles. I noticed that a few servants were beginning the awesome task of setting the whole to order in preparation for another evening of license and revelry. The Oriental finery looked tawdry in the wan morning light, the peacock fans were dusty, and the gilding on the Moorish arches leading into the main parlor was flaking, showing the rough wood beneath.

Madame Isolde herself greeted us, decked out in a pink negligee with elaborate Japanese sleeves and feather trim at the neck. Her finery could not conceal the slackness of the opulent flesh beneath her garment, nor the lines fretting her sharp blue eyes. She wore kohl on her lashes and rouge on her lips and cheeks, and an overpowering attar of roses. Her greeting to Herr Dortmunder was a shade too effusive for genuine good feeling. "What an unexpected honor. It has been too long," she cooed as she took him by the arm. Her accent was more Prussian than Bavarian. "It is always a pleasure to have you here with us."

I hung back, not knowing what to do. How could I face Elizabeth after being in this place? This was not like the English brothels I had some little experience of, where gaming and drinking were as important as wenching and tupping. Here the emphasis was on entertainment, of what nature I could only speculate, though the evidence suggested an abandon not often found in the acceptable London establishments. At my feet I could see a number of wine stains on the Turkish carpet; I supposed that they would blend into the intricate pattern with time. The discarded cigars were another matter, and I could see that the burns they made would mar the carpet forever.

"This is the man I mentioned." He added in English, "Mister Jeffries, come here," he commanded me, all but thrusting me forward. "He is to be presented to the Scotsman. Be good enough to kiss Madame's hand, Jeffries."

I did as he ordered, trying to walk with the slight swagger I suspected Jeffries would have in these circumstances.

"Good morning, Mister Jeffries," said Madame Isolde in German, extending her hand to me, and waiting until I bowed over it.

"Good morning, Madame," I said, also in German, and added, "You have a very unusual place here."

She laughed. "I like to think so," she said with a simper that I supposed was meant for a show of modesty.

"Mister Jeffries is here to enter the employ of MacMillian, as we have already arranged. The Brotherhood is depending on you to make the introduction. He is still here, isn't he?" This last was more an accusation than an inquiry.

"He is asleep with Gretchen and Françoise. He had quite a night with them. They are in the Chinese room, second door on the left at the top of the stairs." She spoke hurriedly, as if she feared a slow answer might gain his disapproval. "Neither girl was remiss in her work, *mein Herr.*"

"Excellent," said Herr Dortmunder as he patted Madame Isolde's arm, for all the world as if rewarding an obedient dog.

"He had four bottles of champagne opened last night; he poured all of one over Françoise, and then licked it off her himself. Like a great, randy puppy. Françoise said his moustaches tickled something fierce." Her laugh was high and nervous. "After such a night, I doubt he will be moving before noon, and then slowly. And his head may ache."

"Good, good," said Herr Dortmunder. "Then he will be less likely to turn away a new servant. He will have to be attended quickly. Did any of your other guests spend the night?"

"Just the Turk," she said apologetically, and hurried on with her explanation, as if delaying punishment. "He refused to leave at the end of the night. He spent the whole evening playing chess. Winning, too. Nothing to drink. No whoring. He said in his country he would not receive such poor hospitality as I would show by requiring him to leave. And he paid very well for the privilege. Didn't even take a girl with him. Didn't have any boys to offer him. For all he did here, he might as well be a monk."

."And you do not want it said that your house does not serve its guests well," said Herr Dortmunder, looking ill used.

"Not at this house, no, and not a Turk. What would

they say if we would not allow him to sleep here?" said
Madame Isolde, as if defending herself before the bench.
Just what threat did Herr Dortmunder hold over her to
gain so timorous a compliance as she provided? Perhaps
she had seen something as hideous as the rite I had witnessed the night before, while MacMillian was pouring
champagne over a whore named Françoise and licking it
off her.

Again the satisfied pat. "Never mind. The Turk might
prove useful."

The relief on Madame Isolde's face was so great that
under other circumstances it would have been comical. I
decided to take what advantage I could of this development. "Tell me about this Turk then."

Herr Dortmunder shot me a critical look. "Why do you
ask this?"

"Because," I said, improvising, "if the man has any
position in the world he might be able to convince
MacMillian he needs me." I looked about as two more
servants began to clean. "I think it would be a good idea,
if this MacMillian is as touchy as you say he is, if I made
it look as if I would uphold the honor of the Queen, don't
you know?" As I spoke I was getting a better idea of my
own strategem, and my enthusiasm for it grew. "If the
Turk were made to pay respects to a mere fellow like me,
your high-in-the-instep Scotsman would be more likely
to employ me." I smiled. "And I think I can show this
Turk a thing or two." I had not yet the slightest notion
how, but I trusted I would find suitable means as I went
on.

Herr Dortmunder stared at me as if I had just sprouted
an extra pair of arms, or some appendages more alarming
still. "Go on, Jeffries," he prompted. "There may be some
merit in your plan." If his dog had spoken to him, he
would not have been more astonished.

"Well," I said, growing bolder. "If this Turk were to
come down to dine, then it might fall out that he and I

would have a word or two, particularly if I pressed the matter. And we have a few bones to pick with the Turks, any road."

"Not in establishments like this," said Herr Dortmunder, prepared to dismiss the notion completely.

"Then I could catch his attention," I went on, letting my improvisation grow bolder. "I could challenge him about certain irregularities in our dealing with the Turks, and ask for some explanation as to how such things came to be. I could make it clear to him that I won't be put off." Again, the vision of my affianced bride came to my mind and I was chagrined at what my work was leading me to do. Nothing I could tell Elizabeth would save me from her scorn.

"If he knows of such things, what convinces you he would respond to anything you tell him?" This question was quick and clipped, the words staccato. But there was also interest; for the first time I sensed he was willing to grant me a hearing.

"Well, *I* would, if I were challenged as I could challenge him, given the chance. If I wrap myself up in the Union Jack, your Scotsman may decide that in spite of my appearance and . . . all the rest of it, I would be a suitable substitute for his missing valet. Otherwise, him being the cove you say he is, he might just go and look for a valet among the servants here. In Bavaria." Just the mention of the man brought back a brief, hideous recollection of the previous night and I steeled myself against it.

"Mister Jeffries," said Herr Dortmunder, "I may not have appreciated you until now. Venal you may be, but venality has its uses." He smiled in that grim way of his, for all the world as if he were going to bite an arm or a head off of someone who displeased him.

"You hired me to do your work," I said, doing my best not to be offended. "Here I am, trying to do it."

"So we did." He looked over at Madame Isolde, who

had the manner of one seeking to escape from a room with no doors. "What do you say, dear lady?"

"If it would suit your purposes, I will order one of the servants to wake the Turk." She laughed unconvincingly and waved her hand to conceal how much she was shaking. "He will have risen before now, in any case, to pray. They all do, you know."

"So they do," said Herr Dortmunder, as if prayer was a disgusting habit. "And several more times during the day."

"Yes," I chimed in, recalling that Jeffries ought to know something of this, having, according to his story, spent time in Egypt. "They have a cove in a tower who sets up a holler when the time's right. They all drop everything they're doing and bow to Mecca. Except for the Jews. And the women. And the Christians, of course."

"So they do," said Herr Dortmunder, his smile still in place.

I could feel his sudden wrath as keenly as if a cold wind had cut through the stuffy room. What was it about the rites of the followers of Mohammed that made Herr Dortmunder so furious, I asked myself. Was it his own dislike, or the notion of the Brotherhood? I did not know how to ask, and decided it best not to think about it just now. Better to think of what I would tell Elizabeth about this stage of my mission, if I told her anything at all.

"So, you bring yourself to the attention of the——" He broke off as a sudden, hard knocking was heard from the front of the house. "Are you expecting anyone?" he demanded of Madame Isolde.

She shook her head. "The butcher brings his wares to the back of the house. I don't——"

He motioned her to silence as the door swung open and a few hurried words were exchanged with her major domo. The three of us stood very still, as if eluding a hunter.

"Madame Isolde," said her major domo—the fellow in the Moorish tunic—as he came into the room. "There is a man at the door. He is in an official carriage, judging by the device on the panel. He claims he must speak to Herr MacMillian at once."

"Herr MacMillian is still abed," said Madame Isolde in an apparent rush of relief.

"I don't think that will be a sufficient answer," said her major domo. "He is most insistent."

"Tell him to leave a message," said Madame Isolde. "He should know better than to come here at this hour. No one comes here at this hour but tradesmen." She realized her mistake and did her best to cover it. "This has no bearing on you, *mein Herr.* Your invitation is without condition. You are welcome at any hour. Any hour." She was becoming flustered again, and kept glancing uneasily in the direction of Herr Dortmunder. "What shall I do if he will not go away?"

"You will have to admit him eventually," said Herr Dortmunder in a fatalistic way. "Make it worth his while to wait."

She nodded and fussed with the feathers on her robe. "Tell him I do not like to disturb my guests. If there is something he wishes to impart to the Scotsman, he may leave word with me. I will have it carried to Herr MacMillian when he rises. That will be as soon as he will be of use to anyone in any case." She waved the major domo away as if driving off a pesky mosquito.

"I will give him your answer," said the major domo in a voice that suggested he doubted that this ploy would succeed.

"Tell him to present himself at noon. He can have a buffet with Herr MacMillian then, if he wishes." This last offer had a breathless quality to it that struck me as an indication of dread, though I did not venture this opinion.

Herr Dortmunder held up his hand for quiet while he listened intently to the discussion at the front door. "The man is from Chancellor von Bismarck's office. He claims to know nothing about any documents. He was, I think, in fact sent by the Krupps. At least he asked if Cameron MacMillian of the ships' engines MacMillians might be

here. He was to extend an offer for such a man to meet
with those who might wish to purchase machinery; he
could ensure himself of a great profit if he could make
such an arrangement." He heard the hinges creak. "It was
not a clever deception. To seek to bribe a fool without any
skill and no subterfuge." He shook his head in patroniz-
ing condemnation. "He deserved to be sent away."

"But—" Madame Isolde looked more distressed than
ever.

"Be quiet," said Herr Dortmunder; she complied at
once.

The front door had just closed when the major domo
uttered an exclamation of surprise. A moment later he
stepped into the parlor. "The Turk is just emerging from
his room."

Madame Isolde sighed. "He must be fed. He expects
his food promptly, or so he told me. Have the cook prepare those lamb chops he ordered last night, and make
sure the pastry is hot." She had lost that bewildered look
and replaced it with an exasperated one. "I had best tend
to it."

"And you, Mister Jeffries, may want to see your . . .
opponent up close before you undertake your little sce-
nario." He nudged my arm.

"Right you are," I said, and stepped into the entry hall,
glancing up the elaborate staircase to the landing where
the Turk had paused in his majestic descent from the
rooms above.

I stopped at the foot of the stairs and prepared to accost
the man in the splendid Turkish robes. I folded my arms,
the better to show my determination, and glared upward.

Into the profound gray eyes of Mycroft Holmes.

FROM THE PERSONAL JOURNAL OF PHILIP TYERS:
*There has been a note delivered from Inspector Cornell,
asking for information about Vickers. M.H. left permission for me to release the basic report he keeps on the
man, and to advise the Inspector to use caution when*

dealing with the Brotherhood. For what good it may do, I have followed these orders.

Mother has once again sunk into complete lethargy. The end is very near.

Chapter Seventeen

HE SALAAMED GRACEFULLY, amusement giving his mouth a wry twist. "Good morning, good sir," he said in terrible German as he came the rest of the way down the stairs, the robe whispering around his ankles. Where, I wondered, had Edmund Sutton come up with it, and on such short notice? Mycroft Holmes' face was slightly darkened and his brows had been blackened; his turban successfully concealed his graying hair.

With Herr Dortmunder standing in the parlor, I had to bluster my way through. "To you it may be," I declared in English, and then repeated it in German far better than his had been.

"You are not German?" asked Mycroft Holmes, still using his ludicrous accent.

"English," I declared, feeling at once very foolish and in extreme danger. I must make no slip now, I realized, for it would put us both into the hands of the Brotherhood, and I had firsthand knowledge of the consequences of such a calamity.

"And you are in Bavaria? You are a traveler, as I am." He beamed at me, as if delighted to find a commonality between us. "I have come from Bursa to see the wonderful castle of King Ludwig. Perhaps these buildings he is making are of interest to you, as well?"

"No, I am not here to see castles. We have castles aplenty, and better, in England," I said, with all the bravado I could summon up in myself, suspecting that we were being closely observed by Herr Dortmunder.

"A pity," said Mycroft Holmes in his Turkish guise. "To see a castle with gaslight, done in the modern way, not as we Turks have done it for centuries, now that is an accomplishment, one I have not encountered before. His Neuschwanstein is heated and lit by gas. A marvel." He favored me with a distant-but-affable smile. "I did not see you last night. Did you arrive very late? I did not stay up much beyond midnight."

"I have only arrived this morning," I said, wishing I could say more.

"Ah. You were detained, possibly, on the road? Some mischance or another? Perhaps the weather? How unfortunate." He turned away from me toward the parlor. "Madame Isolde, would it be possible for me to request breakfast? You had my instructions last night, I recall. I have no wish to impose on your staff, but I have been awake for some time, reading." He paused in the entrance to the parlor, then salaamed to Herr Dortmunder. "Forgive me. I did not realize you were entertaining. And so early in the morning."

Madame Isolde's face went scarlet under her paint and she looked uneasily from Herr Dortmunder to Mycroft Holmes, then back again, as if one man or the other would provide her response for her. When neither did, she said, "Herr Dortmunder is an old . . . associate."

"How fortunate to renew your acquaintance," said Mycroft Holmes, and pointed toward the arch opposite the parlor. "Would you plan to serve breakfast there? The morning sun would be pleasant."

"I'll have Felix tend to it at once," said Madame Isolde, glad that someone had given her something she could do at last. She called out for her major domo. "Set the table by the window. Give Herr Kamir his breakfast there."

"Herr Kamir," said Herr Dortmunder, "did I hear you say you were from Bursa?"

Mycroft Holmes bowed slightly. "Yes, that is where I currently reside. My family, however, is from Izmir, which you and the Infidel Greeks call Smyrna." He stopped, continuing in a conciliating manner which changed again as he became more heated in his sentiments. "I do not mean to offend any Christians, for you are People of the Book, as are we, and the Jews, but the Greeks take advantage of the tolerance and respect we show to the People of the Book, and they seek to intrude into our country. It is a distressing state of affairs. They claim it is theirs by historical right. If we had taken Vienna, matters would be different now." His German was now nearly unintelligible, as if Herr Kamir were being overcome with emotion. I could not but admire his performance and his great composure, for surely he was aware that we were in danger.

Herr Dortmunder showed a little interest in this outpouring. "Is there any danger of actual fighting, do you think?"

"With Allah's help there will be peace," said Mycroft Holmes. "It will be as Allah wills."

I saw a smirk pass over Herr Dortmunder's face as he said, "I suppose that's true enough."

Madame Isolde was becoming nervous again; she approached Mycroft Holmes uncertainly. "Your breakfast will be ready shortly, Herr Kamir."

"Excellent," he approved, and nodded in my direction. "Perhaps you, English, will come and tell me about the castles in the island of Queen Victoria?"

I glanced at Herr Dortmunder and saw him signal his consent. "All right. But I warn you, I will not be impressed by any of the accomplishments of King

Ludwig. He has all the modern machinery and other things to aid him. The men who built the castles in England did it with sweat and muscle and will."

"So it is with most castles," said Mycroft Holmes as he salaamed again and turned away toward the room opposite the parlor, asking as I fell in behind him, "And what is your name, English?"

"August Jeffries," I said at once, trying to keep up the pugnacious character I had assumed. We passed into the drawing room in time to see the major domo Felix supervising the setting up of a table by the window.

"Jeffries," said Mycroft Holmes, as if tasting the name. "Not as hard to say as some I have encountered," he went on in his execrable German, making a quick sign to me to do the same. "Sit down with me, Herr Jeffries, and tell me of the English castles while I have breakfast." He clapped his hands, and when Felix turned toward him, said, "Set a place for Herr Jeffries. He will join me."

"Very well, sir," said Felix resentfully as he left the two servants to tend to it.

"I have a passion for castles," went on Mycroft Holmes, speaking as "Herr Kamir" of Bursa. "Ever since I saw the ruins of the Crusaders' forts, I have been eager to see those that are still occupied."

I smiled, the effort greater than I had anticipated. "You Turks learned something of us English then," I said, hoping my boast did not ring false.

"Yes," said Mycroft Holmes. "We learned that you put on metal clothing to fight in the desert, and that you weighed too much to use our horses in battle, and so had to ship your own from great distances." He bowed to me, and looked toward the table. "Shortly we will eat." He added very softly, and in English. "They are listening."

"I know," I said in German, and straightened up. "Your soldiers might have thought ours unwise to fight in armor, but—"

"And they provided a red or black cross on their chests. Most archers yearn for such targets," he went on in his

Kamir-German. "It made our work so much easier for us."

"And our knights were martyrs to their faith," I blustered.

"So they were. They lost." He nodded approval as the servants brought chairs to the table. As we approached to sit down, he murmured in English, his lips hardly moving. "Your last message was most alarming. I regret circumstances detained me for two days. I had planned to intervene before the situation became so fraught. Say something in German."

"I wouldn't call it lost," I proclaimed.

He answered as Kamir. "No—it is not the way of the West, is it?" and went on again softly, "This has become difficult. More than I guessed it would."

I kept up my German. "It was a glorious war, the Crusades."

"All were lost," said Mycroft Holmes again, with the good humor of a curious scholar with an appreciative student. "And it is not fitting to remark on the losses, not here." He added in an undervoice. "How much danger are you in?"

My answer was for his private question, though I offered it as if responding to the public one. "The risk seemed worth the reward."

"Truly?" asked Mycroft Holmes in his Kamir manner. "My dear Guthrie," he went on quietly, "you alarm me."

"Yes," I insisted; the sound of my own name had taken me aback, and I tried to cover my confusion with indignation. "And no wonder. Germany is a most unexpected place, I have found."

"Assuredly." He looked to be unflappable, the master very much in control of his craft. We were given strong coffee; the bitter scent rose from our cups. I noticed that Mycroft Holmes had taken a packet from his robes, saying in a deferential way, "It is sugar, good sir. I find that sugar is not the same away from my own country, and it

is a taste I miss. Thus"— he added in an undervoice—
"it can so easily contain poison."

I suppressed a shudder and said, "Just so."

"There will be lamb and bread soon. Have some with
me," he offered in his terrible German. "It is good of
Madame Isolde to do this for me, for it is not often she
must cater to one of my compatriots." He coughed,
brought his napkin to his face and while apparently striving to stop the spasm, said quickly and softly, "Is there
any immediate danger for you here? Is that man with the
Brotherhood?" He set his napkin aside, and remarked, "It
is often thus on a chill morning. The fog gets into the
throat."

"So it does," I agreed, and said, "Yes, your observation
is correct."

"About Madame Isolde, you mean?" His strange
accent seemed to be growing stronger.

"Your most recent remark, indeed," I answered, feeling
my vitals tighten. "I have rarely encountered such a
reception as I have had in this country." It was audacious
to say this, but I knew Herr Dortmunder would expect
something of the sort from Jeffries.

"Truly, it is a most gracious and remarkable place,"
said Mycroft Holmes in the cadences of Kamir. "I
stepped out earlier this morning before you arrived, I
think, for a walk, and had a chance to admire the city, as
well. It is a pity the weather was not better. Truly Munich
is a jewel."

I decided to follow his lead. "How could anyone suppose otherwise?"

He nodded, and gestured to the approaching servant to
put silver and napkin before me. "Your coffee will grow
cold," he warned me.

"So it might," I said, and obediently lifted the cup, hes-
itating at my lips while I tested its heat.

The window shattered, and the cup, at seemingly the
same instant.

I was too shocked to do more than freeze in place until I realized that Mycroft Holmes had dropped down under the cover of the table and was pulling at my coat from underneath. Belatedly I responded, all but oversetting my chair in my haste to protect myself.

I could hear shouts in the house, and Herr Dortmunder came rushing into the dining room, a pistol drawn, and his face a mask of ire. Behind him Madame Isolde cowered. Throughout the house was the sound of hurrying footsteps as the servants came to discover the reason for all this upset.

"Good sir, good sir," cried out Mycroft Holmes in his Kamir-German. "Someone is shooting at you. You must get away from the window."

A second shot came, and I felt a hot crease along my forehead. I jerked away from the pain of it and my chair toppled over backward. I could feel blood on my face, hot and wet.

Herr Dortmunder rushed to the door, tugged it open and squinted out into the morning glare. He raised his pistol and fired it once, swearing as he did.

Mycroft Holmes was bending over me, still in the character of Kamir. "Are you hurt, good sir? There is blood in your eye."

"Small wonder," I muttered. "What the devil was that all about?" I demanded in English as I tried to sit up; my head rang like a smithy and my eyepatch was once again smirched. "I'll be right enough in a moment," I said, hoping it would be so.

"Good sir, I cannot understand you," said Mycroft Holmes, whose Kamir was not intended to speak English.

I made myself change languages. "I assume I will be better directly."

Herr Dortmunder slammed the door closed, then came to my side, putting his pistol back into his coat as he neared me. "That was too close, Mister Jeffries."

Madame Isolde was bending over me, fussing. She lifted the corner of my eyepatch, made a face of repugnance, and restored the patch to its place. I was again relieved that I had taken the precaution of giving the lid the appearance of severe scarring. "I will send for a basin, so we can wash . . . that away."

I had taken the napkin offered by Mycroft Holmes. "I would be grateful if you would."

"But Herr Jeffries," said Mycroft Holmes in Kamir-bafflement, "who is shooting at you? Good sir, you must be in some danger from evil men, to have them take so bold a step against you."

"So you must suppose, sir," said Herr Dortmunder for me. "It has been the misfortune of this young Englishman to be attacked three times since he has arrived on the Continent. I have taken it upon myself to see he is not exposed to such hazards again." This was directed as much toward me as to the Turkish version of Mycroft Holmes.

"I cannot think who has any reason to do me harm," I added in an injured tone, in English. "I came here on commission of a gentleman in London, and in the hope that I could make my way back home by taking employment with an English gentleman in need of a servant, so that I would have payment for the second leg of my travels. And thus far all I have received for my troubles is attempts on my life."

"A horrible state of affairs," said Herr Dortmunder.

I finished wiping the worst of the blood from my face, and discovered that the wound was still seeping. Pressing the napkin to my forehead, I did my best to get to my feet. My whole face felt raw, and my muscles were watery.

"Let me help you, good sir," Mycroft Holmes offered, holding out his large, long hand to me. I took it and felt him haul me to my feet. "There. Now you can look at that wound for yourself. Madame Isolde will provide a mirror."

Madame Isolde was grateful for something to do. She hurried off to fetch a mirror for me as I swayed on my feet, shaking as with sudden cold.

"Bring more coffee," ordered Mycroft Holmes to the gawking servants. "At once."

"And put schnapps in it," added Herr Dortmunder. "You will need to sit down a moment, Mister Jeffries."

"So I think," I said, and was grateful for the chair shoved under me, as much as I was embarrassed by the attention.

So great was the confusion that no one heard footsteps hastily descending the stairs, and we were all startled when we heard a voice speaking German well but with a pronounced Scots burr demand, "What the bloody hell is going on here?"

FROM THE PERSONAL JOURNAL OF PHILIP TYERS: *This morning we—that is, Edmund Sutton and I— sustained another visit from Miss Roedale of Twyford, G.'s fiancée. She is most upset that she has had no further word from G., especially since his absence at a family gathering has caused her great embarrassment. She has said that he must make himself available for the wedding of her cousin, which takes place in four days, and she wants no excuses offered. Apparently there are those in her family who are not pleased that G.'s government service should require so much time and effort from him. She has left a note for him, warning him of her dissatisfaction with the turn recent events have taken.*

Chapter Eighteen

MacMillian wore a lavish robe in his own tartan with wide velvet reveres with apparently nothing beneath it. The excesses of the night before marred his countenance, leaving dark circles under brilliant blue eyes. In spite of that, he was an arresting figure. He had luxurious, brindled muttonchop whiskers that blended into an extravagant cavalry moustache, though his rusty red hair had begun to recede, leaving him with a pronounced widow's peak. His nostrils were chiseled and the bridge of his nose so prominent that looking down it came easily. Just at present his wide, thin-lipped mouth was set in a hard line. He pulled a small pistol from his pocket as he looked around the room.

Of all the ways I had imagined presenting myself to this man, I had never considered it would be in this manner. I tried to bow, but vertigo overcame me and I clung to my chair as if to keep the world from moving. I saw my carpetbag lying on its side under my chair. I knew I would have to retrieve it before anyone could examine its contents.

"I thought I heard shooting." He winked in the direction of Madame Isolde, who had just come from the rear of her establishment carrying a mirror. "Dueling for your favor, are they?"

She blushed and hurried to my side, paying this interloper no notice.

I took the mirror and stared at the gash along my forehead. It looked to be about eighteen inches wide and five deep, but I knew that it was actually no more than three inches long, and not deep enough to do anything but bleed a great deal, as so much of the face does. I sighed and took the cloth I was offered in place of the napkin. As I pressed it to the wound, I knew I should have the thing stitched closed so that it would not become infected, and the scar would be as minor as possible. I handed the mirror back to Madame Isolde. "Many thanks."

"You should have that looked at," she said, echoing my own thoughts. "It is a bad cut."

"So I think," I agreed, and noticed that MacMillian had moved closer to me.

"I am able to do this," volunteered Mycroft Holmes. "It is a skill we are taught."

"Good Lord," exclaimed MacMillian as he saw the sodden napkin and had his first real sight of my forehead. "How bad is it?"

"Not as bad as it looks," I answered, trying to sound calm; I realized some of the glass from the window had embedded itself in tiny shards in my forehead and cheek. "But you know how it is with wounds on the face."

"They're the very devil," said MacMillian, regarding me askance. "Do you work here?"

Recalling my mission, I said, "Not precisely. I came here in the hope that you, sir, would employ me." I had managed to stand up without being too shaky on my legs, and I tried to reassure the Scotsman that I was an acceptable manservant. I spoke in English, to the disgust of

Madame Isolde and the apparent confusion of Mycroft Holmes. "I met Angus last night, who was leaving on the first train this morning. He had pressing business at home, or so he said. I thought that with him gone, you would want someone to take his place, so I came along to find out if—"

"What's this about Angus leaving?" he demanded. "He said nothing of it to me."

"Well, he did to me. Said you were busy. Didn't want to disturb you while you were here. Said he had to tend to an estate." It was vague enough that I hoped it would not be questioned. I hooked the carpetbag with my toe and pulled it nearer. This was not the time for any curious person to make an idle exploration of its contents.

"That tangle with the uncle again?" said MacMillian in exasperation. "I thought that was settled at last."

"Apparently not," I said, glad my ruse was successful. I noticed that Herr Dortmunder was looking pleased in that hard-faced way of his. "He was confident that he would have his inheritance at last."

"What man wants to run an inn?" scoffed MacMillian. "He will be nothing but a servant until the day he dies, if he continues that way. Still," he went on with a condemning shrug, "it is what he was born to."

"If it is what pleases him," I ventured, "he will be well satisfied." I swabbed my brow once more. "But his leaving puts you at a disadvantage, sir. I would hope you might be willing to take me on, for a trial period." I did my best to neaten my coat and shirt. "I don't think you'll find another more willing Englishman in all Germany than I am."

"But men are shooting at you," MacMillian protested reasonably.

"Begging your pardon, sir, but I suspect they were trying for the Turk." I indicated Mycroft Holmes, and lowered my voice. "Probably up to no good, for all he says he's traveling to see castles." From what I had been told of this man's character, I supposed he would be convinced that Turks might expect to be shot at for no other reason than being Turkish.

"You're probably right," said MacMillian, putting his hands into the pockets of his robe as if to avoid contamination.

I determined to take full advantage of MacMillian's prejudices. "And the windows are not the best glass. It is not unlikely that the man firing the gun had not so clear an aim as he hoped."

"Very true." He sighed. "Well, when you've had that injury properly dressed, come to my room. I'll be having breakfast. We'll discuss what you are to do." He made a sweeping gesture. "Servant you may be, but you are British, and it wouldn't be fitting to leave you in Bavaria with whores and Turks, and the men who shoot at them. All right. We'll discuss the terms of your period of trial, and what wages you'll receive, if you give satisfaction." He turned to Madame Isolde, who was supervising the cleanup efforts of her staff. "Send breakfast up to me. The tea with milk, not cream. Make sure the porridge has no lumps." With that, he cast a look of intense dislike at Mycroft Holmes and left the room.

"If you will follow me, young sir," said Holmes, his Kamir mannerisms flamboyantly displayed as he salaamed to the room at large. "Acts of charity are required by the Koran. Let me do as my religion commands me."

"Go along. It is preferable to bringing a physician here, for then the police might learn of these events," said Herr Dortmunder in a warning tone. "If this . . . gentleman can stitch you up, so much the better." He frowned at Madame Isolde and began to upbraid her for permitting the attack to occur.

"But how was I to know—?" she protested.

"You hear rumors all the time. I rely on you for that. . . ." The rest of their dispute faded as I started warily up the stairs in Mycroft Holmes' wake, my carpetbag feeling like a leaden weight at the end of my left arm.

In his room I saw that he had put a small rug atop the carpet. "For prayer. They know here that Moslems have such rugs. The incomparable Mister Sutton provided it."

"God knows how he comes by these things," I said, leaning back on the door to assure myself it was closed.

"He's an actor. Actors require props of all sorts, or so he has often explained it to me. Right now, he is essaying the role of Mycroft Holmes, man of strict habits, as he has done so many times before. It is a part he plays particularly well, I think, so long as he does not have to speak. Do come over here to the window and let me have a look at that wound of yours." He chuckled. "And don't fash yourself. I have sewn up more than a few bullet holes in my time. I have tweezers to get the bits of glass, though they'll probably hurt like the very devil. Oh, yes, I noticed them as well." He waited for me as I did as he instructed. "Tell me who was shooting at you, and why? Do you have any idea? And how do you come to be with Dortmunder dogging your heels? Is he responsible for the shot, do you think? Or have you been discovered? There had to be a reason for that botched attempt at murdering you. It would be best if you told me all about it. And let's have none of that farrago of yours about Germans taking potshots at random Turks."

"I had to say something; it convinced MacMillian." I lowered my eye and fussed with the patch. "This is the damnedest nuisance."

"Keep it where it is, if you please. I will work around it." He opened the leather case set out on the nightstand and pulled out a small bottle. "Peroxide. It will hurt a bit, but it will stop infection."

I nodded, and set my jaw as he set to work on me.

"While I'm at this, tell me what's taken place these last few days." He continued his cool, methodical treatment of my forehead, and made a quick inspection of the other minor cuts on my face. "By the look of it, you have been active."

"That is one word for it," I said, and as concisely as I

could, recounted all that had happened since I left
England. I tried not to dwell on the man I killed, though
my distress was surely evident in how I spoke of it. My
narrative faltered while he set four stitches in the gash,
closing it expertly. I clenched my teeth until the worst of
the pain was over, and went back to my account. When he
was finished dressing the stitches, I had reached the murder I had witnessed the previous night. Mycroft Holmes'
mouth grew increasingly stern as he listened.

"I never thought this mission would become so terrible. It seemed simple enough at the outset." He set his
medical supplies aside. "I apologize for placing you in
such danger. But it was not my intention to do so. Nor
was it my intention to leave you without any support in
the field. However." With that, he favored me with a careful look. "It would be more dangerous still to withdraw
you from the assignment at this time. If you want to be
certain that you are safe, you must persevere."

"If I must," I said, feeling both conviction and ill use as
I spoke. "I am appalled by the Brotherhood and I will do
whatever I must to stop them. But I cannot tell what to
think of the Golden Lodge."

"No," said Mycroft Holmes speculatively. "No more
can I."

"You mean you are unfamiliar with them?" I asked,
alarm making my pulse hammer in the wound on my
forehead.

"Oh, I have heard whispers of them, but I know rela-
tively little about them. I wish, in fact, that I knew a great
deal more, so I would be able to assess their role in all
this." He began to tick off alternatives on his long fingers.
"They might—one—wish to continue the status quo and
desire nothing more than to assist our efforts." Mycroft
Holmes's pained smile revealed how little stock he put in
this possibility. "Two: they could wish to expose our work
with the same intended result of the Brotherhood, but with
themselves becoming the rulers of Europe. Three: they
might wish to use the treaty to ingratiate themselves with

the leaders of Europe, either for their own direct gain or for the opportunity it would afford them to destroy the Brotherhood. It is wise to remember they are as fanatical as those they oppose. Four: they might be honestly patriotic and wish to warn von Bismarck of the secret accords of the treaty." He rocked back on his heels. "If they are patriots, however, they have a most quixotic way of demonstrating it, at least to date. Should this be their motive, it would be disastrous for England." He regarded me with a quizzical stare. "Five: they may wish to sell the treaty to the highest bidder. I suspect that Whitehall would be forced to prevail in such an auction, no matter how grievous the cost. We cannot afford the consequences of that treaty being made public, and no matter what we would have to pay, war would be more costly still. And finally, six: the Golden Lodge may not care about the treaty but as bait to lure members of the Brotherhood into a trap, in which case they may want to encourage von Metz to continue his attempts to steal it, so long as it would allow them to bag a good number of the Brotherhood. That would be the most precarious for us, for if the treaty means nothing to the Golden Lodge, the Brotherhood may achieve their hoped-for results by chance. Or mischance."

"Then the treaty is at more risk than we supposed?" I inquired, wanting to define my own apprehension.

"Possibly. It is all a question of which of the motives are truly those of the Golden Lodge. What I particularly dislike is this business about an assassin. Until now, I supposed that all we had to worry about are political machinations, but now that they are killing . . . And using an assassin I am unaware of." He clicked his tongue in self-condemnation. "I thought I knew all those who were operating in this part of Europe. And this is the first I've been aware that the Golden Lodge makes use of them. I knew about the activities of the Brotherhood, as you are aware, but not the Golden Lodge." This confession clearly distressed him. "There is a greater hazard here than we realized, Guthrie, and that is most disquieting."

"Then it is vital that I keep close watch on MacMillian, isn't it?" I did not need to hear his answer.

"Crucial," said Mycroft Holmes, folding his arms and slipping back into the character of Kamir. He salaamed. "On your way, young sir. MacMillian is expecting you. It would not be wise to keep him waiting."

FROM THE PERSONAL JOURNAL OF PHILIP TYERS: *According to Inspector Cornell, he does not have sufficient material in M.H.'s file to link the death of the unknown woman to Vickers, or anyone else for that matter. Were it not for the severity of her wounds, all administered before death and her dumping into the Thames, he would regard the death as a suicide. I have the impression that he would prefer to dismiss the case as that. But as there is little or no water in her lungs and the high degree of blood loss, to say nothing of the brands and other wounds on the body, he must list it as murder, and try to discover who has done it.*

Chapter Nineteen

"THAT EYE OF yours will be black tomorrow," said MacMillian as I stood beside his breakfast table, trying to make myself appear useful to him.

"Better than having a split skull, sir," I responded, doing my best to ignore my headache. At my feet, my carpetbag seemed to radiate my duplicity.

"No doubt," said MacMillian, and looked me over critically, then heaved a sigh of disappointment. "Have you ever tended to a gentleman before?"

"As a clerk for one, and a secretary for another. I began as a clerk. I got the work because I knew German." I felt as if I had been called upon to recite in class and could be birched for answering incorrectly.

"And how did you come to know that?" he asked, his eyes filled with suspicion. "Surely someone of your station has not been abroad?"

"I learned it at school. We could choose to learn chemistry or German or French. I decided German was the most useful. I thought it would make it easier to secure a position." It was near enough to the truth that I felt no awkwardness in saying it. "I can manage French, too."

"That's sensible, at least." He glared down at his porridge. "Do you know what would be required of you, as my manservant?"

"Well, as I understand it, I would have to look after your things, tend to your clothes, see that they are pressed and in good repair. I would have to settle your accounts for you at various establishments, such as this one, and hotels. I would keep records for you, of a confidential nature, and serve as your barber and cook when you needed such service. I would be responsible for the care and appearance of your quarters and I would keep your personal belongings in good repair." I looked down at my shoes. "I can drive a carriage, if you need a coachman."

"What an enterprising fellow you are, but men of your station have to live by their wits, or so I've been told," he said, sounding faintly bored at this. "All right. We're in Bavaria and a lunatic is King here. So I will undertake an act of whimsy, and give you a trial of forty days. At the end of that time if I am pleased with your efforts, I will pay you three pounds beyond the price of your upkeep. If I am displeased, I will pay you one pound ten. This will serve as an incentive for you to excel." He coughed once, for emphasis. "Given the state you are in, I will not ask you to commence your efforts until this afternoon. And while you are healing, take care to stay out of sight. A visage like yours just now would sour milk."

I nodded once, gingerly to avoid hurt. "Thank you, sir. Thank you."

"Thank Angus, if you must, for he is the one who put you in the way of getting this position. If I were not in such straits as I find myself, I would not consider you to take his place, but as beggars cannot be choosers, you have the position by default," said MacMillian. "And tell Madame Isolde that I want to see Françoise. Have her bring two bottles of champagne. And goblets, of course."

His wink was so lascivious I nearly laughed, for he was like a lecher in a play, leering and scheming.

"Very good, sir," I said, and hurried to the door, determined to make the most of my respite. I needed about twelve hours of sleep, but would have to make do with three. But I reckoned without Herr Dortmunder, who was lying in wait at the foot of the staircase.

"Well?" he demanded as I came down.

"He has agreed to take me on for forty days," I told him, and added, "I have to give a message to Madame Isolde for him."

"We will not need forty days," said Herr Dortmunder with great satisfaction. "We will have this settled in ten, or we will fail utterly. Forty days. He must be desperate." He directed a look of condemnation at me that made me long to protest his assumptions of me, for he assuredly thought I was a contemptible creature, feckless and venal at best. "You will be paid for your work," he added, confirming my worst suspicions.

"So I had better," I replied grimly, coming to dislike August Jeffries with a determined intensity that was the more ferocious because Jeffries was only a role, a fiction adopted and molded for the occasion. I passed through the dining room to the kitchen where Madame Isolde was working with her servants to find something to put over the shattered window. "MacMillian wants something from you," I told her, and relayed his orders as crisply as I could. I was growing tired of carrying the carpetbag with me everywhere, though I supposed a man in Jeffries's uncertain position would do just that.

She looked up as I approached her, and put one hand to her bosom. "You are a sight, English, there is no denying it. I hope you will not suffer any greater hurts while you are here."

"You're very kind," I said. "But it is a flesh wound, not so severe as it appears. I will heal. MacMillian has agreed to take me on, and for a first commission, he has asked that Françoise be sent up, with champagne." I could not completely hide my embarrassment at this request, which caused Madame Isolde a fleeting amusement.

"Do not worry about this, English. These girls have done far stranger things for men. Do not doubt it." She clapped her hands. "Hannes, go fetch Françoise and tell her that MacMillian is thirsty again. She knows what to do."

I studied the activity in the kitchen a little longer and then excused myself, claiming—not incorrectly—that I had a headache and needed to lie down. I thanked her again for all she had done.

"But I did so little," she exclaimed, looking about in apprehension. "It was the Turk who stitched up your wound, and Herr Dortmunder who undertook to discover who fired the shot. His efforts so far have garnered no results. We do not know who shot, or why. How can I accept your thanks for that?" She had fear in her eyes and I wondered what Herr Dortmunder had been saying to her since the shooting occurred.

"Nevertheless, I am grateful, Madame," I said, hoping to discover some alleviation of anxiety in her.

I did not succeed. "You should rest, English. If you are not able to work for Herr MacMillian, there will be great . . . displeasure." She coughed delicately, as if she could not risk saying more. "There is a small room adjoining Herr MacMillian's. It is for his servant. I suppose you should lie down there."

"All right," I said, feeling a rush of gratitude for this simple effort on her part. "I will do that."

"The door is to the left of Herr MacMillian's, near the top of the stairs. It is in an alcove." She made a quick motion with her hand. "I should not continue to talk with you here, Herr Jeffries. I should, I think, let you rest and return to my chores. And I will see that Françoise is sent up with the champagne. I trust," she added with a practiced smile, "their antics will not keep you awake."

"I doubt they could, Ma'am; not the way I'm feeling just at present," I said, with a slight bow; even that little motion set my head ringing. I picked up the carpetbag again and trudged up the stairs.

The room was small; hardly room enough in it for a narrow bed and a chest of drawers. There was a single wooden chair near the little window. A ewer stood on a tall, thin stand and lacked a mirror. But it was enough to serve my purposes well. I put down my carpetbag, then tucked it under the springs, removed my coat and shoes, and disposed of myself on the bed with a single blanket over me, thinking with it being light out I would need time to get to sleep.

And the next thing I was aware of, MacMillian was standing over me, shaking me, his face rigid with outrage and fear. "I said *wake up* you idiot! I need your help at once."

I sat up groggily, my head swimming, and I stared at MacMillian, who was partially dressed with his robe flung carelessly over his drawers and singlet. "Is something the matter?"

"Of course something is the matter," he barked at me. "I need your help at once." He tossed my blanket back and all but dragged me to my feet. "Now! Do you understand me? *Now!*"

By now I was awake enough to realize my headache had not left, but merely retreated to another part of my skull. I reached out for my coat and pulled it on, trying to imagine what had happened to MacMillian that he should be in such a taking. "All right," I said as I faced him. "If I do not need my shoes, I am at your disposal."

"And about time," he growled, taking me by the upper arm and thrusting me into his room. He paused and pointed to the naked body of the girl I had to assume was Françoise. "Look!"

I noticed the contorted features and tense body. "When did this happen?" I asked, trying not to be shocked.

"Not ten minutes ago. I . . . I didn't know what to do."
His face was turning as ruddy as his hair. "I suppose I will
have to inform Madame Isolde?"

"I will do it, sir," I said almost without thinking; I made
an effort to pull myself together. "Tell me how it happened." That was a good start, I decided. I would have to
find out for Herr Dortmunder and Mycroft Holmes, both
of whom would have reasons of their own to want to
know about this death.

MacMillian began to pace, rubbing his hands through
his hair as he did, as if he could set his mind in order with
his fingers. "She came as I was finishing breakfast, about
twenty minutes ago. She . . . she brought two glasses and
a bottle of champagne. I removed the cork while she
undressed. She has . . . had a way of undressing that
makes me come to attention at once." He glanced at the
corpse once, then looked away. "She poured a glass of
champagne for herself, then did as I like best, and emp-
tied the rest of the bottle over her shoulders and breasts.
She toasted me and drank what was in her glass. Then she
. . . she came to me so that I could take my share from her
flesh." He coughed. "I don't know. She shuddered before
I touched her, and began to shake, as if with palsy. Then
her tongue protruded and she tried to breathe—"

"And what did you do?" I asked.

"What *could* I do? I tried to stop her from falling, but
her spasms got worse and she fell to the floor." He put his
hands over his eyes and stopped pacing. "Look at her.
That could have happened to me."

So now we have it, I thought. "You think the wine was
poisoned?"

"It must have been," said MacMillian. "How else could
she have . . ." He ended his thoughts with a vague gesture
toward the body.

"But if it is known that you . . . take your champagne
as you do," I said, hoping I was being sufficiently tactful, "wouldn't it follow that you are being sent a warning?" Or a distraction, I added to myself.

He gave me a pointed stare. "That is possible."

"And if that was the intention, all the more reason for me to tell Madame Isolde about it at once, so that whoever is responsible will know his message has been received?" I stared down at the girl again. She had been very pretty until half an hour ago, with a cloud of dark hair and full, rouged lips.

MacMillian prodded me on the shoulder. "Be about it, man. Be about it."

I bowed slightly, and went to the door of his room. "It may be necessary to summon the police," I reminded him.

This earned me an affronted stare. "I will not have to give evidence, surely. This woman was a whore."

"And she was murdered in your room," I added for him.

He dismissed this out of hand. "She died in a brothel. Whores die in brothels every day. The police must know that."

"So they do," I said, and left him to dress. As I came down the stairs, I noticed that Mycroft Holmes was sitting in the main parlor, studying a chessboard, apparently unaware of my presence. Herr Dortmunder was busily supervising the covering of the broken window with a cut board, ordering the servants about as if he wanted to use his postilion's spurs on them.

Madame Isolde, who had been pouring herself a strong cup of coffee, now turned and saw me. "Oh, dear," she exclaimed. "Is anything the matter?"

I bowed slightly, taking care where I stepped in my stocking feet. "Not with me, Madame, but there is something very wrong upstairs. MacMillian has asked me to inform you of it."

This caught Herr Dortmunder's attention, and he swung around. "What now?"

"It appears that Miss Françoise has . . . met with an accident," I said, trying to keep my demeanor as stoic as possible. Had I not already been pale from the cut on my forehead, I would have blanched now.

"An accident? But . . . how could she?" Madame Isolde watched Herr Dortmunder narrowly as she voiced her questions.

"She . . . seems to have drunk some . . . bad champagne," I said, finding the words difficult to get out. "You had better come up."

"Oh, yes, I suppose I had," she said, rattling nervously. "It is always so awkward when one of the girls has something . . . go wrong." She pulled her pink wrapper more closely around her, and started toward the stairs as much to escape Herr Dortmunder as to help MacMillian or Françoise.

"Wait!" Herr Dortmunder commanded. "I should go with you."

Madame Isolde shot a single, stricken look at me, and then said, "Certainly. Your help is always welcome."

His laughter was not pleasant. "You may thank me yet, Madame," he said as he started up the stairs two at a time, his spur-leather chains ringing as he went.

We followed after him. "How bad is it?" whispered Madame Isolde as we climbed.

"Very bad," I whispered back. "She is dead."

Now Madame Isolde went white around her painted mouth. "Oh, no," she said, holding on to the bannister for support. "What a terrible thing."

"She is . . . quite shocking to see," I cautioned her.

Herr Dortmunder was knocking on MacMillian's door as we reached the top of the stairs. "Let me in."

MacMillian responded to the summons slowly, as if answering doors was beneath him. He rolled back his eyes in high-born protest to Herr Dortmunder's officious behavior. "All of you?" he asked in a pained voice. He was almost completely dressed, lacking only his cravat.

"It would be better," I recommended. "So that someone can give the report."

"Ah, yes. That," MacMillian said as he stood aside. "You will need to know what to tell the police."

As I went into MacMillian's room, I saw out of the tail

of my eye that Mycroft Holmes had abandoned his solitary chess game and was standing at the foot of the stairs looking up. I wished I could ask him to join us here, but that would not be acceptable to MacMillian or Herr Dortmunder, and so I held my peace. I moved to a corner of the room so that there would not be a crowd around the body.

Madame Isolde stared in dismay at Françoise, and I saw tears standing in her eyes. She swallowed hard several times, and at last looked away from the dead girl.

"Tell me how—" began Herr Dortmunder.

MacMillian launched into recounting the death of Françoise, emphasizing his own conviction that he was the intended victim. He set his jaw and looked directly at Herr Dortmunder. "It would not be fitting for me to be part of any inquiry into the matter."

"How can you say that, if you were the target?" demanded Herr Dortmunder.

"Because I *was* the target, you cretin. You would expose me to another attack if my name were to come into the investigation. If there is an investigation." This last was speculative.

Herr Dortmunder nodded slowly. "Yes. There is a way it could be managed." He gave a signal to Madame Isolde. "Have your staff bring a tarpaulin up here." When he saw resistance in her · face, he said, "At once, Madame," in a tone that cracked like a whip, and I remembered the cold ferocity with which he had killed Angus the night before.

She capitulated with a nod and went to the bell-pull, tugging it twice. "Hannes and Ernst will be up shortly. You may give them your orders."

FROM THE PERSONAL JOURNAL OF PHILIP TYERS:
Word has just come from M.H. that he has located G. at last, and will be accompanying him and MacMillian to England, though they will probably not travel by Mercury train, M.H. judging such extraordinary measures apt to

draw unwanted attention to the mission. This is good news at a time when such is needed. He warns me, however, that I must not attempt to contact him at any time, for it could increase their danger, which is already very great.

G. has been injured, though not seriously. M.H. expects to be traveling again by nightfall.

Chapter Twenty

BY THE TIME Hannes and Ernst had wrapped Françoise in the tarpaulin and borne her down to her small quarters, MacMillian was becoming anxious to depart. As soon as the body was gone, he left his room and made his way downstairs to put distance between himself and her death. He was increasingly apprehensive and testy, pacing the main parlor, drinking schnapps and coffee alternately, and swearing at the servants when they dared to approach him. Satisfied that Françoise would not be connected to him, he did all he could to behave as if he knew nothing of the matter. He had no wish to return to his room, and ordered me to tend to all packing.

"You'll need this," he said, holding out a key to me.

I took it. "What does this open, sir?" I asked him as politely as I could. I had already made up my mind to drop the most offensive of Jeffries's mannerisms and try to maintain the appearance of an acceptable servant. I doubted MacMillian would tolerate gutter slang or the speech of the lower orders. Let the other assume that I was trying to elevate myself, or put on airs. It was what would be expected of someone like Jeffries.

"It opens a lock, of course, fool," he snapped, then said, "In the closet there is a small chest. You will have to open it to pack it. There is a long leather map case in the chest. For no reason are you to disturb it. Do not open it, and do not move it from its place. It must remain precisely where it is." He tossed back his schnapps, muttering, "They can't make decent whiskey in this place."

"I will attend to it at once, sir," I said, bowing, and wanting to get my shoes on at last. Not only did my head hurt, but my feet were starting to ache from the chill of the day. I climbed the stairs quickly, and let myself into MacMillian's room, taking care not to step where Françoise had lain. There had been too many violent deaths in my life these last few days, and the weight of them was telling on me. As I buttoned my shoes on, I did what I could to put it out of my mind and set about gathering and folding MacMillian's clothes. I wanted that task done before I tended to my own things, for I was reasonably certain he would be annoyed if I put my packing before his.

I was interrupted by a rap on the door, and a moment later, Mycroft Holmes, in his Oriental splendor, came into the room. "Pity about the girl."

"It is," I said with feeling, for as deplorable as her way of life might be, she deserved a better end than this one.

"If I had time, I would want the last of the wine in the bottle that killed her, so that I could determine the poison used. But"——he spread his hands wide——"that would draw attention on Kamir, and that might lead to questions that would be awkward to answer. So I will content myself with warning you to be very careful in all that you do. Our enemies, and there are a number of them, are playing for the highest stakes imaginable, and will not let anyone, certainly not you or I, stand in their way." With this, he bowed deeply and left me alone to my work.

The chest MacMillian had singled out was behind a

large valise, and I pulled it out with a little difficulty. It was a sturdy, leather-covered and brass-bound piece, about twenty-four inches long, sixteen wide, and ten deep, and the lock on it was heavy, though it opened readily enough at the turn of the key. I folded the lid back and saw that there was indeed a long, tubular map case in the bottom of the chest, with a small brass lock on the fittings. I shook it carefully and heard the slither of paper inside. Doubtless that was where MacMillian had the treaty. At least he had kept it under a double lock; that was a little consolation. I laid his hunting jacket and britches atop it, using the boots to steady the map case.

There was a sharp sound below and a moment later I heard the main door open, stern voices asking to see Madame Isolde.

Thinking it was the official from this morning returning, I left my task and went to the top of the stairs. Herr Dortmunder was confronting two men I took to be constables of some sort. I heard his postilion's spurs ring as he paced, making an invisible barrier with the movement of his strides between the constables and the rest of the house. Realizing I would have to hurry, I went back to packing with more dispatch than finesse. When this was completed, I was satisfied that we could now depart. I went to the room I had been allotted, collected my hat, my coat, and my carpetbag, and used the bell-pull to summon assistance in carrying the luggage down to the carriage entrance, for even if we were bound for the train, we would certainly not go to the station on foot.

Though I looked for him in a general way, I saw no further sign of Mycroft Holmes, or his Turkish counterpart, Kamir. Much as I wanted to know what had become of him, I knew it would be unwise to ask about him. Perhaps, I thought, I would overhear the servants mention him as I finished preparations for departure. I listened closely without results.

There was a porter; Madame Isolde summoned him and had him load up the chaise with MacMillian's lug-

gage, apparently as eager to be shut of him as he was to
be out of her place. As he went about his work, he whis-
tled a tuneless little four-note song that he repeated end-
lessly. By the time the trunks and chests and cases were
secure, I was heartily sick of the refrain and knew it
would echo about in my mind for hours to come.

At the train station, MacMillian attempted to commandeer a car for himself, and was told politely but firmly
that this would not be possible. He raged at the stationmaster, demanding an explanation. "I am on a diplomatic
mission, I will have you know, and if anything should
happen to the documents I carry, the consequences would
be heavy for Germany. If I come to any mischance, it will
be laid to your lack of assistance."

I thought about the singular lack of care MacMillian
had shown these same documents while he was at
Madame Isolde's, and had to conceal a sour smile. Such
cavalier treatment would not be viewed favorably by
those who were depending upon him for the safe delivery
of the treaty. Not that it was likely they would ever learn
of it.

"There is no order assigning a private car to you, sir,"
said the stationmaster, bowing as much as his starched
shirtfront would permit, which was not very much. "The
best we can do is give you a private compartment with
empty compartments on either side of you."

"That is hardly sufficient; the arrangements must be
better," said MacMillian with terrible scorn. "My mission
is much more important than you suppose. You surely
know how to take care of foreign diplomats, don't you?
You are not barbarians here, are you?"

"When we are told to by those with the authority to
command us, we perform our duties to a high standard.
We do not offer any insult to those not deserving of such.
It is a tradition in Germany to give superior service," said
the stationmaster, the very picture of affronted dignity.
He seemed about to impale his jaw on the starched points
of his collar.

"Very good," said MacMillian sarcastically. "Then you will attend to getting the private car I require, and then you will see that a waiter and a guard are assigned to it."

The stationmaster grew more formidably stiff. "You have no authorization for such specialized treatment. For what reason do you believe you are entitled to such privilege?"

Realizing that the Scotsman and the German had reached an impasse, I plucked at MacMillian's sleeve, and cleared my throat, hoping it would not be ripped out for my pains. "Sir, if I may make a suggestion . . ."

"What is it, Jeffries?" He gave me a hard stare, as if he had already come to the decision that employing me had been a mistake.

"It is simply this," I said, keeping my voice low. "There have been attempts on your life; why make yourself conspicuous? The more distinction you are given, the easier it will be for those working against you to find you. A private car is obvious, and easily isolated. It would tend to attract the very forces you would most want to keep at bay."

This argument apparently carried some persuasive weight with MacMillian, for he rubbed at his chin and regarded me thoughtfully for a short while. "That is a very telling observation, Jeffries; yes, I take your meaning," he declared at last, and swung back in the direction of the stationmaster. "Your circumstances here have put me at a disadvantage. Under the circumstances, I will avail myself of your offer of a private compartment with empty compartments on either side, and a guard assigned to the car." He raised his chin, the better to look down his nose at the stationmaster. "See to it."

"I will have to get permission to assign you a guard," said the stationmaster, unwilling to compromise even on this point.

"Then *do it,* man," he ordered. "The train for Karlsruhe leaves in twenty minutes and I have my luggage to get aboard yet." He scowled at the platform, where the locomotives were drawn up.

"The Karlsruhe train will not leave for an hour yet," said the stationmaster in the manner of one confessing a fault. "It has been delayed by order of King Ludwig."

"Oh, my God," muttered MacMillian in English. "That delusional madman." He rolled his eyes upward as if petitioning heaven to aid him.

If the stationmaster understood, he did not admit it, though he spoke more sharply. "His Majesty is sending a messenger to France on the Karlsruhe train. This messenger will have a private car."

"A private car," repeated MacMillian as if counting this against the stationmaster. "Very good for him, getting the approval of a man like Ludwig," said MacMillian, once again speaking German. "Well, let him enjoy it. Make note of this, sir: I will change at Karlsruhe for Mainz and then to Bonn. At Bonn, I will change for Liège. At Liège I will change for Ghent. I expect you to wire instructions ahead so that I will not have to repeat this farce again."

"I will endeavor to do as you instruct," said the stationmaster.

I noticed that there was a strange emblem on the watchfob the stationmaster wore, an Egyptian eye, of the sort I had seen over the gates and fireplace at von Metz's schloss. My heart beat more quickly. I did not know if I should warn MacMillian, and if I did, how I would account for my information. I was beginning to fear that everything I had been told about the Brotherhood was not only true, but an understatement. Would it be safe to alert MacMillian in any way?

I was still puzzling over this when MacMillian rounded on me, whiskers bristling. "And Jeffries, from here on out, making these arrangements will be your responsibility. If I am kept waiting or if I am given inadequate accommodation, it will be on your head."

"Certainly," I said, doing all that I could to look prepared for the task. "Just tell me who you want me to talk to."

"There is a private waiting room," the stationmaster

announced as if divulging a state secret. "You may wait there until the train is ready to depart. No one will disturb you."

"And my man?" asked MacMillian with a negligent wave in my direction. "I will need him to tend to me."

"He should remain in the public waiting room." The stationmaster heaved a little sigh. "But if you require him, he can be with you while he is fulfilling your commissions."

MacMillian was pleased at having scored this point, and so pressed for one more advantage. "And as there has been no time for breakfast, you will see that we have pastries and coffee."

The stationmaster set his jaw. "I will tell the baker who has his wagon outside to bring you his best."

"And quickly," added MacMillian, starting down the corridor the stationmaster indicated.

No sooner had MacMillian settled himself in a high-backed, overstuffed chair than the door opened, so suddenly that I spun about in a crouch, expecting trouble and prepared to defend myself. The events of the last few days had truly taken their toll on me.

It was the messenger who had come to Madame Isolde's that morning, armed with nothing more than a walking stick and an overlarge valise. He strode toward MacMillian purposefully. "I was told you would be here," said the messenger. "You have led me a merry chase."

"Oh, it's you, Zimmerman," said MacMillian blandly after he had regained his composure. "You have been on my heels for three days. What do you want?"

"I have a message for you, something that I must tell you in private," he said with a quick glance in my direction.

"I will leave you; I want to have a bite to eat," I said at once, the more to reassure Zimmerman than to appear subservient to MacMillian. I preferred selecting my own food, now that I thought about it; this situation was too exposed and I had to assume we were being watched. I

wanted to be certain I did not eat anything detrimental to
me.

"You are such a fussy old hen of a man," said
MacMillian with a sigh of ill use. "Though I suppose
government needs fellows like you, to tidy up after the
real work is done." He waved me away with a weary flap
of his hand. "Come back in ten minutes." His gaze rested
on Zimmerman. "I don't suppose you will need more
than ten minutes."

"If you have no questions, it should suffice," said
Zimmerman, trying not to sound too put-upon.

"And bring pastry and coffee when you come,"
MacMillian added as I went out the door, taking care to
close it.

The platform was busy, with travelers, porters, and
railroad employees bustling about. The activity was
invigorating, the kind of sensible work that had not been
my lot for some time. How tidy it all was, this determined
industry, how simple and direct. The engines hissed like
tame dragons as they were stoked and readied. Ruddy-
faced men loaded fuel into the car immediately behind
the engine, and I watched these efforts with a degree of
envy that surprised me. Porters with handcarts carried
crates and bales to the waiting trains, stowing them with
the ease of practice. Those men were not being hunted by
unknown cabals, the targets of assassins, sent on missions
that grew hourly more convoluted and dangerous. None
of them had thrown a man to his death. None had stood
helplessly by while an innocent man was ritually slaughtered. At the end of the day they went home, having done
an honest day's labor, to an uncomplicated family and the
pride of achievement. Even as I thought this, I knew it for
the simplification it was, and found little solace in it.

At the baker's cart, I selected four pastries, two of them
filled with soft, sweet cheese and a berry comfit that
looked delicious. At any other time I would have bought
some for myself, but my appetite had not truly returned,
and though it was early afternoon, I could not think of

eating without feeling queasy. I paid for the pastries with a flourish, then wondered if anyone was watching me.

What was Zimmerman telling MacMillian? And what difference could it make to me? I began to walk back in the direction of the private waiting room, pastries wrapped in paper.

I halted at the beginning of the corridor, realizing that I was witness to something important. The stationmaster was standing just outside the closed door of the private waiting room, head slightly inclined for concentrated listening. I had no idea how long he had been there and what, if anything, he had overheard. The notion that one of the Brotherhood had information I could not obtain troubled me greatly. Remembering his watchfob, I hesitated, trying to decide what would be the most truly Jeffries thing to do. Should I challenge the man, or appear to ignore what I had seen? The decision was made for me.

A whistle sounded from outside the station, and the stationmaster raised his head, like an animal testing the wind. He saw me then, and had the temerity to nod at me as he made his way to the front of the station to greet the new arrival.

Watching the stationmaster walk away from the door, I caught a glimpse of a woman in the crowd, a slight, young woman with light-colored hair that reminded me briefly of Penelope Gatspy, though with so many fair women about, it was odd that she should have worked such a powerful response from me. For an instant, I wondered how she was doing with her brother, for surely she had reached him by now. Then I made myself think of more pressing matters. Then I turned my thoughts to Elizabeth, and tried to imagine how I would tell her of all I had done. It struck me then that I might not be permitted to tell her anything of my experiences, which would be bound to displease her. I reminded myself philosophically that I could not deal with the future when the present was so precarious.

I made my way back to the private waiting room and

held out the paper with the pastries to MacMillian. "I hope these are satisfactory, sir," I said. "I purchased four in case you wished to offer one to Herr Zimmerman."

"Why would I want to do that?" asked MacMillian sharply, his attitude suggesting I had taken leave of my good manners if not my senses. "And do not think you can tell me that you don't want one for yourself."

"I have had mine," I lied. "They are excellent."

"You need a taster, do you?" challenged Zimmerman, whose face was redder now than when he had first arrived. "Not that I blame a man for being careful of enemies; you have many to be wary of."

"Meaning that you are one?" suggested MacMillian. "Perhaps when all this is over you and I will have leisure to enjoy our animosity."

"It is a shame that so much depends on a man like you," said Zimmerman with no apology for his insult. He rose, bowed stiffly and all but clicked his heels. "I will leave you, *mein Herr.*"

"At last," said MacMillian with a studied, languid manner. He had looked at the pastries and then set them aside as Zimmerman departed. "Jeffries, my coffee."

As I went to do MacMillian's bidding, I kept wondering how—or if—I would get him to tell me of Zimmerman's errand.

FROM THE PERSONAL JOURNAL OF PHILIP TYERS: *Information is expected from Germany momentarily. What M.H. intends to do regarding travel is not yet apparent, but he has asked that the Mercury train which brought him to Germany be sent back to Paris, but held there in readiness against any sudden need. The Mercury train has performed extremely well, according to M.H. The real trouble is the quality of track over which it travels, for it limits the speeds the train can reach safely.*

Edmund Sutton has reported that three men have asked for M.H. at the Diogenes Club, which causes him some trepidation. He fears that some of M.H.'s enemies may suspect his use of a double and are hoping to find out the truth of the matter for themselves.

Word brought from the Admiralty indicates that the matter of pilfering is now wholly concluded and the scandal is averted.

I am once again called to hospital. The signs are grave.

Chapter Twenty-one

IT WAS THIRTY minutes later that the stationmaster summoned MacMillian to take his place in the private compartment, with the assurance that the compartments on either side would be empty, and the railroad guards would ensure our protection. I looked at his Egyptian eye watch-fob, and could place little trust in his assertion.

"That is fine," said MacMillian, motioning me to hold his greatcoat for him, which I did. "We will have a pleasant autumn day, at least, now that the fog is gone. Nothing is so dismal as looking at river fog, mile after mile."

"It is pretty country," I allowed, thinking that were it not for the danger around me, I should probably enjoy all I saw.

The stationmaster waited impatiently. "It is the third car, immediately after the baggage cars, the middle compartment."

"The Germans are very sentimental about nature," said

MacMillian, ignoring the stationmaster. "Forever prosing on about it."

I made sure everything of his was gathered up, and went to hold the door open for him, suspecting that such attentions were demanded by him.

He regarded these acts with a lack of concern, which only confirmed my suspicion that he expected them. "And which is our compartment?" he asked as we entered the corridor.

"Third car, middle compartment," I said, repeating what the stationmaster had just said.

"Middle compartment. There are five compartments, I presume?" He looked out toward the platform. "And who is that, going into the fourth car?"

"That is the private car," said the stationmaster in a cold tone.

"King Ludwig's crony," said MacMillian, shrugging as he started across the platform toward the waiting train. "I will want my luggage in my compartment. It should not go into the baggage cars."

"I will have the porter tend to it," said the stationmaster, making it obvious he was glad to see the last of Cameron MacMillian.

Now that I was boarding the train, I wished I had been able to have one more word with Mycroft Holmes before I undertook this phase of my assignment. I wanted to know where he would be, and how I could contact him if it came to that.

"Look!" MacMillian's sharp command cut through my reflections. He was pointing to a hunched figure in a wheeled chair attended by a young man in a cadet's uniform. So wrapped and blanketed was the invalid that it was impossible to discern either the age or the sex of the person, or the cause of his condition, if it indeed was a he, and not some ancient *Gräfin* or *Marschallin* being accorded this distinction.

I saw that the chair was being pushed toward our train,

the cadet moving hastily under the instruction of his charge.

"That is King Ludwig's guest," exclaimed MacMillian as two porters struggled to carry the wheeled chair and its tenant into the private car. "If that man has anything infectious, I will hold King Ludwig responsible for any illness I contract."

"It may be that the reason the King ordered the private car was to prevent any contact with other passengers, if the person is ill and not suffering from some other malady," I suggested, thinking that such care was unlikely, but wanting to keep MacMillian from fretting.

"You give King Ludwig a great deal more credit than he deserves," said MacMillian as we reached the steps up into our car. "If he thinks of his people at all, it is only as decorations for his buildings. Having any regard for someone in poor health, or the health of others, would not be deemed important by him."

The center compartment was not unlike other private compartments: a settee that became a bed at night, a little dressing room, a large, curtained window, a small closet.

"You can put my luggage in the adjoining compartments so that I will not be any more crowded in here than necessary," MacMillian announced. "I will want the keys when you lock the doors."

"Naturally, sir," said the senior guard who had been given the task of watching this car. He saluted smartly and went to follow MacMillian's orders.

"The washroom is just there," said the conductor as he came by the compartment. "At the end of the car. You change at Karlsruhe for Mainz. I will summon you when we are thirty minutes from Karlsruhe, to allow you time to make ready."

"Yes," said MacMillian. "And inform my man an hour ahead, so that I will not have to wait for him." He indicated the door. "Where are the valets' compartments?"

"Next to the washroom," said the conductor, who touched the bill of his cap and left.

"You will put your things in order and arrange for the evening meal." As he said this he scowled. "You will have to pass through the private car to reach the kitchen. That is a bad thing. Perhaps at one of the stops the waiter could bring my food up to me, walking on the platform, to decrease the risk of infection." He waited for me to help him remove his greatcoat and put it away in the closet. "I leave that up to you."

This sudden concern for infection struck me as odd in a man who had spent the previous night licking champagne off a prostitute. "Perhaps I should ascertain what is the nature of the invalid's complaint before resorting to so awkward an arrangement," I said, hoping that this would meet with his approval. I wanted to discover for myself who it was who traveled immediately behind us.

"So long as you wash your hands and face thoroughly after speaking to the creature, well enough. Do not bring any contamination into me. And when you have seen him, I will want to know how serious you think his condition is." He had made himself as comfortable as possible on the settee, and seemed inclined to remain there for the afternoon.

"I will, sir," I told him, and backed out of the compartment, recommending as I closed the door that he lock it from the inside. "Better too cautious than too sorry," I reminded him, sounding very like my mother.

"Yes," he agreed, and I heard him move. A moment later the bolt was pressed home and the door was as secure as it could possibly be.

In one of the two valets' compartments on the car, I saw my carpetbag, and the hat I had worn earlier this day. I slipped into the tiny chamber, which was little more than half the size of MacMillian's compartment. And while there were two woolen blankets, it was obvious that the unupholstered wooden bench could not be made into a bed.

I was distressed to see that the door lacked an inside lock, for I was apprehensive about the notebooks I carried. I tried to see if there was some manner in which I might improvise one, when the train gave an experimental lurch and I found myself clinging to the doorframe to keep from falling.

As the train groaned and came to life, I made my way back to the bench and hung on, waiting until we had rattled and huffed out of the station and had begun to pick up speed. Rising, I saw that MacMillian had been right— it was a beautiful autumn day in Bavaria now that the fog had lifted. I reminded myself of my duty and started off in the direction of the private car, wondering as I did why it was so strangely placed in the train. Most private cars were put first or next-to-last of the cars, to keep them private, but this one was oddly situated. I made my way, swaying with the train, to the private car, taking care to knock before I opened the door.

The young cadet faced me in the open door, his fresh face so clean and boyish that it was hard to imagine he was a devoted student of war. He gave me a salute and stood aside.

At the far end of the private car there was a long couch with a high back which faced the enameled-iron stove. The wheeled chair stood abandoned, and on the couch, in a fine English suit topped off with a muffler of cocoon-like proportions, sat Mycroft Holmes, legs stretched out the length of the couch. "Guthrie, do come in. I didn't expect you quite so soon. The chill hasn't quite gone off yet, but be comfortable, do. It will be warmer shortly."

I stared at him, thinking I should have realized he would not leave me to flail about on my own. "I'm relieved to see you, sir," I said as I dropped into the armchair.

"As I am," my employer confessed. "I was not sure this arrangement could be made so quickly, things being as they are in Bavaria." He coughed delicately. "And I do not simply mean about King Ludwig. It is difficult to work around the Brotherhood. Von Metz has his fingers in a great many pies, and we have yet to discover the whole of them." His expression of disgust revealed more than his tone of voice. "But I was fortunate. Von Schallensee was able to arrange all this on extremely short notice."

"Von Schallensee?" I asked, not recalling the name from any of the work I had done for Mycroft Holmes back in London.

This was acknowledged with a nod. He spoke more loudly as if he intended to be overheard. "Von Schallensee is a man who works very much as I do, quietly, for the benefit of all Germany, as I try my poor best to consider all of Britain's Empire in what I do. Von Schallensee is the man who first identified von Metz for me, and provided the information necessary to bridge the gap between Vickers and von Metz. He was able to delay the train long enough to procure this car—it is one of his own, incidentally—and to arrange for its placement in the order of cars, which, as I understand, was more difficult than procuring the car itself." He waved to the cadet. "Kreutzer, pour some brandy for Guthrie here. And be sure the fire is taking hold as it should."

The cadet nodded at once, and opened the cabinet where a number of bottles and glasses waited. "And for you, sir?"

Mycroft Holmes pulled at his lower lip. "I think I'll have the same."

"Very good," said Kreutzer, and set about pouring generous tots into two balloon snifters. He brought these to us, giving a stiff, military bow as he did. "Your brandy, sir."

"Thank you, Kreutzer," said Mycroft Holmes, making a single gesture to dismiss the lad. "I will probably need you later. Before we transfer to the next train."

"Of course, sir," said Kreutzer, and retired to the far side of the car after checking the stove and adding another quarter-cut section of log.

"He is one of von Schallensee's men," Holmes explained with a slight smile.

It had to be something like that, I knew, for the cadet to be here. "You trust him."

"With my life, which I mean quite literally," said Mycroft Holmes after taking a little sip of brandy. "And given the dangers at the station, he served me well. Tell me how it is going with MacMillian."

But I was not going to be fobbed off so easily. "What dangers at the station?" I asked, recalling Zimmerman.

"There were five watchers there, three in railroad uniforms which they must have been provided by those belonging to the Brotherhood." My employer took out a cigar and snipped its end, preparing to light it. "Surely you were aware of them, Guthrie?"

"No, sir, I don't think so," I said. "I was more concerned with MacMillian than with station guards."

"Not surprising," agreed Holmes as he took a deep pull on his cigar. "Well, you will have to accept my word that they were there. They did not wear the correct shoes, and one of them was foolish enough to wear his signet ring. To have the right uniforms and the wrong shoes! It's oversights like that"—he took another lungful of smoke—"which cause me to lose all respect for von Metz's underlings."

"That accounts for three of the men. What of the other two?" I asked, wondering what details I had not noticed.

"Oh, you saw the man with the Prussian accent, didn't you? Tall fellow with brindled whiskers and a stiff arm? No?" He had recourse to his cigar again. "Well, he was pretending to claim baggage at the end of the platform, but it was all sham. He addressed all his remarks to one of the false guards, and he carried two pistols under his coat and perhaps a third in his sleeve." He tapped the ash into a saucer Kreutzer had provided. "The last was the woman in gray, with the very attractive hat and veil. They do deign to use women, now and again." He shrugged. "Tell me about—"

"MacMillian," I finished for him. "You know everything up to when I packed his things." I recounted the events from the last time I had seen him at Madame Isolde's to my arrival at the door to this private car. I

made my report as succinct as possible, including noticing the Egyptian eye on the stationmaster's watchfob, and
the private visit of Zimmerman. I ended by saying I did
not want to be away from MacMillian too long. "So we
are now bound for Belgium, and MacMillian thinks all
the spies of Europe are after him."

"As well he might" was Holmes's answer.

"Is he in much danger?" I asked, finally tasting the
brandy.

"Well, there are many factors to consider: if Mac-
Millian is killed, a more competent messenger could be
appointed. Unfortunately, his death is apt to herald the
theft of the treaty, which must, of course, be avoided. I
am concerned that our Scot is making a public nuisance
of himself. He is demanding too much attention and he is
choosing his company badly. England is not the only government keeping close watch on the Brotherhood. If the
Germans suspect what MacMillian is carrying, then we
will be in the unenviable position of having to deal with
them in their own country. There is also the continuing
presence of the Golden Lodge, and I am not yet satisfied
if we are being aided, observed, or used by them, nor to
what ends. It behooves us not to become complacent
about them. It may be that MacMillian's very ineptness
will serve as a shield. Some may assume that a man who
careers from brothel to brothel boasting of his great secret
mission must be a decoy." He blew a cloud of smoke into
the air. "It would be circumspect to assume we have two
deadly and antipathetic groups who are determined to
obtain the treaty at any cost whatsoever."

I listened to Mycroft Holmes with an increasing sense
of frustration and foreboding. How could I protect
MacMillian from such forces without revealing my mission to him? And if I did tell him of my true purpose in
accompanying him, would he believe me? And if he
believed me, would he cooperate with Mycroft Holmes to
protect the treaty?

Holmes sensed my misgivings. "I hope it will not come

to it, but if you must be revealed, you won't have to tell him anything. If it becomes necessary, I will do it."

"Speaking of what I must tell him, what should I say about the person in this car? He is afraid that he will take some infection from the invalid," I said.

He considered his answer carefully. "I think you should say that the invalid is an important military adviser who was severely injured in battle some years ago. There will be no question of infection, and no need for MacMillian to fear any plague will light upon him." He chuckled suddenly, adding, "You might also say that the invalid is nearly deaf and difficult to converse with. That should stop him wanting to press for an interview."

"You have the cut of his jib," I said with a single nod. "All right. I will give him this tale and I will hope we will be able to squeak through this without any more trouble. If only that treaty were not so crucial."

"But it is," I added, wondering again if any piece of paper was worth what this one had already cost. Certainly safety for the many outweighed the lives of the few, or so I had always believed. But I had seen a man murdered less than twenty-four hours ago, and had killed a man myself two days before that, and the matter was no longer as certain to me.

Mycroft Holmes noticed that I had not taken much of the brandy, but he did not comment on it, merely asking, "When did you last eat?"

"In the morning," I replied.

"You will want to get something into you, Guthrie. I need you to be alert, and for that, you cannot starve. The kitchen can make up a supper for you at my order, if you would like." He motioned to Kreutzer, and the young man stood at once. "Have a good dinner made for Guthrie, here. And take it to him in his compartment."

"I should make sure that MacMillian has something as well," I reminded my employer.

"Naturally," said Mycroft Holmes. "Kreutzer, tend to it, if you will." He watched as the young man passed out of the private car toward the next one, which contained the kitchen. "If MacMillian complains of your long absence, attribute it to the amazing deafness of the invalid. Let him know how painstakingly you had to repeat the simplest questions."

I nodded. "All right. And I will be glad of a meal." I had to admit that as little as food appealed to me, I could feel that hunger was affecting me. "I'll have supper, and make sure that MacMillian does not take it into his head to come and bother you."

"Thank you, Guthrie." Holmes rose and indicated the door leading back to the car where MacMillian rode in solitary state. "He is difficult, I know, but it will not be long before this is over."

My answer was as heartfelt as it was unguarded. "I hope so."

FROM THE PERSONAL JOURNAL OF PHILIP TYERS: *There has been a note for G. delivered by messenger this afternoon. It was sent by Miss Roedale, who has marked the missive "confidential."*

Given that I have had no further word from M.H., I can only hold this note until both men return, and I have sent a note to Miss Roedale to so inform her, so that in future she cannot claim that she was unaware of how matters stood.

Chapter Twenty-two

"CRIPPLED AND DEAF," exclaimed MacMillian as I made my report to him a few minutes after leaving the private car and Mycroft Holmes. "Poor devil. And to think they're still hauling him all over the country."

"He has the cadet to look after him," I pointed out.

"Probably a relative of sorts. That's how these old military families are in Germany." As if they were different in Britain. He indicated the window. "I've been looking at the church spires, and the colors they are painted. It's one of the things I like about Bavaria and Baden, the colors the peasants use to decorate their buildings. So much more festive than England. English peasants have no taste for bright things."

"I took the opportunity to go through to the dining car and ordered supper for you," I went on, trying to show myself a good servant. "It should be delivered shortly."

"Excellent," said MacMillian, whose mood had mellowed as distance was put between him and Munich. "I hope they will have some of that good Rhine wine to serve. It's well enough to drink beer at a country inn, but on a train, only wine is acceptable at a meal. And a French vintage is preferable to a German one, no matter where we are." His expression was filled with satisfaction with his own opinion and approval of his taste.

"The cadet will probably bring the meal, so that his charge will not be unduly disturbed," I said, aware that MacMillian might not be pleased with this arrangement. "It seemed the more discreet thing to do."

"If it will help accommodate the old man, I suppose there's no trouble with it," said MacMillian with a touch of sulking in his manner. He looked toward the window again, and gave a sigh. "I've heard there are trains now that can go at nearly seventy miles per hour. They do not pull many laden cars, of course, but they can keep up that speed for as long as their fuel holds out." His whole demeanor implied that if such a train did exist it should be at his disposal.

"I have heard the same thing," I said, taking care not to mention that it was part of a confidential memo from Whitehall. "But you know how men like to boast. They want to believe that such a train exists, and so they make claims that assure them their wishes are met."

"You're a cynic, aren't you, Jeffries?" said MacMillian with haughty amusement. "I wouldn't be in such a hurry to doubt the train is real." With this he waved me away. I returned to my compartment and sat down, feeling exhausted. But much as I wanted to nap, the least sound jolted me into alertness, and I began to fear I would never be able to rest again. I had reached that stage of exhaustion when a false alertness takes over, demanding wakefulness with jangled nerves. It was growing late in the day and the first streamers of sunset were beginning in the west. At home, I would be getting ready for tea, just finishing up my day's work for Mycroft Holmes.

The tap on my door from Cadet Kreutzer almost sent

me diving for cover, so loud did it seem over the steady racket of the rails. I did what I could to compose myself and went to the door.

"Just what was ordered, sir," said Kreutzer, holding out a tray with three covered dishes on it. "Pork roast with apples and prunes, potatoes with cheese and onions, and cabbage soup with cream and pine nuts." When I hesitated, he added, "I have just served MacMillian."

"In that case, thank you very much," I said, taking the tray and putting it down on the end of the bench near the window. Before I closed the door, I asked, "Is your . . . charge well?"

"He will be sending a telegram at the next station we reach, which will be in an hour or so." He saluted and departed.

I could not bring myself to relish the meal I had been provided, but I did realize that it was what my body craved, and I set about consuming it as methodically as I was able, though it had all the savor of a sack of feathers to me. As I finished the food, I began to be sleepy, and I hoped that at last I could restore myself with sleep. With all the events of the last few days, I had begun to fear I would not be at rest again until I was laid out for my wake. Putting the tray and its now-empty dishes on the floor, I opened one of the blankets and stretched out on the wooden bench, trusting to the steady rhythm of the train to lull me into slumber.

It was quite dark when I opened my eyes again, and at first I could not fathom why I had awakened. Then I became aware of a muffled, scuffling sort of noise coming from the next compartment. The compartment that was supposedly locked. The compartment containing MacMillian's luggage. I sat up, shaking my head as if to sort out my thoughts more clearly, all the while listening to the movement in the adjoining compartment. Were they actually stealthy, or did the thickness of the walls only make them seem so?

At last I decided I had to do something, in case the

thief was in search of something more valuable than cuff links and shirt studs. How much I wished I had my lost pistol and knife now. And how little I wanted to have to use them. As I made for the door, I heard another soft thud, and I moved more quickly. I opened my door with care, making sure it made no telltale sound to alert the miscreants in the other compartment. It would probably be best, I thought, to grab the thief from behind, and pinion his arms to his sides, so that if the fellow had a weapon, he could not easily turn it on me.

The most difficult part was immediately ahead of me. I had to open the compartment door without alerting the person inside. I had put my hand on the latch when I heard a soft oath in English, and the tautness went out of my hand. I rapped on the door. "Herr MacMillian," I called out, wanting to avoid any misunderstanding on his part or the part of the German guard, who was supposed to be watching this car. "Herr MacMillian, is all well with you? Is anything wrong? This is Jeffries."

"Thank God, and about time," he said, pulling the door open and glaring at me. "Where the bloody hell have you been?"

"In my compartment. I . . . went to sleep."

"So early?" he demanded. The lamp in this compartment had been lit, and I saw that MacMillian's cases and trunks and chests were all in a jumble. "I've been trying to find it."

"To find what?" I asked.

"The map case, of course," he said, as if any simpleton would have known the answer.

My heart went cold in my chest, as if it had been filled with ice instead of blood. I tried to maintain an even tone. "It is in the chest you had it in this morning. I packed your boots and hunting jacket with it." I was growing more awake by the moment. "Is it missing?"

"Find it for me," ordered MacMillian in a tone that would tolerate no objections.

With a languor I did not feel, I stretched and said

resentfully, in Jeffries's character, "If you wish. But it is late, and your luggage isn't going anywhere. Why is it so important now?" I realized too quick a compliance might well make him suspicious of my purpose here, and kept up my assumed surliness. "Surely I can do this in the morning?"

"I want it done now," said MacMillian in a flat voice that promised a fine display of temper if I did not set to work at once.

"All right," I said, and sighed as I looked at the disorder MacMillian had already wrought in the compartment. My distress at the confusion was only partly feigned and covered my rising panic well. "If you would return to your own compartment, I will do what I can to find the map case for you." As he started to leave, I held out my hand. "I will need the key, sir."

"So you will, so you will," said MacMillian, and took it from his waistcoat pocket. "It is now ten-twenty. If you have not discovered it in forty minutes, let me know, so that I may inform the guard of what has happened, and appropriate measures may begin to return my property to me. And put all this to rights." With that he returned to his compartment, leaving me with the chaos he had made of his own belongings.

The chest in question was, of course, on the bottom of a stack of cases. It took me fifteen minutes of shifting the various trunks and cases into other piles before I could reach my target. When I opened the lock, I put my hand on the map case almost at once, in the very place I had been told to pack it. Relief coursed through me; the treaty had not been discovered or touched. Holding this trophy in my hand, I ventured into the compartment next door. "This is what you wanted, isn't it, sir?"

"It is," he said with as much visible relief as he could bring himself to express around someone of my station in life. "And the lock is in place?"

I extended my arm so he could see the lock. "Closed all right and tight. You have the key for this. I do not."

MacMillian cleared his throat as if ridding himself of a cud, and gave a single nod. "Very good. I am satisfied that there has been no tampering. Replace it carefully, make certain the lock is set on the chest, and restack my luggage. And ask the waiter to come for the tray." Now that he was assured of the safety of the treaty, he wanted to restore his dignity as quickly as possible.

"What sort of map's in that case, sir, that it's so important to you?" I could not keep myself from asking.

"The map is none of your concern," came Mac-Millian's brusque answer. "It is necessary only that you make certain it is protected."

"That I will," I said, and added, expressing the worry that had taken hold of me. "But what of the guard you've been assigned? Shouldn't he be looking after this?"

MacMillian shot me a startled look. "I should think so. Go and find him. Tell him I want a word with him." His brow darkened, promising that the word would be a harsh one.

"Very good," I said at once, and started toward the head of the car in the other valet's compartment. The guard was not there, though I did see a large cup with the last remnants of chocolate at the bottom of it, suggesting he had waited there earlier in the evening. There was also a faint, drying impression of another glass, for a dark ring remained where a second libation had stood. I made note of this to include in my report.

In the compartment immediately next to MacMillian's the guard lay asleep, his rifle tucked along his body like an ungainly doll. He was snoring gently but with that steadiness that indicates deep sleep. I would not rid myself of the unwelcome suspicion that the fellow had imbibed something in his second drink that had promoted this sleep as chocolate and cream would not. I bent over and smelled his breath: a strong odor of kirschwasser was present; the odor of cherries could conceal many other substances. Reluctantly I woke him, and noticed the groggy confusion that possessed him, and the muddled way in which he formed his words. He had certainly had more than one glass of schnapps or he had had something along with it. "Herr MacMillian has had a disturbance and wants to talk to you."

"A disturbance?" the guard repeated thickly. "I didn't hear anything."

"That is what he wants to talk with you about," I said, and helped him to his feet, feeling I was doing him no kindness.

MacMillian received the fellow with haughty, hearty displeasure. "I heard someone enter the compartment behind this one. You were nowhere about. Are all Germans so lax in their duty?"

"Well, you see," the guard said, his face turning red, "I . . . I fell asleep, *mein Herr.* There is only the invalid in the next car, and when his companion offered me chocolate, I didn't think there was any harm in it."

"Chocolate!" jeered MacMillian. "Brandy, more like."

"No, sir," I interrupted, taking care to speak in English, no matter how rude. "Chocolate. I saw the dregs in the cup." I did not want him pursuing the manner in his hamhanded way, which I was certain he would do if I revealed what I had observed. I had also to consider what might happen should MacMillian take it into his head to confront my true employer.

MacMillian's gaze was intended to turn me to stone. "How dare you defend this coward!"

"I am not defending him, sir, far from it," I persisted, hoping I would not be dismissed out of hand for this. "But it would not surprise me if the chocolate might have been drugged."

"Drugged! What nonsen—" MacMillian burst out. "What sort of fool would—?" Then his eyes narrowed. "Drugged," he mused. "What makes you say that?"

"Well, as you must have noticed, it is early in the evening to sleep, and this man—look at him—is still logy; you might think he had drunk himself into a stupor. If the chocolate were poisoned, it might account for it, mightn't it?"

Now MacMillian ruminated on the question, his face blank with concentration. "It is possible," he allowed. "And if so, all the more reason to demand a competent guard." He switched back to German. "You, sir, have failed in your duty. You will be put off the train at the next station and a new guard will take your place."

The man bowed his head. *"Jawohl, mein Herr."*

"And I will inform the railroad of what took place aboard this train." This addition was intended to impress the guard with MacMillian's importance, and it came near enough to succeeding.

"The invalid's companion brought the chocolate," said the guard, trying to offer some defense of his actions.

"I will speak to him, if you like," I volunteered quickly, wanting to postpone any meeting of those two men for as long as possible. "There may be some explanation I can gain without bringing any embarrassment to anyone."

MacMillian regarded me doubtfully. "Would it do any good?"

"I cannot guarantee it, but it may avoid attention that could . . . . compromise your mission," I said as boldly as I dared.

If MacMillian thought I had stepped out of line, he did not say so. "That might be wisest," he said, as if satisfied that he would not have to sully himself dealing with underlings. He rounded on the guard. "Put yourself at my man's disposal, and I will take your remorse into consideration when I make my report on this incident."

"If that is what you want, *mein Herr,*" said the guard, looking more hangdog than before.

"It is what you have created for yourself, sir," said MacMillian. "And should you ever be permitted such a duty as this again, remember what your poor judgment has brought about here."

The guard did not salute, but his dejection was so complete that MacMillian was satisfied without it.

I realized that before we reached the next stop I would have to have a word with Mycroft Holmes.

FROM THE PERSONAL JOURNAL OF PHILIP TYERS:
When I returned from hospital this evening, Inspector Cornell had brought a number of written questions for M.H. to answer, and was not pleased at being put off. I cannot admit that M.H. is out of the country, and I suspect that Cornell would not believe me in any case. He insists he must speak with M.H. tomorrow, and will not accept that this is impossible. I have claimed that press of work for the Admiralty has claimed all his attention, and that the work is intended to avert a crisis on the Continent, which is true enough, but the Inspector will not be willing to make allowances for this excuse much longer. I will be grateful when word comes from M.H. again and I will have some notion as to when I may expect him to return. If I can provide Cornell with a time when he can put his questions to M.H. in person, much of his impatience will fade, I am certain of it.

Edmund Sutton is now positive he is being watched and has taken every precaution he and M.H. arranged four years ago to be certain they are not compromised and their purpose discovered.

Chapter Twenty-three

"I DON'T LIKE it," said Mycroft Holmes as he drew his heavy dressing robe more tightly around him. "You were right to inform me before you spoke to anyone else."

"I am supposed to be speaking to the conductor. But I could not do that without passing through your car, in any case. I will have to do it fairly quickly, however," I said with an uneasy glance over my shoulder, as if I expected to be pursued by the still-irate MacMillian—which, to some degree, I did.

"I can't imagine that MacMillian is taking this well," he said fatalistically. "He would not let such an opportunity to display his importance go by." He sighed. "We will take on water in another hour or so. There is no telegraph that I know of at that stop, so I may have to send Kreutzer off on an errand from there. I may do it, in any case," he went on enigmatically. He placed the tips of his long fingers together, and continued in a contemplative manner. "It must be either the Brotherhood or the Golden Lodge. They are the ones who would have the greatest access to those working on the railroads, and would be able to enlist their support without any difficulty. And you saw the emblem on the stationmaster's fob."

"Are you certain of that? That it must be German?" I asked, thinking that there were countries that would find it to their advantage to compromise this treaty.

"Yes. Most railroad employees would not endanger their salaries by dealing with foreigners. It is not a German thing to do, given the German character." He slapped his hands together. "Therefore the skullduggery is internal, a matter among Germans. Which is more than sufficient to endanger all our months of negotiations."

"What do you want me to do?" I asked, thinking that I was treading a very uncertain path, with unseen traps all around me. I was not wholly convinced that Mycroft Holmes fully understood the gravity of the matter, but I would have to rely on him utterly, for all other advice that might be offered to me was twice-tainted.

"Speak to the conductor first, and make note of his demeanor. If he is truly surprised to learn of this occurrence, permit him to assign you another guard. If you are not entirely satisfied that the man had no knowledge or suspicion that this attempt might be made, then say you will summon assistance when we reach Karlsruhe."

"And how am I to convince MacMillian that this is a wise course?" I asked, rather more testily than I intended.

"Appeal to his vanity, of course. Say that his mission is too important for mere railroad guards. Tell him you doubt that any of the railroad guards have enough comprehension of his significance to protect him with sufficient care." Mycroft Holmes had a smile that was disquietingly reminiscent of a wolf pursuing prey. He wore it now. "In fact, you might plan to take that tack, in any case. Kreutzer can arrange for it. You will have the new guard in time to be with you when you change trains for Mainz."

"That is an obvious ploy, sir," I remarked.

Mycroft Holmes nodded in quick approval. "Exactly.

And for that reason will more likely be accepted. MacMillian would not expect anything so clumsy from those he fancies are his enemies."

"It would not be good for me if MacMillian discerned my purpose," I said, letting my doubts show.

"Then all the more reason for you to be at pains so that he will not." His lupine smiled returned. "Men like MacMillian make very biddable tools if you will only use their weaknesses as strengths."

I bowed slightly, wondering if this philosophy extended to me. "I will endeavor to keep your instructions in mind."

Holmes chuckled. "Don't cut up rough, Guthrie. It isn't my practice to make tools of men. I need those about me whom I can trust and whose integrity is impeccable." He beetled his brow. "You're certain about the second glass and the kirschwasser?"

"Absolutely, sir," I said with conviction.

He nodded. "I was afraid you were. If you wonder, your observation serves to confirm my opinion of your excellence, and I fear sets the seal of doubt on . . . another."

Was he, I asked myself, flattering me or telling me the truth? Or perhaps some of both? In spite of my uncertainties, I let myself be persuaded for the time being, and I left the private car and went in search of the conductor in order to lodge the complaint for MacMillian. After a brief conversation with that worthy we agreed that a special guard would join MacMillian at Karlsruhe and travel with us.

"For I don't mind telling you," said the conductor as we finished our dealing. "That man who employs you is a difficult and demanding one."

At that moment, as I agreed with the conductor, I thought such could be said, and justifiably, of both Cameron MacMillian and Mycroft Holmes.

By the time I had got back to MacMillian, it was after midnight, and he was cranky with lack of sleep. I recom-

mended he have a brandy, to take the edge off. I did not
want to have to deal with him in the morning if he passed
the night unhappily: he would be hard enough to deal
with as it was.

"A good notion, Jeffries," said MacMillian, who was
still preening over the idea of having a special guard sent
to accompany him, though he also complained that it
should have been offered to him in the first place. "A
brandy would be just the thing. But the waiter isn't available at this hour, is he?"

"I will attend to it, sir," I said, thinking I would avail
myself of some of Mycroft Holmes's supply in the private
car. It would be the least he could do.

I found Holmes preparing a dispatch to go with
Kreutzer, saying as he sealed it, "I will anticipate your
return telegram at the next regular stop. Tell me to whom
you have reported and who is the person we are to have
as escort. Use the code words I have given you so that we
can have no spies foisted upon us."

"Of course," said Kreutzer with a sharp salute as he
took the dispatch and tucked it into the inner pocket of his
tunic. His young face burned with zeal and efficiency. "I
will also forward a full report to your Admiralty, as you
have requested."

"Thank you," said Holmes, accepting the salute and
motioning the cadet to leave us. "Now then, Guthrie,"
Holmes continued when Kreutzer was gone, "what do
you want to tell me this time? And I trust it is not that
Kreutzer is a spy from the Golden Lodge, for that has
been apparent since he first presented himself to me."

"He is?" I asked, feeling either very foolish or quite
astonished. "But you said—"

"Yes, yes, because he was listening," said my employer
impatiently. "And as such he will serve my purpose well
enough. I wanted to alert the Golden Lodge to the possibility of the Brotherhood attempting to seize the treaty
from this train. But now I am just as glad to have him

away from me. There are too many things he could over-hear."

"Do you mean I have spoken out of turn?" I felt stung, for I could not imagine it was my duty to have guarded my tongue when Mycroft Holmes made it apparent he expected me to speak candidly.

"No, of course not," he responded. "I mean only that I did not want him to realize I am aware of his purpose."

"What told you he was one from the Golden Lodge?" I asked. "So I will know what to look for in the future."

"It was his careful attention to all I said in relation to the Brotherhood. He made several attempts to engage me in conversation concerning their activities, with the pretense that he wished to understand the whole of his duties to me." His chuckle was not at all friendly.

"Might that not have been the simple truth?" I suggested.

"It might have been, had I not observed him purloin one of my pages of notes detailing what is known of the Brotherhood's activities in Bavaria." He regarded me severely. "He knew precisely what he was looking for, and made away with it very neatly. I reckon he will pass the information on to his superiors in the organization as soon as possible."

I shook my head. "I don't know. It does not seem sufficient to me."

"In time, Guthrie, you will develop a sense about these things, and will know what to look for." He looked at my face critically. "That bruise is getting ugly, and you should clean that wound on your forehead before you retire tonight. I will supply you with iodine and peroxide for the purpose."

Until he reminded me, I forgot how much damaged my face was. I put my hand to the welt along my forehead. "Thank you. It would not do to have this become infected," I said with an edge to my voice.

Which, apparently, Mycroft Holmes did not hear. "No,

it would not." He went to his cases and took out a small
leather satchel. "You will find what you need in here. Oh,
and you may want to reaffix the—uh—scar over your
eye, in case there is any attempt to—"

"To what?" I interjected. "Throw me off the train?" As
I said this I became aware that the train was slowing
down.

"We take on water here," said Mycroft Holmes. "And
Cadet Kreutzer leaves us. After all, you don't want him
rummaging about in MacMillian's things again, do you?"

"You mean it was *Kreutzer* who broke into the compartment and tried to take the treaty?" I could not take
this in.

"He would not have succeeded in his task, I assure you,
even if he had found the map case." He patted the side of
his coat, and I realized my employer was armed.

It startled me that he knew about the map case. But
then I decided I must have mentioned something to him
about it, or he had learned of it from MacMillian himself,
while at Madame Isolde's. "He was the one who
attempted the search, then?"

"And quite inexpertly" was the answer. "He barely
unlocked the door when he was discovered."

"That would mean it was he who put MacMillian on
the alert, and caused him to search his own luggage." I
was hoping to make some sense of all this, but I was not
succeeding. I recalled it was MacMillian's activities that
had roused me, so it was possible Kreutzer had been in
the compartment first. This thought turned round and
round in my mind, but I could glean nothing from it.

"Is there anything else, dear boy?" asked Holmes at his
blandest.

"A double tot of brandy, so that MacMillian will sleep
the night away. He is so keyed up now that I suspect
another shock would pop him out of his skin." I knew that
some of that emotion affected me as well.

"Take what you want, Guthrie," offered Holmes. "And
if you will look on the lowest shelf, you will see four

small bottles without labels. The liqueur inside is a deep . green. It is made in Bavaria and it should help you sleep without discomfort tonight. The monks at an old Benedictine monastery make it to give to exhausted travelers. One bottle should do you. The taste is not unpleasant."

The train was almost stopped now, and I could feel the sway of the car. I did as he told me and retrieved the bottle, then poured out a hefty portion of brandy into a simple glass, taking care not to spill anything. "Thank you, sir. I will see you in the morning."

"Very good, Guthrie; sleep well. You've earned it," he said, and waved me out of his presence.

As I made my way back to MacMillian's compartment, I saw Kreutzer leave the train and rush toward the siding where an old-fashioned phaeton was drawn up, two restive horses harnessed in line. The driver saluted as Kreutzer sprang into the passenger seat. Then a great cloud of steam obscured the window and by the time it cleared, Kreutzer and the carriage were gone.

MacMillian was fidgeting as I came through the door, and he greeted my return with a look of extreme annoyance. "You took long enough."

"I thought it would be best to gain the cooperation of the old man by telling him the urgency of your mission, sir," I said, annoyed that this self-important fellow required so much flattery. "He allowed me to take a double measure for you, realizing that your work is of such moment."

This mollified MacMillian. "Very good, Jeffries. Yes, very good." He took the glass I proffered, sniffing it critically. "And a good brandy, at that. Not that I would expect a military hero to have less than the best." He took a long sip. "How long are we going to be here?"

"Until the train has sufficient water, I suppose," I said.

"There is no chance of the train being boarded here, is there?" His apprehension would have been comical in less desperate situations. "You will have to keep watch for me, until we have the new guard assigned to us in Karlsruhe."

"I will attend to it, sir," I said, and as I did wondered what provision Mycroft Holmes had made for our protection during the night. There would be something, I was convinced of it.

"Good man, Jeffries." He scrutinized me briefly. "You are not a very prepossessing chap, but I am beginning to think that I had the better bargain when Angus left me and you came to my service."

I could not keep from remembering Angus, dying terribly in that cellar. My God, I thought, was that only a night ago? I bowed once and hoped that all I had seen in the last days would not crowd in on me all night.

"Off you go, then. I will expect you to arrange a breakfast for me before eight."

With a mixture of gratitude and annoyance, I left him to return to my comfortless compartment to clean my injured forehead and then let the grassy-tasting liqueur ease me into sleep.

FROM THE PERSONAL JOURNAL OF PHILIP TYERS: *It has been an eventful afternoon and the evening is proving to be more of the same. Confirmation arrived in regard to the travels of M.H. in Bavaria, with the assurances that he would be accorded every courtesy from Munich to Ghent. He will have the use of a private car for most of the journey, and has arranged to keep his accommodation in close proximity to the one in which MacMillian and G. are riding, the better to inform himself of their progress.*

He has also told me that his activities are being monitored by a group known as the Golden Lodge, who are rivals to the Brotherhood. He has one such monitor with him in the person of a cadet named Kreutzer. It is M.H.'s intention to be rid of this young man as soon as possible, and if he can, to have this serve a double purpose.

I have prepared a packet of information from Inspector

Cornell which I shall have waiting for him in Liège. It is being carried to Europe tonight, to be given into the care of two of M.H.'s most trusted agents on the Continent. It would seem that the police have reached the end of their resources in this case and without the help of M.H. the dastards who murdered the young woman may well go unidentified and unpunished, which is intolerable, given what she endured to get her information to us. My report urges M.H. to make his private material available to Inspector Cornell, with the understanding that those factors impinging on the security of the Empire cannot be divulged in a court of law.

Edmund Sutton was accosted by ruffians as he came back across Pall Mall from the Diogenes Club. He was able to hold them off with his walking stick, which he claims is easier to wield than a sword in Henry IV. Since such activities are rare in Pall Mall, the ruffians fled at this resistance rather than face capture by the police. Sutton says he will not divert from M.H.'s strict schedule, but he thinks that a policeman or two, in anticipation of other mischief, would be a prudent addition to the street when he is about. I have passed on this request to the proper authorities, and I am informed that it will be done.

I had only an hour to spend with Mother this evening, and I am not certain she was aware I was with her. I spoke to her, making the assumption that if she could hear me at all, she would welcome my voice in these last days. I did what I could to assuage any fears she may have, and promised her that she would be in the care of God and His angels, for all the good, selfless things she has done in her life, and the many kindnesses she has offered to so many. The arrangements for her burial are now all but complete, for which I am truly grateful.

Chapter Twenty-four

I AWOKE SHORTLY after dawn as if emerging from a vast field of feathers. Whatever was in that little bottle had surely worked its magic on me, for I felt as close to refreshed as I had at any time since I began this devilish mission.

I dressed quickly and went to the washroom to shave. My face had reached the purple-and-mulberry stage, like a canvas by Cezanne; my single visible eye shone out of a livid cave of swollen flesh. The cut had swollen as well, and the stitches looked like puckers, or postholes for minute fences. I used my razor with care, handling my skin gingerly, for it was unusually tender.

By the time I went into the private car on my way to arrange for breakfast, I was feeling well enough to be embarrassed by my general appearance. I tapped on the door of Mycroft Holmes's car, identifying myself before operating the latch.

"Good morning, Guthrie," he called out in good humor. "We reach Karlsruhe in two and a half hours."

"Where we change trains," I said, not relishing the transfer of all MacMillian's belongings to the next compartments.

"And continue on to Mainz," said Holmes, adding with stern amusement, "with new guards. Guards who have been properly vetted."

I sighed. "What do you require of me in the meantime?"

"Why, hardly anything at all, dear boy, but that you tend to MacMillian and make yourself ready for changing trains."

It was difficult to believe him, and as I went to order breakfast, I could feel my muscles grow tense in anticipation of trouble.

But the time to Karlsruhe passed easily enough, and when we reached the station, we were met by an escort of uniformed officers who saw to our transfer speedily and with a deference that pleased MacMillian greatly. They also carried sealed orders that rerouted us through Strasbourg and Metz, with a stern warning that word had come from Mainz that assassins were waiting for us there, and as a result we were to stay away from the place and leave German-controlled territory as soon as possible.

This news gave me a qualm, for I could not envision how Mycroft Holmes would adapt himself to this abrupt change. But I had the greatest respect for his resourcefulness, and I doubted that any machination now could throw him off the scent. Who knows? I thought, this change may well have been at his instigation. And there were the guards, a total of four given the duty to protect MacMillian. Two remained with us, one at either end of the car, arms at their sides. The other two were put in the compartments flanking MacMillian's. I was not able to see how Mycroft Holmes achieved his transfer to this train, but I was certain he had, and that he was riding, probably in another disguise, somewhere aboard.

We were under way in good time, and passed through

the whole day and the splendid German countryside of the Rhine Valley, with its well-ordered farms and rolling pastureland now dark from the end-of-harvest plowing, in an uneventful fashion except for the lowering clouds which promised rain during the night. Rain was an inconvenience, and given what I had endured in the last week, I felt that if this was the worst that could be offered, I would be glad of it. I had begun to lose my sense of imminent danger, and gain in its place a vague, ill-defined apprehension which was more difficult to banish for being diffuse in nature. But the afternoon went on, mile after mile, with little to suggest that my anxiety was well founded. I began to hope that we had at last won free of our enemies and that all I would have to contend with would be bad dreams. We would shortly be out of Germany and into the rolling hills of France. So tranquil was our day that by evening, MacMillian was growing restive again, needing excitement and distinction, and was casting about for ways to bring attention to himself.

"I want to dine in the lounge car," MacMillian announced when I asked him what I should order for his supper.

"Do you think that is wise, sir?" I inquired, knowing full well it was folly.

"I think I am about to die of boredom here, and that if I do not move about I will run mad. In fact, I would *enjoy* running mad." He stretched, and nodded toward the magnificent river valley through which we were traveling, his expression far from admiring. "I can only endure so much of this, and then I want to burn fields, for variety."

It was tempting to upbraid him for this notion, to point out that his guards were useless here if he went to the lounge car. I began to think it was the drink in the lounge car he sought more than the food or the company of his fellow men. "You have to think about the trouble in Munich. It would be prudent to remain where you are, I think. I could bring you schnapps or brandy, sir, if you would like it."

"I want to see other men," he declared, and added with a lascivious wink, "since I cannot have women here."

"But—" I protested.

"Arrange it, Jeffries. That is what I pay you for." He would not tolerate more opposition.

"I will speak with your guards, sir," I said, stifling an urge to castigate this prideful fellow for his vainglorious hunger for the envy of others.

"Very good," MacMillian approved, rubbing his hands together as if he were embarked on a high treat. "I will want two of them to accompany me to the lounge car. The other two will have to keep watch here. Over my things. They will all have to take their meals later, after I retire for the night." This last provided him the greatest satisfaction, as if in depriving them, he gained something for himself that was more pleasing than an end to his hunger.

"I will so inform them," I told him, not looking forward to the response the men would offer.

Nor was I disappointed. "I and Corporal Hirsh will take the duty," said Corporal Pfosten. "We will see that this courier is protected, in spite of himself." His bearing was so correct that it was a wonder his spine did not crack.

"I will inform him," I told Corporal Pfosten.

"And if you will allow, sir, I will now go to the lounge car and make appropriate arrangements for you."

"Very good," MacMillian declared once more. "Get about it, Jeffries. I am about to succumb to ennui."

"Certainly." I set off with the hope that a high-ranking member of the railroad staff would forbid this reckless arrangement, making it possible to avoid the whole absurd coil. I had reckoned without the German wish to accommodate superiors. I tried to alert the Germans to the trouble that might result—expressed as my own worry for MacMillian—only to be promised that the English Herr's requirements would be met. In forty minutes it had been agreed that there would be a place for MacMillian in the lounge car in half an hour. I returned to report this, making every effort to conceal my frustration and dismay. MacMillian was determined to put himself in the way of trouble and I was in no position to prevent this. Worse still, I was none the wiser as to where my true employer had secreted himself this time.

"I will want my dinner jacket, of course. Do get it out, Jeffries. It is in the closet." MacMillian was mightily pleased with himself, and intended to make the most of this opportunity. "For we will sleep in Strasbourg tonight, and then we will truly speed to our destination tomorrow. It is almost over, Jeffries. And then you may be about your business, assuming we do not strike a bargain between us. You will have to take care to watch my baggage tonight while I . . ." He finished with a flourish of his hand. By which, I was certain, he wanted to take advantage of this chance to be noticed. "Be certain all my things are ready to be carried from the train upon our arrival. And do not suppose you will be allowed to be lax at your post, Jeffries."

I aided him to dress for his supper, and all the while I kept my senses alert for anything that would portend trouble. The worst of it was that after so much upheaval and danger in the last few days, everything had the capacity to alarm me. When ten nerve-wracking minutes had ticked by, accompanied by two sharp reprimands from MacMillian, I tried the opposite tack, shutting out the tweaks and niggles that made me suspect I was still in a nest of Brotherhood members in the same way a man may fall into a nest of vipers. With no opportunity to seek out, or even to identify Mycroft Holmes, I felt truly at sea again.

Corporals Hirsh and Pfosten were waiting when MacMillian left the compartment at last. Pfosten took the lead and Hirsh brought up the rear of their little escort as they bore MacMillian off to eat in the lounge car, the two corporals as stiff as soldiers in a toybox.

I put MacMillian's compartment back in order, obeying his instructions to make all ready for departing the train. I made sure all his things were packed away with as much care as I could bring to the work. I took every precaution in my handling of his things in case some new deviltry had been recently concealed there. I could not say what I suspected—a dart tipped with a rare poison, perhaps, as the dart that struck my attacker in Luxembourg must have been, or a spider with a deadly bite—but I had no wish to find it by accident.

When I had completed my tasks, I went to my compartment, and for the rest of the evening, I made notes for Mycroft Holmes and reviewed the information in the notebooks I had carried in my carpetbag, and dressed the welt on my forehead once more. It was developing a yellowish-green undertinge, with the purple parts fading to a slate-blue. At least Elizabeth could not see me. Just the thought of my fiancée made me suddenly long for England and safety.

All the while as I went about these mundane chores, I tried to convince myself that no one was watching me, or MacMillian, now that we were bound out of Germany by this new path. We crossed the Rhine before ten in the evening, arriving at the station shortly thereafter. From there we were taken to the second-best hotel in Strasbourg for the night. My room was two doors down the hall from MacMillian's, an arrangement I could not like, but knew better than to protest while the guards were with us.

The next morning I woke with the true beginnings of optimism in my heart and the first real appetite I had had since Luxembourg, which I lost almost at once when I recalled all those warning tales which spoke of foolish adventurers who allowed themselves to relax their vigilance before they were completely beyond reach of harm, and paid for this indulgence tenfold. I poked at my food with my fork and tried to rekindle my relish without success.

Such glum thoughts did not possess MacMillian, who declared that he had passed a capital evening with the other men in the lounge and had made a gentlemanly amount of money over two rubbers of whist. He was glad to be on solid ground, if only for a few hours more. "For once we reach Metz, we will be as good as on English soil," said MacMillian confidently.

"I hope it may be true, sir," I said, and began to stack his cases, chests, and trunks, in preparation for our departure to the train station. I could not banish the realization that on English soil there was Vickers, who had started me on my way here.

"I've always liked Strasbourg," said MacMillian as he gazed out the window. "It is so . . . European. Not at all like England or Scotland." He indicated the heavy clouds. "More rain today. It could slow down the train." His annoyance at this inconvenience was apparent in the downward turn of his mouth.

"So it would appear, sir," I responded, trying not to look at the sky.

"Our guards should be waiting by now," he said a bit later, with a faint sigh.

"They are a wise precaution, sir," I said, trying to sound unconcerned, for I was in the grip of a growing apprehension that boded ill. In vain I told myself it was only the distress of the last week that made me feel so vulnerable with no obvious reason.

"Did you sleep well, Jeffries?" asked MacMillian, a note of complaint in his voice, as if my passing a poor night would necessarily impinge upon him. "You do not have any cheer about you this morning. Perhaps that cut on your forehead is troubling you again. While we are in Strasbourg you may want to have a physician look at it, in case there is an infection."

"I slept well enough," I replied, fingering the cut as I spoke. It was starting to heal and it itched. "And my wound is improving."

"Gives you a reprobate air, no doubt of it," said MacMillian in disapproval. "Still, you got it honorably, I suppose. That bullet could have done far worse than strike you."

"Yes, indeed, sir," I said, recalling how near it came to Mycroft Holmes.

MacMillian is unaware of my meaning, but favored me with a complacent expression of his own superiority. "It is good that you realize these things, Jeffries. It bodes well for your continued employment."

I could not bring myself to thank him, but I bowed, rather stiffly, and went to look over the baggage that must be carried to the train station this morning in order to have it aboard the train for Metz, which departed at ten-forty-five and was supposed to arrive ten hours later at our destination. We had been assured by Corporal Hirsh that another guarded compartment was reserved for MacMillian's use, and that there would be no other occupants of the car but MacMillian, the guards, and me.

There was a charabanc drawn up at the front of the hotel drawn by two big, square-bodied Hannovarians, their coats fuzzy in anticipation of winter's cold. The coachman was much like his horses, a massive fellow, big-shouldered and tall, with a bad limp and a slouch hat pulled down low over a scarred visage. He spoke a fast and ferocious mixture of French and German in a guttural roar which gave me a moment's dismay until I sorted out his dialect while he lugged the baggage onto his vehicle, securing it in place with a number of wide straps. "That fop of a foreigner get you here, and quickly," he ordered, or so the instructions sounded to me.

"It seems he has been assigned to you," I told MacMillian as I held his coat for him. "He will travel on the train with us, and will give us transport from Ghent to our ship." I shrugged at this arrangement. "He says he has done work of this sort before. At least, I think he has, for I am hard-put to understand him when he speaks quickly, his patois is so—"

"All peasants speak in that way," MacMillian informed

me, dismissing the matter. "Probably an old soldier, if what you say about his face is accurate. Someone they've kept on in service because he might otherwise starve." He made a swipe with his hand to banish the matter from his mind. "Well, come, then. We must continue the mission."

"Certainly," I said, as I opened the hotel doors for MacMillian and followed him down the few broad steps to the waiting charabanc. I held the panel open for him, then climbed up, taking the backward-facing seat.

The coachman, already on the box, saluted us with his whip before he gave his team the office. The carriage was well sprung and the coachman was very skilled. As a result there was little sway in our passage through the streets to the train station. It was a quiet day, with few people abroad. At the train station the porters were ready for our arrival and went to work at once. Our car had been set apart, and the guards took up their posts immediately once we boarded the train, having arrived at the station well in advance of MacMillian and me. With the determined aid of the coachman, the luggage was shifted to the train in rapid order, and shortly thereafter we were under way for Metz.

FROM THE PERSONAL JOURNAL OF PHILIP TYERS: *M.H. is still with G. and MacMillian, but his telegram of this morning expresses some fear that the travel changes may not be enough to keep the Brotherhood from attempting to ruin all that the treaty seeks to achieve. M.H. has identified two spies aboard the train MacMillian and G. rode yesterday and is afraid that there will be more today, for the nearer MacMillian gets to England, the more determined the Brotherhood will be that he shall not arrive. If it would not draw more attention than any of them want to the mission, he would order the Mercury train to Metz, to carry them all to the coast as quickly as possible. But a fast-traveling train presents an impressive moving target, and for the time being, he is convinced the Brotherhood would rather not draw much attention to their activities. He states that MacMillian is proving to be a greater liability than he had supposed at first, and therefore he is going to remain with G. and MacMillian all the way to England, in whatever persona seems most useful for the task. He asks me to offer his congratulations to Edmund Sutton, for he believes that G. has not yet recognized him in his current guise, which has given him a great deal of amusement.*

Early this morning another missive came from Miss Roedale for G. It would appear that she is deeply displeased with what she considers his thoughtless neglect in staying away without any word to her for a week. It is her intention to deliver an ultimatum to G. upon his return regarding what she believes is an unreliable factor in his character of which she was not previously aware. She is afraid this may mean that their married life would be irregular as well, which does not please her. I have not violated her confidence in stating these things, for she sent the note unsealed with instructions that M.H. was to be made aware of its contents as well as G., so that he could see for himself how his demands have compromised G.'s hopes of happiness.

I have obtained the information M.H. has requested in regard to Brotherhood centers in France, including those private holdings of members which have been used by the Brotherhood, and have had it wired to him. I trust he received it before he had to leave. I will send a duplicate copy to Metz, so that he will have it in hand should he not receive the information at Strasbourg.

I must go to hospital shortly. Edmund Sutton has offered to remain at the flat all through the morning, although he often has his own time in the morning for tending to his own affairs. He leaves in the clothing of a rag-and-bone man, and returns a few hours later all rigged out as a sailor. I am astonished at how complete a transformation he achieves, for even I, who have known him for years, do not recognize him at once. In my current situation he is willing to give up his time for himself to enable me to be with Mother. Say what you will, actors are not without compassion for those in trouble, as I have discovered these last few days. I had not realized how much sympathy he has for those as unfortunate as Mother is.

It is my hope that I will soon have further word from M.H. in Germany. These delays and silences are the very devil to endure.

Chapter Twenty-five

By NOON THE rain was falling in steady sheets, taking most of the light out of the day and turning the world a monochrome sepia shade of ill-defined shapes beyond the streaming windows. The train had slowed to half its usual speed and its headlight shone as much as warning as to light the way ahead. Though the countryside in this region was not generally difficult terrain, it was hilly and there was always the chance of slides blocking the way in such weather and the engineer was not willing to risk an accident, for which sensible precaution I could heartily have cursed him.

"What sort of cowardly fellow is he, to delay us in this way?" MacMillian demanded as he checked his watch for the fifth time in the hour. Boredom had long since made him surly, and he had consumed more brandy than was prudent. With the windows steamed up, he had wiped half a dozen circles on the glass but could not find a view to suit his purposes. "We will miss our connection to Liège, and then what will we do?"

"The engineer has the safety of his passengers at heart," I answered rather more curtly than I should have.

"Don't be insolent with me, Jeffries," warned MacMillian. "I can still end your employment if you displease me. Remarks like that one do displease me." He rocked back in his settee as far as it was hinged to go. "If only this infernal rain would stop. We might make up for some of the time we have lost."

"We might," I agreed in the best sycophantic manner I could summon up. "And then it should be no later than midnight when we reach Metz." My problem with feeling safe, I had decided, originated with the ill-at-ease feeling that possessed me when I added a *von* to the city ahead, and recalled that this region had been changing hands between France and Germany for more than a thousand years. Von Metz was undoubtedly German, and just as undoubtedly, the territory from which he took his name was now part of France, a prospect that ended any small degree of comfort I could take from our current location.

"Let us hope so," said MacMillian, soothed by my deferential attitude.

I shared his concern about the slowness of our progress and reminded myself that it was of necessity having the same effect on our pursuers. Assuming, my thoughts continued in an unwelcome manner, that they were, in fact, behind us and not waiting in ambush up ahead, in which case they might well be as restive as we were.

My fears proved prophetic. About two in the afternoon as we were crossing over a series of rills and freshets made into brooks by the rain, the train gave a lurch, then its brakes shrieked, the whistle howling in alarm. There was a loud, metallic scream echoed almost at once by human ones as the first of the cars buckled free of the track, and the two behind, including the car in which MacMillian and I were riding, canted and sagged away from their rails, to lean against the hill as if taken with a sudden severe cramp.

MacMillian swore heartily, struggling to get to his feet, thrashing about in his effort.

"Sir," I said as I sat up gingerly. "It might be better to move more carefully. We do not know how precariously we are balanced." Though I doubted even his most forceful activities could cause serious damage to us now, the notion of him blundering about in the car, where our armed guards were most certainly taking every measure to protect us, filled me with apprehension. Having escaped assassins, I had no wish to be shot by those assigned to keep me safe.

"But—" protested MacMillian, only to have this drowned out by what sounded like an explosion ahead of the train.

Now I moved quickly, making my way on the leaning wall to where the door yawned over the slope beyond the tracks. In fair weather it would be an easy drop to the ground, but not now. Taking what measures I could to minimize my risk, I dropped out of the car, and pulled myself to my feet quickly, brushing mud and fine gravel from my hands as I did. The rain was everywhere; it quickly soaked through my coat to my skin and drained what little warmth I had been able to preserve for myself from me.

Ahead I saw the two conductors and their assistants walking along the side of the derailed cars, shaking their heads and gesticulating. Behind a small number of the passengers were emerging from the cars that were still on the tracks, many of them dazed, a few clearly upset.

We would not be reaching Metz tonight, not even by midnight. Another unwelcome thought intruded on this unhappy reverie—if another train were expected along behind us, it could be on top of us before it could safely stop, and then there would be a true disaster. I began to think I should warn someone of this possibility—which seemed the more likely to me because I supposed I was still being pursued—when I saw one of the two conduc-

tors take a lantern in his hand and begin to trudge down
the length of the train. I hoped this meant he would continue on to some siding where a warning could properly
be posted. Two of the assistants were preparing to assess
the damage, tugging on oilcloth coats and taking lanterns
and crowbars to help them in their work.

A short, burly fellow came rushing by me from one of
the cars behind me, calling out loudly that he was a physician and was volunteering his services. He held a leather
bag in one hand and clapped his hat to his head with the
other. I swung around again to look behind me, and
noticed that more people had left the train and were
beginning to mill about in the wet.

One of the guards came out of the car, moving with
exaggerated care. "What now, sir?"

"You ask me?" I wondered aloud. As I recalled, his
name was Dieterich. "What does MacMillian tell you?"

The guard—Dieterich?—laughed once without any
amusement. "He tells us to put the engine back on the
tracks, set the cars to rights and get us moving."

"Of course," I said, still not sure why this fellow should
come to me instead.

"They told us you were to be consulted in an emergency," said the guard in a lowered voice. "This appears
to be an emergency. So—"

"Yes, it does appear to be one," I agreed slowly, wondering where the guards had been given their orders, and
by whom.

Ahead, the physician began to bustle back down the
line of cars, stopping first at the one in advance of
MacMillian's, calling out if any of the baggage-handlers
had been hurt.

"Nothing but cuts and bruises," came the unconcerned
answer. "Worst of all is the mess."

The physician went on, arriving at MacMillian's car
next. He glanced at me. "Is there anyone else in there?"

"Yes," I said. "Three guards and a Scottish nobleman."

The physician nodded portentously, and declared, "I

must see how they are. You seem to have been injured yourself, sir."

"Two days ago," I said. "The Scotsman is in a terrible temper," I added, thinking it only fair to warn him.

"I will strive to keep that in mind," he said as he began to climb up the leaning car toward the door to the interior, his bag clutched tightly in his hand.

"So, sir," the guard said when the physician was gone into the train, "how does it strike you? An accident or something more?"

I had no answer for him beyond remarking, "Whichever it is, we are in as much of a pickle for one as for the other."

"True enough," he agreed, and took up his place underneath the door into which the physician had just vanished.

We were to the west of Sarrebourg, at the edge of the area called Étang de Lindre, where a number of large ponds turned marshy in winter. Our next station was Bénestroff, some considerable distance ahead—I assumed it was a good eight miles; Sarrebourg was perhaps a mile farther than that behind us. At this time of year and in such weather, few would be willing to walk to either place, especially so late in the afternoon.

I approached the knot of men gathering around the engineer, who held his shaking hand to his forehead. "I don't know," he said. "It was as if there was an explosion. Water can do that sometimes, build up behind some impediment, and then blast free, but . . ." He stared at the way this engine straddled the tracks. "I would have sworn there was an explosion."

"But who would be blasting here, at this time of day, and in such weather?" asked one of the passengers in Dutch-accented French.

"I don't know. We're warned about such things," said the engineer, his dazed voice sounding as if he were a child. "Someone will have to be told."

I knew I must not leave MacMillian, especially if the engineer proved right, and it was learned there had been an explosion that put the train off its rails. I felt I had to make some recommendation. "If anyone goes, let it be two men together, in case of any mishap."

"That's a sensible notion," seconded the senior conductor. "Yes, two men, walking together, in each direction. That should take care of us." His elaborate moustaches drooped and dripped. "There's also the Canal. We might find barges on it where word could be taken to the next lock."

"With night coming on, is that likely?" asked one of the firemen. "They tie up for the night, those bargemen." He gave a very French shrug. "And why should they help us, anyway? Besides, the Canal is farther away than Sarrebourg. We would reach the town first."

"Is anyone hurt?" I asked, feeling shamed that it had taken so long for such a consideration to gain my attention.

"Nothing worse than a broken arm, as far as I know," said the senior conductor. "The physician should be able to tell us something more shortly."

I nodded once and hunched to turn my collar up. It did little but keep the worst of the rain off my neck, though it quickly soaked through. As I did this, I noticed out of the corner of my uncovered eye the coachman emerging from the next-to-last car where his carriage and horses were held. "Wait!" I called out, vexed that it should have taken so long for me to remember this. Over my shoulder, I said to the rest around the engineer, "He has horses. He can ride back along the tracks for us, or ahead, for that matter."

The senior conductor slapped himself on the cap. "He's right. How can I have forgotten? Yes, there are the two horses and the carriage." He stopped and gave me a suspicious look. "Do you think your employer will permit us to commandeer them?"

"If he wants to reach Metz, he will," I said with purpose. "Let me deal with him."

The engineer moaned and swayed on his feet, but when

eager hands reached out to steady him, he brushed them away. "I will be better shortly," he informed us with all his dignity intact.

"Very good," said the senior conductor, who was not at all convinced. He motioned me aside and said, "It's not my place to tell you your work, but it would probably be best to give the coachman his orders before speaking to your master. Just to hurry things along."

I nodded twice at this suggestion. "Very sensible of you." I had not thought of being quite so audacious, but under the circumstances, I reckoned it was the wisest thing I could do.

"Men like him don't always grasp the problems quickly," added the senior conductor, and managed to look encouraging.

"No, they don't," I said, and squared my sodden shoulders before going in search of the coachman when one of the private guards—not Dieterich—assigned to protect MacMillian came up behind me and tapped my arm.

"Begging your pardon, sir," he said quietly, "but the doctor says you'd best come quickly."

I faltered, but only for an instant. As soon as I ascertained what the physician wanted, I would deal with the coachman. "What's the matter?" I asked as I set myself to accompany him back to the car.

"He didn't tell me. Just said he had to talk to you at once." The guard, I noticed, had a bruise on his jaw and a tear on the sleeve of his tunic.

"All right," I said, and added, "Has the physician seen to you?"

The guard looked startled, then laughed a little. "Why, thank you, sir, we get worse in drill. This is . . . nothing." He nodded along the track to where Dieterich was helping construct a makeshift shelter toward the rear of the train. "I'm going to give them a hand. There's still two of us to look after the Scotsman, and heaven knows no one is getting away from here at any time soon."

I gestured a resigned acceptance of this necessary-but-unwelcome fate, and as I did, I thought I heard the sound of a scuffle. At any case, I looked up the hill, and blinked as the rain sluiced into my eye and around my patch, and though I could see nothing, I was more certain than ever that something untoward was going on not twenty paces up the slope.

"There," the guard explained, pointing out a group of men struggling to bear a broken tree branch down to the shelter. "For a fire. We will want a signal as much as the means to keep warm."

"An excellent notion. We'll need it before it gets much later," I said with feeling. Damning though it may be for a man of my heritage to say it, but there are few things I dislike more than being cold and wet. "Are the ovens still working in the kitchen?"

"I understand that they are, which is fortunate," said the guard, and paused near the entry to MacMillian's car. "If you like, I'll give you a leg up, sir?"

"That won't be necessary," I answered, hardly paying any attention to him now. I was concentrating on securing a grip on the hand-rail so that I could swing myself aboard. I had just scrambled to my feet on the canted floor when I saw that the physician was bending over MacMillian, who lay sprawled in the corridor.

"He lost his footing," said the physician, one hand on MacMillian's wrist as if to check his pulse. "I'm afraid he struck his head. He's bleeding." He indicated the mat of carmined hair just above the temple.

"Call the other guards. They will help you," I responded at once, trying to make my way toward them without mishap.

"They are busy," said the physician, taking something from his bag, a small object like a leather-covered egg. "If you will lend me your support?" He motioned me to his side.

As I bent over MacMillian, I saw something embossed or branded on the bag the physician carried—an Egyptian eye. I could not believe it and was about to demand to know what the fellow was doing with such a mark when I felt two strong arms seize me from behind.

In the next instant the side of my skull erupted and I heard more than felt myself fall into darkness.

FROM THE PERSONAL JOURNAL OF PHILIP TYERS:
It has been an endless day, with no further word from Germany, but to confirm that M.H. and G. have not yet arrived at Metz, and that the train they were on is missing. That is the word they have used: missing. As if somehow the train has abandoned the tracks and gone careering off over the countryside to places unknown. A second telegram confirmed that the train has not arrived at the stations where it was expected, nor have there been any accounts of it on subsidiary lines. The railroad authorities fear there may have been a blockage on the tracks, or, worse still, a derailment, all of which will take time to locate and repair, given the inclement weather and the late hour of the day.

To add to these festivities, I have this evening sustained an irate visit from Inspector Cornell, who has threatened to compel M.H. to testify in regard to what he knows in the case of the murdered young woman, for the circumstances of her death continue to trouble him. He is determined to question Vickers as well. I have sent word around to the Admiralty to request they provide a few more days' delay so that M.H. may be located. Willing though he is to impersonate M.H., Edmund Sutton draws the line at misleading the law.

I will not return from hospital tonight until quite late, by which time I hope there will be news from the Continent more welcome than any I have had of late.

Chapter Twenty-six

THE FIRST THING I saw as my wits came back to me was the coachman bending over me, the rain forming a peculiar halo, provided by the lantern, around his slouch hat. The next thing I felt was a raging headache above my left ear. I half-sat, wincing as I did and pressing my hand to my head in the process. "What happened?"

"You were coshed," said Mycroft Holmes, keeping his voice low. "About twenty minutes ago, judging by what we've been able to piece together. Quite a competent job of it, too. Enough to knock you out, but not enough to put you into a long stupor." He shoved himself to his feet and went on in the loud, puzzling mix of languages he had assumed for this disguise. "The Scotsman by criminals has been taken away."

I did my best to rise, taking care to steady myself as the world went fuzzy around me. When I was certain I would not stumble, I took a tentative step back toward the car where MacMillian had been riding.

"I wouldn't do that, dear boy," said Holmes quietly, coming to my side again. "There's a bomb inside."

"A bomb?" I repeated, thinking I must have misunderstood the word. My hands were shaking, and it took me several seconds to identify this as fright.

"It would appear so," said my employer in a dry undertone. "If you are well enough feeling, good sir," he went on in his dreadful Alcasian growl, "you to your feet I will help get. Be to take care that you fall not."

"Thank you," I said, first in French and then in German. My legs were as uncertain as a newborn foal's, but I managed to keep atop them.

Mycroft Holmes turned to those gathered around us, straightened to his full height and addressed them in German so impressive that it would pass muster with von Bismarck himself. And probably had, I added inwardly as I listened. "Good people, you are the unfortunate victims of enemies of all the European states. You have had to take the brunt of the assault of an organization sworn to disrupt the carefully negotiated affairs of these countries. They have made attempts on the lives of the Scotsman and his servant before. This time they have succeeded in taking the Scotsman, as you know, and it is now imperative that his servant and I follow after them. Did anyone see which way they went?"

There was a confusing chorus of contradictory answers.

"Please," said Holmes in his impeccable German. "It will only help us if you are able to give accurate information. Think very carefully before you answer. If we chase after shadows, these villains may yet triumph. So. You." He pointed to Dieterich. "What did you observe?"

The guard straightened, and I noticed two bruises on his face that had not been there before. "Well, I noticed a commotion up the slope from us, and I saw that there were three or four men on horseback, with three more horses on leads. They came as far as the cover of the trees and the angle of the slope would permit them to, and when one of the men gathering wood attempted to hail them, asking for help, he . . . he was shot."

"You all agree that was the start of it?" Holmes asked, and waited for a few minor contradictions—there were four men and eight horses. No, there were eight men and nine horses. No, all the horses were mounted.

"All right. Men came on horseback to a place where they clearly anticipated finding someone." He held up his gloved hand and ticked off this information. "Who saw what happened at this car?" he went on, indicating the car in which MacMillian, I, and our guards had ridden.

"I think someone dropped a case out of that door," said one of the men, with less certainty. "There was a piece of luggage, that I do remember."

"And the Scotsman," added the senior conductor. "He was taken out by the physician. Draped him over his shoulder like a sack of meal and went off with him, that guard bringing the luggage behind him." He looked very pleased with himself for giving so complete a report. Now, I thought as my eye became more accustomed to the waning light, if only it is accurate.

"Very good," said Mycroft Holmes. "Can you describe the luggage?"

The senior conductor screwed up his face and scowled. "It was a good-sized leather one, about as large as a nightstand, possibly a little smaller." He looked at me. "You know which it is?"

I had already feared the worst, but this served to confirm my most hellish nightmares. "I know," I said heavily as the full weight of my failure came near to overwhelming me.

"The contents are important?" Holmes asked me in German.

"Crucial," I answered in the same tongue. "My employer will not forgive this lapse, I fear."

"Your employer," came the answer, still in German, "knows that you have done everything you could to protect him and his mission. He will not be harsh in his judgment of you as you are of yourself."

"Possibly," I said, sensing that in Mycroft Holmes's perceptions the game was not over yet. "What are we to do?"

"There is no point waiting around to be rescued. The railroad will manage all that. We, Jeffries, are going to take the coach horses and ride after the abductors." He said this in German and heard the protests from the people gathered on the track. "Do not worry, good citizens," he soothed them. "When a train bearing such an important personage as the Scotsman is traveling, it is monitored very closely. We know that help is coming, but we must take action now, to prevent the worst from happening. The search for the train has begun, but we cannot wait for—"

"But what about the rain?" asked one of the cooks.

"They will first discover when we passed through Sarrebourg and then will realize we are too late. A handcar or tie-testing engine will have been sent out at least half an hour ago. Help should be arriving shortly."

"Are you certain?" asked the engineer, who was huddled near one of two smoking fires.

"I have it on the authority of the governments in Bruxelles, Paris, and Berlin." He straightened up. "Dieterich, select one or two men to go with you and start back along the tracks, carrying torches, so that those coming will see you. And you." He pointed to the other two guards, both of whom looked very hangdog. "Do the same going up the track toward Bénestroff. It will protect us all."

"How did Dieterich get those bruises?" I whispered to Holmes as the men began to obey his orders.

"The . . . physician struck him when he tried to stop them carrying off MacMillian. He acquitted himself very well, did Dieterich." He glanced around, as if he feared new disruptions. "Are you fit to ride? It will have to be bareback and with coaching tack for bridles. Cut the reins so that they will be of riding, not carriage length."

The very thought of being on horseback made me queasy, but I nodded. "Yes. I will manage."

Mycroft Holmes gave me a quick smile. "Stout fellow, Guthrie. We're almost to the end of this, I promise you."

All I could do was nod, which made the world swim a little before my single eye. "May I at least take this infernal thing off?" By which I meant the eyepatch.

"When we're away from here, yes. We'll both need all the eyes we can get then." He glanced over his shoulder and resumed his upper-class-military German speech and deportment. "Have the horses bridled and brought out. We will need two lanterns. We will take them from the car with the horses, do not fear. And we will have to rely on all of you to give a full and accurate account to those men who come to find you."

There was a flurry of activity as three of the baggage handlers went to prepare the horses for us.

By the time the two big Hannovarians were led out, one of the men who had started down the track with Dieterich was running back, shouting that a train was coming, and would be here in fifteen minutes.

With the help of an undercook, my carpetbag had been retrieved from the train and was now sitting in the shelter of the next car.

"Tell them about the bomb in the Scotsman's car," Mycroft Holmes reminded them in his Berlin best. "It is with the rest of the luggage, in an oilskin bag. You do not want a tragedy now that we have overcome so much." He looked up at the gelding being led to him. He noticed the horse was mincing, performing little *piaffes* in his eagerness. "That had better be spirit instead of nerves, old fellow, or a loose shoe; it won't do to have you go lame on me tonight, or to toss me in a ditch at the first sign of trouble," he warned the animal as he gathered up the reins, took a handful of mane and vaulted onto the tall, broad back. He was in scale with the horse, tall and big of bone and frame, with weight enough to keep the animal in check. He secured his seat with his lower legs, which was possible only because he was so tall. I knew I, slighter and shorter, would not fare so well.

With my head still aching, I knew it would be stupid of me to attempt to get aboard in the same way. I settled for a leg up, provided by the senior conductor, who then handed us the lanterns Holmes had requested.

"We will climb the slope and head to the west, I think," said Holmes as we moved away from the train.

"What you told them about rescuing trains—was that true?" I asked as I at last flung away my eyepatch.

"Yes, as a matter of fact, it was. Though there is also a train from Selestat to Saarbrücken due through here at seven tonight." He pulled in his brown Hannovarian—who, like all brown horses, looked black except on the belly and around the mouth—and signaled me to do the same. "Listen."

From down the slope and some distance away I could hear the urgent whoop of a train whistle. "That's a good thing, given all the passengers went through."

"Guthrie, dear boy, those passengers will dine out on this story for the next four years at least, or I know nothing about the human love of adventure," said Mycroft Holmes in the same manner as he would speaking across the table at breakfast. "One of the misfortunes of our sort of work is that we are not allowed to talk about it. If we were, every hostess from New York to Buda-Pest would be after us, and we should never have any time to do our work." He chuckled as he started his horse moving again, and now his attention was fixed on the ground, the beam of the lantern searching out the telltale signs of recent travel.

At last there was a mass of recent hoofprints in the damp ground. They picked up a narrow trail leading off to the west.

"I think I know where they're bound," said Mycroft Holmes about an hour later. It was full dark now, and though the rain had slacked off, the wind was sharper and I felt stiff with cold; my legs and back ached from hold-

ing the Hannovarian with my knees and calves and my
head thrummed when I moved. "We will reach the town
of Dieuze in another two hours. We can spend the night
there. The horses will need rest and you and I, Guthrie,
will have to thaw out, have a good meal, and let Tyers
know that all is not lost."

"It isn't?" I asked quietly.

"No, Guthrie. For I have obtained one significant piece
of information that will help us, since the Brotherhood
are not aware I know this." He indicated the path between
the ponds ahead. "Stay on this and we will reach Dieuze.
Take the north fork when we reach it."

"North fork?" I asked, baffled. From where I was, I
could see only the single, narrow path stretching away
into the darkness between the lakes. The weight of my
carpetbag was immense and growing with every passing
minute. Were it not for the notebooks it contained, I
would have been tempted to abandon it along the trail,
but could not bring myself to commit such an irresponsi-
ble act.

"The track splits at the head of one of these ponds. The
south fork goes off to the village of Heming, back toward
Sarrebourg." He recited this easily, with the familiarity
that often meant long acquaintance with the region.

I shook my head, too tired to question how he came by
all this information. But I could not keep from asking,
"What is the one thing you have learned that the
Brotherhood is unaware of?"

He looked intensely pleased with himself, though the
upward-flaring light of the lantern gave his face a certain
demonic cast. "I know where von Metz's château is. I discovered it by accident three years ago, when I chanced
upon some coded records of the Brotherhood which
revealed a number of their holdings. Thanks to what we
learned then, four of their strongholds in Austria and the
Bohemian region have fallen. But those in France, Italy,
and Germany are untouched. This knowledge is my one
advantage at the moment, and I must use it while I may."

He indicated the hoof marks on the track ahead of us. "And by the looks of this, so do they. That is why I want us to stop at Dieuze, so that we will be as fresh as they will be when we encounter them tomorrow."

How had he managed, I wondered, to obtain this coded record? And what had the cost of it been? I wanted to put these questions to him, but I felt too cold and miserable to shape the words. I also had to confess that I dreaded what the answer might be. I let my mount pick his way after Holmes's, and tried to keep from imagining vast steaming bowls of stew with dumplings, which to me were now taking on the qualities of ambrosia.

It seemed to be eons later when we finally entered Dieuze and made our way between the stone houses to an inn at the north edge of the town with the promising sign: *Le Chat Pêcheur,* showing a smiling tabby pulling a fish from a stream. With the Canal and the Seille so near, the sight must not be an uncommon one, I thought as Mycroft Holmes called out for assistance.

A groggy ostler came rushing out in an oilskin to take our horses, and to inform us politely that Madame would be with us directly. If he thought two men arriving riding on carriage horses at ten at night was unusual, he made no indication of it, but accepted the reins as we slid off our mounts and led the horses off in the direction of the stable, promising them both warm mash and a rubdown before he left them.

"Now there is a capable groom," remarked Mycroft Holmes in approval as he strode up to the entrance of the inn and rapped hard twice, waited and rapped thrice more. When the door opened, he bowed and said in perfect French, "Good evening, Madame. We are sorry to present ourselves so late, but we are in need of rooms, as you can see." Then he held out a considerable amount of money, bowed again and said, "For the inconvenience we have caused, arriving hungry at this hour."

Madame was a middle-aged woman in a widow's cap and dark dress with a plover's body and a wry expression worked into her face from years of use. She took the money without mentioning it, and held her door open for us. "We are not so busy tonight, Monsieur, that you are at any disadvantage. There is a joint of lamb still in the kitchen, and a cheese pastry with onions. I can provide wine as well, if you like." She indicated her guest book and watched as Mycroft Holmes signed as E. Sutton of Bruxelles and London, and his valet, Josue.

"Josue?" I asked in a whisper.

"In case we should need to raze the walls of Jericho, dear boy," said Mycroft Holmes very quietly. "And now Madame . . ."

"Thillot," she supplied. "You are cold and hungry. While your rooms are being readied, come to the morning room, and I myself will tend to your supper. Leave the carpetbag. I will have the maid take it up."

I did not want to surrender it, but I knew that holding it would cause her to wonder about its contents and our activities. It would not be wise to do that. And at this hour, there would be few people likely to come to the inn and search my luggage with impunity. I saw a quick signal from Mycroft Holmes, and I complied, leaving the bag by the entry counter.

Madame Thillot smiled as she led the way to the back of the inn. "You are fortunate. I have only two rooms taken tonight. One is a young woman traveling to meet her family. The other is a gentleman whom I think is a military man, though he is not in uniform." She held the door to the morning room open, and at once apologized for the chill. She bustled over to the hearth and prodded the embers into a semblance of warmth, then put down two more short logs. "It will be warmer shortly."

"Very good," said Mycroft Holmes, at last shrugging out of his tremendous coachman's coat and removing his hat, which had long since lost any semblance of shape in the rain. He put these aside and chose one of the upholstered chairs. "We have been traveling a long time."

"Where did your carriage break down?" asked Madame Thillot. "I saw your horses. No saddles, and harness for driving, not for riding. I must assume your coach is in a ditch somewhere." The wry expression of her face became stronger.

"Very true, Madame Thillot," said Holmes. "In weather like this, what can one expect?"

"What, indeed?" asked Madame Thillot, and went off to bring us our supper. When she returned with a platter of lamb and brussels sprouts cooked in butter, Holmes thanked her profusely, and added, "Would you be willing to help me further? Is there a telegraph office in this town?"

"Yes," she said after a brief hesitation. "It is for those using the Canal."

"Would you be able to take a message for me to be telegraphed, first thing in the morning? I would give you the message in full and pay for it twice over." He was holding a sliver of lamb on his fork, waiting for her answer.

"For three times the amount, I will tend to it myself," she said at once. "Write your message and give it to me with the money."

"Thank you, Madame Thillot," he said. "When I have finished this excellent supper, you may be sure that I will." He paused again, then asked, "Would it be too much of an imposition to request a bath for my man and me when we are finished with our meal?"

She chuckled. "Not at all. In fact, had you not asked, I would have recommended one." Her nose wrinkled. "I do not mind the tang of honest sweat, but when there are machine odors, burning, and marsh-mud in the mix, it is no longer pleasing."

"My very thought," said Mycroft Holmes, cutting more of the lamb.

"I will arrange for water to be heated. You may have the first tub, and your man the second," said Madame Thillot as she left us to our meal.

*   *   *

FROM THE PERSONAL JOURNAL OF PHILIP TYERS:
At last there is word from M.H. It arrived with the milk-man this morning, and assures me that he and G. have almost reached their goal. He also tells me that MacMillian has been kidnapped, and adds that he supposes the kidnappers got more than they bargained for in their captive. He is going to get the man back, for he does not want the man to complain of the reward he has had for his service.

G. is slightly injured again but up to the task they must perform. M.H. informs me that it will be a day or two before they have concluded their work there, and then they will turn toward home. It will be good to have this mission completed, for it has been a precarious one from the start. M.H. claims that it keeps him in fighting trim to match wits with such lethal enemies.

I cannot but worry when M.H. takes on his jaunty tone, for in the past it has always meant great danger. If I do not hear from him by nine this evening, I will do as he instructs and warn the government of possible trouble.

Chapter Twenty-seven

IT WAS NOT the sunlight that had awakened me, I realized in the first seconds. I shook my head several times, trying to force the last dregs of sleep from my mind as I wondered what had startled me out of my dreams so abruptly.

"At last, Mister Guthrie," said a cool, feminine voice that banished the last of sleep.

I sat up, tugging the sheet and blanket with me—to have a woman discover me so improperly!—and saw at the foot of my bed the slim, pale figure of Penelope Gatspy, no longer dressed in mourning but rigged out in a riding habit of the first stare, and holding a Navy revolver pointed directly at my chest. I tried not to goggle, either at the pistol or at Miss Gatspy.

She held out my personal notebook from my carpet-bag, where I had done my best to keep a record of all that transpired on this mission; I had hoped my entries were obscure enough to foil most inspections. "This is most interesting reading. I had no idea there were so many desperate persons in Europe. And all of them after you." The gun did not waver as she spoke.

"I . . ." It was a feeble beginning, I realized, but no other words came to mind.

"You. Yes, you. You appear to be at the crux of things, and what a tangle it is! Had you revealed yourself, you might not have had to contend with one . . ." She broke off, calling herself to order once more. "You are not August Jeffries, messenger for the Brotherhood and initiate of the Servants of the Valley of Kings. If only we had known this earlier we might have managed matters rather differently. How did you contrive to come by that tattoo on your wrist? You must tell me the whole, one day." Hearing her, I felt color mount in my face. "You are not the valet Josue, either. You are Paterson Erskine Guthrie, employed by a British governmental functionary named Mycroft Holmes. And lucky for you we discovered this in time, or you should not be alive at this moment." She held out the notebook while retaining the pistol. At that instant, I would have preferred the opposite arrangement.

As I took the notebook, I saw that she had been reading about von Metz. "Miss Penelope Gatspy. If that is who you really are."

"Oh, it is," she said with a kind of formal cordiality that did not bode well for this encounter. "Your government is not the only group to have bones to pick with Herr von Metz and his pernicious Brotherhood. They murdered my brother last year." Her blue eyes shone with such purpose that I was struck with a notion.

"Is that the opinion of everyone in the Golden Lodge?"

If I had hoped to disquiet her with the question, I failed. "Yes, it is. We exist to stop them."

Her dedication was convincing, but for all that she was a young woman tangled in affairs much too complicated for her to grasp. I did what I could to soften the blow. "But Miss Gatspy, the British and the French and the Germans are all doing their best to stop the Brotherhood.

Why should the Golden Lodge succeed where these countries have not?"

"Because countries have other matters to attend to. Treaties, for example. And they cannot devote themselves to ending the activities of the Brotherhood as we of the Golden Lodge can. And they have no real understanding of the power of the Brotherhood, which we do." She slipped her pistol back into her purse and sat on the edge of the bed. "We know them as you do not, as you cannot. And, unlike you, we have no hesitation in doing all that must be done to exterminate the Brotherhood as the vile thing it is."

"If you have such a mission in life, how is it you did not kill me when you had the chance on the train from Calais?" It was a foolish question and I did not honestly expect an answer, so it was all the more surprising when she gave me one.

"It was Guilem's idea. He got so little from you the night before that he thought we had better be sure you were not just a lackey." She smiled at me with what passed for warmth. "He thought you were nothing more than a hireling, and an uninformed one at that. The final decision of your disposal was left up to me."

I regarded her with fascination. "I don't know what to say . . ." I began, and broke off.

"Of course you do," she countered winningly. "You want to wring my neck. I would want the same thing in your position." She leaned toward me, her eyes bright. "And now that the Brotherhood has taken MacMillian, you will have to be willing to work with us to get him back."

"And why is that?" I asked her sharply. If she had not that pistol with her, I might have been tempted to act more forcefully, for all that she was a female.

"Because we know where the Brotherhood has taken him." She wore a look now that was at once smug and righteous. It did not become her. "Oh, I know your

employer, Mycroft Holmes, has the location as well, but
we have a record of the guard posts and the various traps
which protect the château. You may find the place but you
will not reach it alive without our help." She cocked her
head, and I noticed a low whistle from the floor below.
"Your Mister Holmes is coming in from the stable.
Guilem is waiting for him." She tossed my blankets back.
"Come, sir. You must rise at once. We have no time to
lose."

I rubbed my face and felt the stubble under my fingers.
"I need to shave and dress, Miss Gatspy," I said, hoping
she would step out of the room.

"I have seen men do both before, Mister Guthrie," she
said without a hint of a blush. "Do not be embarrassed on
my account."

I sighed, and went to my carpetbag, putting the notebook back into it before I took out my inadequate shaving kit. I went to pour water into the basin and readied my
soap for the brush. Looking into the mirror, I saw that my
black eye had been revived by the blow on the head I had
received the day before. It was a bright purple with deep
purple shadows and a trace of green and yellow where the
old injury was fading. It was reassuring to see both my
eyes for a change, though the right eyelid still looked
swollen from the glue I had used to fix the supposed scar
to it.

Penelope Gatspy appeared over my shoulder in the
mirror behind me. "I think I would cover one eye, too, if
mine were like yours," she said with a faint smile. "I
thought when I met you in the compartment to Paris that
you were not used to wearing the eyepatch."

"What mistake did I make?" I asked her as I lathered
my brush.

"Nothing obvious. But you were not yet used to turning
your head as far as you would need to see with one eye. I
noticed that from the first." She favored me with a pursing
of her lips. "It was one of the reasons I didn't kill you."

"Thanks very much," I said, and stopped spreading the

lather on my cheeks as I heard a scuffle downstairs, followed by a sharp oath in English.

"Keep on, Mister Guthrie," said Penelope Gatspy. "We will want to join Mister Holmes directly."

"If you do him any harm, you will aid the Brotherhood beyond all reckoning." I took my razor and began to shave. It was in need of a proper stropping, but I did not have the leather for doing it. "What are you planning to do?" I asked as I progressed down my cheek to my jaw.

"We have as much interest in getting the treaty as you do. We would just as soon it remain secret, as your government must." She favored me with another smile that did not reach the brilliant blue of her eyes.

I finished shaving in silence, and as I tugged off my nightshirt, I could not keep from blushing when Penelope Gatspy did not decently turn away, but watched me with an eagerness I found disconcerting. I dressed as quickly as I could, and allowed her to order me down the stairs. She, I noticed, carried my carpetbag.

We found Mycroft Holmes in the taproom, a German newspaper open, a cup of strong coffee steaming on the table beside his chair. Across from him was seated a man I had not seen since he thrust me under my bathwater in Calais. He held a pistol negligently in one hand and watched Holmes with the appearance of boredom.

"There you are, dear boy," said Holmes as we came into the room. "I see you have met one of our new . . . allies." He coughed once, to make his point, and then regarded me narrowly. "I think it would be best if you would take the time to look at this piece in the paper." He folded the pages back and handed me the paper, indicating a report from Munich.

ENGLISH ADVENTURER SOUGHT IN
DEATH OF PROSTITUTE

MUNICH: An Englishman posing as a valet and calling himself August Jeffries is wanted for questioning in the poisoning of a prostitute named Françoise. Police have established that she received the fatal dose from this man, who appears to be the associate of known criminals.

"You may thank your old friend Dortmunder for this. He is making sure you cannot return to Munich and make any claims against him." Mycroft Holmes nodded once in a decisive manner. "The Brotherhood is very powerful indeed."

"So we have been trying to persuade Berlin, but all in vain," said Guilem in a voice I remembered all too well. Now that I saw him properly, I realized he was a personable man of about thirty, with dark hair and blue eyes. He was not nearly as tall as I had assumed he was, and while he looked strong, he was not massive.

"Not as much in vain as you might think." Mycroft Holmes accepted the paper back from me. "There are those in high places who are in sympathy with the Brotherhood, and who have done all they can to misinform their superiors in regard to the Brotherhood. Sadly, there are many venal officials in every government. Flattery, advancement, favor, bribery, blackmail, all may be used to suborn the greedy and ambitious. And once the Brotherhood has tainted you, they increase their hold by providing the protection their power provides. Dear me," he interrupted himself. "What dreadful alliteration."

"Where does it begin?" Guilem demanded. "How do we stop it?"

"It begins in little things, of course," said Holmes. "Nothing to frighten off the willing clerk or burgermeister, just a minor token: an improvement for civic buildings, or a fête for a visiting official. Perhaps an underminister is suffering an embarrassment; the Brotherhood makes him a trifling loan. It becomes an easy thing to reward your pawns and punish those who threaten to betray you. If one of the Brotherhood gains public position, he wraps himself in patriotic fervor so that his motives will not be closely questioned. If anyone attempts to abandon the cause, there are so many accidents that can claim him. Many of their creatures know this, and do nothing that would put them in harm's way."

Penelope Gatspy had tightened her hands into fists. "Despicable."

My employer nodded once. "On this mission we have encountered guards and other functionaries purportedly sent by the railroad or government who were in reality agents of the Brotherhood." He looked penetratingly at Miss Gatspy and her companion Guilem. "The Golden Lodge is not exempt from suspicions. You began by attempting to harm Guthrie, as you have told me, and then sent your cadet Kreutzer to keep a watch on me. I cannot forget that because we share a common foe we do not embrace the same ends."

"From what you are saying, we are all you can trust," said Penelope Gatspy in a quiet voice. "You cannot approach local authorities in case one of their number is with the Brotherhood. We may be the best of the bad bargain, but we are all you have."

This time Mycroft Holmes sighed deeply. "I realize that. And much as I would prefer to deal with agents who have earned my trust through years of service, it is as you say."

"Then why are we lingering here?" asked Guilem when Mycroft Holmes had completed his remarks.

"Because we must be prepared to deal with a very malign group," said Holmes quietly. "As powerful as they are in Germany, they also have great influence in France, which they believe should be in German control." He took a long sip of his now-cool coffee. "You know their goals in terms of metaphysics. I am far more concerned with their politics. But just at present our aims are the same." He gave me a thoughtful look. "If only they didn't know you, Guthrie."

"But they do," I said. "And we must consider that when we go against them."

"Which will be shortly. Our horses are being brought round." He saw me wince and managed a look of apology. "I am sorry to require more bareback hours from you, but there isn't time to procure proper saddles, and if we did we would draw attention to ourselves." He patted his coat under his arm. "My pistol is ready."

I was surprised that he was armed. I glanced at Guilem, then back to Holmes. "I didn't realize—"

"We had a brief misunderstanding upon my return," said Holmes nonchalantly. "I think we have ironed it out." His eyes flicked over Guilem, then to Penelope Gatspy. "For the time being, we are agreed that we oppose a common enemy, and act accordingly?" He waited for an objection which did not come. "Very well."

I had the uneasy feeling that we were taking too great a risk, but I kept my thoughts to myself. As we prepared to leave, Holmes stopped to leave payment with Madame Thillot. "Thank you for attending to that matter for me, Madame," he said as he handed over a doucement in addition to the sum of our bill.

"It was my pleasure, Monsieur." She showed no trace of curiosity as to why all her guests should be leaving together, though the wry lines in her face deepened significantly as she took Miss Gatspy's money, and then Guilem's.

As we went to climb aboard the Hannovarians, I whispered to him, "Aren't you afraid of what may become of the treaty if we throw our lot in with them? You said yourself that their goals are not ours."

"No," Mycroft Holmes declared as he swung aboard his big gelding.

I could not believe what I was hearing. "But don't you understand? They cannot be trusted. Once we have MacMillian, they could demand the treaty for their own purposes." I felt a familiar soreness begin to settle into my hips and thighs as I found my seat on the Hannovarian's back.

"That assumes that MacMillian has the treaty," said

Mycroft Holmes with a wink. "He doesn't." And with that, he turned his mount toward the road and let him begin at a steady, long trot.

I waited only long enough to see Penelope Gatspy and Guilem climb onto their horses before I rushed after Mycroft Holmes, with so many questions in me that I felt all over bristles.

FROM THE PERSONAL JOURNAL OF PHILIP TYERS:
I have spent an hour with Mother, and I now concur with her physicians—the end cannot be more than a few hours away. I have promised to return there by noon, and will remain as long as is necessary.

Edmund Sutton has offered to remain at the flat and receive any messages that may come while I am away. It is most generous of him, and I am grateful to him for this help at so critical a time.

No more word from France, but I had not expected any, not yet. It is never pleasant to have to wait for developments, which is what must be done now. If the mission is successful, we will know it by morning. If it fails, we may never know how that came about.

Chapter Twenty-eight

A STREAM LED us toward a fold in the hills which was filled with trees, making it difficult to discern how deep the fold was, or how much of a defile was concealed there. We had been riding for over three hours and the sun was nearly overhead, suggesting rather than imparting warmth. The shadows were far more honest in their chill.

All through the ride, I had been pondering that last, enigmatic remark of Mycroft Holmes's—that Mac-Millian did not have the treaty. Did that mean he had never had it, that all this was a diversion, or that the treaty had been stolen, and if so, by whom? And when? And if he did not have it, why had the Brotherhood taken him? And least pleasant of all, what would they do to him when they discovered he did not have the treaty? Much as I might dislike MacMillian, I would not wish the wrath of the Brotherhood upon him were he a thousand times more offensive.

"That's where the château is, back in those trees," said Mycroft Holmes, drawing his horse in with care. "We had best go the rest of the way on foot. And prepared for trouble."

"But it's at least a mile, perhaps more," said Guilem, pulling his handsome mare in beside Holmes. "Why not get closer?"

"Because they will be watching. They have Mac-Millian and they expect someone to come after him." Holmes pointed toward the trees. "And now they have the advantage of cover."

"But if we don't approach directly—" Guilem protested.

"They are not fools, man," Holmes interrupted them. "As you should know better than I. They are vicious and evil men who are trying to undermine the fabric of European and British society for their own ends."

"Yes," said Penelope with deep feeling. "And we cannot permit it to happen. Mister Holmes is right, Guilem. We must take no chances." She slipped out of her saddle and took her horse's reins firmly. "Where can we tie them safely?"

"I would think we could leave them at that church, back at the village behind us," said Holmes. "No Christian, of whatever stripe, can want the Brotherhood to succeed."

There was a startled moment as the others considered this remark, and then I said, "True enough," for all of us, and gratefully swung my horse around.

Penelope Gatspy climbed back into her saddle and pushed her horse to a steady trot. "It is not long until noon. We will have to move quickly if we do not want to be at that château at night. You know what their rites are. It would be best to be gone before sunset."

"Because they invoke powers of darkness," said Guilem. "They are willing to seek out the worst—"

Holmes gestured him to silence as we entered the little village. "Not here. People listen. And some will understand English."

The Abbé at the little church was willing to look after

our horses for a small donation to his parish. He also provided a wheel of cheese and two loaves of bread, which he took care to bless before handing them over.

"If we are not back by midnight, please send a telegram for me, to this place," Mycroft Holmes added as we were about to depart. He handed over a folded note and another few francs, and then led us out of the village along the road that ran in the general direction of von Metz's château.

After a brisk half-hour's walk, we turned off the road and wandered along the stream, still moving at a good pace, but not with any obvious purpose but to enjoy the autumn scenery. As we walked, we shared the bread and cheese among us, nothing more than travelers taking a respite at midday.

"At that next group of trees, turn toward the château," said Mycroft Holmes as we neared the place. "Keep well to the west side of the grove. We will be under cover of the trees, and if we are being watched, they will not know where we have gone."

"You still think we are being watched?" I asked, my thighs now as sore as my calves and my head the worst of all. "In spite of all our precautions?"

"Don't you think we are?" Holmes countered. "Ask these two, if you doubt me." He nodded toward Penelope and Guilem in turn. "Killers are always sensitive to these feelings."

Penelope bridled at the word *killers,* and defended herself by saying, "We kill only our enemies, only those of the Brotherhood who threaten the welfare and safety of millions."

"Yes," agreed Holmes at once, his voice soothing. "Your purposes are admirable. But your victims are dead, all the same." He smiled at her, no trace of condemnation in his face.

"Are you any different because your deputies pull the trigger?" she asked sharply.

"No, I am not," he said with such simplicity that I was fully convinced of his sincerity. "And for that reason, if no other, I must thank you for sparing Guthrie for me. I would be truly at a loss without him."

We were now well under the cover of the trees, and at a motion from Holmes, we began to walk separated from one another, silently, toward the deepest part of the little defile, where the château had to be. With a number of simple gestures, Holmes reminded all of us to watch the trees for lookouts, and take care where we put our feet, for fear of traps.

As I walked, I could not put aside the sense that I had mistaken what Mycroft Holmes had implied to Penelope Gatspy—that she had been planning to kill me when we met in the train. Though she had admitted as much to me, how was it that her purpose was so clear to everyone but me? And had she completely abandoned those intentions now that Mycroft Holmes had intervened? These profitless speculations were interrupted by a terrible, gurgling cry off to my left. I turned in time to see Guilem fall to the ground, a small crossbow quarrel no larger than a dart lodged in his chest.

I had a single, sharp instant of recollection of the second man dying at the edge of the abyss in Luxembourg with just such a small dart or quarrel in his neck. Was it the Brotherhood that had protected me then, thinking I was working on their behalf? And what would they do now, knowing it was untrue? I had to keep myself from imagining just such a dart biting into my flesh.

Holmes made a sharp gesture, and we were all still, and I no longer felt I was back in Luxembourg fighting for my life. He signaled us to move cautiously to a stand of hawthorn, which I did, resisting every instant the urge to break and run from this sinister place.

Once in the shelter of the hawthorn, we waited, and in a short while heard footsteps approaching. One of the two men wore postilion's spurs, and even on this damp, leaf-strewn ground, the chains rang softly. I did not need to look out to know that Herr Dortmunder was standing a dozen feet away, bending over Guilem.

"Take him back to the château," Herr Dortmunder ordered. "There may be information on his body."

"Are there others?" asked his assistant.

"They've probably fled by now, if they have any sense left to them." He chuckled and headed back in the direction of the heart of the defile.

"Don't move," Holmes whispered so quietly that I was not at all certain I had actually heard him speak. "Wait. Wait."

Penelope sat watching with that dazed, glazed way people have when death confronts them. For all the killing she may have done, she had not yet come to terms with those who have been killed. I felt sympathy for her, and an irritation that she would be so willing to risk all our lives without preparing to face death herself.

She must have realized I was watching her, for she looked up over her shoulder and glared at me, daring me to express any commiseration. I looked away.

"The guard has withdrawn," Holmes told us softly.

"Guard?" I asked, feeling foolish once again.

"The fellow in the branches of the tree," said Holmes, pointing ahead to a large oak. "He was left to see if anyone else was coming. He would appear to be satisfied that we are gone." He pulled his coat around him. "Come. We must be quick. They are on the alert now."

I scowled as I tried to get out of the thicket without tearing my clothes, and almost succeeded. A bit of my coat snagged on one of the barbs and ripped free. I would have left it, but Holmes stopped me. "If they find this, we might as well carry torches and cymbals."

Sheepishly I made sure that the bush was free of all bits of fabric, and then I followed Holmes and Penelope through the woods, taking care to keep off the two small paths we encountered, and trying to go from thicket to hedge in an effort to be in range of cover. It was cold with a chill that did not come wholly from shadow.

Finally, up ahead, I saw the looming stone walls of an ancient tower, a squat, round, forbidding fortification going back to the time when the Kingdom of Germany reached from Verdun in the west to Breslau in the east, when Frederick II reigned. It was a magnificent piece of history, but now the sight of it filled me with dread. I could not help but think of those men-at-arms who had marched against it when it was new, and I felt myself at one with them.

"I suppose it's too much to hope for a confessor's door," Holmes mused softly.

"Not in a place like that; that is not a bailey, it is a bolt-hole," Penelope Gatspy said in an undervoice. "How are we to get in?"

"Are you certain this is where they have taken MacMillian?" I could not keep from asking.

"My dear boy," Holmes told me, keeping his voice low but speaking with great precision, "this is one of the strongholds maintained by the Brotherhood I've told you about. You have already seen the one in Bavaria, which they would be foolish to return to, with the police looking for MacMillian. The one remaining in Austria is near Salzburg. Another is near Zagreb. This location is most convenient for them. Nothing would serve their purpose better. Where would they bring him but here?"

"All right," I said. "I only thought they might have hidden him in another place."

"They do not know we know this location," Holmes reminded me as he drew his pistol from under his coat. "It would be nice to have one of their crossbows. They're much less noisy than pistols are. Perhaps once we get inside we can claim one as our own." He nodded toward the tower. "If we work our way around to the back of it, we may find the means to get in."

Penelope Gatspy held up her purse. "I have a revolver with me. And a length of wire." She was pale but composed, accepting Guilem's death with a professional calm that told me more of her experience as an enemy of the Brotherhood than any words would do.

"Excellent," Holmes approved, and motioned us into silence again, indicating the tangle of underbrush nearby. "Stay out of that. It makes noise," he warned us, his words hardly louder than breath.

We worked our way around the bulk of the wall, holding to the shadows of the trees while avoiding the brush where our passage would give rise to noise. It was nerve-wracking, and with each step I still half-anticipated the jolt of a quarrel smashing into my body. At least I would not fall into a chasm.

Finally we were at the rear of the place, in a steep, narrow part of the hill where berry brambles mixed with the bushes. We had all been snagged by the thorns in our trek along the hillside.

"Just as I hoped," whispered Mycroft Holmes as he pointed to a pen with half a dozen pigs in it. "Where there is a kitchen, there must be a door." He smiled at Penelope Gatspy and me, then motioned us to start forward.

One of the sows grunted as we approached, hoping we were bringing food. She was a good-sized animal, more than two hundred pounds, and her little eyes were bright with cunning.

"There is the door," Holmes said softly, pointing to a narrow opening near what was clearly an abandoned bakery-and-creamery. "We must be very careful here. They will expect some attempt, I am sure."

We were about to move when the wooden door of the old bake-house swung open and Herr Dortmunder strode out, two dark-clad men in his wake.

"He is lying. He knows where the treaty is. Alert van Meter, and tell him that we may have to stop that train again, and get the rest of his luggage."

"He will not take much more questioning," said the fairer of the two men. I noticed there were dark patches on his sleeves and the front of his tunic. "If he goes off in

another swoon, I don't know how long he will be unconscious."

"Use hartshorn to rouse him," said Herr Dortmunder,
then stepped inside the kitchen door, his postilion's spurs
ringing on the stone floor.

"Do you think they have MacMillian in there?" I whispered to Holmes.

"Either they do, or they want us to think they do," said
Penelope in the same low tone.

"Precisely," said Holmes. "And we will have to find
out which. Although it appears they have made a classic
mistake and are guarding only the front of the tower, and
not the rear, assuming that nothing can come from behind
them. That is a naïveté I would not expect from the
Brotherhood. And so we must not indulge in the hope that
they are not alert. They have Guilem's body, and that
ought to make them worried about more trouble." He
frowned. "If MacMillian has been badly beaten, it will
not be an easy thing to carry him out of here." He stifled
a cough. "We must first determine if MacMillian is
indeed being held there."

"I will go," I said, hating myself for volunteering.

"They know you," said Holmes, shaking his head.
"And you, Miss Gatspy, are not dressed to climb onto
roofs." He squinted up at the sky. "It is my task. Besides,
I am much too large a man to hide with a knot of a tree.
Better I should act." There was grim amusement in his
gray eyes. He motioned us to lie down at the base of two
big elms. "You are well hidden here. If they take me,
leave at once. There will be nothing you can do to save
me then; you would only sacrifice yourselves need-
lessly."

I nodded, having no intention of following this order,
for I had seen what would become of him, and could not
desert him in the face of such danger. I began to plan
what I would have to do to protect Holmes from these
malign men even as I watched Holmes slip away from us
down the slope toward the little kitchen-yard.

"What do you think?" I whispered to Penelope when two infinitely long minutes had dragged by.

"I think we could all be killed," she said with amazing calm.

"Good Lord, woman!" I exclaimed, my voice no louder than the sound of the wind.

"And if we can stop the Brotherhood, it will be worth it," she added, with such coolness of mien that I was taken up short. "They have a long, hideous history and if no one will oppose them it will go on indefinitely, gathering power as they go. In time they will have their wish of conquest because no one was willing to refuse them what they want." Her eyes were shining with purpose. "Well, I will not stand by and permit them to triumph."

"If they are so strong, what use is it for three of us to stand against them?" I asked her softly.

"Because if three do it now, six might have courage enough to do it later, and then twelve. If no one opposes them, then they are right and they are the masters of Europe. And all we have done will be for naught." She put one hand to her eyes, the first indication of emotion I had seen in her. "Guilem."

I could think of nothing to say to comfort her, or to give her hope, for I had almost none to spare. To have come so far, and to risk so much, and for what? If the treaty was truly not in MacMillian's hands, what was the point of this?

There was a flurry of activity off to our left down the slope. Penelope Gatspy pointed her revolver in that direction, then dropped the muzzle as Mycroft Holmes came into view, pulling himself arm over arm along the ground in a fast, powerful wriggle. He made very little sound, which surprised me, and again made me wonder how he had passed his earlier years.

As soon as he reached us he said, "MacMillian's not conscious. They've been cruel with him. Even if he regains consciousness he will not be able to walk. One of his arches has been smashed. He will be fortunate to walk with a cane after this." His face was set in an expression of condemnation I had not seen before and trusted I would never have to see again. "There was a guard on him who will not waken for some time; I was able to put him out of the way. But there are still two guards with small crossbows at the entrance to the kitchen. They are the ones we must do something about if we cannot get to MacMillian without alerting them."

"Are there any more, do you think?" Miss Gatspy asked with a calm that still had the capacity to astonish me.

"We must assume there may be," said Holmes. "The Brotherhood do not often leave themselves open to attack."

"What kind of chance will we have—" I began, hating myself for sounding craven.

Mycroft Holmes looked at me and grinned. "Why, all the chance we need, dear boy. All the chance we need."

FROM THE PERSONAL JOURNAL OF PHILIP TYERS:
Still no word from Germany.

I have received another missive from Miss Roedale, this time delivered by the lady herself in the company of her uncle, who has given it as his opinion that the trust of the Roedale family was sadly misplaced in G. Miss Roedale brought a small, sealed box for G., and ordered me that I am to inform him that she considers their engagement to be at an end, no matter what pain her decision may mean to their mothers. She added that had she known of his unsteadiness of temperament when they were younger, she would have prevailed upon her parents to inform G.'s parents that the match was not suitable; she holds him to blame for allowing her to assume their life together would be of a far different nature than what it would be given what he has chosen to make his work. His letters and his ring, she told me, were in the box. I have given my word that I will present them to G. immediately upon his return. And I pray that he does return.

Edmund Sutton has spent the day at an audition and has just returned in time for tea. He is not eager for this part, but says that a man in his line of work must make himself available. It is dangerous to have him away for so long during the day, and he has apologized for it more than once. He has no other commitments beyond this one between now and the end of the week.

I must go to hospital one last time.

Chapter Twenty-nine

APPROACHING THE BAKE-HOUSE was tricky, even with Penelope Gatspy just behind us on the slope covering our actions with Holmes's pistol and her Navy revolver. Any discovery would be, I knew, the most terrible death the Brotherhood could give us—which would surpass anything I could imagine.

As we made our way through the trees to the bake-house, I had the feeling that something hot was on my skin. I realized I thought it was the eyes of lookouts in the trees, and not the result of exertion that gave me this particular sensation. The bake-house seemed a long way off, and bristling with danger.

Holmes motioned me to stop, which I did. My whole body was sore, and I did not know how to shut it out, though I would have to if we were going to succeed. After all they had done to me, I refused to capitulate to them. At this point I knew I would not give the Brotherhood the satisfaction of beating me. It did not matter why Mycroft Holmes had sent me on this mission, it was now a matter of pride with me, as much as any service I could render to the British government. With this resolve, I listened while Holmes outlined what we would have to do.

"It would be useful to get one or two of those little crossbows," he reminded me. "To even the odds a bit."

"So you've said," I replied. "And if I can, I will get one."

Holmes must have sensed my resolution, for he gave me a swift, measuring look, and nodded. "Off we go, then."

The last few feet were the most dangerous, for they would mean moving in the open, and past the pigs.

"A pity we haven't a sack of cabbages for them," Holmes whispered as he prepared to slip across the little kitchen yard. "The door does not make too much noise. That, at least, is in our favor."

I gestured my endorsement, and crouched in the pitifully small shadows of the trees at the edge of the yard in the early afternoon light.

Holmes moved with remarkable swiftness through the yard and to the side of the bake-house, his big, drab cloak blending with the old stones. Carefully he made his way to the far corner, and, after a quick, meticulous inspection of his surroundings, he vanished from my sight. I immediately followed after him, wishing now that my coat was not the deep brown shade it was, for it served to make me a shadow where none should be, and therefore conspicuous.

The stones of the bake-house were cold, and as I inched forward, I had the uncomfortable notion that the building was in actuality a crypt. I made myself set such notions aside as I at last swung around the end of the place and started for the door, which was now ajar. I reached it without incident, pulled it open and slipped inside, taking care to close the door as Mycroft Holmes had. Then I turned and saw Cameron MacMillian for the first time. And tasted bile at the back of my throat as I did.

Herr Dortmunder had done an unholy piece of work on

him: his eyes were grotesquely swollen, and huge bruises on his jaw showed where a few of his teeth had been knocked out. Three of the fingers of his left hand were broken, there were burns on the palm of his right, and his right instep was crushed, leaving his booted foot in a mass of blood. He stank of urine and feces, his pulse was fast and irregular, and each breath he took was a whimper.

"Help me gag him," said Mycroft Holmes. "We can't have him screaming when we move him."

I saw at once the logic of his demand, and did all I could to accommodate him. I located at once a length of cheesecloth, and held it out.

Holmes was not pleased at its flimsiness, but accepted it, and secured it swiftly around MacMillian's battered head. "Help me get him over my shoulder."

"But shouldn't we—" I began, indicating I had expected to help carry him.

"No. In this terrain we will do better if I carry him." He indicated another length of cheesecloth. "Tie his legs together, too, so that he will not be able to thrash about."

I did this quickly, having a mushrooming sense of peril within me.

"Quickly now," said Holmes as he wrestled MacMillian over his shoulder, so that the Scotsman's head and arms hung down his back. "Open the door and move aside for me. I depend on you to protect my back, Guthrie."

"I will, sir," I said, and moved to obey his instructions.

The guards at the kitchen door were nowhere in sight. I suspected that at this hour they were having their dinner, for even men of the Brotherhood ate. Cautiously I motioned Holmes to come out, and as soon as he did, I closed the door behind him, taking care to put the bolt in place.

We went swiftly across the worn stone paving of the yard, past the pigs, who squealed in anticipation of a meal, and into the cover of the trees, where Holmes, panting from the exertion, came to a halt in the cover of an oak. He strove to keep MacMillian in place, and I rushed to help.

"Well done, thus far, dear boy," Holmes said, using a breath for every two words. "Now, if we can get away altogether, we will have done something."

The chilling implication of his words caught my attention. "Then we had better get moving. I will carry MacMillian for a way, if you like."

He nodded. "In time. For now, I will manage." He looked carefully about, and added, "We will need Miss Gatspy with us."

"I'll go fetch her," I volunteered, remembering the little notch where she had hidden, and beginning to wonder why she had not joined us.

"Excellent," said Holmes, and steadied his burden against the tree.

She met me some fifty yards along the swell of the hill, making her way back toward us. "You did that very well," she approved as she came up to me, and though her voice was low, her words gave me a reward I had not anticipated.

"It isn't over yet," I reminded her.

"Hardly," she answered, the stern purpose back in her face once more. "If we get away, it will not be over."

In spite of myself, I asked her, "How many of them have you killed? Of the Brotherhood, I mean?"

"In total? Eleven. Not nearly enough." Her last words gave me an odd moment.

We were once more back with Mycroft Holmes, and I was relieved to see him breathing more evenly. "It will be best, I think, to go over the hill, instead of back the way we came," he told us as we came up to him. "They will have a harder time following us. And you may be sure they will follow us."

"And make an example of us if they take us," added Penelope Gatspy.

"That is true," said Holmes somberly. "Let us be under

way. We want to put as much distance between us and the tower as we can before they realize MacMillian is gone." With that, he started away up the slope, trudging steadily while doing his best to keep under cover. As we hurried to keep abreast of him, he said, "Miss Gatspy, please give Guthrie my pistol. You still have your revolver."

As she handed me the weapon I could sense her reluctance to surrender it.

"You haven't had to kill before now, have you?" she asked as I thrust the pistol into my coat pocket.

"Yes. Once." The man in Luxembourg came swiftly to my mind. "I did not like it."

"That is what worries me about you. You may well hesitate when you must not, and we would all be the worse off for it." She was not interested in hearing any protestations from me, and made this very clear as she continued up the slope, struggling from time to time with her skirts.

We had almost reached the brow of the hill when there was a loud cry from the kitchen-yard below. This was followed almost at once by more shouts and alarms. MacMillian's disappearance had been discovered.

"Now it begins in earnest," said Holmes, and pointed to the steep descent ahead of us. "They are coming after us."

"But they don't know which way yet," said Penelope Gatspy. "That may be in our favor."

"Let us hope it is," said Holmes, and started down into the narrow valley. "Hurry." He gestured our course down the hill with his free hand. "When we reach the stream, we will cross it, and then work our way back toward the farmer's lane."

I felt the pistol in my pocket and wished the heft of it would be more reassuring than it was. I kept slightly behind Holmes, protecting his back as he had ordered me to do.

It was rough going. Twice we surprised deer taking their afternoon ease in the thickets. They bounded away with such grace that the noise they made was almost unimportant. Then it struck me that they would provide the Brotherhood an indication of where we were.

The hill was much steeper here, and the footing uncertain. As we were making our way down this difficult part of the slope, Penelope Gatspy slipped, and, thanks to her voluminous skirts, ended up sliding and rolling some distance away from Holmes and me.

"I'd try that myself if it weren't for MacMillian," said Holmes, trying to keep enough air in him to continue. "I doubt it would do him much good."

"Given what has already been done, a few scrapes and bruises should not be an issue," I said, trying to make light of our predicament. "We had best try to find Miss Gatspy. She may be injured."

"Scrapes and bruises?" suggested Mycroft Holmes drily. He was crabbing his way down, his feet placed sideways against the damp earth in an attempt to keep from sliding. It very nearly succeeded. But at last MacMillian regained consciousness, and began at once to struggle, his muffled cries louder than either Holmes or I wanted.

I reached out to offer Holmes the support of my arm, but was a fraction of a second too late. With a shout, Holmes was toppled and he, with MacMillian tangled up in his flailing arms, went careening down the side of the hill. I watched in dismay as they were lost to sight in the first thicket beneath this steep section.

I hurried down after them, all but tripping myself. I was no longer concerned about the Brotherhood behind us, but all my attention was intent upon the fate of Mycroft Holmes, MacMillian, and Penelope Gatspy.

As I reached the foot of the rise, I saw MacMillian lying, as if discarded by a careless farmer, against a tree, his head and shoulder to one side, for all the world like a horrendous doll. He was muttering through his gag, and his mauled left hand flopped on the leaves. I paused long enough to assure myself he had taken no new serious hurt, and plunged on, looking for Holmes.

I found him a short while later, fetched up in a stand of berry vines, his face much scratched and his clothes snagged. "Where's MacMillian?" he asked as I approached him.

"Back there," I said with a hitch of my thumb. "Not moving yet. I'll go back for him as soon as you are extricated."

"Very good," said Holmes, working at freeing his cloak from the snags and spikes of the vines. "I have a few knocks, but no real injury. No bones broken."

"Thank God for small favors," I said, and lent a hand to getting him out.

"I'll manage for myself. You go fetch MacMillian. It wouldn't do to let the Brotherhood get their hands on him again." He indicated with his elbow that I was to hurry. I made a half-salute and began to retrace my steps.

I was within thirty feet of where MacMillian lay when I heard a sharp sound to my right and behind me. Hoping it was Penelope Gatspy, I turned without taking the pistol from my pocket, and found myself looking at the notched quarrel of one of the small crossbows. Herr Dortmunder was smiling as he came toward me, the ching of his postilion's spurs muted by the damp earth and fallen leaves.

"You have done enough damage, Mister Jeffries, if that is your name. It is now time you answered for it." He aimed the crossbow at my thigh, where the dart would disable me but not kill me.

"Pleasure to be of service," I said, in order to hide the cold, gut-numbing funk that had stolen over me. I held up my head. "It is too bad you did not get the treaty."

"Oh, we will. Never fear." There was an edge of panic in his grim announcement, as if he was terrified of the ramifications for him should he fail to fulfill his mission.

"Not this time, I think," I answered, wondering how I could draw my pistol and fire before Herr Dortmunder could put that little quarrel into me.

"You may change your tune before we give you to the altar. You know what will happen then, of course. You have seen it." He said this with the clear intention of increasing my dread.

Would I have the courage, or the desperation, to bite out my own tongue before the Brotherhood could force the story from me? Would I be able to trick them to kill me before I gave it all away? I wanted to force myself to break and run so that he would possibly kill me.

"Stand very still, Mister Jeffries," said Herr Dortmunder, seeing my intent. "I will put this through your lower back. You will not die, and you will regret that bitterly."

I had already begun to do just that.

FROM THE PERSONAL JOURNAL OF PHILIP TYERS:
I have brought my mother's things back from hospital. They seem so very few for so long and worthy a life. She would be saddened, I think, to discover how few things are representative of her. I have arranged to keep a few of them in memory of her, but the rest will be donated to the charities she so long supported. Her funeral will be in three days.

No word has yet come from Germany, and Edmund Sutton has admitted some trepidation to me. It is not like M.H. to undertake such dangerous ventures in so unguarded a way, and as a result, both of us fear he may have come to some harm. But we are not permitted to act for several hours yet.

I can but hope that my anxiety in this regard proves groundless and that the telegram we have been told to expect will arrive in the time designated. But it would be less than candid for me to claim that I am sanguine regarding the outcome of this mission. There are those who would say that the death of my mother has made me anticipate the worst, and given my outlook a morbid twist, but I must confess that I cannot look upon the current circumstances of M.H.'s investigation with anything other than the gravest apprehension.

Chapter Thirty

THE GUNSHOT WAS little more than a pop, so that I did not at first realize it was a shot, or that it had struck Herr Dortmunder. He seemed unaware of what had happened, and so I supposed the shot had either been for me, or had not found its mark.

Then, very slowly, his grimace still fixed on his face, Herr Dortmunder collapsed, like a puppet with severed strings, landing in an untidy heap on the ground.

I stared at him for almost a minute before I could make myself move. When I did, I was shaking so much I could hardly take the little crossbow from his dead hand.

"It's ironic, really," said Penelope Gatspy from the shelter of the trees immediately behind us, "that I should be sent here to kill you, and I have kept you alive." She had a smudge of dirt on her cheek and her bodice was torn at the shoulder, but other than that she showed no signs of more serious harm. She held the Navy revolver easily, not quite pointed at me, not quite pointed away. "Do not make the mistake of thinking that we are on the same side. We are allies for the moment because our purposes are similar, just as Britain and Germany are in that precious treaty you are trying to preserve. I have my reasons for wanting to keep you alive, or you would be laid out beside that offal." She kicked at Herr Dortmunder's corpse with such feeling that I was distressed to see it.

I looked down at the crossbow in my hand. "There will be others nearby, I fear."

"Yes. We must not linger." She looked around. "Where is the Scotsman? And where is Mister Holmes?"

"Mister Holmes," said he as he came up to us, "has just done away with two of the Brotherhood guards. You are to be congratulated, my dear, for so wise a decision in regard to Guthrie here. I would have not liked to kill you." He offered her a slight bow which looked raffish with his clothes showing the depredations of the berry vines.

I had brought my trembling under control now, and the shock of the moment changed to a more pervasive feeling that I was extremely vulnerable and could not be sure of any protection. I held on to the crossbow with one hand and felt for the pistol with the other. I wanted to say something that would convey my gratitude as well as my misgivings, but no phrases came to me, and I gave up on the attempt, devoting myself instead to listening for the approach of other hunters.

"Guthrie," said Holmes as he started off to where MacMillian was lying, "get Herr Dortmunder under cover, enough so no one will trip over him. We don't want to speed his deputies after us."

At last I said what had most troubled me. "How is it that it was Herr Dortmunder who found us, and not one of the others?"

"He saw you from those narrow upper windows," answered Penelope Gatspy, her manner as cool as when I met her. How could she manage it, I wondered? For I was doing all that I could to put my inner turmoil aside and get out of danger, when I would have to deal with another death on my hands. "When the alarm went up, he took his glass and looked over the slope. I saw the sun on the lens, and I recognized his clothes."

"You're very attentive," said Holmes over his shoulder.

"Any assassin must be," she answered, following after him while I dragged the body of Herr Dortmunder to the shrub-grown base of half a dozen elms.

It was disturbing to feel the utter deadness of that body, no trace of anything alive in it. I could well understand now how it was that people claimed the dead weighed more than the living. Penelope Gatspy had shot him at the base of his neck, and his head lolled most appallingly, though there was not as much blood as I would have expected in so fatal a wound. I heaped an armful of leaves over the corpse and was about to go after Mycroft Holmes and Penelope Gatspy when I noticed another of the Brotherhood guards making his way cautiously through the woods. On his current path he would find Mycroft Holmes, Penelope Gatspy, and MacMillian in a matter of minutes. I could not allow this to happen. I took a position and braced my arm, then aimed the crossbow and pulled the trigger.

The little dart sped unerringly to the place between the man's shoulder blades. He grunted, staggered, and fell, embracing the trunk of a tree as he went.

Working mechanically now, my thoughts masked from me by the demands of the moment, I hid this man as well, this time in a thicket of hawthorn. I hoped that these precautions had bought us at least as much time as they had taken. Then I rushed to where MacMillian had been left and found Holmes just settling MacMillian over his shoulder.

MacMillian was half-awake, and he kept muttering through his gag. "Don't know. I don't know. I don't know."

"We know that, old man," said Holmes soothingly as we made our way through the lengthening shadows of afternoon.

Twice we had to hide in the shadows of trees as

Brotherhood guards went by, and once we surprised a local poacher with a rabbit in his bag, who nearly used his sporting gun on us. But by four-thirty we were once again at the outskirts of the village, and Holmes stopped to take MacMillian from his shoulder.

"There will be guards in the village, you may be certain of it," he said. He was quite gray with exhaustion, but his stamina had not yet failed him. "It will be necessary to get the horses without alerting the guards."

"But . . ." Penelope Gatspy held up her revolver.

Holmes regarded her with such exaggerated patience that I wondered at her tolerance of it. "My dear girl, we can't go shooting every member of the Brotherhood we see, no matter how laudable a project that may be. There are more of them than there are of us, and so circumspection is called for. And we don't want to be kept here answering questions for the French authorities."

"You are a most irksome man, Mister Holmes," she informed him, by way of agreement. "Very well. I will not press you on that head again."

I reckoned she had conceded the matter much too quickly and simply, given what I had seen of her zeal in her cause, but I kept my opinion to myself, not wanting to bring about any discord at this juncture.

We went toward the church via the backs of several houses, and as we arrived, we saw the Abbé preparing for Vespers. He was kneeling before the little altar, his hands joined.

"I hope we do not disturb you, Father," said Holmes as we came in the rear door. "If you wish, we will wait until your service is finished." He went and eased MacMillian down in the front pew, making sure he would not fall onto the floor. "Our friend here has met with an accident, or we would not intrude."

"You do not intrude," said the old man, cocking his head once in the direction of the confessional, but otherwise unmoving. "You know where your horses are. They have been fed and watered."

"Thank you, Father," said Holmes, his eyes flicking toward the confessional. I did the same, and wondered if one of the doors was supposed to be ajar. "We have to reach the station at Château Salins to make our train to Metz this evening."

At the word *Metz* the Abbé flinched slightly. Mycroft Holmes nodded once. I saw that Penelope Gatspy was moving toward the confessional, her pistol drawn.

The door was flung open, and two shots were fired. One struck Penelope Gatspy in the shoulder—she staggered, but maintained her hold on her pistol—the other missed Mycroft Holmes by inches, for he had dropped to the floor at the opening of the door.

And I put my hand on the pistol in my pocket, and without drawing it, pointed it at the confessional and fired twice into its interior, completing the ruin of the garment I wore and killing von Metz at the same time.

For several seconds after the body sagged out of the confessional the church was silent. Then the Abbé rose, blessed himself three times, and went to say the offices for the dead even as Mycroft Holmes and I went to tend to Penelope Gatspy's wound.

"He arrived a little more than an hour ago," the Abbé said when he had completed his initial blessing. "He doubted you would live to return, but he wanted to be prepared, in case one of you should slip his noose." His expression was somber. "He said other things, things so obscene that I cannot repeat them. I fear they will leave a stain on my soul. God will have to forgive him, for I cannot, and that will add to my sin."

"We have some notion of what he told you, and if God is the fair judge you claim He is, you will have nothing to blame yourself for," Holmes remarked as he inspected the crease in Miss Gatspy's shoulder—she winced at his touch but made no sound. "Painful and bloody, but not dangerous. No bone was hit. It will heal if you have it attended to at once, and I am certain the Golden Lodge can arrange for it," he said. "And it will not hamper you in your work, for what gratification it may bring you to know that."

"Thank you," she said in her self-contained manner. "The Golden Lodge is grateful for all you have done, with me and for me."

Holmes hesitated before he spoke again. "I am sorry we could do nothing to save Guilem."

"So am I. But he died for what he believes in, as I will one day." She might as well have been talking about the weather for all the concern she expressed.

The enormity of what I had done struck me then, with such force that I did not trust myself to remain on my feet any longer. I held on to the nearest pew, steadying myself. I had killed von Metz. He was actually dead. I was glad and sick at once. I gripped the pew with all my strength.

"Guthrie, dear boy, you look as if you could use a drink," said Holmes.

"*I* should have one first," muttered MacMillian. "How could you take so long to find me?" His words were slurred but his tone carried his complaint eloquently. "What kind of incompetents are you?"

Holmes had taken a flask from inside his voluminous cloak. He had offered it to me, but now he went and lifted it to MacMillian's lips, saying to me as he did, "Make allowances, Guthrie."

I shrugged, absurdly relieved that amid the chaos MacMillian had not changed. "When you are through, sir."

MacMillian cried out as the brandy touched his broken lips and missing teeth, and this gave me pleasure it should not. I wanted some distraction. Penelope Gatspy provided it.

"If you will come and help me onto my horse, Mister Guthrie?" she said. She had completed wadding her neckcloth into a bandage and packing it under her torn habit to protect her wound.

"But—" I began, rather stupidly.

"My people are expecting me. They are not far away.

They are never far away from the Brotherhood." She made a gesture of farewell to Mycroft Holmes, and then hastened to the door.

Sunset bloomed around us, the sky a magnificent display of rose and orange, with long, blue shadows crossing the hills.

"You will need a lantern," I remarked as I escorted her to the little stable at the back of the church.

"I don't have far to go, and I know the way." A hard amusement lit her blue eyes. "The world is not what you imagine it to be, Mister Guthrie. Your Mister Holmes knows that better than most, especially for a man working in a government. If you want to be in it, listen to him. If not, then—" She found her horse and watched as I tightened the girths. "It has been an unexpected mission in many ways. I am almost sad to leave you." She reached for her reins. "I will accept a leg up, if you will give it," she said.

I held my hands linked at my knee, and as she stepped into them, I lifted her into the saddle. She was lighter than I had supposed, a strong girl with the mind of a Hindoo fanatic. "I thank you, Miss Gatspy, for all you have done for me. I wouldn't be alive now but for you."

"No, you wouldn't," she said as she gathered her reins and adjusted her leg over the horn. "Nor would I but for you. So all debts are canceled. Remember that next time we meet." And with that she turned her horse away and rode out of the barn, and I supposed, out of my life.

Mycroft Holmes looked me over as I came back into the church. "You look rather steadier," he informed me as he offered the flask to me.

I took it gratefully, and let the welcome burning go down my throat so fast that I coughed at the impact.

"What is Jeffries doing?" demanded MacMillian in a quarrelsome tone. "How could you let them take me, Jeffries?"

"He isn't Jeffries, he's Guthrie," said Mycroft Holmes. "And he does not work for you, he works for me." He gave his attention to the Abbé. "I am sorry for this disturbance, Father, but I trust you will pray for us. We will be going now, with your permission. We are almost out of danger."

"Go, my son," said the Abbé with a very French shrug. "We will take care of this fellow"—he motioned to von Metz—"in our churchyard. And may God be merciful to us."

"Charity is a great virtue, Father," said Holmes as he began to pull MacMillian upright.

"And this misguided man has much need of it," said the Abbé as we left him in his church and went to prepare for the ride to Château Salins.

FROM THE PERSONAL JOURNAL OF PHILIP TYERS: *Thank God they are safe, and aboard a train headed for Antwerp. The message came at a few minutes to eight this evening, and I have rarely been so pleased to have news. I have sent word round to the Admiralty to inform them of these welcome developments.*

MacMillian and the treaty are both safe, though MacMillian is much in need of medical help, which will be provided to him on his travels, as much as is possible, and then he will be given over to the best surgeons in England once he is home again.

Edmund Sutton was delighted to hear this news, for now he can tell Inspector Cornell that there will be answers for him shortly. And he can return to the boards once again, until he is needed here. I often think it is unfortunate that the finest performance of his career must go unrecognized and unhonored. Perhaps in time he will be allowed to reveal what he has done. That would be fair.

Epilogue

"BUT WHO HAD the treaty?" I asked Mycroft Holmes over tea that afternoon. It was six days since our return and autumn had turned soggy. His flat was made warm by two fires, and with the last of the reports on our mission now finished, it was pleasant to find answers to questions without the fear of imminent death to lend urgency to them.

"Why, you disappoint me, dear boy. I thought you knew that." He took a bite of a scone covered with clotted cream.

"Well, I didn't," I responded. "I thought it might have been hidden aboard the first train and carried out of Germany by another route."

"Clever, but incorrect." Holmes was enjoying himself.

"All right. It could have been moved to other parts of MacMillian's luggage." Given all the cases and chests he traveled with, it would present a puzzle, I thought.

"Another good notion, but again, wrong." Holmes poured more tea into our cups.

"Then where was it?" I demanded.

"Why, with me," he said, with innocence worthy of a baby. "I took it while you were convincing MacMillian to hire you."

"At Madame Isolde's?" I asked, astounded in spite of myself.

"Certainly. I took the case while everyone else was downstairs. When I had the treaty, I put it into the special lining of my coat and substituted a map of Europe so that the case would not be empty." He smiled at me. "I thought it wiser not to tell you."

"No doubt," I responded, stung.

His face lost its cherubic aspect. "You were so green, Guthrie, that I could not be sure you would be able to do all we had to do." He stared into the fire. "And I am very sorry you have paid so high a price."

"Others paid higher," I said, taking some of his somberness. "Guilem. Françoise."

"True enough," he said. "But I think it has been worth it. The treaty will ensure that for the next two decades no nation in the Balkans is able to draw all Europe into war. In time, I suspect, the Balkans will be the fuse on the powderkeg primed by the newly united Germany. For the time being, Russia has every reason to enforce peace in that region through diplomacy, not trial of arms. There is nothing like the Royal Navy and British gold to serve as incentives to the Tsar. All in all, a difficult but worthy month's effort." He regarded me in that sleepy way that has no trace of inattention about it. "Would you agree, dear boy?"

I nodded and sipped my tea. "I wonder if MacMillian thinks so."

"When he is given his knighthood, he will," said Holmes with world-weary certainty. "He will boast of his part in it, and very possibly take credit for things you and I, and Miss Gatspy, did."

That seemed all too likely to me. I stretched out my

legs and sighed, glancing at the red spot on my wrist where Mycroft Holmes had used his chemicals to dissolve the tattoo he had put there. "It will not be easy to listen to that."

"You will learn how to do so with grace, if you stay in my employ." There was a speculative light in his eyes as he said this.

"Why should I not?" I asked with some alarm. I had thought I had done well enough for a novice, but did not know how to protest on my own behalf.

"Well, this work may not be to your taste. Not everyone has a talent for it, and of those who do, not all will do what the . . . employment demands," he told me in a steady way. "As you have discovered, my secretary does not always have the usual sorts of duties one would expect in a secretary's venue. It is unpredictable, the work I require. And it has already been the cause of your broken engagement. To say nothing of three attempts on your life." Again he looked at me, waiting.

"As to Miss Roedale, I am sorry she could not accommodate herself to the work you give me to do, and I am no doubt a cad for bringing disappointment to her. My mother will be severely displeased and I cannot blame her; my union with the Roedales was her dearest wish. But it is far better to know of this . . . unhappiness before we were married, for as great an injury as I have done her and her family, I am afraid it would have been magnified many times had we actually been married." I did not like to confess that I had, over the last two days, come to regard the termination of our engagement as a deliverance—no gentleman likes to think so poorly of his judgment or his word. "As to the attempts on my life, they will be made, either on me or on another who undertakes this necessary work. It cannot all be left to Miss Gatspy and her associates. How can I permit another to fall in my place?" I met Holmes's eyes and smiled. "And I suspect that a return to the humdrum work of records and letters and translations would pall on me now. Besides, there are enemies of Britain out there who cannot and must not be allowed to act with impunity."

"Good fellow, Guthrie," said Mycroft Holmes, and went himself to fetch the brandy.

FROM THE PERSONAL JOURNAL OF PHILIP TYERS:
A sleety Boxing Day, and G. is off to Amsterdam, with instructions to send a telegram when he arrives there. Mister Watkins will be waiting for him. We will have the packet in our hands by the New Year.

Word came from Inspector Cornell that Vickers appears to have gone to ground, much to his distress. The case of the young woman's murder will remain unsolved as long as Vickers is at large, a situation which satisfies neither the Inspector nor M.H.

Available by mail from

BURNING DOWN THE HOUSE • Merry McInerny
Burning Down the House is a novel of dazzling storytelling power that peers into the psyche of today's woman with razor-sharp insight and sparkling wit.

CHOSEN FOR DEATH • Kate Flora
"I enjoyed *Chosen for Death* immensely. Kate Flora is a fine new talent."
—Barbara D'Amato, author of *Hard Tack*

PLAY IT AGAIN • Stephen Humphrey Bogart
In the classic style of a Bogart and Bacall movie, Stephen Humphrey Bogart delivers a gripping, fast-paced mystery.

IRISH GOLD • Andrew M. Greeley
"May be Andrew M. Greeley's best effort yet....A first-rate adventure story with the love interest intertwined in the mystery."—*Baltimore Sun*

COLUMBO: THE HELTER SKELTER MURDERS •
William Harrington
The most popular detective on television returns to face the legacy of one of history's most infamous killers.

STAGE FRIGHT• McNally
For five years, Hayley's been tormented by guilt over the murder of her fiancé. Now a vengeful ghost has come to claim her, and Hayley must defend her life and the man she has come to love.